I was a Stranger

*

The central character of this novel is the
Rev. John Ash. As chaplain to the forces
he was decorated for bravery at Dunkirk,
and then invalided out of the army as a
result of wounds received during the
evacuation. He goes straight to the care
of a large North London parish, a post
for which his experience in a monastic
order before the war had scarcely fitted
him. *I was a Stranger* deals with his
impact upon the various social circles
in this parish, and also with his efforts
to avoid getting involved in personal
relationships with certain of his
parishioners

I WAS A STRANGER

A Novel by

Martin Mewburn

1955

THE HOGARTH PRESS
London

Published by

THE HOGARTH PRESS LTD

42 William IV Street

London W.C. 2.

★

CLARKE, IRWIN & CO LTD

Toronto

To
MARY HITCHIN

Part One

PARIS

Paris

AMONG the passengers on one of the first boat trains to leave for the Continent after the war, were a couple who roused a certain amount of interest, though they seemed quite unaware of it, she being so wrapped up in him, he in his own thoughts.

He was a well-made man of about thirty-five, of medium height, and looked as if he might have been something of an athlete but for a slight limp in his right leg; and at the same time he had the look of a man of intellect. But his manner was the most remarkable thing about him, and the way he treated his companion; for in the moments when he was not speaking to her there was a brooding expression in his deep-set eyes, which, when she spoke to him or attracted his attention in any way, was immediately replaced by a look of almost painful concern, as if he distrusted his power to please her.

Any woman of the world who saw them together for only two minutes would have known that in this he need have had no fear, for his companion's manner showed the absolute devotion of one for whom life hardly existed outside his person. When he was not looking at her and was lost in his brooding thoughts, she would glance at him anxiously, her strangely coloured violet eyes worried; and when he looked at her she seemed to try with all her being to read his thoughts and to set at rest his obvious anxiety. But he seemed unaware of this, and though always treating her with manners almost old-fashioned in their correctness, he showed no warmth towards her. And the experienced observer would have seen that this caused her pain.

To guess his occupation would have set the most experienced sociologist a problem; his limp suggested a war wound, but some gentleness in his manner made it most unlikely that he was a soldier; something courteous and almost unworldly about the way he treated the various officials he came into contact with on the journey, suggested a life unusually sheltered; whilst the patience and lack of irritation he showed at the delays and troubles inevitable on journeys abroad,

A* 3

showed that he had a more satisfactory philosophy than that enjoyed by most of his fellow travellers. In fact it was only towards his companion that he showed uncertainty.

Had those who wondered about him been able to read his passport, where it was revealed that his name was John Ash, his occupation Clerk in Holy Orders, and his address a vicarage in an unfashionable quarter of north London, and had they known that he had been married only the day before, they would have thought that much about his manner was explained.

But they would still have wondered why he was so distant from her, whilst she was so close to him.

This too worried Katharine Ash, and had done since the ceremony on the previous day. It had worried her during the afternoon when she had helped him finish his packing, and during the evening at the concert where neither had heard more than a few notes of music; and it had worried her more than ever during the night which she had spent in her digs, and he in the spare room at the vicarage, where already he had handed over to his successor. It struck her as curious that he had not managed to book a room in a hotel for that night.

It still worried her as she sat beside him in the deck-chair on board the boat that took them across the Channel. Even when he became animated in telling her that the boat they were on was the very one that had taken him away from Dunkirk, she still did not lose her anxiety, for she was aware that he was speaking to her as if she were a stranger. Continually she asked herself what was on his mind, but she did not dare to ask.

But as they sat in the train near the wrecked docks of the French Port, waiting to be taken to Paris, she asked softly:

"What is worrying you?"

And he looked quickly away from her, out of the window.

"There is something . . . something fundamental, isn't there?" she persisted, when he remained silent. "Can you tell me what it is?"

"I cannot even tell myself," he replied, almost beneath his breath.

"What kind of a thing is it?"

To this he was a long time in replying. Then at last he said:

"In the last two years my whole life has been turned upside down. My whole scale of values seems to have been ... reversed. ..."

"Since when?" she asked.

"Since ... well, no definite date. It has been happening slowly, ever since I took over the living ...."

Again there was a long silence between them. Then she said:

"Would it help to tell me everything that happened, from the moment you entered the parish? Try to remember every significant detail, every little conversation that meant anything. ..."

He looked at her quickly, almost eagerly, but the eagerness soon vanished, and a slight smile touched his lips.

"It would not be much of a holiday for you," he said.

But now it was her turn to look eager.

"But it would," she said. "Nothing would interest me more than to hear it all, everything that happened to you, from your point of view—both before and after I came on the scene ..."

For the first time he looked into her eyes.

"Perhaps it would help. ..." he said. "Perhaps if once I got it off my chest, told it all to you, matters would begin to straighten themselves out in my mind ...."

"Yes," she said. "Begin now, at once .... And any time you feel like it during the next few weeks, continue, until you've told everything ...."

And so it was that he began to tell it to her, slowly and hesitantly at first, but gradually with more confidence, with more of the smooth colloquial style which had made his sermons, for a brief period during the war, famous in north London.

"When I left the army," he said, as the train moved slowly out of the station, "there were some who doubted the wisdom of my taking a living in north London, or anywhere else for that matter. A padré in the next bed at the hospital was quite vehement in trying to dissuade me. 'You are too close to God and remote from man to ever be able to bridge the gap,' he said.

'Your idealism will never survive the great disillusionment you will experience.' He of course knew that most of my adult life had been spent in a monastery, away from the world, and that I had emerged only to enter the Chaplains' Corps; not many people knew that. He said I should either go back to the monastery or become a missionary in some wild part of Madagascar or Borneo, where only simple emotions were met with, that I was not the kind to wrestle with the complicated depravities of a civilization I did not understand. I laughed at him and told him I was just the kind needed in a civilized world—that my innocent mind (I did not of course believe in my own innocence) would enable me to see clearly; that I depended in no way on my fellow men, but only on God, and would never become emotionally entangled with them. This was a rather mean hint at his own life, for he had previously confided in me the story of his unhappy marriage, which I believed had embittered him. For I had decided in my brief few months in the army that the fault with the average working clergyman was that he became so involved with the people whose souls he was supposed to tend, that he could no longer see their problems impartially. But at this my friend had only smiled ironically, and the subject was not mentioned between us again.

"Well, the living I was eventually assigned to seemed to be just what I wanted; it was poor, with only one area (in the corner of a neighbouring borough) in which people of means lived; the rest was slums, and tough, with a reputation before the war of razor-gangs and the lowest Church attendance in the whole of Britain. But most of the young toughs were now serving their King and Country, and it was quieter; or so I was informed. I was quite confident that I would change the nature of the whole parish. . . .

"I had of course been briefed as to the state of the parish—that my predecessor had been killed in an air-raid three months before, and that the living had been vacant since then. An occasional service had been held by a neighbouring vicar (when he had had time) but otherwise the parish had been entirely neglected. I felt in fact quite flattered that I should have been chosen for a parish in such dire need, not realizing then that the diocese was in such urgent need of clergy that almost anyone would have been offered the living. . . .

"It was not until I took up residence in the vicarage—that large gloomy Victorian mansion—that I realized not only had the parish been neglected during the preceding three months, but also during most of the twenty years of my predecessor's reign. I found all his belongings still there, his furniture, even his clothes, the latter, and all his personal belongings, neatly locked away in wardrobes by the housekeeper, Mrs. Taylor. It seems he had no relatives to claim them. Apparently he had lost his wife soon after accepting the living, since which he had led a life almost of complete retirement, writing a book on some obscure aspect of religious dogma which he never finished, emerging only to conduct his services and fulfil those functions of the Church which even the most un-Christian of congregations never seem willing to dispense with—marriage, christening and burial. I told myself with some satisfaction—remembering my friend's arguments in hospital—that this man had failed because he had become too much involved with temporal things, for, it was said, it had been on the death of his wife that he had virtually ceased to live.

"However, standing for the first time in the dark study of this my new home, I cannot help admitting that I felt some misgivings, a kind of helplessness, a feeling of not knowing how to begin. I even felt a sensation I had never expected to feel—regret at no longer hearing the sound of German guns. I thought of the Battalion and realized for the first time how much I had enjoyed life in the army; even the sense of numbness in my right calf, where certain tendons had been cut, roused in me pleasant memories.

"However, I quickly pulled myself together, and called to my side Mrs. Taylor, almost the only person in the parish with whom, at that time, I had spoken. I quickly found that in her I had not only an excellent housekeeper, but an unlimited source of information, and a person of very strong views on most subjects.

As you know she was a woman of remarkable ugliness, short and squat, with a deformed hip which caused her to walk at an odd angle, but with a face so beaming with good nature that I had no difficulty in understanding how it was, in spite of her grotesque appearance, she had once had a husband (a person to whom, incidentally, she never referred), and understood this even better when I had sampled her cooking. It soon came out that she had had a profound respect for my predecessor; when referring to him she invariably said that "e was a real gentleman who kept hisself to hisself' as if the fact that this characteristic of keeping himself to himself (which caused him to neglect his parish) was of no importance compared with the fact that he was a gentleman. At first I found it difficult to make her talk, as she seemed to suspect my comparative youth—she seemed to think that no clergyman should ever be on the right side of fifty—but as soon as she noticed my limp and found out its cause, she seemed suddenly to melt before me and to take on the qualities of a doting mother in the presence of a favourite child; from that moment onwards I found myself being looked after with every care.

"She was also full of information and good advice. She let me into the secrets of the geography of the parish, advising me to 'wash my hands of them streets', indicating with a sweep of her arm the general direction of that part of the parish remote from the small expensive quarter which she referred to as 'Carlton Court' because that was the name of the largest and most expensive block of flats there; for Mrs. Taylor was a snob and despised with all her heart the kind of people who hung their washing in their back-yards, who ate their meals in shirt-sleeves, or who (being women) appeared in public in hair-curlers; such people were not worth the attention of the Church, she considered. She advised me to concentrate on the small, select area of Carlton Court, where 'real nice' people lived, and where she did a little charring for 'pin-money'. She would, she magnanimously informed me, let it be known there that the new vicar had come and that he was 'a real gentleman who had been wounded at Dunkirk', and she had no doubt I would immediately be invited to tea by at least four different people, among them a certain Mrs. Carrington-Smith who had 'county connexions' and a Mrs. Robinson who was a very genteel lady. Also, she informed me, there were 'them there Committees' of which my predecessor had rather unwillingly been a member—'A.R.P. and whatnot'—and to one of which he had been on his way when 'the bit of shrapnel got him'. Nearly all the members of these Committees apparently lived in Carlton Court and held 'real good meetings' with tea and refreshment 'very friendly-like', and this had been about the only contact the previous vicar had had with the world. ''E really enjoyed hisself once 'e got there,' Mrs. Taylor informed me, 'though 'e grumbled something awful when 'e 'ad to go. Yes—' she had finished this particular conversation, on a note of profound philosophy, '—don't you bother your 'ead with them people—' nodding her head once more towards the slums, 'it's a task beyond the power of 'ercules and the Augean stables!' she added, triumphantly, and a little surprisingly, apparently mis-quoting one of my predecessor's favourite quotations.

"So it was that, though feeling that it was not the true direction in which lay my duty, I started off my career in the parish by making contact with Carlton Court. I did, it is true, in those early days, venture into the slum area and knock at various doors in an effort to make myself known, but found myself met with such suspicious stares and listened to so uncomprehendingly when I tried to make conversation, that I came quickly to realize that Mrs. Taylor's advice, if defeatist, showed common sense. I decided that the time was not yet ripe for such excursions, that first I should get my Church in order. Those first visits to the wilderness were not however fruitless, for they showed me one way at least in which I could be of practical use to the neighbour-hood, and this was in the looking after of the large numbers of apparently forgotten old people who were living alone; with something of a feeling of horror I found that there were dozens of such people, hardly able to look after themselves, often dying through neglect, often ignored even by their immediate

neighbours; in a few cases I at once set my teeth and personally
set about the task of cleaning out their rooms, a job nauseous in the
extreme, but which my sense of pity made it impossible for me to
avoid. During the next months I was to spend a large part of my
energies organizing a small group of people who undertook this
work, and it is in this connexion that something happened of
the importance of which I do not have to remind you. . . .

"But that is recent history to which I will eventually return;
I am now concerned with those early months in which I soon
found myself so involved with matters directly connected with
hostilities, that I had far less time to think of the real needs of my
less fortunate parishioners than I liked. But always they were at
the back of my mind, like an uneasy conscience.

"Meanwhile, I made the acquaintance of the principal people
of the Carlton Court area. As Mrs. Taylor had foreseen, a few
days after my arrival, I was visited by the chief Air-Raid Warden
for the district, one William Barlow, who was proprietor of the
Carlton Arms; he was a large powerfully built man of about
sixty, with a broken nose. I soon found out that he had been a
professional middle-weight of some renown, who had managed
to save enough from his purses to buy the Carlton Arms out-
right. From then on I found conversation easy, for one of my
duties in the Battalion had been to organize recreation, including
boxing, and I had picked up quite a useful amount of information about the subject from the men, and had even heard them
mention the famous Billy Barlow. This both astonished and
gratified Mr. Barlow. 'Thank Gawd,' he said, 'we've got a 'uman
parson at last. The bloke 'ere before you weren't a man at
all. 'E was—', and he hesitated as if searching for a simile that
would not be too insulting to the Church but adequately express
his meaning, '—'e was a little feller, all dried up like a pea, looked
as if a puff o' wind would blow 'im away; 'e wrote books too.
Brainy maybe but with no real understandin' of life if you
know what I mean. . . .' And he looked anxiously at me as if
wondering if he had gone too far.

" 'I know what you mean,' I said quietly.

"Mr. Barlow looked relieved as if his only remaining doubt about the new vicar had been removed. We then went on to talk for half an hour about boxing until he rose to go; then, casually, from the doorway, as if as an afterthought, he mentioned the object of his visit:

" 'We 'ave meetings,' he explained. 'An' your presence would be welcome, sir. When there's an air-raid we often 'as need of the services of the Church. An' the old vicar—,' he came back into the room, speaking confidentially, '—'e was scared stiff. Went into 'is cellar and stuck there till the all-clear. Not that I blame 'im—'e was timid by nature. But you, sir, you could be a lot of use. . . .' And subtly, by his manner, he managed to suggest he was referring to my record at Dunkirk.

"I tried to feel annoyance but in fact felt some pleasure at the implied compliment.

" 'I shall be pleased to come to your next meeting,' I said. 'Let me know when it is.'

" 'Next Wednesday, six-thirty, in my private sitting-room— you know, the Carlton Arms, just down the road. You come in at the private door round the back.'

"And with a nod, he withdrew.

"Scarcely had the front door closed behind him, when the telephone rang, and almost before the caller had introduced herself as Mrs. Carrington-Smith, I found myself invited to attend a meeting of the local W.V.S. on the following Monday evening; she profusely made excuses for introducing herself to me so informally, and for not coming round personally for that purpose, but she was so busy, and in these days of national emergency, she said, unconventional methods had occasionally to be resorted to; but it would be such a relief, she went on, to have the Church once more represented on her Committee, to which it was in a position to give such valuable advice; and quite apart from our official contact, she added, she was *so* looking forward to meeting the new vicar, whose great record at Dunkirk had preceded him; she suggested that everyone was quite excited about my arrival.

" 'I too,' I said politely but perhaps a little coldly, for I hated, and still hate, gushing women, 'I too shall be looking forward to meeting my parishioners.'

"And after a few more unnecessary compliments, she rang off. At the same moment Mrs. Taylor came in, carrying the tea-tray, and looking at me expectantly.

" 'Might I inquire if that was Mrs. Carrington-Smith?' she asked.

" 'It was.'

" 'I thought so. I told 'er all about you, and she's rung, like I said she would.'

" 'You seem to have told her much more about me than was necessary, Mrs. Taylor.' I said.

" 'Oh, no, sir, I didn't. I only told 'er you was a hero at Dun-kirk and was wounded in the leg and got a medal.'

" 'All of which has no bearing on my position as vicar of this parish,' I said sternly, 'and anyhow is strictly untrue. I was not a hero, Mrs. Taylor. I received my wound whilst in the act of running away from the enemy. Will you please understand that I do not want any exaggerated stories spread about what I might or might not have done at Dunkirk.'

"A look of slight alarm had appeared on Mrs. Taylor's face.

" 'I'm sure I'm very sorry, sir,' she said, 'but it was all in the paper, about you being an 'ero, so I thought it could do no 'arm——'

" 'In what paper?'

" 'The local paper, sir, the Gazette. None of them up at Carlton Court ever reads it, they reads only The Times or The Telegraph so they didn't know nothing about you, not even that you'd come, so I told them. I'm sure I'm very sorry, sir, if it's not what you wanted.'

"The look of anxiety on her face at once dissipated my an-noyance.

" 'That's all right, Mrs. Taylor,' I said. 'Only I don't like these ridiculous stories that get around about heroism. I did far less than ninety per cent of the troops over there, and much less than most of you people who have had to endure these air-raids. So from now on, please realize that I was not a hero and that it annoys me to be called one.'

" 'Yes, Mr. Ash,' she said humbly, but the expression on her face seemed to indicate that her opinion of my supposed heroism was in no degree altered.

"And so at last I settled down to a cup of tea and the composition of my first sermon. But scarcely had I put pencil to paper when I heard the door-bell ring, then footsteps come along the passage; and my door opened once more to admit Mrs. Taylor, beaming with satisfaction.

" 'Another visitor for you, sir,' she said. 'Mrs. Robinson of Carlton Court.'

"And seeing for the first time the smiling face of that woman who was to play so important a part in our lives, I could not help feeling some slight trepidation. For I saw at once that she was the kind of woman I had never met before but about whom I had heard much and had always wondered how I would deal with. Knowing her so well as I do now, it is difficult to recall exactly what my first impression of her was; I know that in the first moments before she came near me, I put her age at twenty years less than it was, and that even after she had sat within a few feet of me for half an hour, I was still ten years out in my guess; for the rest, I was conscious of clothes that were very smart and which everywhere accentuated her full figure a little too much without actually being vulgar, and of eyes of a most vivid blue. She came towards me with hand outstretched, her eyes looking into mine unwaveringly, with a look in them part questioning, part teasing, the expression with which, I was to learn later, she greeted all men on first meeting them.

" 'But how young you are!' were her first words on taking my hand and holding it a little longer than necessary, and I think I can say with honesty that for the first time in my life I was for a moment at a loss for words, for I read in her eyes an interest that had never been shown in me before. Before I could bring forth an intelligible sentence, she said:

" 'This room always gives me the creeps. . . .' And looking round almost fearfully, she gave a scarcely perceptible shudder. 'But now that *you* are here,' she went on, with a look at me that seemed to take me into the warmth of her personality, 'you, a young and imaginative man, will do something about it, won't you? I mean——' and with a gesture of her hand she indicated the entire room, the drabness of which I had hardly until that moment even noticed, '—I mean all this gloom, this fustiness, this brown paint—it's the environment of an old man who's finished with life . . . promise me you'll alter it before it gets into your bones and . . . makes you old too. . . .' And once more I was aware of those blue eyes looking into my own, more searchingly now, a little bolder, on the verge of impropriety.

"With an effort I pulled myself together, having become unpleasantly aware that I had allowed to enter into my relationship with another person an element not strictly controlled by my intellect, which was contrary to my strictest principles of life. With this woman I felt something emotional and instinctive that could not be explained by logic, and I did not like it. So I suppose that when I spoke, it was a little coldly.

" 'I doubt whether,' I said, 'I shall have time to bother much about my personal environment, at any rate for some time to come. There's too much to do in the parish. . . .'

"I was aware then of her looking at me quickly and curiously, with an interest I had never seen in a woman's eyes before; there was an extraordinary acuteness about the way she looked at me, as if she understood with some feminine instinct something I did not understand about myself. It was as if in some way I had unconsciously revealed myself to her. I felt confused, almost abashed. But doing my best to hide this odd feeling, I asked her to sit down, rang for Mrs. Taylor, requested her to bring another cup, and then gave my visitor tea. Seated near to her so that she was within the ring of light cast by the table-lamp, I was able to observe her more closely and to realize that she was not as young as I supposed, but probably just over forty rather than thirty (as you know she was actually fifty) but still a woman of considerable beauty, of a rather florid kind. Having made this effort of intellect, I became again complete master of myself, again the parish priest in the presence of a parishioner whose sex was not of the least importance, interested in the well-being of her soul, quite impersonal; in fact the complete clergyman I had always pictured myself as being. She talked about the parish, about some of the people in it, and with surprisingly little malice; surprising because I had a fixed idea that women of this kind always talked maliciously about their neighbours. Only once during this first meeting did I again become aware of her as a woman, and this was when she again looked into my eyes as she took her leave; in this moment I again saw that searching, veiled look which made me feel uneasily that there were perhaps some aspects of my own nature which I did not yet fully understand, and again I felt disturbed, dissatisfied, as if there had appeared a rawness in a personality which I had always regarded as fully developed. . . ."

At this moment the narrative was interrupted by a waiter putting his head into the carriage and announcing that the first luncheon was being served.

Mr. Ash looked inquiringly at his wife.

"I am hungry," he said. "Shall we have an early lunch?"

She nodded.

At lunch there was again the brooding, far-away look in his eyes and she had great difficulty in making conversation. After an almost silent meal they returned to the carriage, where she said gently:

"Go on."

He looked at her and again there was on his face that anxious, almost diffident look.

"Are you sure I am not boring you?" he asked.

"Of course not . . . . Go on, and try to remember every little thing that might be important. . . ."

At once the brooding look vanished from his eyes, and he started

speaking again, and once more she found herself carried away, fasci-
nated, by his pedantic, but extraordinarily descriptive flow of words.

"The next incident I remember clearly," he began, "was my
visit to the W.V.S. meeting. I know that in the intervening days
I was very busy organizing the Church—even the verger had
resigned—and on that first Sunday I preached to a congregation
of twelve persons, including six elderly spinsters who seemed to
have come for the purpose of inspecting me. Later I asked Mrs.
Taylor who these women were, and she said they were nosy
parkers who did nothing in the parish but discuss their neighbours, and who were by now no doubt discussing me. Asked
why no one from Carlton Court was present, she seemed
momentarily confused and said lamely that they had 'lost the
'abit' in the last few months, but that no doubt, when I had been
to one or two of the Committee meetings, they would come
back.

"Well, go to one of the Committee meetings I did, on the
next evening. I found Carlton Court to be a vast modern building
full of self-operated lifts and labyrinthine corridors, and I had
some difficulty in finding the right flat. This caused me to arrive
late, and when I entered I found the Committee members
already assembled. Five or six women and one man were seated
round a table, and one youngish woman in rimless glasses, who
looked like a model private secretary, had open before her a book
in which—I surmised—were written the minutes of the previous
meeting, and from which she had seemed to be about to read.
This woman waited in a kind of icy silence as I was introduced,
as if I had interrupted some kind of ritual of which she was high-
priestess, and she only slightly inclined her head when it was her
turn to be introduced.

"These introductions were effected by Mrs. Robinson as the
only person present who had met me. During these introductions I did little more than grasp that a rather dominating
looking woman with thin lips at the head of the table—the very

antithesis of Mrs. Robinson—was Mrs. Carrington-Smith, the Chairman; that a pretty young woman with a rather impertinent look in her eyes and a slight cockney accent, was Mrs. Bartram—'our young bride'—as Mrs. Robinson described her, at which description the young woman had pulled a rather sour face; that the one male present, a fat man of about fifty with horn-rimmed glasses, was a Dr. Kynaston, and that the icy young woman was Miss Cooter, 'our very efficient secretary', as Mrs. Robinson described her. The others present, nondescript women in their forties, made no particular impression on me. Throughout the introductions I formed the opinion that Mrs. Robinson was not altogether popular with the others, and that her tone, when she described each of them, was a little facetious. Then, after a short and rather formal speech of welcome by Mrs. Carrington-Smith, at which she expressed the Committee's appreciation at once more having the Church represented at a meeting, the business proceeded.

"From the first moment I was impressed by the efficiency of these women. Miss Cooter read her minutes in a cold and expressionless voice, and I had my first surprise—at the amount of work that seemed to have been got through on the occasion of the last meeting, only a fortnight previously. These minutes were duly approved and signed, and matters proceeded quickly and efficiently. I understood little of the details of what was going on, previously only having experienced the W.V.S. from the other side of the counter, as it were—in the canteens I had visited in the short time I was in the Battalion before it went abroad—and I was astonished at the amount and the variety of the work done. There were even casualties to record—Mrs. Carrington-Smith's first action after the reading of the minutes was to make a grave little speech expressing regret at the death of two of their workers in a recent raid, a speech which was received, though gravely enough, with no particular emotion, and caused me to realize at once that I was in the presence of a body of women who not only knew there was a war on, but who were in the front line. The proceedings lasted for over an hour, various propositions were made, with speeches for and against, votes taken, and motions carried, and I was able to get a very good idea of the respective degrees of efficiency of the various members of the Committee.

"Mrs. Carrington-Smith seemed to be very intelligent; she bided her time, listened to everyone's point of view, and then added her own, and when the vote was taken, it turned out that her point of view was almost invariably carried. I noticed that young Mrs. Bartram seemed automatically to vote for whatever was proposed by Mrs. Carrington-Smith, and that Dr. Kynaston and one of the nondescript women seemed to do the same. Only Miss Cooter seemed to vote consistently against her, and I began to wonder whether these women were carrying on their meetings quite as impartially as they should. I suspected undue influence on the part of the Chairman. I did not however at the time take these impressions very seriously.

"Finally, proceedings came to an end, the meeting declared closed, cigarettes lit, and the eyes of most of the members turned towards me. Only Miss Cooter packed her papers in a brief-case, and with a short nod which included everyone present, abruptly took her leave.

" 'I have another meeting to attend,' she said shortly, as she disappeared through the door.

" 'Does she ever relax?' asked one of the nondescript women.

" 'No, dear,' said Mrs. Robinson, 'She's just one of those restless spinsters who must always be having some passionate interest to distract them from their single state. I've known her slightly for nearly fifteen years. When I first met her she was a little shorthand typist in a solicitor's office, determined to become the perfect private secretary. She was spending half her life in night-schools. She has absolutely no sense of humour and never makes a mistake——'

" 'I won't have a word said against her,' interrupted Mrs. Carrington-Smith abruptly. 'She's invaluable to us and the bravest woman I've ever known. If she isn't always quite of my way of thinking, I don't blame her for it. It's useful to have a little opposition. Mr. Barlow told me yesterday that she was standing almost beside Margaret and Mrs. Cartwright when they were killed. She didn't turn a hair and did all she could with bandages until the Red Cross people turned up. They were taken to your post, weren't they, Marjorie?' she added, looking at Mrs. Robinson.

" 'Yes,' said Mrs. Robinson quietly, 'and she came with them. I must admit she has courage. She was quite unmoved. . . .'

" 'You can't tell, you know, by people's outward appearance,' said Dr. Kynaston. 'She may merely have exceptional self-control.'

" 'She's got ice in her veins, not blood,' suddenly broke in Mrs. Bartram. '*I* saw her that night, too. She came into the canteen after leaving the Red Cross post—they were all three on their way to relieve us. Any other woman would've called it off, gone home. I was down in the shelter myself, dead scared. I'm human. She came down and found me—I didn't know what had happened then, and she didn't say a word. She just looked at me a little scornfully—you know, as if she'd found me signalling to the enemy or something—and told me I could go. I asked her if she'd seen anything of the raid and what it had been like, and she only shrugged her shoulders and gave a little smile—you know, with her lips only. "Nothing much," she said, "you needn't be scared—it's all over now, the all-clear will go at any moment." I nearly slapped her pale face— *I'm* not ashamed of being scared of getting killed. I have a husband to think of, which is more than she has. I suggested we closed the canteen for the night—there was less than an hour to go. But she wouldn't hear of it. So I left her to it, calling the others from the cellar and making them heat tea and what-not. I suppose I should have stayed, but I thought Margaret and Mrs. Cartwright were coming in at any moment—I didn't know they'd been killed. I think she enjoyed not telling me so that I'd feel small when I realized I'd left them short-handed. She may be a brave woman—if having no nerves is being brave—she may be invaluable to us—but she'd be more at home with the Nazis; she's cold-blooded, like them.' And stubbing out her half-smoked cigarette, she lit another, and I knew that at any rate this woman's nerves were not all they should be.

"The others had looked at her whilst she was talking with the wrapt attention of gossiping women—they were human at last, I thought—and when she had finished, they looked at each other expectantly, as if all were wanting to speak at once, to add their own tale of the inhumanness of Miss Cooter. But again Mrs. Carrington-Smith took charge. She seemed again to remember my presence, to become conscious that tonight there was more male company than usual, and she apologized profusely, with a touch of the gushing manner she had used on the 'phone, and at once started acting the hostess, just a little artificially, I thought.

"From then on the evening became more of a social occasion. Mrs. Robinson and one of the nondescript women went into the kitchen and soon came back with coffee and sandwiches, and conversation became normal. Gradually members of the Committee drifted away, and finally I myself left with Dr. Kynaston.

"Outside, I remember the doctor looked up at the sky.

" 'Cloudy tonight,' he said. 'Jerry won't be over.'

" 'Do you get it badly here?' I asked.

" 'Not specially. There's no particular target, but it's London. And they seem to jettison a bit here on their way out. . . . What's wrong with that leg of yours?' he asked with professional interest.

"I explained, going into as much medical detail as I was able.

" 'I must look at it sometime,' he said. 'It sounds like an interesting condition. But no doubt the medicos have done all they can. I don't expect it can be cured altogether, but it shouldn't give you much trouble. Glad to be out of the army?'

"I did not at once reply. This was a question to which I didn't know the answer myself, because I liked being honest and couldn't quite understand how it was I had almost enjoyed war.

" 'I don't know,' I said after a moment. 'Of course I'm glad of the chance of getting on with the kind of work I feel a vocation for—looking after a backward parish. Here I feel there's real

work to be done, if ever I find out how to set about it. In the
Army it was merely a question of fulfilling a function already
laid down by King's Regulations—improvising Services that
were automatically attended by men wanting to get out of more
wearisome fatigues—attending Church Parade was preferred,
on the whole, to cleaning out the latrines. Generally, I was
looked upon by the men with a kind of amused tolerance which
gave the illusion of popularity; they rather liked to see me about
because I wasn't an ordinary sort of officer likely to insist on
clean boots and short hair, and they didn't have to be too particular about calling me "sir". I was a sort of advice bureau on
their home affairs—when they learnt their wives were carrying
on with other men, which was frequently, they would ask me
what they should do about it. . . .'

" 'And what did you tell them?'

" 'Oh, if I thought it genuine, I usually managed to get them
compassionate leave; and almost invariably they came back with
the news that it was only family gossip. Sometimes it was genuine, though. Once a lance-corporal of mine stabbed the other
fellow with his bayonet and then came back to his unit and shot
himself. Sometimes they just failed to come back from leave.
Once or twice I was asked to start divorce proceedings—as if I
had the power of ending as well as starting marriages! I was
general adviser on all welfare matters, particularly wives' allow-
ances, which was the men's main preoccupation, besides chasing
other women. It all had very little to do with God. . . .'

" 'Yet you liked it?'

" 'In a way. There was plenty to do without having to seek it,
even if any competent welfare officer could have carried out my
functions. And there was always the companionship of the mess.
. . . And then, of course, when the retreat started. . . .'

" 'Yes?' asked Kynaston.

" 'I saw men die. I saw how they behaved when face to face
with their Maker.'

" 'And how did they behave?'

" 'All they wanted from me, usually, was a cigarette. . . . But you see men die, too, doctor. How do they behave to the man of science?'

" 'Almost always, to the last, they think I can do something.'

" 'A sign of the times,' I said. 'There is more faith now in science than in God.'

"There was then a long pause during which the doctor filled his pipe. Soon he stopped at a front door.

" 'Here's where I live,' he said. 'Come in for a drink, won't you?'

"I hesitated. I did not want to be a nuisance, but would have liked half an hour beside a homely fire. The doctor saw my hesitation.

" 'Come on,' he said. 'My wife would like it. She's often rather bored.'

" 'I'm afraid she would be more than ever bored with me,' I said. 'I am not a ladies' man.'

" 'On the contrary,' he said. 'She would probably find you very interesting. She's a passionate student of human nature. She studies the mind, I the body.'

" 'And I the soul,' I said. 'All right, doctor. I cannot refuse a challenge like that.'

"My first impression of this other woman who was to play so important a part in our lives, was very different from that made on me by Mrs. Robinson. She was a small, neat person, with bright, mocking eyes, about forty years old. She offered me coffee or whisky, and I chose the latter.

"At first conversation was difficult; my host and hostess seemed slightly embarrassed; I thought, rather naïvely, that this might be due to their being atheists—I considered myself an expert at sensing this in anyone. And almost at once she seemed to put my thought into words; I was often to experience this power almost of thought-reading in her—which was in fact nothing more than quick wits.

" 'I'm afraid you're in the presence of a couple of atheists,' she said, with a certain amount of boldness, almost as if wanting to provoke an argument.

" 'That, presumably,' I said, 'worries you more than me.'

" 'It should worry you a lot,' she said. 'Isn't it your job to bring straying sheep back to the fold?'

" 'It is,' I replied. 'But I don't advertise my methods.'

" 'I see,' she said. 'The subtle approach. I must be on my guard. Actually, it doesn't worry me in the least being an atheist.'

" 'Then you must be a fatalist.'

" 'Perhaps.'

" 'So are the Japanese.'

"She looked at me sharply, not liking this. The Japanese were not popular at that time. But she was quick to make a reply, the exact nature of which I do not remember, but it started the kind of argument I had often engaged in before, only this time it was more amusing than usual, because she was a woman with a sense of humour, and, as I have already said, and as you know only too well, very quick-witted. Compared with her, her husband was like a bull-dog competing with a whippet. I began to understand what he had meant when he said she was sometimes bored. Occasionally he put in a word, almost deprecatingly, as if afraid his wife had gone too far. I enjoyed this, my first crossing of swords with Mrs. Kynaston. But of course then I was full of self-confidence.

"Soon the subject changed to the Committee meeting.

" 'How did you get on with the rival Queens?' asked Mrs. Kynaston with a twinkle in her eye.

" 'Who are they?'

" 'The Honourable Mrs. Carrington-Smith and the dis-honourable Mrs. Robinson.'

" 'Really, my dear——' protested her husband, looking uneasily at me.

"But by now I was in the mood for Mrs. Kynaston's wit; I had by then had two whiskies and hardly anything to eat since lunch, and her conversation seemed more amusing to me than it probably was. I laughed, laughter in which, after a moment of hesitation, Dr. Kynaston joined, whilst his wife watched us gravely. After a moment she asked:

" 'Which of the two ladies impressed you most?'

" 'Well,' I said. 'Mrs. Carrington-Smith hasn't yet made any very definite impression. . . .'

" 'She wouldn't. One learns about her gradually. But of course Mrs. Robinson has made an impression on you?'

" 'Well——' I began.

" 'Don't be afraid of admitting it, Vicar. In short, you adore her?'

" 'A slight exaggeration——'

" 'Well, you should adore her if you don't. We all do, except Mrs. Carrington-Smith and her cronies. She's a wonderful creature, a woman without vice. The only complete unadulterated woman I've ever met. Though perhaps "unadulterated" is not quite the right word! But you know what I mean—the scientists say that none of us is completely sexed—that all men have something of women in them, and all women something of men. But Mrs. Robinson is all woman. One hundred per cent. You watch out, Vicar. She is quite unrepressed. . . .'

" 'Really, my dear,' protested Dr. Kynaston. 'You're not in a medical ward now, you know. My wife,' he said, turning to me, 'was a hospital sister and also studied psychiatry up at Cambridge. She's inclined to be a little outspoken about these matters. . . .'

" 'You sound as if you think I might be shocked,' I said. 'You have an odd idea of the Church, Kynaston. We are far less likely to be shocked than most people.'

" 'You are an interesting vicar, Vicar,' said Mrs. Kynaston. 'You see, we are used to the Church being out of contact with the facts of life. To be quite honest, I don't think your predecessor knew them. If anyone mentioned sex, particularly a woman, he would clear his throat rather obviously, and peer anxiously over his pince-nez, like this——' and she gave a remarkable imitation of an elderly cleric looking shocked. Again we both laughed. She was a born mimic, and as the evening wore on, she became funnier and funnier and more and more daring. I too have a certain gift in reproducing the way people speak, and so was able

to enter into the spirit of her comedy. In fact, Dr. Kynaston was
somewhat left out of it. I began to feel very pleased with myself—
this was the first time I had been such a success with a woman,
and I felt it was only partly due to the whisky. And when finally
I left I was indeed in a happy frame of mind—the happiest I
ever attained in the parish, except perhaps for that brief period
when we worked together; but then, as you know, there were
very good reasons why my happiness was not complete. . . .

"But on my way home from my first evening with the Kynastons, there was nothing to spoil my optimism. I was full of hope,
on the threshold of a new career, and had just had an unexpected
success with two of my parishioners. I had also had two glasses
of whisky."

*And Mr. Ash turned to his wife, his face flushed with the emotions
recaptured from that day nearly two years before; but she saw, as he
returned suddenly to reality, an unhappiness come into his eyes. He
seemed conscious of this, for he made some effort at a smile, and her
heart went out to him in his attempts at disguising the strange weight
that was on his mind. She wanted to put out her hand and touch his,
but did not dare do so.*

*He turned to the window of the train which was now rolling through
the outskirts of Paris.*

*"Look," he said, "there's Montmartre and Sacré Coeur. That
virgin Cathedral which has not yet been taken into the hearts of the
Parisians. Personally I don't find it ugly. There is something attractive about its isolation. . . ."*

*She tried, looking out of the window, to feel excitement at this, her
first visit to Paris. But she could not. Instead, she found her eyes returning to his face in profile, searching it, trying to find the meaning
of his expression.*

*"I was in Paris once before," he said. "At seventeen I was sent
on a tour of Europe with other young men destined for the Church.
It was supposed to broaden our minds. But we only saw with our eyes
the places we visited—we were not allowed to experience them with*

our senses. It really meant very little to us. If anything it put a greater distance between us and life. . . ."

It was as if he were trying to excuse himself to her, and she took some comfort from the fact that he had now at least told her something about his life before the war. Until this moment, he had not even mentioned having been to the Continent before.

They found their way to their hotel, where she discovered that at least a double room had been booked, though it had twin beds. In their room she at once began to change, whereupon he hurriedly made an excuse for going out "to see the management". He did not return and she had to go downstairs to find him. She discovered him in the lounge, waiting for her.

"Would you like to stroll to the Étoile tonight," he said, "and sample some of the famed French food in a good restaurant?"

"That would be lovely," she said.

Over the meal he was almost gay, obviously trying hard to make himself as amusing as possible. But again he treated her as a stranger, as an acquaintance to whom he was trying to give a good time. Back in their room, he started running her a bath, generally made sure she had everything she needed, and then, before she had even let down her hair, he went downstairs "to have a final smoke".

When he returned she was already in bed. He retired into the bathroom and returned not long after, clad in pyjamas and dressing-gown. Quickly he got into his own bed, and after courteously wishing her good night, switched out the light.

She was late going to sleep that night, and so was late waking. When she did so she found him already almost dressed and about to shave. Seeing she was awake, he said:

"Shall I have coffee and rolls sent up to you, the traditional Continental breakfast?"

"I would rather have it downstairs with you," she said, and started to get out of bed. He shut himself in the bathroom. With a sigh, she sat down at the dressing-table, and started to brush her hair.

They spent the morning in the Louvre, and the afternoon wandering along the banks of the Seine. She found they had many interests in common, and a happy enough companionship was established between *them. But still there was no warmth in his manner towards her and she dared not show any on her side for fear of embarrassing him. They dined at the hotel, and it was after dinner, over a café arrosé, that he resumed his narrative.*

He began as if there had been no interval since he had last spoken, which made her realize how much he had been thinking about it.

"The morning after that visit to the Kynastons," he said, "I awoke almost with a guilty conscience, wondering whether I had behaved quite as I should the previous evening. I was aware of having listened to malicious gossip and enjoyed it, engaged in theological argument without caring whether my opinions prevailed or not, and even drunk enough to affect my powers of judgement. I tried to tell myself this was nonsense, that I had behaved as I had in order to show the Kynastons that the Church was not out of touch with life, and that I had in fact succeeded in impressing them.

"But this did not entirely satisfy me, and to quell my slight uneasiness I flung myself with all energy into organizing the parish, and in the next few days did more work than most men do in a week. And in the process I nearly forgot to attend the A.R.P. meeting on the Wednesday evening; however I remembered in time, and duly arrived, once more a little late.

"The atmosphere of this meeting could hardly have been more different from that of the other. I entered Billy Barlow's smoke-filled parlour and found seven or eight not altogether pre-possessing men, aged between fifty and sixty-five, and Mrs. Robinson. Tankards of beer were on tables and window-sills, and there was a great deal of noise, which I noticed grew less when my presence was observed. I had time to see Mrs. Robinson sitting surrounded by men and looking as much at home as she had in Mrs. Carrington-Smith's flat or in my study the previous week. Never, in fact, at that time did I see her in the smallest degree ill at ease, and this was possibly why I formed for her an admiration which went against all the evidence, which was why perhaps many of the people who met her in those days of danger felt for her a respect in spite of themselves, as if sensing in her a unity of personality which neither themselves nor anyone else of their acquaintance possessed. And this unity of personality she retained until there was no longer the danger in which she thrived—only then did it begin to disintegrate. . . .

"When she saw me and came across to me with hand out-stretched and china-blue eyes wide with pleasure, I could not help feeling some embarrassment at being so greeted by this woman whose attention every other man in the room had so obviously been trying to attract. Again I felt her soft hand grasp mine and hold it a little longer than necessary, again I was aware of perfume a little too strong but not unpleasing, and at the same time I thought I sensed in her manner the faintest suggestion that she was a little put out by my presence. . . .

" However, she introduced me to all the men, who were staring at me almost with hostility, and with each of them she seemed to be on terms intimate enough to permit her to crack jokes which to a stranger would have seemed almost brazen. In fact throughout the evening I saw an aspect of her new to me, for she seemed almost to take on the characteristics of a barmaid, even her accent became appreciably more vulgar, her laugh louder and more frequent, and throughout the evening she disappeared often into the public bar, to return with trays of pint-mugs which she distributed with almost a professional air. I was surprised that a woman who two evenings before had seemed such a lady, should now so obviously not be one; and even more remarkable than this sudden change of personality was the fact that she should be willing to undergo it in my presence, as if quite unconscious of letting her other self down. I was to notice on more than one occasion this odd ability of hers to merge, yet at the same time not quite merge, with the particular social environment in which she found herself, particularly, a few months later, at an Area Red Cross meeting where there were several titled people; for on this occasion she so took on the air of a slightly florid but quite convincing dowager—perhaps one

of those who once so delighted the Gaiety audiences, but none
the less a dowager for all that—that I could hardly believe it was
the same woman whom I had seen disporting herself in Billy
Barlow's parlour; admittedly, there was about her manner at the
Red Cross meeting a slightly spurious air which anyone really
used to 'good' society would have spotted at once, and which
would have caused them to realize that she had not been born
there, or even been there on sufferance for a decade or two, but
then so was there this slightly spurious air about her in Billy
Barlow's parlour, and in Mrs. Carrington-Smith's flat, which
seemed to prove equally, that as well as the upper, neither the
lower nor the middle classes were her proper environment. And
as I came to know her better I realized that whilst never being
exactly ill at ease, Mrs. Robinson was never quite at home, and
it was then that I first began to feel pity for her. . . .

"Rather to my surprise I found that this A.R.P. Committee,
which was all men with one woman, was less efficient than the
W.V.S. Committee which was all women with one man; in
fact it was scarcely a Meeting at all, but more an excuse for the
air-raid wardens to get together, drink beer, and enjoy Mrs.
Robinson's company. Billy Barlow did get to his feet, call for
silence, and read one or two official leaflets about new kinds of
German incendiary bombs, and then give details of various
training programmes which the members of the Committee
were supposed to carry out, but which no one seemed to
take very seriously. He then asked if anyone had anything to say,
obviously hoping that no one had, and he seemed quite surprised when two members of the Committee rose to their feet.
They both voiced the complaint that they just hadn't enough
personnel to carry out an efficient duty roster, and it seemed to
me that the second of these two, when he came to the end of
what he had to say, looked rather pointedly at me. Upon this
Billy Barlow had once more stood up, cleared his throat as if a
little embarrassed, and looked hesitantly at me.

" 'It has been wondered,' he said, 'seein' as Mr. Bateman is
short-handed, whether you, sir, could lend a hand. Mr. Bateman's

the warden for your area, you see, and there's a scarcity of the able-bodied in 'is section. . . .'

"And with a deprecating manner which went oddly with his lusty exterior, he stood looking at me, and I was aware that everyone else was looking at me too, and in a not particularly friendly manner. I was about to stand up and offer my services when I was forestalled by Mrs. Robinson.

" 'Oh no,' she said. 'Mr. Ash has more than enough to do. Now that he's come among you sinners he's hardly got time to go to bed, let alone take on A.R.P. duties. You know, he's got an awful lot of praying to do if he's going to save *your* souls. . . .'

"This remark was greeted with a burst of laughter—anything she said intended as even remotely funny would have brought the house down in that company—but it quickly ceased as I in turn stood up. I was feeling a little nervous, aware of not being looked upon with entire approval.

" 'I think,' I said, 'that the time to consider souls will come when our bodies are in a little less danger. . . . I propose to leave them severely alone until Mr. Goering has ceased paying us his attentions . . . and whilst I appreciate Mrs. Robinson's concern for your moral welfare—no doubt she knows more about it than I do—I shall on this occasion resist the chance of accepting her protection. If Mr. Bateman thinks I can be of any use, I am at his service. . . .'

"This speech went down reasonably well, and there were even one or two cries of 'good for you, Vicar', and I sensed that the prejudice against me was probably largely due to the example set by my predecessor, and that there was no personal grudge against me. A little later I found myself being slapped on the back by Billy Barlow, and shaking hands with Bateman, a rather good-looking, tall man of about fifty-five—I mention this man's looks for reasons which will emerge later. He was apparently some kind of builder in a small way, and he informed me that he would drop into the vicarage some time to arrange my place on the roster. I felt that the air of hostility that had greeted my entrance into the room had already to a large extent disappeared and I felt a certain amount of pleasure at this. From this moment onwards all pretence at holding a meeting vanished, and most of the Committee went into the public bar carrying their mugs, after first taking a fond farewell of Mrs. Robinson. Soon only I, Mrs. Robinson, Bill Barlow and Bateman were left and for a few moments there was a sense of slight awkwardness which I did not understand. At last however Mrs. Robinson stood up to go, and I with her, and as she took leave of Bateman I thought that for a moment there was a look of slight dissatisfaction in his eyes, as if he were mildly annoyed about something. However, it lasted for only a second and his manner was very friendly when he shook hands with me.

"So I found myself outside with Mrs. Robinson, and though it was a clear night and the black-out not so dense as usual, she seemed to find it sufficiently dark for it to be necessary to take my arm, and in this way we proceeded along the street, her hand on my arm. She seemed quite oblivious to the fact that it might be thought odd by some people for the vicar to be seen arm in arm with her in the act of leaving a public-house, and I cannot help admitting that I hoped we would not meet anyone.

"She looked up at the sky much as Dr. Kynaston had done a few nights before.

" 'Just the night for Jerry to come over,' she said. 'Oh well—we've survived his visits so far and there's no reason why we shouldn't go on doing so.'

" 'Do you never feel like leaving London?' I asked.

" 'Leave London?' she asked. 'Good heavens no, Vicar. I was born here—I wouldn't leave at a time like this. I'd never be able to look the place in the face again. Besides, I have certain business interests to look after.'

"For some moments she was silent and I sensed some kind of uneasiness in her. Soon she said:

" 'Vicar . . . I know you're not a gossiping sort of man, but . . . if Mrs. Carrington-Smith or any of the others question you about the A.R.P. meetings, you won't tell them on what good terms I am with the men, will you?'

"And before I could reply she went on hurriedly:

" 'You see, I'm one of those people who can never have anything to do with anyone without getting on friendly terms with them. I like people, Vicar, whatever walk of life they come from. . . .'

" 'An excellent characteristic,' I said. 'The true Christian spirit. . . .'

" 'But some people don't understand it. Mrs. Carrington-Smith for instance—she has funny ideas about class and that sort of thing. If she knew how friendly I was with Billy Barlow and the others she might take it the wrong way. . . .'

" 'You mean Mrs. Carrington-Smith is a snob?' I asked.

" 'Exactly,' she replied, and I thought I heard in her voice a note of relief that I had put this interpretation to her remark. 'And as I have to live in the same flats, I find it simpler to keep on good terms with her. One has to make compromises with one's ideals sometimes, Vicar. So you won't say anything about it, will you?'

" 'You have no cause to worry,' I said, perhaps a little stiffly. 'As you say, I am not in the habit of gossiping.'

" 'Of course not, Vicar. But it's so easy to let something slip out without intending to. Mrs. Carrington-Smith is a dear person and I'm very fond of her, but she just loves finding things out about people. Forewarned is forearmed, you know. . . .'

"By this time we had reached Carlton Court, and I felt with some relief that now I would be relieved of my duties as escort; but she expressed great surprise when I started to say good-bye, and said she thought it had been mutually understood that I was to step up to her flat for coffee. And as I looked at her in the dimly-lit entrance-hall, for a moment I thought I saw a hint of mockery in her expression, as if she were daring me to go up; and perhaps out of curiosity, or perhaps because of an odd little strain in my character which always responds to a challenge, I accepted.

"In the lift she smiled at me, and said:

" 'You needn't worry, Vicar. I shall be very surprised if we are alone in the flat.'

" 'You have visitors in your absence?' I asked.

" 'Oh yes—frequently. You'll see. . . .' And her smile became almost teasing.

"After leaving the lift, we went along two corridors and eventually stopped before a door which she opened, ushering me into a small hall. The flat was very similar to Mrs. Carrington-Smith's which I had already seen, but seemed larger, there being more doors leading off the hall. Exactly what I had expected to find there I do not know, but I was certainly not prepared for what I was immediately faced with; for almost at once I had my first shock—my foot caught in something on the floor, and, looking down, I saw a bed consisting of what seemed to be a mattress and two blankets, made up army fashion; I would in fact have tripped up altogether but for Mrs. Robinson's steadying hand on my arm.

" 'Sorry!' she said. 'There are liable to be obstacles like that in my flat. I've got rather an overflow tonight—I'd almost forgotten. But I'm used to it, you know. This time it's the Polish Army.'

"At this moment I became aware of conversation and loud laughter coming from behind one of the doors, and also the smell of what seemed to be Turkish cigarettes. Without further explanation, my hostess opened the door of the room from which the noise was issuing, and indicated that I was to follow her in. On the threshold I paused; for a moment I couldn't see clearly, partly because of the glare of light after the black-out, partly because of a haze of tobacco-smoke, but it seemed to me that the room was full of men in strange uniforms, all standing rather stiffly to attention with unnaturally broad smiles; to these men Mrs. Robinson seemed to be paying no attention, but was talking to a youth in civilian clothes who was sitting negligently astride the arm of a sofa with his hands in his pockets, a person she seemed surprised to see there. As my senses became used to the atmosphere, I realized there were five men in uniform present, all members of the Polish Forces—only one an officer—and that three of them were holding between their fingers cigarettes in long black holders. They were all standing very politely waiting to be noticed, but their hostess continued to ignore them as she went on with her conversation with the youth on the sofa; in fact this moment became so prolonged that I felt it necessary to make some gesture of friendliness to the Poles, so I smiled and slightly inclined my head, upon which two of them saluted, the others bowing from the hips and all smiling more broadly than ever. After a moment's hesitation, two of them said together, 'Good evening, Father', whereupon the one in officer's uniform said in very broken English, rather sharply, 'No—in England it is padré, as in France—you say "good evening, padré",' upon which the other two looked somewhat abashed and the two who had not spoken burst out laughing. This commotion attracted Mrs. Robinson's attention, and she looked round as if she had forgotten the existence not only of the Poles but of me too.

" 'Oh, I do apologize, Mr. Ash,' she said, 'not that I'm capable of introducing these gentlemen, their names are quite beyond me, but as you've no doubt guessed they're members of the Polish Forces on leave in London. I found them sitting about in the canteen last night looking bored but behaving so politely, so I thought I'd ask them up for a cup of coffee and they've been here ever since. They must have misunderstood me in some way, but it doesn't matter because I'm quite used to it—there are quite a number of men who drop in when they're on leave in London—you know, soldiers we've struck up an acquaintance with in the canteen—they seem to find it more comfortable than the hostels, and it stops them going to worse places perhaps, you know what troops are, and so many women have been cashing in on the war—you know what I mean. But at least I can introduce you, with your nice plain English name.' And turning to the Poles, she smiled graciously, saying:

" 'This is Mr. Ash, our vicar, I don't know the Polish word for vicar——'

" 'Please?' asked the officer.

" 'Oh well, it doesn't really matter, this is just Mr. Ash, a friend of mine who has dropped in for a cup of coffee——'

" 'Dropped?' asked the Polish officer.

" 'Oh well, just come, you know—arrived—mon ami est arrivé poir boire une tasse de café——'

"Comprehension dawned on the Pole's face.

" 'Oh yes,' he said, and held out his hand to me, which I took, this procedure being repeated with each of the others, after which Mrs. Robinson said she would go and get something to drink, but before she could leave, the Polish officer said:

" 'Excuse me.'

" 'Yes?' asked Mrs. Robinson brightly.

" 'We are drunk already,' said the Pole.

" 'Good heavens—really? I hope not too much so. . . .'

" 'He means,' said the youth on the sofa, "that he *has* drunk already. . . . They've been messing about in the kitchen most of the evening. . . .

"Mrs. Robinson gave a laugh in which there was a certain amount of relief.

" 'Oh, I'm so glad,' she said, 'for a moment I thought . . . well, Poles have a certain reputation when the worse for liquor. . . .'

" 'I make joke?' asked the Polish officer politely.

" 'Yes,' said Mrs. Robinson, 'at least—not intentionally. You see, when you said "we are drunk" it meant you're tight, I mean that you've drunk too much——'

" 'I drink too much?'

" 'No, no, not you. I mean generally. You see, you used the wrong phrase. When you say "we are drunk" it means you've drunk too much alcohol, beer, whisky——'

" 'No!' said the Pole indignantly. 'We are drunk only with coffee. By God I swear it.'

" 'Oh dear,' said Mrs. Robinson, looking rather helplessly towards me, 'now he thinks I've insulted him. . . .'

The Poles had in fact gathered round their leader, looking insulted.

" 'I'll try them in French,' I said.

" 'Oh, can you? My French is quite unable to cope. . . . Only the simplest phrases. . . .'

"In my French, such as it is, I managed to explain the misunderstanding, and the faces of at least three of the Poles showed immediate comprehension, and once more smiles spread over their faces, and they burst into bellows of laughter, slapping each other on the back, and explaining in explosive Polish to their companions who did not understand French; whereupon they all insisted on shaking hands, not only with Mrs. Robinson and myself and with the youth on the sofa, but with each other, a procedure which took nearly five minutes. When it was at last over, Mrs. Robinson started to leave the room once again, only to turn round at the door to say to me;

" 'Oh, I almost forgot, but this is Peter, my son,' and she indicated the youth, who had by now left the sofa, and was standing by the window, smoking. 'Peter—Mr. Ash, our new vicar. Do get to know each other.'

"And at last she went out, after calling for volunteers from among the Poles, who again seemed to misunderstand her, for they followed her out to a man.

"The youth came towards me rather unwillingly, and held out his hand.

" 'I had heard the Church was once more represented among us,' he said, 'though I hardly expected to meet it here. It's a new venture of mama's to fraternize with the clergy. . . .'

"As I shook hands with him, I looked at him keenly, not much liking his tone; his slight build, neat, thin features, and restless dark eyes that would not meet mine, and his black hair brushed meticulously, made it difficult for me to believe he was Mrs. Robinson's son; he seemed to be her very opposite in type. However, it was his expression I noticed most, and most distrusted; for there was an odd ironic twist to his lips which gave him the look of a cynic twice his age. In reply to his remark I said, amiably enough:

" 'I had no idea Mrs. Robinson had a son.'

" 'Thank the Lord for small mercies,' he said. 'So many mothers talk of nothing else.'

" 'You are still at school?' I asked.

" A look of slight annoyance came into his eyes.

" 'Do I look so young?' he asked. 'No—I am up at Cambridge. Or at least, I shall be next term. I've just sat for a scholarship.'

" 'And heard that you've passed? Congratulations.'

" 'Oh, I haven't heard that I've passed. But I know I've passed. You see, I don't suffer from false modesty, Vicar. I've no doubt I've won the scholarship. I've sat for many exams., for some of which I've worked, others for which I haven't worked. And I've passed them all. For this one I worked hard, and know I've done superlatively well. In fact I needn't have worked nearly so hard. But I did so in order to have the pleasure of refusing one of the most sought-after scholarships of the year.'

" 'Rather a waste of time, surely? Doesn't your mother want you to take it?'

" 'Mother?' he laughed. 'My dear vicar, my mother has nothing to do with it. She would willingly pay for me at Cambridge, and could well afford it. But I prefer to pay for myself. If I go at all. But as I've said, I shall probably refuse the scholarship.'

" 'And what will you do?'

" 'Why, serve my King and Country, of course.'

" 'Surely you would have to do that anyway?'

" 'Oh no. The scholarship would exempt me. It would cause my country to consider that my brains are of more use to it than my body. Which of course they are. . . . But for that very reason I intend to deprive my country of their use. It amuses me to do so.'

" 'But does it amuse your mother for you to do so?'

" 'My dear vicar, you have a positive obsession with mothers. Or is it this mother in particular? Surely you too haven't fallen for her?'

" 'I don't know what you mean,' I said stiffly.

"Again there came to his lips that ironic smile of a man twice his age.

" 'Don't you, Vicar?' he asked. 'You soon will. . . .'

"I was about to reply sharply, when the door opened, and three of the Poles, defeated in their efforts to become Mrs. Robinson's assistants, came in. There then began one of those conversations in a mixture of languages which are often so much easier to conduct than conversations in only one language, because so much explanation is needed to say so little. Soon Mrs. Robinson returned with the other two Poles, carrying a tray of coffee and sandwiches.

" 'I've just been instructed in the Polish way of making coffee,' said Mrs. Robinson, and she did in fact have the appearance of having been enjoying herself, for her eyes were shining and she seemed to be on an almost flirtatious footing with the Polish officer; she seemed to realize I had noticed this, for she said to me almost apologetically;

" 'These Continentals have such gay manners.'

"Scarcely had she said this, when the air-raid warning suddenly started; this was the first time I had heard it since being in London—there had been a remarkably quiet spell—and it rather startled me. At first the others took no notice of it, and went on talking as if nothing had happened. But after a few moments, quite close, there came the bark of anti-aircraft guns. There was a moment of silence in which we all looked at each other.

" 'Oh bother,' said Mrs. Robinson. 'And I'm on duty tonight. That's the worst of being on so many Committees—there's always something. It's nine o'clock, isn't it?'

"I looked at my watch.

" 'Two minutes past,' I said.

" 'Then I must go down,' she replied. 'And I hope none of you people are going to be foolish and not go down to the air-raid shelter. You will, won't you, Vicar? Please don't argue. It's a great nuisance to all of us when people start being brave and staying in unsafe places to see the fun. Because then when buildings start falling down everybody has a great deal of trouble trying to dig you all out and writing to relatives and winding up estates and so on. So I'll rely on you to see that everyone goes down to the shelter—it's quite easy to find, down in the basement.'

"And she hurried out, only to put her head back round the door a moment later—unexpectedly surmounted by a blue tin-hat—to say:

" 'And don't leave any lights on—in case the windows blow in. . . .'

"Meanwhile the noise had increased; the drone of aircraft could now be heard, and the quiet rustle of people moving along the corridors outside on their way to the shelter. I felt excited, almost exhilarated, as I always did when hearing British guns firing, whether in defence or attack. The others had gone to the window where they had pulled back the thick curtains and were staring out, apparently regardless of the black-out. I switched out the light and joined them, unable to resist the temptation of seeing London in the midst of an air-raid; at this moment however there was a sudden increase in the amount of anti-aircraft fire and through it could be heard the unmistakable whine of a falling bomb. At once the Poles—old soldiers—instinctively flung themselves face downwards, an example I immediately followed, and at once I felt the building shake alarmingly, and my ears were deafened by the noise of the exploding bomb. For a few seconds there seemed to be silence though the guns must still have been firing. Cautiously I looked round the room; the Poles were flat on the floor near the window, but Peter was still standing at the window with his hands in his pockets and with a cigarette drooping from a corner of his mouth; as I was looking at him he removed the cigarette and gently tapped it so that the ash fell onto the sill.

"The Poles began to pick themselves up, dusting themselves down, chattering among themselves, laughing a little; but again the gun-fire increased and this time we could hear distinctly the uneven throb of a German bomber; the Poles looked at each other, and then, as if motivated by a single brain, made a dash for the door, and I then heard them going hell-for-leather along the corridor towards the stairs. Slowly I got to my feet, whilst Peter looked round at me, his eyebrows raised.

" 'Not following our Polish friends, Vicar?' he asked. "It's much the best policy, you know. Personally I rather admired their unanimity of action. But then these Continentals have no repressions—they're not afraid of being afraid. . . .'

" 'You are?' I asked.

" 'Of course. All English are, aren't they? And of course we enjoy being foolishly heroic, as mother calls it. It's our particular form of self-indulgence. I, for instance, have been in several air-raids, and find that I never feel so vividly alive as when threatened with sudden death, as the novelists would say. I feel proud of being so brave. . . . And then war is so beautiful. Look, Vicar. . . .'

"And he indicated the window. I joined him there, and for a moment looked curiously at his face; his thin, pale features were white and his eyes had in them an almost feverish look, but the hand which lifted the cigarette to his mouth was quite steady. I then looked out of the window, and saw what was fascinating him. It was the first time I had seen a London air-raid. And it was certainly beautiful—the beauty of an infernal firework display; pink tracer bullets were pouring upwards, the orange light from an incendiary bomb on a nearby roof was flickering over the buildings, the white beams of a dozen searchlights moved restlessly across the sky, and from above a full moon was casting a disdainful light over the whole proceeding; and as I watched I saw suddenly the silver wings of a 'plane glisten in a searchlight beam; immediately all the other beams raced across the sky to the same spot, followed by streams of pink tracers, and once more the noise of firing rose to a crescendo. I had the sensation of tons of molten metal being hurled up at that one small aircraft, and fiercely, in that unthinking moment, I wanted to see it escape, that beautiful little machine with so much opposed to it. But at once my intellect came into play and told me that this was an enemy bomber which might still cause the death of dozens of my countrymen and I told myself that I wanted to see it burst into flames and come hurtling to the ground. And as had happened to me more than once during the war, I did not know which of these was the more Christian feeling, and for a moment—the first since I had left the army—I felt ill at ease, disorientated, unsure of myself. . . . The phrase 'Do not blame them for they know not what they do,' floated into my mind. And fascinated I continued to watch that beautiful battle going on in the sky, until I was brought back to reality by Peter's voice saying calmly:

" 'They won't get him—he's far too high—they're wasting ammunition. . . .'

"And sure enough the searchlights seemed slowly to lose contact with the machine as it gained height and became smaller and smaller, eventually to vanish altogether; simultaneously the noise of firing died down, though it could still be heard in the distance.

" 'My God, that was good. . . .' he said.

" 'Good?' I asked.

"Then he seemed to see me for the first time, and the feverish look left his eyes as his expression returned to normal. The ironic, mocking look came back to them.

" 'Perhaps the wrong word, Vicar. . . .' he said. 'Infernally beautiful would be a better description. . . . Have a cigarette?'

" 'No,' I replied. 'I don't smoke.'

"Peter threw himself into a chair and switched on a table-lamp.

" 'It was fun whilst it lasted,' he said. 'And thank God it's got rid of those infernal Poles. Mother chooses the strangest friends. . . .'

" 'That bomb was near, wasn't it?' I asked.

" 'No—at least two blocks away. If it had been any nearer it would've blown the windows in, and my face with them. The Poles were quite right in ducking—blast can do funny things in streets. It stripped a woman naked a few weeks ago, not far from here. Or so they say. I wasn't there, unfortunately. I wonder how our Polish friends are?'

" 'And your mother. . . .'

" 'Oh, she'll be all right. . . . It'll take more than a little war like this to finish her off. She's survived far worse things. . . .' He drew deeply at his cigarette, swallowing the smoke. 'I don't know about you, Vicar, but I'm turning in soon. I'm going to claim my bed before I find one of the Poles in occupation. I don't care for their perfume. . . .'

" And he looked up at me, and as I stared back I saw fully into his eyes for the first time, and felt almost a shock; for never before had I looked into the eyes of a human being and seen no sign of the soul lying behind them. Fundamentally they were quite expressionless in spite of the mocking look that lay on the surface. He quickly looked away from me as if sensing he had given something away. I felt a wave of dislike for him pass through me, but I quickly pulled myself together. For always I have hated making instinctive judgements of people—I have always thought that instinct is the province of women. So with a gentleness which I believe rather surprised the young man lolling insolently on the sofa, I took my leave of him.

"I only saw Peter once more before that party held by Mrs. Robinson on the occasion of your arrival among us. . . . Then, of course, the war was nearly over. The other time I saw him was a few months after the air-raid, when the news had just come through that he had succeeded in his examination—he had come second in the whole country—and he was surrounded by half a dozen people (a W.V.S. meeting had just broken up, when he arrived in the flat) who were congratulating him. He was accepting these congratulations in a manner typical of him, with exaggerated politeness, and with his usual ironical smile, but obviously enjoying himself. When they had all expressed their admiration sufficiently—though not very enthusiastically because he was not liked—he came out, as if as an afterthought, with the news that he wasn't taking the scholarship, but volunteering for the Forces. There was a moment of silence, then a storm of protest, which he accepted quite unemotionally; and there was in this general protest a note of admiration, and some surprise, because his reputation was not of the highest among the people of the flats from the patriotic point of view. But he spoiled this—as if hating to be popular even for a moment—by assuring everyone that he was doing it not for any reason connected with patriotism—for he cared not in the least who won the war—but because it would give him great pleasure to take part in this orgy of slaughter; for what other chance in life was he likely to get, he asked, to satisfy the lust to kill which is in all men, and actually be praised for it? And he smiled round at his audience as he asked this question, obviously delighted by the looks of distaste on their faces. And everyone looked very uncomfortable, obviously not knowing whether to take him seriously, or to regard it as just another of his not very funny jokes.

"But, watching him, and half admiring the skill with which this youth played upon the emotions of his audience, I thought I saw through his pose; I thought I saw that this making of excuses for a conventionally courageous action was merely his peculiar way of saving face, of excusing himself to himself, a not unusual attitude for sophisticated, war-time youth, and I felt for him a little pity, thinking how tiring it must be to cloak such simple motives in such complicated metaphysical garb. Little did I suspect then my own innocence. . . .

"So when, on being myself asked, as vicar, to add my own to the general effort at persuading the young man to accept his scholarship, and I used, without the slightest hope of success, Peter's own argument—that his brain was of more use to his country than his ability to kill—I received a shock when, after listening to me in silence, he looked at me with an odd little smile—almost as if he had been waiting for me to speak—and said that certainly he would not combat the authority of the Church and would immediately reconsider his decision, and take the scholarship. At this reply I felt sudden anger, thinking it a deliberate piece of sarcasm, and was about to administer a rebuke in no uncertain terms, when I caught in the boy's eyes a look of delighted expectancy, and realized instantly that this was the very reaction he was wanting me to show. So instead of annoyance, I smiled back at him, perhaps the first really ironic smile I had ever achieved, and congratulated him on his change of mind. For a moment he hesitated, and in that instant I knew that I had to some extent scored a hit.

"I have no doubt that the rest of the occupants of the room were somewhat mystified as to what was going on between us, for they must have sensed that there was more meaning to what we said than appeared on the surface; so they laughed a little as people do when out of their depth, asked Peter what he was really going to do, and accepted his assurance that he would in fact accept the scholarship, with a certain amount of suspicion, still unable to judge when he was being serious. They also managed, by their manner, to express disappointment that he was now going to follow the course they had themselves been urging only a moment or so before, instead of volunteering for the Forces. Only Mrs. Robinson seemed to have some understanding of what was going on, for I was aware of her looking at me with a kind of puzzled respect, though I could not make up my mind whether she did in fact understand the workings of her son's mind, or whether she thought simply that it had been the power of my argument that had caused this change of plan. I did not realize then that I was far further from comprehending the mother than the son."

Mr. Ash stopped speaking, and smiling slightly, looked at his wife. "You are not asleep?" he asked.

"No," she said, her violet-coloured eyes unsmiling. "I want you to go on talking. . . ."

"But my throat is dry. I've been talking for over an hour."

Suddenly she wanted to ask him why it was he was so obsessed over his recent past, what it was he was trying to find out; but instinctively—with the instinct which, she remembered wryly, he had rather disparagingly described as "a woman's province"—she knew it was too soon to do this. So she said:

"*Then let's go for a stroll before turning in, and relieve your poor throat with something in a café . . . it's only nine-thirty. . . .*"

So they went out, this time crossing the river, and sitting down in a rather garish students' café in Montparnasse. For half an hour they sat watching the students' antics, half-amused, half-irritated. As they left, he said:

"*They made me feel quite middle-aged. . . .*"

"*Me too. . . .*" *she murmured. Quickly he looked at her as if about to say something and for a moment she thought he was going to pay her a compliment about her appearance such as other men pay their wives; but instead he said nothing, and looked away, and as he did so she thought she caught a look of self-dissatisfaction on his face. Unthinkingly she took his arm, for the first time since they had been together; she felt his arm stiffen, and he kept it awkwardly crooked so that she could keep her hand there. And this she did until they reached the hotel.*

In their room they went through much the same procedure as on the previous evening, and once more she was in bed when he returned from his final smoke. This, she learnt, was the only cigarette he smoked in the course of the day. The next morning the same ritual was gone through as on the previous morning, and this went on throughout their six days in Paris. They established a regular programme; in the morning they went sight-seeing, in the afternoon he accompanied her round the shops, and in the evenings they sat in the hotel lounge and he talked, and finally they went for their stroll on the way back from which she took his arm.

During it all she was far from unhappy because a firm companionship was being established between them, and they were growing to depend on each other's company; and slowly she was learning to understand him. But still they were no more to each other than good friends, and she began to long for the next stage of their holiday—by sleeper to Florence. . . .

And still, each evening, he went on with his story.

"I soon almost forgot young Peter Robinson," he went on, "in my preoccupation with parish affairs. The actual organization

of the Church had meantime gone on smoothly enough—the
Services were now conducted with the necessary ceremony,
and the congregation was increasing; but in spite of this, I was
not satisfied. I knew that those who came to my services were
only those who traditionally went to Church, mostly from the
older generations—the naturally pious who had in recent months
been going to other Churches in the neighbourhood—and who
had only come back to their parish church on hearing that it was
now in the hands of a comparatively young vicar who had been
—the newspaper report had had its effect—something of a hero
at Dunkirk. And once back, they stayed, partly because of the
geographical convenience of the building, partly because—here
perhaps I flatter myself—my preaching still had a certain freshness,
for I had not yet exhausted all my themes.

"But all the time I knew I had not extended the influence of
the Church by a single soul but had merely relieved some of
the neighbouring clergy of part of the congregation they had
poached during and since my predecessor's term of office. And
among the 'slum' people so despised by Mrs. Taylor, my
progress had been nil, and I was conscious of a certain air of
triumph in my housekeeper's manner when I returned unsuccessful and discouraged from my treks round this neighbourhood.
For try though I did, I had made no contacts in this area, though
I had made some progress in helping the old people who had
no one to look after them, and had actually succeeded in interesting the Council in their plight. But this, I knew, was something
a competent social-worker could have done just as well, and for
me the Church had to be more than a social welfare organization.

"However, life had settled down into a period of comparative
calm—the calmest I was to experience in the parish—and though
interrupted by air-raids and my attendance at the various
Committees—to the W.V.S. and A.R.P. had been added the
Red Cross—I did much hard work.

"At the same time I paid regular visits on Mrs. Robinson, the
Kynastons—where I had mock-serious religious arguments with
the nimble-witted Mrs. Kynaston—and on Mrs. Carrington-

Smith. Mrs. Kynaston gave me much information about various people, and I could not always decide when she was being serious and when gently pulling my leg. But on one aspect of Mrs. Carrington-Smith's character I found her observation to be most acute; she told me a peculiarity of this lady was that when she had any kind of an audience she seemed to lose her head and become almost a caricature of a snob, but that alone she was quite a reasonable person. Again and again I found this to be true. I had many a private talk with her, when she was sensible and unusually intelligent; but as soon as someone else entered the room, she seemed, as it were, to go off the rails, and talk to impress. I formed the opinion that at heart she was an unhappy woman, determined that everyone should know she had once seen better days. And all the local people, with Mrs. Kynaston almost the only exception, seemed to take her at her own valuation, swallowing whole her stories of her life before the war, which I believe were at least partly true. And she was certainly a most accomplished organizer, the W.V.S. Committee being the most efficient of those with which I had any contact; this was perhaps partly due to the fact that it was run more or less on the lines of a dictatorship, with Mrs. Carrington-Smith the dictator. But on the whole I found her most difficult to bear. For, though a woman who perhaps, if life had treated her better, could have been a most useful member of society, it was her personality as it was, and particularly her personality in public, which was effective, and this was most dangerous to the whole fabric of our little society. For you see, she had the power of influencing people, and chief among her followers was young Mrs. Bartram, who, having originated in a social environment lower than that enjoyed by most of the inhabitants of Carlton Court, was wholly impressed by her, and had become a kind of satellite of hers, avidly swallowing her stories of mink coats and Rolls-Royces. It took me some time to realize why Mrs. Carrington-Smith put up with this sly young woman's company—because in theory she was the type the older woman instinctively despised. I soon realized however that she found in her the ideal 'stooge', a perfect little maid-of-all-work who could run her messages and support her on the Committee—to which Mrs. Carrington-Smith had engineered her election—and listen awe-struck to her nostalgic tales of before the war. Had Mrs. Bartram been an 'innocent little thing' I could have pitied her and would have done something to get her away from the clutches of the other woman before it was too late, before they became the most dangerous combination in the parish; but I soon learned that Norma Bartram was as dangerous as the other, sharing all Mrs. Carrington-Smith's worst characteristics and having none of her merits, and I did not realize then quite how dangerous she was, not only to us but to Mrs. Carrington-Smith herself, for you know as well as I do how she used the older woman as a stepping-stone, learning all she could from her, and then abandoning her. But I am anticipating. . . .

"The only woman in the district who seemed at that time in any way able to stand up to Mrs. Carrington-Smith was Mrs. Robinson, and I soon began to understand what Mrs. Kynaston had meant when she had insinuated how these two hated each other. Occasionally, by little acts of insubordination, Mrs. Robinson showed herself to be completely her own mistress, for though she was obviously far from being what Mrs. Carrington-Smith would describe as a 'lady', and could obviously lay no claim to ever having been 'in society', she sometimes displayed a knowledge of society at least the equal of the other woman's. More than once she had, as if accidentally, or—some said—as if suddenly unable to resist the temptation, revealed an acquaintance with the most fashionable hotels both in London and on the Continent, and on three separate occasions in my presence she had sweetly corrected Mrs. Carrington-Smith on points of detail concerning a certain restaurant, a Parisian fashion-house, and a society coiffeur in the South of France; and on each occasion I saw a look on Mrs. Carrington-Smith's face which revealed that the other woman was right. It was at about this time too that I began to notice that, unlike Mrs. Carrington-Smith, Mrs. Robinson never talked about her life before the war, and this, in view of the fact that she was a very talkative woman, was very surprising. She would merely say gently, when challenged by Mrs. Carrington-Smith about a restaurant or a shop in Paris, that she had 'been there', or 'used to shop there', and would never go into details as to when or with whom this had happened. All this, of course, annoyed Mrs. Carrington-Smith enormously, and she would retaliate in her own subtle way, by holding 'intimate' little dinner-parties, to which, she let it be known secretly, she invited only the 'best' people, and to which she never invited Mrs. Robinson.

"But at this time I took none of these petty rivalries seriously, being so preoccupied with the more serious business of the parish; I never thought that later they would become so important to me. At that time my main worry was my failure to make any impact on the poorer quarters and so it was with a sense of relief and renewed hope that one night I met outside the Carlton Arms a man whom I had known as Sergeant-Major White, a man intimately connected with the award of my notorious decoration, and who, I soon discovered, was living in the very area where so far I had failed to gain a foothold—in the tenements behind the Carlton Arms; and because it is important in my future relationship with this man, I will here digress a little to tell you the truth about that little act of 'heroism' of mine.

"My connexion with Tom White started long before the retreat to Dunkirk, during the time when the Battalion was sitting somewhat listlessly in reserve somewhere near where the Maginot Line met the Belgian frontier. I had known Tom White as one of the hardest and most brutal C.S.M.s in the Battalion, and the most uncooperative from my point of view. For he was one of those soldiers who disliked all padrés, begrudging the very rations we ate, and considering us a waste of manpower; it had been one of his favourite grudges—and he had many—that the War Office not only had the idiocy to encumber every Battalion with a padré to whom they allocated a valuable vehicle, but that they should also provide us with able-bodied batmen who could be much better employed in the line. Whenever I had visited the Company to which C.S.M. White was sergeant-major, I had found myself given as little encouragement and as few facilities as possible, and discovered that the Church Parades of this particular Company were by far the worst attended of any in the Battalion. Consequently, being, as I have already shown, unable to resist a challenge, I made a point of visiting this Company as often as possible, and a kind of private war developed between myself and C.S.M. White, a war far more interesting to us both than the real one which at that time was supposed to be going on.

"So it was with a peculiar kind of pleasure that, not far from Dunkirk itself, I had taken the opportunity of saving C.S.M. White's life. During the retreat each Company had taken it in turn to act as rearguard, with the enemy gradually drawing nearer, until, with Dunkirk in sight, and just before the French troops took over from us for the final defence, there had developed a series of hand-to-hand skirmishes, during which I had been called upon to make many a man's final peace with God. B-Company (Sergeant-Major White's) was unfortunate enough to have to act as the final rearguard and had been almost wiped out in the process; and at the very end of the final skirmish, whilst I was making a dash for my parked truck within sight of the enemy after having carried out a final duty by the roadside, I came across C.S.M. White, covered with blood, crawling along the middle of the road, not away from, but towards the enemy. And it was only after the exercise of a considerable amount of physical force that I and my batman succeeded in half-dragging, half-carrying the barely conscious body of the wounded man over the two hundred yards or so separating us from the truck, a process complicated by enemy mortars persistently falling in the vicinity, a splinter from one of which must have entered my right calf just before we reached the truck, a fact of which I was hardly aware until half an hour later. During this rather hectic little walk C.S.M. White had been sufficiently conscious to resist his forcible and undignified removal from the battlefield, and swore vividly at me, telling me to 'get off home to Battalion H.Q. where I belonged' suggesting that this unit was no doubt by now happily billeted in the best hotel in Dunkirk; he also asked to be allowed to go back to his 'boys up the road' unaware that those of the 'boys' still alive were by now being marched in the opposite direction under German escort.

"In fact we succeeded in reaching the truck, in which, with two tyres punctured, and after picking up half a dozen walking-wounded on the way, we managed to reach the outskirts of Dunkirk, from which point a stern military policeman told us we must walk. So we carried the sergeant-major to the beaches, from where, with great luck, after a day or so, we had gone over the water in the cross-channel steamer which brought us here. In England we had parted, going to separate hospitals, and I had not heard whether White had recovered from his ugly chest-wound or not.

And I did not know until, one evening, returning from one of Mrs. Carrington-Smith's 'exclusive' dinner-parties, and feeling rather more disillusioned with myself than usual, as I passed the Carlton Arms, the door opened, and in a crack of light caused by an imperfect black-out, I had for a fraction of a second seen the features of C.S.M. White. For a moment we both stood in the darkness saying nothing, then I had felt my arm gripped above the elbow so hard that it hurt, and through an aroma of beer-fumes—presumably C.S.M. White's breath—I heard the harsh, well-known voice say:

" 'Padré Ash or I'm a——! It is, ain't it?'

" 'It is,' I said quietly. 'What in the name of all that's wonderful are you doing here, Tom White?'

" 'I live 'ere—just down the road. Come into the light, padré, and let's 'ave a look at you.'

"At that moment I was astonished by my own feelings, especially in view of the fact that I had never liked Tom White; for we had not really made friends, not even during the trip across the water; but it was as if, in spite of this, something had been established between us which made us a part of each other's life, however much we might dislike each other. I even felt an odd excitement, a sudden feeling that this meeting was more important to me than all my principles, a feeling which caused me to allow Tom White to hustle me into the public bar, up to the counter, through a curiously staring crowd of men, and place in my hand a pint tankard of beer, almost before I knew what was happening. And then Tom, once more gripping my arm, ushered me towards a comparatively secluded corner of the room, looking me up and down as he did so, saying, "S'truth! It's you all right, padré! Dog-collar an' all! 'Ow's the leg, padré?'

" 'Patched up pretty well, Tom,' I heard myself saying. 'Just a little limp, that's all. How's yourself?'

" 'Good as new—though they won't let me go back to the army. Given me a pension, they 'ave. Silly bastards—I'm fitter than all the brass-'ats put together and a bloody sight more use than the civvy-street warrant officers they're makin' up now-adays. Know what I'm doin' now? Trainin' the 'Ome Guard—me!'

" 'Well—they might be needed, I suppose.'

" Tom gave a laugh in which there was a bitterness that startled me.

" 'Don't you believe it,' he said. 'The way the war's goin' it'll all be over in a few months with us chasin' Jerry 'alf across Europe an' me not there to see it. And as for my boys—the poor old bastards' fingers tremble so as they can 'ardly pull a trigger. And d'you know what they've give us for weapons now? Bits of old bedstead called Sten guns—won't fire more'n fifty yards and then in the wrong direction. But what're you doin' 'ere, padré?'

"I explained my situation and there then began one of those conversations of reminiscence which can go on almost inde-finitely and in this case went on until closing-time; during it Tom went back to the bar more than once and returned with the pint mugs refilled, refusing to let me take my turn, and insisting on my draining my glass each time. It was as if I were allowing

my will to be dominated, not so much by another man as by the
whole circumstance of this unexpected meeting, and as I drank
all that was brought me I did not protest, and even capped Tom's
stories of the Battalion—not all of them decent—with tales of my
own, which I hope were decent, and I was only vaguely aware
that by now we had been joined by a little crowd of Tom's
friends—including a tall, Italian-looking man—to whom Tom
introduced me as Padré Ash, a hero of Dunkirk who'd saved his
life, and he looked round threateningly as if daring them to
dispute it. I had never before found myself getting on so well
with people of this kind and was quite unaware of what I have
since suspected was a certain amount of ridicule in the general
attitude towards us both. Because we must by then have been
more than a little tight, and I suppose the spectacle of a vicar
swapping army stories with a sergeant-major in a public bar
was rather unusual. However, I quietened without much trouble
the small part of my conscience that was still active by telling
myself that by behaving like this I was gaining the respect of
these people, that in drinking their beer and capping their stories
I was seizing the key to their homes; I remember that this rather
clumsy metaphor actually occurred to me.

"Eventually closing-time came and I found myself standing in
the cold air outside the Carlton Arms allowing Tom to persuade
me to go home with him 'to meet the girls'—whoever they were
—and next I was aware of myself walking not very steadily
through the black-out, on that night fortunately very intense,
arm-in-arm with Tom, who was insisting in rather slurred tones
that 'this time he would do the carrying'; actually in my own
defence I must say that I was quite capable of walking, but was
aware of Tom having reached that stage of drunkenness when
it would have been dangerous to contradict him in any way, so I
submitted to his support.

"I allowed myself to be conducted along several dark streets
only vaguely aware of the direction in which we were going,
until eventually I was relinquished rather abruptly and told,
'down these steps, padré—mind your leg,' and found myself

at the top of an almost vertical flight of stone steps down which
Tom was clattering ahead of me. I followed with some difficulty
to find myself once more gripped by Tom at the bottom and
conducted across what seemed to be a yard; after much fumbling
by Tom at a door which suddenly opened unexpectedly, pre-
cipitating us both into a room where the darkness seemed even
more intense than outside, I was then aware of Tom stumbling
about ahead of me, swearing ferociously. And so for a moment
I had only my nose to tell me where I was, and from the smell of
rancid fat and a general effluvia of cooking, I decided the room
was some kind of kitchen. There then came the click of a switch
and the room was flooded with light which for some moments
dazzled me, so that for a while I was aware only of Tom clattering about apparently angry about something, for he was still
swearing, interspersing it now with calls for someone called
'Anna' and muttering something about 'dirty——, ain't
cleaned up again, Millie's been to the pitchers, see, so nothin's
done. . . .'

"As my eyes grew accustomed to the glare, I slowly took in
the details of the room. It was indeed a kitchen, with a bare deal
table against which there was a wooden form and three hard
kitchen chairs, with a dresser on one side of the room and a gas-
stove and sink on the other; but it was evidently a living-room
too for there were two easy chairs, their covers black with dirt,
in front of the fireplace. It was a large room which obviously
had once been the kitchen of a mansion, and the fact that it still
smelt of human habitation in spite of its size indicated that the
windows were probably never opened even in the day-time
when there was no need for the black-out. I looked round
dizzily, having some difficulty in focusing my eyes, and had a
confused impression of an extraordinary untidiness; there were
dirty dishes piled on the table and in the sink, there was a towel
flung over a chair, a pile of film magazines strewn half-across the
floor, and a piece of feminine underwear draped across the
wooden form; in a corner on an old packing-case was a radio
which suddenly, startlingly, began to blare forth dance-music,

apparently having been connected with the same switch as the electric-light and not switched off when last in use. Meanwhile Tom had opened another door and was shouting violently at someone in the other room and was being answered by a shrill feminine voice, and to add to the babel there came the thin wail of a child crying in another room.

"I began to wish I hadn't come but at the same time I was excited; I was aware that this was the kind of household I had been trying to gain a footing in since I had come to the parish, and, my intellect dulled, but my emotions excited, by the four or five pints of beer I had consumed, I felt as if I were about to make some great stride forward in my career, that I was about to discover, by contact with these people, more about the basic nature of man and the substance of his relation to God.

"By now Tom had come back into the room, and with strained attention I watched him as he blundered about seizing dirty plates and almost throwing them into the sink, and grasping clothing and flinging it into a corner of the room; he was in a blind rage, and his appearance, with his stocky, powerful body with its great breadth of shoulder, his tiny, close-set, curiously light-blue eyes which were sometimes cunning, sometimes fierce, but at this moment bloodshot with anger, seemed almost to be that of a different species from the neat, smart C.S.M. White of the Battalion. Suddenly he stopped in the middle of the room, staring at me, screwing up his eyes as if having difficulty in seeing me, and for a moment he seemed startled at my being there at all, as if he had forgotten my existence; then he seemed to pull himself together and said:

" 'Sit down, padré, make yourself at 'ome.'

"And with a curious gesture I had seen more than once in the slum houses I had visited in my abortive wanderings in the area, he wiped one of the wooden chairs with a dish-cloth he was holding, and offered it to me. But as I half turned to walk round the table, I stood suddenly still as I became aware of a third person in the room.

"For standing just within the door through which Tom had

been shouting a few minutes before, was a woman; she was tall and thin with straight black hair, a parchment-yellow complexion, and dark, slanting eyes set in a face quite without expression; she was dressed in an old dressing-gown made out of some kind of towelling, dirty and threadbare, and a soiled cotton nightgown could be seen round her calves, whilst her feet were in carpet slippers too large for her and out of which her yellow ankles emerged awkwardly. Aware that she had been seen she looked away indifferently and started to cross the room to the dresser, and as she moved I received my second shock for she walked with the grace of some lithe animal, which seemed to render almost beautiful her tall thin body, which I now noticed had remarkable poise, straight and upright; her manner registered a kind of proud indifference to the presence of both her husband —for I assumed she was Tom's wife—and myself.

"It took me some moments to grasp the simple and obvious explanation of her presence—that Tom, an old soldier who had seen service in India and Burma, had no doubt married her out there and brought her home. This I still assume to be the truth though I have never been told so.

"Meanwhile the woman had bent down before the dresser from which she took several bottles of beer, as if she knew from experience what was wanted; and looking suddenly from her to her husband I was surprised to see that the anger which previously had possessed Tom and of which this woman had presumably been partly the cause, had suddenly vanished, as if extinguished by the indifference of her manner. In future I was to notice more than once this strange element in the relationship of these two— as if she had some kind of moral ascendency over him which vanished as soon as he was out of her actual presence.

"Tom began to question her in undertones which sounded almost pleading in tone, to which she replied with shrugs and shakes of the head, a whispered consultation which went on for several minutes. I began at this moment to realize that it was nearing midnight and that for the last two hours I had been behaving in a manner not at all befitting my position. I began to feel the shame and self-criticism which is an inevitable part of the sobering-up process, when Tom seemed to realize my uneasiness, for he looked at me anxiously, and it occurred to me suddenly that he was for some reason very eager for me to remain.

" 'Sit down, padré,' he urged, again offering the chair. 'you must accept the 'ospitality of my 'ouse or I shall be insulted. . . .' He leaned across the table as I at last took the seat, and winked broadly. 'Me an' my ole woman,' he went on, nodding towards his wife—this was the nearest I ever got to an introduction to her —'me an' my ole woman may not be beauties, but we ain't done so badly in the matter of kids. . . . You wait till you've seen Ruby. . . .'

" 'You have children?' I asked politely.

" 'Four—though two of them's only kids yet. But the other two's grown up, seventeen an' fifteen they are, and Ruby—that's the eldest—she's a real smasher. . . .'

" 'But surely you're not getting them out of bed at this hour?' I asked, suddenly understanding his intention.

" 'Don't you worry, padré,' he replied. 'This is a special occasion, see. Besides——' suddenly into the small eyes there came one of their few variations in expression, a look of craftiness, 'besides, it'll do 'em good to meet the likes o' you . . . you 'ave a glass of beer, padré, whilst I 'urries them up. . . .' And pushing a bottle and glass towards me, he disappeared through a door. He was gone some minutes and I was about to attempt conversation with Mrs. White—who was now sitting in one of the armchairs staring at me unblinkingly—when Tom came back, looking pleased with himself.

" 'They're just comin',' he said, and started moving about the room, strangely restless, pouring himself out beer, picking up the glass and then putting it down again without drinking. To me he seemed to be in a strange state of expectancy, and was continually looking towards the door through which he had come, and even I began to feel quite interested in what it was I was about to see.

" I was in fact looking at Tom when Ruby came through the door, so it was reflected in the father's eyes that I first saw the daughter; for Tom suddenly became quite still, his hands dropped to his sides and onto his face there came a curious expression—half-proud, half-worshipping. Quickly I looked round and saw standing framed in the doorway a young woman. Now often I have seen illustrated on the front of cheap novels of a certain kind which somehow get into the hands of troops, glamorous young women in a state which I believe is generally described as *déshabille*; always they have on dressing-gowns open almost down to the waist, hair over their shoulders, and legs, usually clad in sheer silk stockings, visible almost up to their thighs, whilst they invariably have figures of the most improbable voluptuousness; now when I tell you that Ruby could have served as a model for such a novel, I am in no way exaggerating. For over her nightgown there was a house-coat as luxurious as her mother's was threadbare and soiled, a garment fastened tightly by some invisible fixture round her waist and which fell open at both waist and neck, revealing, vaguely seen through the thin stuff of her nightdress, the firm smooth limbs of youth. Unexpectedly she had a mass of blonde hair brushed carelessly back, which set into startling contrast the black Eastern eyes set slantwise in her face—eyes which might have been her mother's—but then you know what she looks like as well as I, though you have never seen her dressed like that. Her expression was the only thing that really let her down—for she could not disguise her youth and lack of experience, try though she did to look at me out of half-closed eyes like a Jezebel, or more probably like her favourite film-star.

"Exactly what effect she was supposed to produce on me, I do not know, but I am afraid my reaction was rather disappointing to both her and Tom. For I showed neither embarrassment nor lust but merely stood up and shook hands with her as if being introduced to a prospective Sunday-School teacher, for now I was completely sober and in full possession of all my faculties. As I shook hands with her she looked at me for a moment

uncertainly, as if not knowing whether to giggle or look affron-
ted, and as she came slowly towards the table and sat down on
one of the hard kitchen chairs her lips pouted and for a moment
I thought she was going to burst into tears, and I realized suddenly
that I was indeed in the presence of a child of seventeen caught
out in a rather unpleasant game. For it occurred to me that this
was probably not the first time Tom had displayed his daughter
before men brought back from the pub half-drunk late at night,
and I wondered what kind of a game he was playing, and looked
over at him angrily. But he was sitting there looking at her with
such an expression of devotion in his small eyes that I couldn't
believe he really meant her any harm, but was only proud of her
and too drunk to understand the harm he might do. I determined to speak to him about it when he was sober, having
enough sense to realize that at this moment such an action might
be dangerous.

"It was then that I became aware of Mildred, the second
daughter. She must have come into the room some time after
her sister, and by the time I become aware of her, she was already
busy at the gas-stove, and on Tom telling her to 'come and meet
the padré', she merely glanced round, giving me a cursory glance
with her large brown eyes; it was these eyes that first attracted
my attention—eyes are always the first thing I notice about a
person—for though the same colour as those of her mother and
sister, they were more European in shape, though set in a face if
anything more Eastern than her sister's, for it was darker-skinned
and her hair was still black and straight, not transformed by the
peroxide bottle as was her sister's; and the look in those eyes was
intelligent, and, what surprised me most, as she looked at me
they seemed despising, as if already she were judging her father
and the kind of friends he had, of which I was just another. Her
figure was less impressive than her sister's—she was short and
stocky, though well-developed—as you know. Her clothes on
that occasion, and on every other occasion that I saw her, were
modest—she had on some kind of clean, faded cotton frock. The
strange thing was that though dressed almost like a child she gave

me an impression of much greater mental maturity than her sister. It was soon obvious to me why she had come into the room, probably why she always appeared on these occasions, for she at once set about preparing something to eat, and I gained the impression that this was her normal function, that she, rather than the mother, was the housewife.

"In fact I found my attention being distracted continually by this little figure at the stove, and in spite of the fact that both Tom and Ruby seemed to be doing their best to entertain me, I never altogether lost my awareness of Mildred. Ruby's entertaining consisted of catching my eye and smiling languorously, and occasionally leaning forward so that I was provided with a more than adequate view of her figure, whereupon she would look at me keenly to see what sort of effect it was having on me. It was obvious the whole time that she was acting the part of someone she had seen on the films. It was Tom who did most of the talking, embarrassing me more than Ruby did with his talk about Dunkirk, so exaggerating my part that in self-defence I had to retaliate by describing to his women-folk how brave he had been himself; at this a look of self-satisfaction came into his eyes, for of course he had never before had the opportunity of having his courage described by an eye-witness. As I watched Tom carried away by enthusiasm at his memories of that campaign I realized how his heart was in the army and wondered how he would stand up to full civilian life when once the war was over. If only I had known, then. . . . At that time of course he still had a finger in the conduct of the war, training his Home Guard recruits and no doubt showing off in his capacity as an old soldier with much service behind him; he also had the war itself to talk about in pubs, and his part to play in the excitement of air-raids, his uniform to wear with its double row of campaign medals and his M.M. . . . But when the war was over he would have no work even remotely connected with the army, and there would be no troops about with which he could reminisce, and he would have no uniform to wear . . . and as I looked into his close-set, cruel little eyes which would never look into my own, I remembered his reputation for brutality in the Battalion, and wondered, with a sense of fear, what his future would be. . . .

"In spite of the lateness I stayed with them on that first evening for more than an hour, for soon plates of fish and chips were produced by Mildred which I hadn't the heart to refuse, and which were in fact well cooked and appetizing. Conversation became more general and I tried to talk to both Milded and Mrs. White; but to all questions I put to the latter I received back only an incomprehending stare, until I began to wonder whether she spoke English at all; only when I mentioned Malaya did any sort of intelligence come into those enigmatic eyes, and then they looked wary and resentful as if I had broached a forbidden subject. Mildred answered me always in monosyllables, her face expressionless and hostile, but with an occasional flash in her dark-brown eyes which I can only describe as contemptuous, as if she had some secret reason for despising me.

"So after talking to her for a few minutes—during which Tom made almost irritated efforts to distract my attention, and Ruby watched with a surprising degree of jealousy—I finally took my leave. And as I made my way back to the vicarage through the black streets, lit only by some distant searchlights which moved restlessly across the sky, I felt more excited than at any time since leaving the army. For here was a new kind of people, human material which up to then I had only seen in the artificial environment of the army, and then only the men-folk.

"It was as if my soul was again touched by the excitement of the great world into which I had at last come, a world in which there seemed so much for me to do. I felt more than ever convinced of the rightness of my action in not returning to my secluded life of before the war in which I had spent so much of my youth, and as, on entering the vicarage, the air-raid warning sounded, I remembered I was on duty; and whilst I was taking my new blue tin-hat from its peg in the hall, I felt excited that I was now a part of, rather than apart from, this life that throbbed round me in this greatest city on earth which was at that time going through its biggest trial. I understood in that moment what Mrs. Robinson had meant when she had said that she could not desert it in its hour of need.

"During the next few months I became almost obsessed by the Whites, visiting them several times a week, much to the disgust of Mrs. Taylor, who knew the family well by reputation and insisted they were no good.

" 'Not that you can blame *'er*,' she said, referring to Mrs. White. 'She can't 'elp the colour of 'er skin, poor soul. But it's 'im, Tom White, that's the bad influence in that family. 'E drinks and mixes with bad company and spoils that there eldest daughter something awful. Already she's been seen with Yanks. . . .' she added darkly, and went on to say that before I knew where I was she would be 'on the streets'. Asked to specify precisely what 'bad company' Tom was in the habit of keeping, she said something vaguely about 'a bad lot in the Market', but would explain no further, and I came to the conclusion that her tales were based on hearsay and worth nothing. So I told her I had known Tom White for some time and had personal knowledge of his heroism at Dunkirk, at which she looked sceptical and uttered one of her aphorisms.

" 'That's as maybe,' she said, 'but them as is 'eroes in war-time ain't necessarily 'eroes in peacetime. . . .'

" 'But don't you think,' I asked her gently, 'that someone who cheerfully risks his life for his country must have some good in him?'

"But apparently she had had enough of philosophical argument and went grumbling out of the room, muttering under her breath that 'no good would come of mixing with the likes o' them', and looking generally far more put out than the occasion seemed to warrant. I remember I laughed at her to myself and then put her warnings out of my mind altogether. I remembered them, however, a year or so later. . . .

"Gradually I came to know the family better and succeeded in breaking down some of the resistance of the children, especially Mildred; with Ruby there was never any resistance to break down, in fact it was a case of keeping her at a distance, because the more I saw of her the more friendly she became, a friendliness that was a queer mixture of spontaneity and wickedness; I admit that I was somewhat out of my depth in her company and did not know whether to treat her as an over-affectionate child or as a young woman in need of a severe reprimand. I had an odd idea that she was using me as a sort of guinea-pig to test out the effect of her new clothes—of which she had unlimited numbers—yet at the same time I could not believe that a girl of only seventeen could be so worldly. I did my best to show neither surprise nor dismay at the creations in which she appeared before me, though I was by no means sure that I was taking the right action. I was particularly doubtful when, on my fourth visit to the family, she appeared before me in her dressing-gown which she suddenly removed to reveal herself in a two-piece bathing costume so brief that it did not even cover her navel; she posed before me with her hands on her hips and her eyes half-closed and asked me if 'it suited her'.

"'Made it myself,' she said. 'Copied it from one I saw Betty Grable in.'

"'And who is Betty Grable?' I asked.

"At this she looked at me hard, as if trying to decide whether or not I was joking. In fact, looking back, I think that at that time she must have been very puzzled by my reaction to her various attempts at captivating me—for that of course was what it was —and when I remember how sometimes I used to catch her staring across the room at me with a curious expression in her eyes, I realize that she was probably very divided in her mind as to whether to regard me as being quite oblivious to her charms— and therefore to be despised—or as having a sophistication worthy of Clark Gable (which I believe is the name of one of her favour-ite film-stars), and in that case to be very much admired. In fact at that time there must have been established between us a mutual lack of comprehension so complete as to render us permanently at cross-purposes.

"Whatever her final conclusions about me at that time, she

quickly seemed to come to regard me as her personal property, as she regarded everything brought into the house by her father. And Tom certainly seemed to lavish on her every spare penny he had, and it occurred to me even in those early days that he had far more to lavish on her than he could reasonably be expected to earn; however this thought was not strong enough to really develop into suspicion, unfortunately. The contrast between the possessions of Ruby and those of Mildred and her mother was extraordinary. For Ruby seemed to have a wardrobe worthy of the film-stars she worshipped, whilst Mildred and Mrs. White went about almost in rags. Throughout my acquaintanceship with the family at this period I saw Mildred in only two different cotton frocks—both threadbare and too small for her, but very clean; whilst Mrs. White, besides her dressing-gown—which seemed to be made of a number of army towels sewn together—appeared to have only a greasy woollen dress of pre-war vintage which she put on for special occasions. However, the aspect of Ruby which at that time irritated me the most was the way in which she monopolized my company, making it almost impossible for me to talk to Mildred, which I was very eager to do. In fact it was not until I learnt that on two evenings every week—Mondays and Fridays—Ruby went to the cinema, whatever was on, that I was able to carry on a single conversation of any length with her sister. Even then it took me several evenings of patient effort before I established any trust in the younger girl, for she seemed to resent my efforts at conversation as an interruption to her labours. For not only did she do all the cooking and what cleaning there was done, but also everything practical towards bringing up the two younger children. She dressed them, washed them, sent them to bed, and, I discovered later, saw that they went to school. She did all these tasks in a strangely unemotional way, almost as if she disliked the two children as much as she seemed to dislike the rest of the world, and I could not make out why she allowed herself to be the slave of the family, because she obviously had the strongest character of all the children. In fact there was little love lost between any members of the family, with the exception of Tom's infatuation for Ruby, and Mrs. White's love for the youngest child—a boy. This boy was a pathetic little creature, with tiny arms like sticks and enormous scared brown eyes, who almost gave the impression that he ought to be brought up in a specially heated room, like a hot-house plant; between him and his mother there was a special bond of sympathy even though she never seemed to do anything for him; he was always hanging round her, clinging to her skirt or sitting on her knee, and she was obviously passionately devoted to the child. Watching them together, I thought sometimes that he was the woman's only interest in life, for she took none in the rest of the family or in her home; she would only move herself at all when ordered to do so by her husband, and then not through fear but as if from a tradition of servitude to the male that went back for generations. The few times I tried to speak to the boy, he seemed overwhelmed with terror and merely clung to his mother, hiding his face in her skirts; he gave me the impression that he regarded all grown men with terror, and I wondered whether Tom had anything to do with this. . . . On my fourth visit I tried the effect of giving him toys which he took gingerly and then went straight over to his mother, depositing them in her lap, and never in subsequent visits did I see him playing with those toys or any others. In fact these two, mother and son, remained always a mysterious puzzle, unapproachable, sufficient unto each other until the end, and eventually I came to ignore them altogether as everyone else did, even visitors, and this they seemed to prefer, for then they appeared almost happy, sitting in a corner muttering together, sometimes even bursting into shrill laughs.

"The fourth child was another girl of eleven or twelve who seemed to hero-worship Ruby, though having more of the appearance of Mildred, and for some reason not clear to me even now, I disliked this child from the start; there was a cheeky look in her eyes when I spoke to her and I gained the impression that she was jealous of Ruby's interest in me. I noticed that Ruby seemed to encourage the child's infatuation with her, making outrageous use of her as if she were her personal servant, and rewarding her occasionally with a smile or a discarded garment, either of which seemed to delight the child. . . ."

"During those weeks of feeling my way with the White family," went on Mr. Ash, resuming his story where he had stopped the previous evening, "before I took any action towards interfering with their lives—which I was to do so disastrously— I met several of the people Mrs. Taylor must have meant when she talked about the bad company kept by Tom. At first I took little notice of them being obsessed as I was by the Whites themselves, but after a few weeks I began to realize which of these people were regular visitors and which casual; but still I was hardly aware of them until one evening three of these regular visitors forced themselves upon my attention in no uncertain way, three people who were to play their part in later events.

"On that evening I had called at about seven, to find only Mildred and the youngest girl, Jill, at home. Mildred let me in, showing neither pleasure nor surprise, in fact with her usual lack of any kind of emotion, and I thought that this would be an excellent opportunity of having a talk with her. In fact she raised my hopes by doing something she had never done before—she offered me a cup of tea, which I accepted almost with enthusiasm, thankful for this small token of recognition from this strange child. Jill meanwhile was sitting in one of the two easy chairs rather sulkily reading one of Ruby's film papers, and apart from a rather resentful glance at me when I came in, she completely ignored me.

"In spite of this I decided to have a few words with her, and when I sat down near her I could not help feeling something of a shock at her appearance, for though scarcely twelve years old and still at school, she had her hair up, was using lipstick, and wearing high-heeled shoes and a cast-off frock of Ruby's, crudely cut down to fit her; and the worst part was that she didn't look like a child dressed up like an adult—but at first glance gave the impression of a girl past the age of consent. She was not good-looking, having a large aquiline nose, but she made up for this lack of facial beauty with bold, malicious black eyes, and the beginnings of a figure which promised one day to rival Ruby's.

"I glanced at the magazine she was reading, tried to take an intelligent interest in films, and generally did my best to draw the girl into conversation. Jill however answered me only in monosyllables, stared at me ironically out of her black eyes, and made it only too plain that she did not want my company. Discouraged, I soon left her to herself and went over to Mildred, who as usual was washing up piles of dishes; without a word I took from under her arm the dishcloth and started to dry whilst she washed.

"I honestly believe that this was the first time anyone had done this for her, because she paused and looked at me as if completely put out, in fact throughout my acquaintance with her I never saw more expression in her eyes than at that moment.

" 'You don't 'ave to do that, Mr. Ash,' she said.

" 'I know I don't have to,' I replied, 'but I choose to,' and I grinned at her.

"With a shrug of her shoulders she went on with her washing, but allowed me to do the drying; and as I looked at her it seemed to me that there was a slight relaxation in the usual severity of her expression. For some minutes we continued washing-up in this way, without speaking, and then gently I started to question her, about her life generally, about how she had liked school, about her friends outside the family, about her hopes and her fears. At first I had no more response than usual, but gradually she started to talk. She told me a little of what she could remember of her life before the war, part of which she had spent in Hong Kong where Tom White had been stationed. Her powers of self-expression were limited and crude, but in an odd way vivid, and I had an impression of a state of affairs very different from now. In those days she had admired her father; now she despised him. For her mother too in those days she had had a kind of respect, and I gathered that in some way or other

her mother had been a celebrity in Hong Kong—as some kind of a dancer. But Mildred's memory of those days was very hazy, and she seemed generally to look upon them as days of prosperity when everyone had been happy—'not like now,' she added.

" 'Why are things so bad now?' I asked.

"For a moment she made no reply; then, quite suddenly, she said, with almost startling bitterness:

" 'It's the sort Dad mixes with.'

" 'What sort does he mix with?'

" 'You've seen 'em 'ere. Les an' Al an' Molly Cohen. From the Market, they are.'

"Vaguely I distinguished these three in my mind from among the others I had met in the White house. The two men I remembered as young—or comparatively young in those days when all young men were in the Forces—Les, a small cheerful cockney with only two fingers on his right hand, and Al, a tall Italian who, as far as I could remember, seemed to have nothing wrong with him. I remembered they had both stared at me curiously, and even addressed remarks to me which had seemed at the time inoffensive enough, but which for some reason had caused Ruby to go off into a fit of giggles. The woman I remembered as a handsome Jewess of about forty, who had been particularly polite to me, and who had struck me as being unusually intelligent.

" 'Why don't you like these people?' I asked Mildred.

"She shrugged her shoulders.

" 'They ain't no good,' she said, and again her voice was expressionless, as if she had withdrawn herself suddenly from the conversation. And before I could press forward my inquiries, there came an unexpected interruption from the other side of the room.

" 'Don't you take no notice of 'er, padré,' said Jill. 'Them two boys is all right. They give Dad money.'

" 'Give him money?' I asked. 'How do you know?'

" 'Why, I've seen 'em of course—how d'you think? They've always got money, loads of it. Al give me money once.'

"Suddenly Mildred strode across the room and seemed to stand over her sister, with her whole stocky body tensed.

" 'Liar,' she said softly.

" 'I ain't,' replied the younger girl, and it seemed to me there was fear in her voice.

" 'What did 'e give you money for, then?'

" 'Nothin'.'

" 'What did 'e give you money for?' Mildred's voice was still soft and menacing.

" 'I told you, ain't I? 'E just give it me, as a present. To go to the pitchers, if you must know.'

"Without any warning, with the flat of her hand, Mildred caught the younger girl a blow on the cheek which sounded like the crack of a whip. Jill set up a howling and without attempting to retaliate, ran into one of the bedrooms and slammed the door.

"Mildred came back to the sink and continued the washing-up as if nothing had happened.

" 'Why did you do that, Mildred?' I asked.

" 'For lying.'

" 'But what if she wasn't lying?'

" 'She was.'

" 'Are you sure?'

"To this she made no reply, but only shrugged her shoulders.

" 'Wouldn't it have been better to . . . talk to her?' I asked.

"She gave the nearest approach to a laugh I ever heard her make.

" 'She don't take no notice of words, Mr. Ash,' she said. 'You must do something for 'er to take any notice. Besides, talking about taking money from men might put ideas into 'er 'ead.'

" 'Surely not, Mildred.'

" 'Blimey, Mr. Ash—you don't understand the likes of Jill— nor Ruby neither. They do what they wants to, regardless.'

" 'Regardless of what, Mildred?'

"But once more she had withdrawn into herself, and question her though I did, I could get nothing more out of her; she would only answer me in monosyllables or with a shrug of her shoulders. She did not seem to listen to my questions. At last we finished the washing-up, and I decided to take my leave. Before I could cross the room to the door, however, we heard the noise of several people in the yard outside, singing and talking loudly, as if drunk, and almost at once the door opened, and Tom came in, blinking after the effects of the black-out.

"He looked sharply round the room, and without having noticed my presence, said sharply to Mildred:

"'Where's Ruby?'

"'At the pitchers, of course,' she answered, equally sharply. 'It's 'er night, ain't it?'

"Tom swore, went back to the yard and shouted to the others who were making a great deal of noise and apparently helping one of their number who seemed to have fallen down the steps. Catching my eye, Mildred said:

"'You'd better go.'

"'Why?' I asked.

"'Anythin' might 'appen—they're boozed.'

"The last thing I wanted to do was to go; I wanted to stay and see what would happen. Besides, to go I would have had to pass through them in the yard, which I didn't much want to do.

"Anyhow before I could do anything the door opened once more and in came Mrs. Cohen and another woman I did not know; their hair was dishevelled, their faces flushed, and they were talking over their shoulders to someone behind them in excited, almost hysterical voices.

"'Bring 'er in, boys,' said Mrs. Cohen. 'Disgraceful, this is, comin' 'ome dead drunk—not used to war-time gin, that's what it is!'

"And into the room staggered Les and Al, each with an arm round Mrs. White, whose face, pale beneath the coffee-coloured skin, had on it a silly, fixed grin, as she allowed herself to be half-carried into the room, her legs moving automatically, giving little help to her supporters. Her progress was somewhat lop-sided, for Al, the Italian, was over six feet tall, whilst Les was scarcely five foot four. Les was loudly singing some refrain, the words fortunately incomprehensible, and not very gently, they deposited Mrs. White in one of the arm-chairs. They were followed into the room by another woman I did not know, and two middle-aged men, one of whom, to my surprise, I recognized as one of the air-raid wardens whom I had always looked upon as a particularly respectable citizen. The rear was brought up by Tom, carrying two shopping-bags bulging with bottles of beer. Everyone was talking at once but above the din Tom's sergeant-major's voice was shouting:

" ''Ere, you clumsy——, you've busted 'alf the bottles!', and he held up one of the bags, which was dripping.

"Les made a dive towards it, took it out of Tom's hands and held it up over his head so that the drips fell into his open mouth, amid cheers and laughter.

"Suddenly Tom became aware of my presence, and stood stock-still staring at me, and I became unpleasantly conscious of all eyes being directed towards me.

" 'Well,' said Tom, 'so the padré's 'ere. Where you bin hidin', padré?'

"And amidst silence his little blue eyes travelled slowly from me to Mildred, who was still standing by the sink, imperturbably stacking crockery.

" 'Been 'elpin' little Millie with the washin'-up, padré?' continued Tom, looking round at the rest of the company with what was almost a leer. 'Likes little girls, our padré does—tryin' to keep 'er to the straight an' narrer, that's what 'e's doin'!' he went on, and for some reason the others laughed as if there were some special joke implied by this. I was aware of being stared at half in ridicule, half in hostility, and I had a moment of painful disillusionment, for until then I had thought myself rather liked than otherwise. The tall dark, almost saturnine Al, in particular, was staring at me with definite enmity. But before this impression could really sink in, Tom's manner suddenly completely changed, and he came across the room, slapped me on the back, and said in loud tones:

" 'But you're welcome, padré, to join our little celebration. No doubt you'll excuse our merriment seein' as we've 'ad a little—what you might call—unexpected luck. Moll 'ere—' and he indicated Mrs. Cohen, ''as bin lucky with an 'orse—won eighty quid, she 'as,' and I was aware of a moment of silence as Tom looked at the others, eyebrows raised, and a half-grin on his face; at once there was an air of relief, faces seemed to lose some of their hostility, and the deep-red-haired Mrs. Cohen smiled almost ingratiatingly at me, and took up the refrain.

" 'That's right, Mr. Ash,' she said, 'I got a treble—first in my life. Not that I gamble regular—only a little flutter now and then. I 'ope you'll be my guest and drink my 'ealth in a glass of ale,' she added politely.

" 'Thank you for the offer,' I said, 'but it's really time I went.'

" 'Oh come off it, padré,' said Tom, 'you can't pretend you don't like a glass of beer after what you put back the other night. Millie my love—' he went up to Mildred and put his arm round her waist, in which embrace Mildred stood stiffly, an expression of dislike on her face, '—now don't be stand-offish, girl—' and still holding her by the waist, Tom turned to me, saying, 'our Millie don't approve of our little celebrations—quite old-fashioned, she is—', he turned back to Mildred, 'seein' as your mother 'as what you might call overdone it, and seein' as Rube is still swoonin' over Clark Gable or 'ooever the latest is, do you think, lovie, that you could be friendly-like for once and get out some glasses for your pa's guests?' And he turned round to the others, winking and grinning, at which they all laughed, and Les said:

" 'That's it, pa, show 'oo's master 'ere!' which raised more laughter.

"Mildred, quite self-possessed, evaded her father's grasp and with a face as expressionless as ever started to collect glasses from a cupboard.

" 'Ain't she hoity-toity!' said Les, and minced across the room with a hand on his hip, which caused the two strange women to go almost hysterical with laughter.

"Feeling with some regret—for I was most interested in the proceedings—that it really was time for me to go, I started actually to move towards the door, when it opened, and in came Ruby. As usual she was dressed like a film-star, and much more heavily made-up than usual, with her artificial blonde hair piled high on her head, and for a moment she paused in the doorway, as if she were indeed an actress making an entrance. Then things happened so quickly that for a moment I lost count of events.

"As far as I remember it all started when Ruby began to cross the room, in order to do which she had to pass near to Al, the surly-looking Italian, who had been steadily drinking beer from bottles since he had arrived; as she drew near to him she looked at him out of the corner of her eye with a curious expression, half-wary, half-inviting, and suddenly Al made a lunge at her, grabbed her round the waist, and pulled her onto his knee; at once, with all her strength, Ruby caught him a smack on the cheek, whilst Mrs. Cohen, sitting on the other side of Al, and apparently in defence of her sex (I was to learn much later why she was so concerned for Ruby) repeated the operation on his other cheek, upon which Al seized her round the throat and proceeded to squeeze with considerable strength—whether in fun or absolute earnest I have never been able to decide—whereupon Les sprang to Mrs. Cohen's aid, catching his mate a heavy blow on the cheek, sending him sprawling on the floor with Mrs. Cohen under him and Ruby on top of him, and then Les himself overbalanced and fell into the mass of writhing limbs; the other men present then waded in to part the combatants, making matters worse, whilst the two women guests stood in a corner screaming like cockatoos; only Mrs. White remained seated in her chair watching it all with the same silly smile. Mildred too stood calmly looking on with arms folded, as if it were a state of affairs to which she was by no means unaccustomed.

"Meanwhile Tom, by means of grasping Les by his jacket collar and by a heave of his great shoulders hurling the little man into a corner, and then, wading into the middle of the scrimmage, extricated Ruby and, carrying her like a baby, deposited her in the other arm-chair, her clothes somewhat torn, from where she watched with interest the progress of the fight, which I am sure she was delighted at having caused. It did not however last much longer for already the combatants were sorting themselves out, and there was a moment of silence during which they all looked at each other as if wondering whether they had been in earnest or not. Al alone among them seemed disposed to serious anger, and he moved threateningly over to Les, who was picking himself up from the corner where Tom had flung him, and said:

" 'What you want to 'it me like that for?' and I could see his large hands were clenched as if he intended to let fly at the smaller man.

"But suddenly Tom said, in his sergeant-major's voice:

" 'Cut it out, Al, unless you want to go out on your neck—not for the first time, neither. You started it—what did you want to make a pass at Rube for?', and he strode forward until he was standing just in front of the big Italian—a small, stocky, but very powerful figure; for a moment the two men stood glowering at each other, and I had a sense that there was some kind of long-standing enmity between them. Another fight, more serious this time, seemed about to start when Mrs. Cohen, her dark-red hair hanging over her face, a rent in her skirt from waist to hem—revealing unexpectedly exotic underwear and legs able to display it to advantage—stepped between them, saying:

" 'Here, boys, that's enough, this is a celebration, ain't it?— not a blinkin' peace conference at the League of Nations. And 'ere's me pal Rube turned up to 'elp celebrate my bit of luck,' and as she looked from one to the other, in her intelligent, rather fine eyes, there was a look almost of command, and this was the first hint I had of the importance of this woman in the relationships of these people; for the men themselves relaxed almost sheepishly, Al sitting down on the nearest chair and seizing another bottle of beer which he gulped down rapidly, whilst Tom slowly walked to the other side of the room, and sat moodily down on a chair near Ruby.

"Slowly as people began to brush themselves down and drink

beer, the atmosphere again became convivial, and the irrepressible Les let out a whistle when he caught sight of Mrs. Cohen's underwear and the smooth expanse of flesh above her stocking, whereupon the latter, suddenly aware of it herself, let out a mock scream and hurried across the room to Ruby, and after a moment or two they disappeared into one of the bedrooms to repair the damage to their clothes.

"There was then a moment of silence during which Les rather half-heartedly started to clear up some broken glass from the floor, whilst the other two men and the two women strange to me gathered in a little group and talked in undertones, whilst Tom and Al sat apart, avoiding looking at each other, and so indicating that they were only too conscious of each other's presence.

"This was the moment I chose to leave, and I believe my exit was hardly noticed. . . ."

"That evening with the Whites," went on Mr. Ash the next day, "left me both exhilarated and depressed. At last I had seen the aspect of life in which there was the greatest need for the influence of the Church, yet I could not see how I could exercise that influence. My part in the proceedings had been in no way admirable—I might as well not have been there for all the effect I had had—and I had learnt with something of a shock that not only was I not looked upon with any particular respect by these people, but that I was regarded with something like derision. But at least I knew what I was up against, and as always when faced with a challenge, I was more than ever determined to do something effective.

"I spent some days thinking it out whilst going about my parish duties, and at last I came to a decision. I decided that my first step should be to remove Mildred, if not wholly, at least partly, from the environment of her home. For it was this girl that I had most hope of helping, and it seemed to me—and I still believe that in this I was right—that her strange disposition was due to her being starved of affection, and that therefore it was my duty to get her into a more human atmosphere, and at once I thought of Mrs. Robinson. She had mentioned she was looking out for domestic help, and whatever my opinion of this lady was in other ways, I had no doubt she was overflowing with affection for her fellow creatures. So I decided, after the next W.V.S. Committee meeting to be held in her flat—they were held alternately in her and Mrs. Carrington-Smith's flats—that I would discuss the matter with her.

"Well, the next meeting was held in her flat, and when it was over, I waited patiently for the others to leave. Miss Cooter and Dr. Kynaston left almost at once, but the other women remained behind to gossip, and almost at once the conversation got onto the very subject of domestic help. This was not surprising because getting back to peace-time conditions was on everyone's lips, as the war seemed at last to be drawing to a close, the Normandy landings having just been successfully accomplished, and though London was being subjected to flying-bomb attacks, we were all very optimistic. Mrs. Carrington-Smith—becoming even more reckless than usual in her reaction to an audience—started to talk about the numbers of servants she had been accustomed to before the war.

" 'It will be such a relief,' she said, 'when the girls come out of the factories and start begging us to take them into service again. Of course, they will need an awful lot of training. Almost a generation of girls has grown up with no experience whatever of domestic service. But no doubt we shall get back to pre-war standards eventually. . . .'

"Then Mrs. Robinson, who seemed to be in a particularly mischievous mood, said sweetly:

" 'Did you have many servants before the war, Mrs. Carrington-Smith?'

"Looking at her a little suspiciously, the other replied guardedly:

" 'Yes, of course. We always had a full staff.'

" 'That would be in your house—where did you say it was?'

"Mrs. Carrington-Smith hesitated.

" 'In Hertfordshire,' she said.

" 'Really? I could have sworn you said Bedfordshire . . . .
However, no doubt I am mistaken. That would be the place with
a drive a mile long and with thirty acres of land?'

" 'Yes.'

" 'The place so very quiet and secluded that you hardly knew
there was another place for miles around?'

" 'I may have described it in those terms.'

" 'I have always wanted, my dear, to congratulate you on what
I consider an act of real heroism—for you to have left so lovely a
place in so safe an area in order to come and live here, in these
flats, in the centre of London, with bombs falling all round you.
I must admit that if I had had such facilities, I would not have
been nearly so noble. . . .'

"Again Mrs. Carrington-Smith hesitated, looking at the other
woman very hard. Then she said quietly:

" 'The place was requisitioned. It's now the headquarters of
one of the women's Services—an Area Command I think they
call it. . . .'

" 'And you chose to come here, into London? My dear, you
are a brave woman. I'm afraid *I* should have gone deeper into
the country.'

" 'Well—', as if gaining confidence, Mrs. Carrington-Smith
looked round at the others with an air of modesty, '—I didn't
want to feel out of things. And I must admit, that when my
husband died, I was quite glad to be rid of the place, and to come
to live in these flats, with their modest rent. Don't forget, dear,
that when war started everyone flooded the countryside and
London was almost the only place one could get anywhere to
live. . . .'

"And she, in turn, smiled sweetly at Mrs. Robinson.

" 'After the war,' she went on, 'I will return to the country,
but to a smaller place. I shall be content with four or five bedrooms—perhaps somewhere in Buckinghamshire—a charming
county. And with only a few servants—three or four. . . .'

"And so it was that this little clash between these two women—the first of many I was to witness as peace drew nearer—ended with honours about even.

"Soon afterwards, the others left, and at last I was left alone with Mrs. Robinson. She seemed a little put out, and her mischievous mood of earlier in the evening had quite gone.

" 'I am really angry with myself,' she said to me, 'for that little scene with poor Cynthia. But she really does annoy me at times. . . . She really thinks people believe her stories of her life before the war. . . .'

" 'And might they not be true?' I asked.

" 'My dear vicar, you are so sweet, and so trusting. Of course they are not true. *I* never heard of her before the war.'

" 'And should you have done?' I asked gently.

" For a moment she looked as if she were about to confide something in me—and if she had, how much trouble would have been saved!—but she thought better of it, and merely shrugged her shoulders.

" 'Perhaps not,' she said. 'After all, I did not live in county society.'

" 'Exactly,' I said, and then went on, perhaps a little severely, for in those days I was still inclined to lecture people, 'I must admit, Mrs. Robinson, from my observation of your sex, that you are all rather too much inclined to be—how shall I put it?—preoccupied with petty bickering.'

"At once her mischievous mood seemed to return.

" 'Vicar, you look absolutely sweet when you preach to me. If I were ten—no, eight—years younger, I would be madly in love with you. You are so handsome.'

" 'If I may say so, that remark is an excellent illustration of the kind of frivolous mentality your sex is so much inclined to.'

" 'Oh Mr. Ash—what a low opinion you have of women. I had always suspected it—now I know.'

" 'Not at all,' I said. 'During the last few months I have had all the evidence I need of the heroism your sex is capable of. . . .'

" 'Vicar, that is a sweet remark. But you know, life is not all heroism and serious intention. There is the lighter side. And we women represent that lighter side. We exist to be flirted with and to be taken out to the theatre, to make men forget how serious life is. Have you ever flirted with or been kissed by a woman, Vicar?'

" 'Indeed I have not,' I said.

" 'Then you should be,' she said, and before I knew what she was about, she put her arms round my neck and kissed me on the lips; I was aware of a confused impression of the softness of her arms and of the strong perfume she used. She then sat back in her chair and looked at me, her head on one side.

" 'How did you like that?' she asked.

"I was aware of having gone somewhat red in the face.

" 'A somewhat indelicate action,' I said.

" 'Vicar, your confusion flatters me. It was a purely maternal kiss.'

"And she stared deep into my eyes, with a look I remembered having seen in her face on her first visit to the vicarage, a look of both curiosity and knowledge, as if she were probing into my mind to a depth to which I had never ventured. But as I looked back at her—so inexperienced was I in those days—I was able to persuade myself that her kiss had been purely maternal, and I remember thinking vaguely that it probably had something to do with starved maternal love, as I thought of the cold look in Peter's eyes when he had referred to his mother.

"At the same time I felt even more convinced that there would be room in her life for Mildred. Looking back, it is astonishing that I should have so misinterpreted her emotion. . . . But I at once broached the subject of Mildred, telling Mrs. Robinson all about her, about my fears for her welfare, about the lack of affection in her life. She listened quietly, staring at me curiously as I talked.

" 'And this father of hers,' she asked when I had finished, 'Am I to understand he's a bad lot—mixed up in something not quite honest?'

" 'By no means,' I said, wondering from where she could have got this impression. 'He's only become a little careless in his associates, that's all.' And I went on to explain how brave Tom had been at Dunkirk, and what an excellent soldier he had been.

" 'I see. . . .' she said thoughtfully, 'and you suggest I take this girl into domestic service?'

" 'Yes,' I said. 'I know Mrs. Taylor comes to you only once a week, and that you need someone more permanent. . . .'

" 'One thing only puzzles me,' she said. 'Why have you chosen me, and not Mrs. Carrington-Smith, or Mrs. Kynaston, or one of the other women, all of whom are crying out for help?'

" 'Because,' I said, 'I feel the girl should be in an atmosphere where she will get a little human sympathy—not be treated merely as an employee. I feel that you have—how shall I put it?—the warmth of personality she needs.'

"To my surprise, at this, she stood up suddenly and turned her back to me, and though it did occur to me for a moment that she did this to hide some emotion from me, I dismissed the idea at once as ridiculous. For why should my remark have caused in her any kind of emotion? Anyhow, all she did was to take a cigarette from a table behind her chair, which she lit before turning back to me, and when she faced me once more I was able to put down the slight moisture in her eyes to the effect of the tobacco smoke. In fact her face was strangely without expression as she looked at me.

" 'So you think I am the most suitable person from among all these women to influence a young girl?' she asked.

" 'I think,' I said quietly, 'that of all the women I have met in this parish, you have the kindest heart. . . .'

"Her fingers trembled slightly as she removed the cigarette from her mouth.

" 'Thank you, Vicar,' she said. 'I will try to live up to your opinion of me. Yes, I'll have the girl if she will come. Now I really must ask you to go. It's late and . . . I have to get up early tomorrow.'

"And as she almost hurried me out of the flat, I noticed for the first time since I had known her, that her face was a little tired

and strained, almost as if it were taut with hidden emotion. This
worried me as I made my way to the vicarage, until I remembered that lately there had been more flying-bombs than usual,
and that they were beginning to prey on all our nerves. . . .

"I decided," went on Mr. Ash, "before mentioning my pro-
ject to Mildred herself, to approach Tom about it. This I did not
expect to be easy, knowing only too well the amount of work
done by Mildred in the house. So with some vague idea of
gaining an advantage of terrain, I did not go round to the Whites
whom I had not visited since the night of the fight, but sent a
note to Tom asking him to drop into the vicarage the following
evening, to discuss an important matter.

"I was not at all sure he would turn up, but promptly, at the
exact hour I had suggested, there was a ring at the front door and
a moment later Mrs. Taylor, looking disapproving, ushered
Tom into my study. Mrs. Taylor's disapproval could not have
been due to Tom's appearance, because he was very smart. He
was in uniform—not the shapeless Home Guard but one of those
pre-war khaki uniforms with highly polished buttons down the
front, which Tom must have been allowed to retain when he
was demobbed, and it showed unmistakable signs of the loving
care he had bestowed upon it, for it had the almost inhuman
smartness which only sergeant-majors know how to achieve,
the crowns on his forearms shone like gold, his boots were boned
so that they shone like black glass, and the crease in his trousers
had the appearance of having been sewn in, whilst the sleeves of
his tunic had creases so sharp that it looked as if he had never
bent his arms at the elbows since putting it on; he had bestowed
equal care upon his person, for his hair was nowhere more than
the regulation two inches long, his little grey moustache was
waxed into two points on either side of his lip, and the skin of
his face and bull-like neck—which bulged over the tight collar
of his tunic—looked as if it had just been scrubbed with carbolic.
And as I looked at him standing there holding his peaked cap in

his hand, I felt a sudden pity, for there was an almost defensive look in the little blue eyes which in the past had stared at me so ironically, in those days not deigning to show me more than a token respect. It occurred to me that he had got himself up like this as a kind of expiation for the way in which, that evening three weeks before, he had let down not only himself, but the entire British Army.

"Looking at him standing there with an expression half-defensive, half-truculent, I realized this was the first time I had seen him really sober since meeting him again, and it occurred to me that Tom sober was a very different proposition from Tom drunk, and wondered whether I would be able to take advantage of this. For I thought that quite possibly his conscience would be more active when not under the blurring influence of drink, that he might be less certain of himself and easier to manage, so I decided to put on a cold manner in dealing with him. Rather abruptly, without shaking hands, I asked him to be seated, which he did slowly, his back as straight as a poker, on his face a look of wariness I did not quite understand. For a moment I hesitated, not quite knowing how to put into words what I had to say. At last I said, rather sternly:

" 'It's Mildred I want to talk to you about, Tom.'

" 'Mildred?'

" 'Yes. In my visits to your home I have noticed how hard the girl works, and I'm rather afraid the rest of the household are inclined to make a drudge of her. Now that is not good for her, Tom. I have reason to believe it's having a bad effect on her character, and I have a suggestion to make which I hope you will consider seriously.'

"I paused, waiting for him to say something.'

" 'Is this the important business you 'as to discuss with me, padré?' he asked slowly.

" 'It is.'

"A faint smile seemed to touch the corners of his lips for a moment, to be immediately replaced by a look of great seriousness.

" 'Carry on, padré,' he said, 'I'm listenin'.'

"I then proceeded to explain in great detail my plans for Mildred's future. I had it all worked out, having decided that at first she would go to Mrs. Robinson for only a few hours a day, and that later, as the rest of the White family became used to doing without her and gradually began to do more for themselves, she would start to work full time, and eventually, if possible, live in. Thus not only would she benefit, but the whole White family would learn to be less lazy. It was a pathetically optimistic plan, but one which it did not occur to me could possibly fail if only Tom would view it sympathetically.

" 'Well,' I said. 'How does the idea strike you?'

" 'This 'ere Carlton Court,' he said. 'It's that posh block of flats at the end of the road, ain't it? You pays about ten quid a week for a few rooms?'

" 'That is the place,' I said.

"He looked at me thoughtfully, his eyes a little narrowed. And had I not been convinced at that time of his fundamental simplicity, I would have thought there was an almost calculating look about him.

" 'You think it would do 'er good, Vicar?' he asked. Then, before I could make any comment, he went on: 'You see, Mr. Ash, I've known for some time that little Millie works too 'ard. P'raps I've been inclined to spoil Ruby, 'oo is, as you might say, the beauty of the family, an' the first born an' all. And then the missus ain't what you'd call in the best o' 'ealth—she ain't properly adapted 'erself to English conditions. So it's all fallen on little Millie's shoulders of late. I sort of found out that was what was 'appenin' when I was demobbed, and I've sort of let it go on since. There 'asn't been much I could do about it.'

" 'You could have let Ruby do more.'

" 'You're right there, Mr. Ash. I've always been intendin' to discipline 'er a bit, but it ain't easy with girls. Give me a platoon of recruits now—I'd know 'ow to 'andle them. But girls—it's different. It's not as if they 'ad a mother—not a real mother—to bring 'em up. My missus, Mr. Ash, as you know, is a woman of the East. And where she comes from they 'as funny 'abits, which the kids, with me not bein' there much an' all, 'ave picked up. For instance, when there's a daughter in a family what's a real good-looker—I mean leaves the others standin' like—then the others kind of take a back seat, quite voluntary. They take it as quite right they should serve 'er 'and and foot. There's some sense in it too, out there, because when this beautiful daughter marries some rich man, they all 'as a share in 'im as it were—the bloke kind of marries the whole family, poor——. 'Course I don't agree with it 'ere—but it's just 'appened. Ruby, bein' such a smasher, an' Millie not bein' much to look at, Ruby's sort of— 'ow do you say?—sort of queened it over the rest of them. An' I must admit, Mr. Ash, that girl, when she smiles at me, when she sort of wheedles me, there ain't nothin' much I can do. Women, they've always been my downfall. Like clay in their 'ands, I am.'

"This argument seemed to have such obvious truth in it, to explain so much I had observed but failed to understand in the White family, that I quickly forgot the slight uneasiness which something ingratiating about Tom's manner had caused me.

" 'In that case,' I said, 'it seems to me all the more imperative for Mildred to get away into a more healthy environment.'

" 'It's all right by me, Mr. Ash—it's up to you. I mean if you can persuade Millie. . . . She's an obstinate little cuss, you know.'

" 'Oh, you can leave her to me—I think I can persuade her,' I said. 'I think Mildred and I understand each other quite well.'

"And I stood up, at last holding out my hand, which he took.

" 'It's very kind of you to concern yourself with my family, padré,' he said.

" 'It's my duty, Tom,' I said as I accompanied him to the door. 'You forget I am your vicar and that every one of my parishioners is my personal concern. The Church still performs some useful functions, you know.'

" 'I don't doubt it, padré. I ain't ever been a Church man myself, that I admit, but then I ain't ever been what you could call against the Church, either.'

" 'Come, come, Tom. That was hardly your attitude to

Church Parades. I know you had something to do with the poor attendance in B-Company.'

" 'Well, in the Army—that's different. I don't rightly see what place the Church 'as in the Army. In the Army there should be only fightin' men, Mr. Ash. But in civvie street—that's different. There ain't no discipline in civvie street, and it's discipline what keeps a man to the straight an' narrer. So there 'as to be a Church to show people what's right an' wrong. In the Army there ain't no doubt what's right an' wrong—it's all laid down in King's Regulations.'

"I could not help smiling at this man's faith in King's Regulations, and in that moment thought, in my confidence, that I understood him perfectly.

" 'Well, Tom,' I said, 'that's a theme which perhaps we'll discuss some other time.'

" 'Yes, Mr. Ash—I'll look forward to doin' that.'

"And it seemed to me, just before Tom turned and went down the steps, that I saw again the gleam of irony which I had so often seen in those little blue eyes during my visits to B-Company. This for a moment made me uneasy, but I quickly dismissed the thought as I remembered that I had achieved my main object— of getting Tom's agreement to my plan for Mildred.

"I felt, in fact, that I had acted with considerable cleverness, and little did I suspect that at that very moment Tom was walking away congratulating himself on his own cunning.

"A few days later I called at the Whites', during the early evening, when I knew Tom would be on duty with the Home Guard. I found the rest of the family assembled and there was about them a faint air of expecting me. The door was opened to me by Ruby, who was dressed with greater restraint than usual, having on a summer frock the only immodesty of which was a rather too plunging neckline and rather too much tight-ness round her hips; her hair, instead of being piled high on her head, was on her shoulders, a cascade of fair tresses varying in shade from pale yellow to ash-blonde, according to how the bleach had taken. She could not resist drawing my attention to herself, twirling round so that her skirt rose to above her knees revealing the fringe of a lace-bordered petticoat, and asked me how I liked her 'new look'. And on receiving my usual guarded compliment she pouted a little and tossed her head, saying in very lady-like tones:

" 'You won't 'ave to endure my company for long, 'cos I'm off to the cinema.'

"This surprised me a little because, though it was her evening for the cinema, she never went until the last house, which was some hours away, and she usually made use of every available minute of her time in my presence in her efforts to captivate me. Almost as if aware of my consciousness of this variation in her usual routine, she added rather hastily that tonight she had an escort who was giving her a bite to eat 'before the show'.

" 'A Technical Sergeant Class I,' she added with some pride as she went through the door into the yard, 'and you can't keep the Yankee Army waitin'—them boys is tough.'

"Being now permitted to pay attention to the rest of the family, I turned round to find that Mrs. White had vanished with the boy, and that only Mildred and Jill were in the room. At this moment the latter, with a shrug of her shoulders and with a pile of film magazines under her arm, left the room too, so that I was alone with Mildred.

"From all this I guessed that Mildred knew about the proposition I had to make, and that probably her mind was already made up. She was not doing her usual washing-up but was seated in the other arm-chair staring in front of her. She seemed in one of her less communicative moods for she said nothing and did not look up as I took my seat opposite her.

" 'Well, Mildred,' I asked, 'has your father told you about our plans for your employment?'

"She looked up for a second, her big brown eyes quite expressionless.

" 'Yes, Mr. Ash,' she said.

" 'Does the idea appeal to you?'

" 'I don't mind.'

" 'You mean you would like to work for Mrs. Robinson?'

" 'I don't mind.'

" 'I don't want you to do anything against your will, you know.'

" 'It ain't against my will.'

" 'But you do want to do this work?'

"She nodded.

" 'Mildred,' I said, again very gently, 'look me in the eyes and tell me honestly whether you really want to work for Mrs. Robinson?'

"Slowly the big brown eyes met mine and to my astonishment I saw they were swimming in tears.

" 'Mildred, what's the matter?' I asked.

" 'Nothin'.'

" 'But you're crying.'

" 'No, I'm not, Mr. Ash.'

" 'But there are tears in your eyes,' I said helplessly.

" 'Don't worry about that, Mr. Ash. It don't mean a thing.'

"And looking at her closely I could see no other sign of grief in her expression—just the tears welling out of the brown eyes. Otherwise her face was as expressionless as ever. I felt strangely helpless; I had rarely in my life had to deal with tears, and I felt that beneath the girl's unemotional exterior, beyond the passionless tears, there was some deep emotional disturbance which it was my duty to get to the bottom of. This is what my instinct told me, and perhaps it would have been better had I acted on my instinct; but ever distrustful of all thought that did not come direct through the intellect, I tried to explain her emotion by reasoning. I told myself that she had probably been told by Tom to take the work for her own good, and that she did not like the idea but was too afraid of Tom to refuse; that these tears, in fact, were merely the nervous reaction of a child faced with the prospect of going among strangers for the first time in her life. The more I thought about it from this angle, the more convinced did I become that this was the situation.

'So I decided not to inquire too deeply into the cause of her tears, and so perhaps lost whatever chance I had of really gaining her confidence.

" 'Well then,' I said, 'if you really want the work, I will set about arranging an interview for you with Mrs. Robinson. Shall I do that?'

" 'Yes, Mr. Ash.'

" 'You really want me to?'

" 'Yes, Mr. Ash.'

"And so it was that, after a few more abortive attempts at getting her into a more talkative mood, I took my leave of her. . . ."

"I arranged for this meeting between Mildred and Mrs. Robinson," went on Mr. Ash on the last evening before they were due to set out for Florence, "to take place early in the afternoon a few days later, and sent round a note to the Whites informing them of the time arranged and telling them I would be round for Mildred twenty minutes or so beforehand.

"In due course I arrived, and on opening the door leading from the yard to the living-room—I had developed the habit now of walking straight in without knocking—I saw Mildred sitting in a chair facing the door looking sulky, with Tom standing in front of her talking in a low voice. And although Tom came forward pleasantly enough to greet me, I had an impression of the smile on his face chasing off some less pleasant expression, as if father and daughter had been having words. Tom took me to one side and explained in a low voice that Mildred could be an obstinate little devil when she chose, and that he had had to take a strong line to persuade her to go at all; he said this almost apologetically as if excusing himself for something.

"Mildred however stood up meekly enough when I suggested it was time to go, and on her face there was the usual look of complete lack of emotion. In the street I tried to talk to her, but she would reply only in monosyllables, so I soon gave it up and we walked on in silence. Half-way to Carlton Court however she started unexpectedly to talk herself.

" 'Ruby's been called up,' she said.

" 'Has she?' I said. 'And is she pleased?'

" 'She ain't 'alf cut up about it. Been lyin' on 'er bed all day—won't speak to no one. She 'oped they'd call 'er into industry, but it's the A.T.S.'

"I remembered that a few weeks previously Ruby had had her medical, an experience she seemed to have enjoyed rather than otherwise, and which she had described to me with much unnecessary detail, telling how she had 'took everything off' and been examined by five doctors—'not 'alf interested, they were'—and how they had prodded her all over so that she started to giggle; and she had looked at me as if looking for signs that I regretted not having been present at this interview. But no one had thought much about it, thinking it a mere formality, the general impression being that the war was virtually over—Allied troops had crossed the Rhine and the Seventh Armoured Division was racing towards Hamburg—and that she wouldn't be called up at all. But now that she had been, I could not help feeling a certain satisfaction—I felt it would do the girl good, cause her to do some work for the first time in her life. Mildred seemed to share my opinion though perhaps for different reasons; though she would not talk about it much, she gave me the impression that she was pleased her sister was about to be made to do something against her will.

" 'Not that she will, though,' she added.

" 'What do you mean, Mildred?' I asked. 'She will have to—or go to prison.'

" 'Not Ruby—she always gets out of things.'

"I felt slightly amused that she should have enough faith in her sister's ability to 'get out of things' to back her against the War Office and the entire police force of the country, and it made me realize with something of a shock that the girl was still a child, with childish ideas; I was apt to forget this. Later, I was to remember this conversation.

"Soon we reached Carlton Court, and Mrs. Robinson greeted the girl in a manner which confirmed me in my belief that I had chosen wisely in making her the girl's first employer. For there was about her manner nothing of the haughtiness of a mistress interviewing a prospective maid.

" 'Come in, child,' she said, and with one scarlet finger-nailed hand resting on Mildred's shoulder she piloted her across the hall and into the sitting-room where she made her sit down in one of the best chairs. Mildred seemed quite overcome not only by this treatment but by Mrs. Robinson herself, who was dressed in a silk afternoon dress which was rather more flamboyant than usual. And with her impressive figure, her blue-tinted hair, and the animal magnetism of her personality, she was evidently someone Mildred regarded as coming from another world.

"The girl looked round the room with eyes which I, who knew her so well, realized were positively awe-struck, but which a stranger to Mildred would have thought merely mildly interested. As you know, Mrs. Robinson's sitting-room is quite impressive, especially on first sight; that taste for bright colours of hers, though inclined to make her clothes too loud, is ideally suited to interior decoration of a certain kind, and her bold choice of blues and reds—I always thought—in that room, was entirely successful. There was also the impressive array of silver on the sideboard, and her modern furniture, including that cocktail-cabinet almost beautiful in its vulgarity, which positively glittered with glassware of different colours. To Mildred it must all have been very dazzling; in fact Mrs. Robinson made one or two remarks to her before the girl realized she was being addressed. At this Mrs. Robinson exchanged an amused smile with me, and I could see that her interest in the girl was aroused. But when at last Mildred realized she was being spoken to, she seemed to shrink into herself, as if the curtain of inscrutability through which she normally faced the world, was again drawn across her features. She looked at Mrs. Robinson and said tonelessly:

" 'Yes, mam?'

"The question was repeated, and Mildred replied with her usual monosyllable, giving similar replies to the rest of Mrs. Robinson's gently put questions. In the end the latter said, with a faint smile:

" 'Well, you certainly aren't over-talkative, child. Which is all to the good because I'm inclined to chatter all day long, and if you decide to work for me, at least I shall have someone to talk *at*.'

" 'Yes, mam,' said Mildred.

" 'Does that mean you want to work for me?'

" 'Yes, mam.'

" 'Well, that's fine. We seem mutually suited. But perhaps you'd better see the rest of the flat before you finally decide, and I shall outline what I shall expect you to do. Then, if you're still in the same mind, we'll clinch the bargain.'

"And with a bright smile, and again with one hand resting on the girl's shoulder, she proceeded to lead her round the flat, whilst I followed.

"As we went from room to room, Mildred's eyes, normally large, seemed to grow bigger. Seeing the whole flat for the first time, I was myself surprised by its luxury; from the sitting-room, before I quite realized where we were, we went into her bed-room, and I was a little taken aback by the reproductions of rosy-fleshed Renoir nudes on the walls, the pink ceiling and pastel walls—one wall a different colour from the others, a new idea to me—and most of all, by the contents of the enormous wardrobe which Mrs. Robinson opened to show Mildred where she kept her clothes, revealing an array of nightdresses of a kind I did not know existed. In fact so embarrassed was I that I turned my back and looked out of a window, an action noticed by Mrs. Robinson, who, as we left the room, apologized in a whisper, saying, 'I am so sorry, Vicar, but I quite forgot you were in the room—and anyhow, I can never regard a man of your profession in the same light as an ordinary man,' a remark which did not altogether please me.

"The bathroom with its sunken bath, its row of taps, its array of glass bottles containing various mysterious feminine potions, one wall entirely covered by a mirror, and its perfume of bath salts and dusting powder, seemed particularly to impress Mildred, for she stood there for some moments, staring round warily, as if afraid. I was almost as impressed as Mildred, in fact the whole tour of the flat was just as much a revelation to me as to Mildred, for I had not realized in what sensual luxury the people of the world lived. It confirmed me in my belief that women were by nature extravagant, both with their purses and their emotions, and it did not occur to me that Mrs. Robinson was in any way exceptional.

"In the kitchen, with its electric range and rows of cooking utensils, and dresser full of crockery, I felt more at ease, for I knew that Mrs. Robinson had the reputation of being a good cook, and I did not feel that the squandering of money here was so culpable. Mildred however seemed more awed here than elsewhere, in fact it was here that she ventured her one remark.

" 'I ain't never used anything but gas,' she said, a little forlornly.

" 'Oh, I shan't expect you to cook, dear,' said Mrs. Robinson. 'I shall only expect you to do the cleaning and some of the washing-up, and perhaps later, if you decide to live in, I might teach you a little cooking.'

" 'Live in?' asked Mildred.

" 'Yes—I thought that perhaps later, when the war's over and you know me better, and if we find we suit each other, that you might like to live here.'

" '*Sleep* here?' asked Mildred, as if astonished, looking round as if expecting to see some dark corner with a mattress in it.

" 'Yes—in the small bedroom,' said Mrs. Robinson, referring to a room hardly smaller than her own bedroom and almost as luxuriously fitted, which we had just seen. And as she made this remark she looked hard at the girl, as if interested in seeing her reaction. A look of incredulity for a moment passed over the girl's face, to be replaced at once by her usual impassiveness, perhaps now with a touch of scepticism.

" 'No, mam, that ain't possible,' she said, 'there's too much to do at 'ome.'

" 'Oh, well, perhaps we'll discuss that some other time; let's go back to the sitting-room and talk about when you can start coming to me.'

"This was duly done, and fifteen minutes later, a little dazedly in possession of the information that she would be receiving the sum of thirty shillings for a mere three hours' work a day (excluding Sunday), Mildred was once more in the street, and I was accompanying her home. I found her even more monosyllabic than usual. She did however ask one question before we reached home.

" 'Bit of hot stuff, ain't she?' she asked.

" 'What do you mean, Mildred?' I asked.

"She looked at me hard for a moment, and then shrugged her shoulders.

" 'Oh, forget it, Mr. Ash,' she said.

" 'If you mean Mrs. Robinson is not all she should be, Mildred,' I said a little severely, 'you are quite wrong. She's a woman with much more money than anyone you're accustomed to, and therefore it's natural for her to dress as she does and furnish her rooms in that way. But she's a very generous, kind woman.'

" 'Yes, Mr. Ash.' said Mildred, and we did not speak again until I bade her good-bye."

"However," went on Mr. Ash, "Mildred's remark about Mrs. Robinson being 'hot stuff' worried me more than I realized at the time, for it tied up so well with what seemed to be the opinion of many of the people who were supposed to be our mutual friends, an opinion that was making itself more than ever felt now that an end to the war was in sight. For already the flying-bombs had ceased, and with the decline in the sense of emergency, people were beginning to look round them and to wonder who some of the people were they had been co-operating with in the cause of national emergency, and Mrs. Robinson seemed to be one of the first to be looked at doubtfully. I noticed, in the rare moments when I had leisure enough to give the matter thought, that the guarded admiration with which she had been regarded when I had come to the parish nine months before, had given way, first to amused tolerance, and now, in some cases, to open disapproval, but of exactly what, I still did not know. In fact this general attitude caused me some indignation, for I put it down to the lack of a sense of proportion possessed by people of the world, who were so much subject to the petty rivalries and jealousies that went on around them that they were unable to see Mrs. Robinson in her true colours. It seemed to me that I, with my unprejudiced point of view, saw her more clearly, and there was certainly no doubt whatever that I had found in her far more of the true Christian spirit of forgiveness than in almost anyone else I had come across in the parish, and if she was a little careless of appearances—such as allowing strange troops to sleep in her flat and getting rather too quickly onto familiar terms with the husbands of her friends when they came on leave—this, I was sure, was due more to her natural friendliness of disposition than to any fault in her character. For I had myself experienced this friendliness, and knew that it was fundamentally innocent, whilst I knew at the same time that certain other poeple, had they witnessed the way in which she had spontaneously kissed me that evening a few weeks previously, would have put the most black interpretation upon her motives and probably spread the most dastardly rumours; whilst I knew it had been maternal instinct that had been the main cause of her action. So it was that I reasoned it was this kind of misinterpretation of her motives that had given her the reputation she seemed to have, and I determined to be her champion whenever the occasion arose. There were many other things I admired about Mrs. Robinson; the way in which she never said an unkind thing about her neighbours—in contrast to many of the others, who rarely said a kind thing about each other, let alone her, and the way in which she had absolutely no class prejudice.

"It was at this time that I became aware that there seemed to be almost an organized plot against Mrs. Robinson, and that the prime movers in it were Mrs. Carrington-Smith and young Mrs. Bartram; by thinly veiled insinuation, covered up by many endearments, they seemed gradually to be ostracizing the other woman; and Mrs. Robinson, surprisingly, seemed to be taking it without protest, almost lying-down, in fact. All this confirmed me in my belief that most women were fundamentally superficial in their attitude to life, unconcerned with true values but only with their own petty rivalries. There was only in my mind the faintest uneasiness, connected with Mrs. Robinson's blue hair, her provocative clothes, the contents of her wardrobe, and the way in which she occasionally looked into the depths of my own eyes with an expression that was not entirely maternal. . . .

"I found myself thinking about all this at night, and not sleeping well for the first time in my life, which was absurd, because it played only a very small part in my parish life. I could not understand why it seemed so important to me, and one evening, when I happened to be passing Dr. Kynaston's house, I felt a sudden desire to discuss it, not with the doctor, but with his wife, whose understanding and experience in the ways of the world I had considerable respect for. So I stopped, and on the spur of the moment, knocked at their door.

"The door was opened by Mrs. Kynaston herself, and when she saw me there appeared on her face the expression with which she always greeted me, a smile half-mocking, half-pleased, and which for some reason I always found refreshing.

" 'How nice to see you, Vicar,' she said. 'It's some weeks since you did us this honour, but no doubt you have been grappling with the immoralities of this ungodly parish. Do come in— for a long time I've been hoping you'd drop in for a real *probing* chat without the inhibiting presence of my husband.'

" 'Dr. Kynaston is out?' I asked, doubtfully, though it was what I had hoped to hear.

" 'Yes, dear man, but do not let that dismay you. I assure you I will behave with the utmost restraint, and I have no doubt that your religion will help you to keep within bounds the great passion you no doubt have for me.'

"And taking my arm she closed the door behind me and led me into the sitting-room, where she made me sit in the best arm-chair, perching herself on a stool at my feet, and, clasping her knees in her hands, looked up at me with a smile. I knew, with what was a kind of pleasurable anticipation, that she was in fact about to embark on what she called a 'probing' chat.

" 'Women are a source of never-ceasing wonder to you, Vicar, aren't they?' she asked.

" 'Why do you say that?' I asked.

" 'Well, I have always been something of an amateur psy-chologist, and now that I am past the first flush of youth, and have become old and unattractive—I am past forty, Vicar——' Here she paused, as if waiting for me to say something, but when I did not speak, she went on. 'There!' she said. 'That's proof that you are unaccustomed to the society of women—if you had the least understanding of them, you'd have said, "you don't look forty, and are still most attractive" .'

" 'I thought it so obvious that it didn't need saying.'

" 'Not bad, Vicar—not at all a bad second thought—but a little late. But at least it shows you are capable of learning. But such replies should need no prompting. But to resume. Having studied psychology for twenty years—oh, quite seriously, I read it at Cambridge—and not having had the fortune—or otherwise—of being blessed by children, I have had plenty of opportunity of studying human nature—of applying my know-ledge, as it were—and the first time I met you I said to myself, "Such a good-looking young vicar—what on earth made *him* go into the Church?" For I am always intrigued when I come across a man of both intelligence and sincerity who dedicates his life to God. So I studied you very hard, Vicar. I wondered, among other things, whether you were one of those men who— to put it politely—are biologically disinclined to marriage—oh, don't look shocked, it was a natural suspicion in view of your looks—too many men with blue eyes, curly hair, and fresh complexions, are that way inclined. But there was a certain masculinity about you which made me think this was not the answer. And I flirted with you a little, and found that you reacted satisfactorily. But though you reacted, you at the same time gave me the odd impression that you did not realize it— as if there was about you an extraordinary innocence—as if—as if you had led a very sheltered youth and suddenly been cast out into the world without any of the usual worldly preparation— such as the conversation in breaks at a public-school. . . . In fact yours is a psychology I have never come across before. I found it particularly odd in view of the fact that you must be— well, past thirty. How old are you, Vicar?'

" 'I am thirty-four.'

" 'There you are, then. A man of thirty-four, normally sexed, yet completely unaware of at least one-half of his nature. So I came to the conclusion that you must have had a very unusual upbringing. Have you, Vicar?'

"And removing her hands from round her knees, she sat forward on her stool, resting her chin on her clenched fists, and looked at me attentively, her intelligent, quaintly-attractive face serious.

"And though feeling slightly perturbed that I gave such an impression of innocence, I felt no annoyance, for I was accustomed to these cross-examinations by this cynical but stimulating woman, and had for some time been looking forward to pitting my principles against her nimble, if superficial, intelligence; because though intelligent, I knew her wits lacked the sheet-anchor of religion, and I was quite confident that I would be able to defeat her in argument. So I replied with the confidence of one who had nothing to hide, one who had no dark corners in his mind which he preferred to hide from public view. Rather, I was proud of my innocence.

" 'I have been brought up in the Church,' I said, 'whose text-book is the Bible, not Freud, and from which one can learn more wisdom than from any worldly upbringing. You, Mrs. Kynaston, seem to be biased very much in one direction—you talk as if sex were the main motive for all human behaviour.'

" 'Well, being a psychologist, I have been brought up to have more respect for Freud than for God—but unlike some Freudians, I do recognize the existence of other motives. Vanity, for instance, and greed for riches. But to return to the Bible. Do you really believe what you just said? Do you really believe that the study of a book, however wise, is a substitute for practical experience? Christ, in whose existence you presumably believe, is supposed to have learnt his wisdom, not from a book, but from life.'

" 'I too have experience of life. You forget I was in the Army.'

" 'For how long?'

" 'Almost six months.'

" 'And before that?'

" 'Before that I was in a monastery.'

"A look of interest came into her eyes.

" 'How long were you there for?'

" 'Over ten years.'

" 'Ten years! That would make you twenty or so when you went in. Where were you at school?'

" 'I never was at school. My parents died when I was a child and I was brought up by an uncle, who gave me private tutors.'

" 'A bachelor uncle?'

" 'Yes, Mrs. Kynaston. No feminine influence, if that's what you are trying to get at.'

" 'And was this uncle in the Church too?'

" 'He took Orders but never had a living. He was something of an amateur philosopher—he wrote several books on metaphysics and religious philosophy. More of a philosopher than theologian, I fear.'

" 'Of what did his household consist?'

" 'He was very wealthy—is, I should say, for he's still alive. We lived in a large house with a full staff of servants, as Mrs. Carrington-Smith would say.'

" 'Who brought you up—the servants or this eccentric scholar?'

" 'He was not eccentric, but a very wise man, and he showed me great affection; he—and the tutors he chose—brought me up.'

" 'You must have been a lonely child.'

" 'I am not conscious of having been. I was always very busy.'

" 'Studying metaphysics?'

" 'Not until a later age—and I soon discarded metaphysics as an attempt to explain by reason that which gives us the power to reason, which is so much waste of time. I preferred faith. But as a child I was not lonely, for my uncle's estate was full of all the creations of God—ponies, dogs, trees, flowers, all the life of a model farm he ran as a hobby. How could I be lonely?'

" 'And the people who ran this estate, this farm, did you have much contact with them?'

" 'Very little—always I was accompanied by my uncle or a tutor. For some reason my uncle seemed to consider the workers on the estate unsuitable company. And he maintained strict discipline—they never tried to make contact with me.'

" 'In later life didn't you consider this upbringing a strange one?'

" 'It was unusual, certainly. But then it was quite a logical one in view of what my uncle intended me for. He was trying out some philosophical theory or other on me, and wanted my intellect to remain pure and uncontaminated by what he called the distractions of civilization, so that I could lead a life of the intellect.'

" 'Which you did until the war came?'

" 'Not exactly. Metaphysics and religion are poles apart. One is intellect, the other faith. In my monastery I did not think about mankind, but contemplated God.'

" 'And so were completely "uncontaminated by the distractions of civilization," as your uncle called it?'

" 'Yes.'

" 'And then, suddenly, you were called up?'

" 'Oh no. I was exempt. I volunteered.'

" 'Why, Vicar?'

"I shrugged my shoulders.

" 'Like most of us, I disliked the theory of the totalitarian State. You see, there was no place for God in it.'

D*

" 'So your only experience of what we know as "life" is less than six months in the Army and a few months in this parish?'

" 'Yes.'

"She paused, and for a moment there was silence between us. Then she said, her voice soft, and full of what I can only describe as compassion:

" 'And here you are, exposed suddenly to the evils of a post-war society, like a child from a primitive world with no resistance to the diseases of civilization.'

"This slightly annoyed me—she so misunderstood the situation. It was I who should be showing compassion for her, filled as she was with all the irrelevant theories of civilization, a woman without faith.

" 'You forget,' I said, 'that I have learnt all I need to learn about life from the Bible.'

" 'The Bible!—it is only one book in millions. There is only one source from which we can learn—that is life itself. You will find your Bible useless when you become entangled with this post-war life we are about to embark on. You will be like the Australian aborigines, Vicar, who, on their first contact with civilization, began to die like flies from tuberculosis. Only your tuberculosis will be of the mind.'

" 'But I have that experience of the Army,' I said mildly, 'which is a notoriously contaminating society. And as far as I know I have come through unscathed.'

" 'My dear vicar, you were protected by your cloth. You had virtually no contact with the Army, which anyhow is the most conservative of societies. There are no women in the Army, Vicar. It is a society lacking the two principal causes of corruption —women and money. It is a community almost as simple and as far removed from civilization as the society of the Australian aborigines I have just mentioned—especially for you, a padré, the man in whose presence even fellow officers curb their tongues and behaviour. No, Vicar, you know nothing of life. You will indeed need the protection of God to get through the next few years. Personally I would rather see you under the protection of a good woman. For already I have seen how helpless you are in the hands of the other sort.'

" 'What do you mean?' I asked sharply.

"It was some moments before she replied, and she seemed to be thinking deeply, as if really worried about the effect of what she was about to say. At last she said quietly, with all vestige of facetiousness gone from her voice:

" 'I know I'm in the habit of talking about my neighbours— often I say cynical things about them. I have shown more than once in your presence, for instance, that I consider Mrs. Robinson worth most of the rest of the women in this district put together, possibly including myself. In fact, in my heart, I do prefer her to myself, and to the others—one cannot help preferring absolute generosity of instinct to natures more restricted by the needs of society—so long as one is not subjected to the effects of this absolute amorality, which fortunately I am not, which is perhaps why I am able to like Mrs. Robinson. My husband, you see, is a doctor, and sees women, however attractive their flesh, as potential guinea-pigs. But in spite of this I am not blind to the fact that within the bounds of society—in which, for better or for worse, we have to live—Mrs. Robinson is a greater evil than all the little meannesses and hypocrisies practised by women such as Mrs. Carrington-Smith and her little crony Mrs. Bartram. Their catty, gossiping, nasty ways are their only defence— and a legitimate one—against the power exercised by women like Mrs. Robinson. Their means—by which they are slowly achieving her social ostracization—may be despicable—they may even be destroying something noble—but theirs is the only way possible. This is the kind of thing I mean by life, Vicar, about which you know nothing—the need to know when to compromise and how to reconcile it with your conscience. . . .'

"Suddenly she stood up and walked quickly over to the window, out of which she looked, much as Mrs. Robinson herself had turned from me a few evenings before to hide emotion, emotion she was ashamed of and afraid to show; realizing this, I felt sudden affection for her, the compassion I had been unable to feel a few moments before. I felt also a slight feeling of triumph.

" 'Do not be ashamed,' I said quietly, 'of showing that you are moved. Concern for the state of the human soul does you credit rather than otherwise. It shows how skin-deep is the worldly, cynical attitude you are always at such pains to keep up.'

"She turned round, and her face had again its slightly mocking look.

" 'Thank you, Vicar,' she said. 'But I prefer to maintain my pose, as you call it. And I am not in the least concerned for the state of the human soul—I am merely interested in it. But I admire your self-control. It almost makes me think that your faith is superior to my logic.'

" 'Almost?' I asked.

" 'Yes—almost, not quite. For much though I might want faith, I cannot have it just because I want it. And my scepticism, which at least gives me a working, if unsatisfactory, way of facing life, has stood the test of time. It has stood up to much, Vicar. I only hope your faith is proof against the realities of life you are about to face. But enough of this high-falutin talk. You have been sitting here now for half an hour and I have offered you no hospitality—I have merely subjected you to an inquisition, and I am grateful to you for allowing me to add another leaf to my psychological case-book. Let me get you some coffee.'

"And without waiting for an answer, she left the room.

"Alone, I felt as if I had gained a moral victory in this little exchange; knowing that faith, being a thing felt rather than understood, could not be explained by words, I had developed the practice, in arguments of this kind, of allowing the other party to talk themselves into a realization of the futility of their own argument, thus giving a practical demonstration of the superiority of faith over intellect. But in spite of this supposed victory I remained uneasy, for Mrs. Kynaston had disturbed my faith in Mrs. Robinson, if not in God, and since I had committed Mildred to her care, Mrs. Robinson was very much in the forefront of my mind. And having lived in the district for some years,

Mrs. Kynaston perhaps had some very good reason for disapproving of Mrs. Robinson, a reason which would force me
to reconsider my opinion of her; for in spite of my liking for
Mrs. Robinson, deep down in my heart I trusted no woman. So
I made up my mind, on Mrs. Kynaston's return, to find out
exactly what she knew about Mrs. Robinson, and if I found
out that her opinion was based merely on supposition and feminine intuition, to disregard it altogether.

"So on her return, I at once broached the subject. As she poured
out coffee, I asked:

" 'Apart from the self-protective instincts of the ladies of
this parish, is there anything definite known against Mrs.
Robinson?'

" 'You mean,' she said, 'is all this supposition based on anything concrete, or is it merely irresponsible feminine jealousy?
Well, Vicar, I know nothing definite against her, but then I
always champion her rather than otherwise. Not, however, for
that reason. I am personally quite certain that these other women
are right—this is something women understand without having
to "know anything definite". Now don't look sceptical, Vicar.
I assure you it is so.'

" 'I am more than sceptical. These other women have evidence
of the fact that Mrs. Robinson attracts men, but, as far as I know,
nothing else to go on. And on this flimsy evidence they jump
to the conclusion that she will take the first opportunity of
stealing their husbands. Mrs. Robinson cannot help being
attractive.'

" 'My dear vicar, this is another indication of your ignorance
of women. She can help being so attractive—haven't you noticed
her clothes? Is it necessary for her to draw such attention to her
figure? The woman has not yet been born who, aware of this
power over men, does not make use of it. Especially if they are
widows.'

" 'Mrs. Kynaston, you are allowing your cynicism to cloud
your judgement,' I said.

" 'Well—a little exaggeration perhaps, but nine times out of

ten it is so. And in Mrs. Robinson's case there is plenty of cir-
cumstantial evidence. Since you've been in the parish, comparatively few husbands have been on leave—but in the early
part of the war, there were many incidents. And her flat has
been a kind of clearing-station for troops at a loose-end in
London throughout the war—Americans, Poles, Free French,
every nationality under the sun.'

" 'I know,' I said. 'I have been in her flat several times when
troops have been there. And I can assure you she has had them
there solely out of the goodness of her heart.'

" 'I'm glad to hear it. You may be right. As I say, I make no
accusations. I am only giving you the reasons for the other
women's attitude. And anyhow, if a woman behaves as indis-
creetly as she does, she deserves her reputation. Not that I think
she cares—I think she positively adores creating scandal.'

"I remembered suddenly the look in Mrs. Robinson's eyes
when I had left her after introducing to her the subject of Mildred's employment; at the time the look had disturbed me, but
I had dismissed it from my mind. Now it came back vividly,
and I felt more than ever that my opinion of her was justified,
and that these women were wrong.

" 'No,' I said, 'I think it gives her great pain.'

" 'Well, Vicar,' she said with a sigh, 'I don't want to malign
anyone, especially a woman I like as much as Mrs. Robinson.
By all means continue to think her an angel who can do no
wrong. But in my opinion she is a very different kind of angel
from the ones you are accustomed to dealing with. Shall we
change the subject?'

" 'By all means.'

"But somehow, though we made several attempts, conversation would not start again. It was as if we now knew too much
about each other to be completely at ease. The odd idea occurred
to me that Mrs. Kynaston was in some way jealous of my
championship of Mrs. Robinson, and so I came to the conclusion
that fundamentally she was no different from other women, only
a little quicker-witted. So I soon left, feeling a little disillusioned,

but convinced that I had found out what I had set out to discover
—that no one in fact knew anything definite against Mrs.
Robinson.

"Although annoyed with Mrs. Kynaston for what I considered
to be her unjust attitude towards Mrs. Robinson, I was more
annoyed with myself for having what had almost been a quarrel
with her for so small a cause. I could not understand why I had
felt something very like emotion, for I was accustomed to being
moved only by causes of universal significance, and could not
understand my preoccupation with an individual. Matters were
made worse by the fact that almost whenever I met a group of
people who knew Mrs. Robinson, she was invariably brought
into the conversation, and almost always I found myself feeling
irritation at something that was said. On one occasion in Mrs.
Carrington-Smith's flat, after listening for twenty minutes to
insinuations and hints about her, none of them complimentary,
I became unable to control myself any longer, and said with
some irritation:

" 'Just why is it you all find so much to criticize in Mrs.
Robinson these days? Not long ago she was one of the most useful members of your Committee, and you all made as much use
of her as you could.'

"At once there was silence, and I was aware of everyone looking at me—the entire W.V.S. Committee with the exception of
Mrs. Robinson herself and Dr. Kynaston, were present, even
Miss Cooter having been prevailed upon to have a cup of coffee
—and immediately I regretted my question, feeling that I had
probably qualified myself as a subject for gossip.

" 'My dear vicar,' said Mrs. Carrington-Smith after a moment,
'We are very fond of Marjorie. She is one of my very best
friends. If we are sometimes a little critical of each other, don't
pay too much attention—it's only idle women's gossip. And after
all, Marjorie does lay herself open to a little friendly criticism—
she has such a weakness for the other sex, and uses such—how
shall I put it?—such conspicuous methods for drawing attention
to herself.'

"All the other women seemed to approve this explanation, except Miss Cooter, who remained silently staring in front of her, her eyes expressionless behind her rimless glasses.

" 'Almost pathetic, I call it, at her age,' said Mrs. Bartram. 'She must be nearly fifty, with a grown-up son, and all. Why, when my husband came on leave last, she made a pass at him, and he wasn't half amused. Old enough to be his mother, she is.'

" 'And the way she splashes her money about,' said one of the other women. 'We all of us have to be careful these days, but not she. She's had her flat decorated each year since the war; how she gets the labour, beats me.'

" 'Oh, I can explain that,' said Mrs. Carrington-Smith. 'She has friends in the building trade.' She leant forward in her chair, and all the other women—again with the exception of Miss Cooter—did the same. 'You know that rather good-looking Mr. Bateman who's on the A.R.P. Committee? He does it for her on the quiet—at night. She knows all the men on that committee, and positively queens it over them. Fetches their beer from the public-bar, I'm told—with almost a professional air, my informant tells me. But the vicar will be able to tell us about that,' she added, leaning back in her chair again with a slightly shamefaced air, as if remembering suddenly that there was indeed someone present who had first-hand information on the subject. 'You attend the A.R.P. meetings, don't you, Vicar?'

" 'I do,' I said, 'and Mrs. Robinson is as useful on that Committee as she is on yours. She does occasionally bring in refreshment for the Committee, just as she does for yours, Mrs. Carrington-Smith. And not with a particularly professional air.'

" 'Oh, I've no doubt she's useful,' said Mrs. Carrington-Smith. 'She's a great committee-woman. Knows everyone—from the lowest to the highest. Why I've known her, when in my company, actually greet the man who cleans her windows, in a public street. As I say, I have a great respect for her. One cannot help admiring the way she has crept into every aspect of life in this district, and made friends on all levels. By dint of using little Mrs. Kynaston as a stepping-stone, she even managed to make herself noticed at the Area Red Cross Meeting a few months ago. I'm told she was fawning round Lady Castleby who was Chairman on that occasion. She was quite put out when I told her I knew Phyllis Castleby twenty years ago, when she was the Hon. Phyllis Clyde-Ponting, you know, Lord Canonbury's daughter. I was at a house party given by him in '31—rather an insufferable woman, actually.'

"There was a moment's silence while everyone digested this information, pretending not to be particularly impressed, but in fact showing that they were.

"'Talking of Mrs. Kynaston,' said Mrs. Bartram suddenly, 'there's a person I can't stand. So sarcastic, she is—thinks she's the Marchioness of What-not just because she got a degree at Cambridge. Anyone can get a degree if they work for it, and it's not a woman's place, I always say, to go in for that sort of thing—takes the bread out of men's mouths. She isn't half sarcastic—if that's what Cambridge does for you, I don't think much of it. Lowest form of wit, I've always called it. And she doesn't half discuss people—no one's character's worth tuppence when she gets going. I'll tell you what's wrong with her—she's got starved maternal instincts, that's what she's got. It's my belief the doctor's not capable—these fat men often aren't.'

"And Mrs. Bartram looked round at the other women, a confiding expression on her pretty, sly face. For a moment it looked as if she were going to be snubbed—I had noticed more than once that she was not popular with the other Committee members, and was borne with at all only because of the protection given her by Mrs. Carrington-Smith; I think they disliked her more because she came from a lower class than themselves rather than because of her sly disposition, and because she had an embarrassing habit of always going too far in conversation. However, once more Mrs. Carrington-Smith came to her aid, and took her up warmly on the subject of Mrs. Kynaston, and an animated discussion began on the iniquities of that lady's character. After a moment or two, Miss Cooter, finishing her coffee at a gulp, stood up, and in her usual abrupt manner, took her leave. As the door closed behind her Mrs. Carrington-Smith looked round at the others, and again leaning forward, said in a low voice:

" 'Now, if the truth were known about *her*. . . .'

"This was too much for me, and with as much politeness as I could muster, I followed Miss Cooter's example, and fled, feeling, as I left, that probably my character was in turn being pulled to pieces in the room behind me.

"I hurried down the corridor, and found Miss Cooter still waiting for a lift, and as we descended together, I found myself more or less obliged to make polite conversation with her. I had never spoken to this rather forbidding young woman alone before and knew little about her, not knowing where she lived, what her occupation was, or even whether she was one of my parishioners; our conversation in the lift was limited to the workings of that unreliable piece of machinery; in fact, being unable to coax it into movement at all, I had to relinquish the controls to Miss Cooter, who with her usual efficiency managed to get it going. She even gave a pale smile as I complimented her.

" 'We shall all be efficient in the post-war State,' she said, a remark the relevance of which I did not altogether understand.

"I found myself still beside her in the street outside, and in desperation for some subject to talk about, and with my usual habit of making straight for the point, I asked:

" 'Do you share the rest of the Committee's dislike of Mrs. Robinson?'

"Miss Cooter shrugged her shoulders.

" 'I neither like nor dislike her,' she said.

" 'You knew her before the war, didn't you?'

"She looked at me sharply.

" 'Look here, Mr. Ash,' she said, 'if you think I'm going to indulge in gossip too, you're making a mistake.'

" 'I have no desire whatever to gossip,' I said. 'I am merely trying to find someone who can confirm my own opinion that these rumours about Mrs. Robinson have no basis.'

"Miss Cooter looked at me a little oddly.

" 'Whilst I agree that the undisciplined tongues of my fellow-committee-women are extremely annoying, I am not prepared to express an opinion as to whether or not they are justified in this instance. It seems,' she went on, 'that you and I, rather to my surprise, have something in common. We both dislike irresponsible gossip, but no doubt for totally different reasons.'

" 'Why for totally different reasons, Miss Cooter?' I asked mildly.

" 'Well, you see, I find these women typical of the decadence one is only too liable to find in this country. But I confess that they have a certain fascination for me. I even feel a certain nostalgia when I think that soon they will be a thing of the past—that they will be swept out of existence in the great revolution.'

" 'Are you expecting civil war, Miss Cooter?' I asked politely.

" 'I doubt whether it will come to that. I have little doubt that the heroic example of the Union of the Soviet Socialist Republics has made the world realize that there is only one sane way to govern a country, that is, by the people for the people. And the actions of the partisans in the oppressed countries—all of them Communists, as is well known—all this has laid already a foundation for a comparatively peaceful take-over in most European countries. It is only here and in America that there may be a little trouble—we have not been occupied, and so the Party in Britain and America has not had the chance to show conclusively its superiority over all others. But I don't expect much trouble.'

" 'Indeed,' I said. 'And what do you think will be the fate of my profession in the great take-over?'

" 'Well, it depends on your reaction. If you attempt to organize public opinion against us—which I don't for one moment expect, for there is no drive left in Christianity—but if you do, we will have no alternative but to liquidate you, for the good of the people. If on the other hand, as I think probable, you work in the interests of the Party, then you will be tolerated for a while. You will be allowed to fade gradually out of existence, until the people, no longer fed from an early age with nonsense about immortality and life after death, come to realize by their own free will your uselessness, and cease to tolerate the wasted space taken up by churchyards and churches, and the waste of man-power in maintaining them. But until then you will be allowed to carry on a kind of welfare organization for the benefit of the older generations.'

" 'Generous of you, I must say,' I said. 'May I ask what is the principal improvement you expect to effect in the life of the community by this revolution, peaceful or otherwise?'

"Miss Cooter looked at me as if I were a rather backward child aged four.

" 'Such ignorance,' she said, 'in one brought up under the narrow, bigoted influence of the Church, does not surprise me.'

"By now we were standing outside the local Underground Station where Miss Cooter had stopped, and where she continued the conversation in a clear, emotionless voice, audible to a small group of passers-by who seemed to have stopped to listen. She continued to talk even more loudly when she noticed them, as if for their benefit.

" 'Our object,' she said as if reciting something learnt from a text-book, 'is to create a society in which every citizen is able to make use of his natural abilities free from the oppressive in-fluence of class-prejudice, a society in fact, in which everyone is recognized as having been created equal.'

" 'Are you not aware,' I said quietly, in fact so quietly that one rather drunken member of our audience shouted, 'Speak up, Holy Joe', an interjection greeted with a mixture of laughter and cries of 'quiet—let 'im 'ave 'is say', during which I stopped speaking, waiting for silence. When at last they were quiet, I went on, still mildly but in a stronger voice:

" 'Are you not aware that the Christian Church has for nearly two thousand years preached that all men are equal, in fact that it was from our Church that your Party got the idea?'

" 'And it has taken you two thousand years,' said Miss Cooter, looking round at the audience with a faint smile, 'to achieve these living conditions,' and with a sweep of her arm, she

indicated the decaying mansions, such as were lived in by the
Whites, and which could be seen from where we were standing.

" ''Ear, 'ear,' said the wag in the crowd, which had now
doubled. 'One up for Joe Stalin. Now let's 'ear what 'Oly Joe
'as to say.'

" 'I say,' I continued, now using my trained voice to full
effect, 'that in two thousand years—a mere moment of time in
the billions of years since life was created—yes, I say created—
we have raised man from a state of tribal warfare in which he
had no time to employ his mind on anything but the necessities
of living, to——'

" '—to blowin' 'imself up with flyin'-bombs,' the wag in the
crowd finished for me.

" '—to be willing to lay down his life to save his fellow-men
from oppression,' I finished, in a way I had not intended, but
which seemed to take the crowd by surprise and to some degree
impress them, for they made no ironical comments, but looked
towards Miss Cooter for her reply. Slowly she looked round the
faces surrounding us, and I could see from her eyes behind the
rimless glasses that she was in her element, that I was in the
presence of a born street-corner orator.

" 'Comrades—' she began impressively, but before she could
get any further there was an interruption in the person of the
large figure of George Baker, the local policeman, a man well
known to me, and a humorist in his own right, who slowly
pushed his way through the crowd.

" ''Ere, 'ere, what's all this?' he said. 'A political meetin' in a
public thoroughfare? I can have you all locked up for creating
a public nuisance.' He caught sight of me. 'Well, well,' he said,
'and what might you be doin' 'ere, Mr. Ash? You are the last
person I expected to find creating a public disturbance. Now
Miss Cooter 'ere is well known to us—regular thorn in our flesh,
she is. Now, Miss, a public hall or Marble Arch on Sunday
morning is the place for this, you know that as well as I do. And
you, Sir, if I may respectfully suggest, can talk as much as you
like from the pulpit of your church, where all these good people

can come and listen to you.' And he winked at the crowd who gave this remark a better reception than they had either me or Miss Cooter.

" 'I apologize, George,' I said, 'but Miss Cooter and I were rather carried away by our own eloquence.'

" 'That's all right, Sir, but don't let it occur again. It's my duty to keep the public thoroughfares free from congestion, and I don't want to 'ave to exercise the majesty of the law in order to do so. Now Miss Cooter, Miss, you take my advice, and go back home and get your people to 'ire you a hall where you can much better exercise your talents for public speakin'. . . '

"And as Miss Cooter, once more the rather prim and very proper Committee secretary, moved off in the direction of the Underground, George Baker gave her a by no means unfriendly grin. When she had gone—by which time the crowd too had dispersed except for a few lingerers, I found myself walking in the direction of the vicarage in the company of George Baker, with him saying:

" 'Not a bad woman, Miss Cooter. Known 'er since she was a kid, I have. She was born 'ere—not ten doors from the vicarage. 'Er parents still live there, respectable workin' folk they are,— ain't never given no trouble, very law-abidin'. But she's one of those women—always spinsters, they are—'oo keeps getting bees in their bonnets. Not long ago it was Fascism—quite a follower of Mosley, she was. Now it's this 'ere Communism— not that she knows anything about it really—she just reads it all up in books. . . . But there ain't no real 'arm in 'er—a terror for argument, that's all. You mark my words, after the first General Election, when the Communists'll be ignored as you might say, she'll forget all about it, and take to dress designin' or something. More suitable for a woman, too.'

"I was not sure that George's usual optimistic view of human nature was quite so justified in this instance, but I was in no mood for more argument, so I said mildly:

" 'You know many of the people in this district, don't you?'

" 'Should do—lived 'ere all me life, and spent most of it in the Force. I was just reachin' retirin' age when the war come along, so they kept me on. And as I ain't what you'd call an ambitious officer, they've kept me all the time in this borough, except for a year or two I 'ad down Hackney way. So I knows the district as you might say like the palm of me 'and.'

" 'Has Mrs. Robinson been here for long?'

"For a moment he was silent, and I had an odd idea there was a slightly evasive note in his voice when he did finally speak.

" 'Mrs. Robinson?' he asked. 'There's 'alf a dozen Mrs. Robinsons 'ereabouts. Which d'you mean, Mr. Ash?'

" 'Mrs. Robinson of Carlton Court.'

" 'Ah, I know 'er. I thought it was 'er you meant. Came back to this district just before the war, she did. I've 'eard rumours she was born in a house where Carlton Court now stands. But that's just rumour. Grand lady, she is now. I've 'eard rumours she wasn't such a grand lady once.'

" 'You didn't know her when she was a young woman?'

" 'No—can't say I did. She left 'ere when she was a girl, and come back like I said, a grand lady.'

"Again I had the impression there was something evasive about the usually voluble George.

" 'Do you know anything against her, George?' I asked suddenly.

" 'Against 'er, Mr. Ash? No, I can't say as I know anything I would describe as against 'er. And if I did I couldn't reveal professional secrets, as you might say.'

" 'No, of course not. I only ask because rumours are starting about her, and as far as I know they have absolutely no foundation. And I don't like that sort of thing.'

" 'No more do I. What sort of rumours, Mr. Ash?'

" 'Oh—nothing definite. The ladies of Carlton Court seem to have their knives into her, that's all.'

" 'Oh, ay, they would. Strikes me she's the sort of woman who'd rouse other women's hatred, as you might say. Too popular with the men, eh? I wouldn't take no notice of it if I was you, Mr. Ash. Let the ladies look after themselves. Always fightin' among themselves, they are. Some is fated to be popular with the men and unpopular with the ladies. That's the way of life. But Mrs. Robinson is able to look after 'erself. She's done so up to now.'

" 'Yes, her husband seems to have left her comfortably off. Did you ever hear who he was, George?'

" 'No, can't say as I 'ave. As I say, Mr. Ash, don't you worry yourself about Mrs. Robinson—there's many worse than 'er about. If she 'as erred, she's erred what you might call on the right side. Well, Mr. Ash, 'ere's the vicarage, and I must take my leave of you—due to meet my relief up the road in five minutes, and 'e might get nervous all alone, bein' a youngster. . . .'

"And rather hurriedly he saluted, and strode off up the road with his usual ponderous stride, leaving me more perplexed than ever about Mrs. Robinson."

This was the point in his narrative reached by Mr. Ash on their last evening in Paris.

The next day they spent in final sightseeing before joining their train early in the evening. After depositing their luggage in the sleeper, they went straight along to the dining-car, just as the train moved off. Katharine enjoyed that meal in the moving train with the lights of the French villages flashing past.

Back in their sleeper, it was natural for him to go into the corridor for a smoke whilst she prepared for bed, for there was hardly room for two to undress at the same time. When he returned, she was already in the upper bunk.

As he prepared for bed, she lay reading.

"I don't suppose I shall sleep," he said. "I didn't in my only other experience of a sleeper."

"I don't suppose I shall either," she replied.

"What a pity the noise of the train is too much for me to go on with my story," he said. "I would have liked to have got on with it."

After a pause, she asked:

*"Why don't you come up here? There's room beside me if we
don't intend to sleep."*

There was a moment's silence before he replied.

"Are you sure you don't want to sleep?" he asked.

"Quite sure. Would you like me to come down to you?"

*"No. . . . There's no need for you to get out of bed. . . . I'll bring a
blanket up and lie beside you if you're sure there's room."*

*He was some time coming up and when he did so she found he was
fully dressed except for jacket and shoes. He lay beside her rather
stiffly and arranged the blanket over him. She felt the warmth of his
body for the first time, but did not dare move nearer to him. She felt
instinctively that if she did so she would forfeit his trust, which she was
slowly building up.*

*He began talking, his head a few inches from hers, his voice just
audible above the rumbling of the train.*

"From the evening of my talk with Miss Cooter and George
Baker onwards, the hints, insinuations and veiled admissions of
everyone connected with Mrs. Robinson became too much for
me. Up to then I had brought the conversation round to her
more by chance than by design, but from that day onwards I
deliberately sought information, though trying to hide my object
from the people I questioned. But just how unsuccessful I was
in these efforts at dissimulation—the first I have ever attempted—
was brought home to me one afternoon by Dr. Kynaston.

"In actual fact I had gone round to him for the perfectly
genuine reason of having my leg looked at, which had been
giving me a little trouble, and had not intended bringing up the
subject of Mrs. Robinson. However, after completing his
examination and giving me his advice, the doctor leant back in
his chair, looked at me over his half-lensed glasses, and said, with
an odd little smile:

" 'Well, Vicar—proceed.'

" 'Proceed with what?' I asked.

" 'With the inquisition. Your main reason for seeking my

professional advice was to find out what I know about our
mutual friend Mrs. Robinson, wasn't it?'

"My face must have shown my astonishment, for he went on:

" 'Don't be embarrassed, Vicar. Curiosity is a natural human
failing. And in any event it's no doubt a part of your professional
duties to find out as much as you can about the moral character
of your parishioners. After all, you look after their souls as I look
after their bodies. . . .'

" 'But what makes you think I intended speaking to you about
her?'

" 'Well, to be quite honest, it was my incorrigible wife who
put me up to it. It wouldn't have occurred to me in a hundred
years. But apparently, on the female bush-telegraph which is so
highly developed in the vicinity of Carlton Court, the news has
gone out that you are systematically combing the neighbourhood
for the truth about the fascinating widow, and as I seem to be
about the only person you haven't cross-questioned, my wife
came to the not unnatural conclusion that my turn would come
this evening. . . .'

" 'I am astonished,' I said. 'I must have been extraordinarily
clumsy.'

" 'Not at all, Vicar. All you've done is to underestimate the
power of female gossip. It is one of those things that has to be
experienced to be believed. It's a form of hysteria—it can sweep
through a community like a super-contagious disease. And the
devil of it is it can be just as virulent when unjustified. In this
instance there is a certain amount of justification, if you don't
mind my saying so—you have been looking for information
about Mrs. Robinson, no doubt for a very good reason. But
sometimes gossip can start with no foundation whatever—for
instance a combination of circumstances pointing momentarily
to a certain conclusion, but in fact being only coincidence, can
set the tongues of fifty women wagging, so that enough cir-
cumstantial evidence is built up—all absolutely imaginary—
to convince a jury. Character can be blackened with no foundation in fact, and the only way the poor devil can defend himself

is by starting a libel action for which he usually hasn't enough
evidence, or by leaving the district.'

" 'I had no idea,' I said, 'that I was an object of such interest
to the ladies of this parish. Judging by their Church attendance
I was under the impression they were barely aware of my
existence. . . . But as you have brought up the subject, Doctor, I
might as well pursue it. What is your opinion of Mrs. Robinson?'

" 'I'm afraid that on that score, Vicar, you've come to the
wrong shop,' he replied, with an air of hearty frankness which
I did not find altogether convincing. 'As you may have noticed
I keep myself entirely apart from the idle feminine gossip with
which I am surrounded, and although my wife's tongue, I regret
to admit, often amuses me, I pay little attention to the content
of what she says. And believe me, Vicar, she's not the worst
offender. With her, matters go no further than myself; she's a
connoisseur of gossip—she collects it, hoards it, turns it inside
out when she gets home, but never spreads it further. As for
myself, I know very little about Mrs. Robinson. I'm interested in
people only as patients. I know of course that for some reason
she's made herself unpopular with the ladies of Carlton Court,
but no more than is inevitable for a woman with her disregard
for the conventions. Otherwise—well, she's a patient of mine,
in theory at any rate, but she's hardly ever had a day's illness. I
did however on one occasion have cause to give her the once-
over, when she had 'flu a couple of years ago, and believe me,
Vicar, she's one of the healthiest women of her age I've even seen.'
He leaned forward in his chair, and his pale, rather expressionless
eyes seemed to glisten with the impersonal enthusiasm of the
scientist, the artificial note having completely vanished from his
voice. 'This may be a breach of professional etiquette,' he went
on, '—as a doctor I should not discuss a patient outside the profession—but I don't mind telling you that if I had cause to find
a perfect specimen of a woman of ripe years to illustrate a lecture
to a group of students, I would have to look no further. Physically she has reached a perfect state of development at an age

when most women begin to deteriorate. I'd always admired her figure, her movement, the way she carries herself, but had always thought her appearance was largely due to the many artificial ways in which a woman can deceive the eye. But in her, nature is virtually unassisted. For instance, though her body's well covered —her figure is what one would describe as well-developed— nowhere is there any ugly accumulation of fat, there is not the least inclination to sagging or flabbiness, everywhere the flesh is firm and resilient. Her skin is as clear and unblemished as it must have been when she was eighteen. She's a woman who would delight the heart of a Botticelli, though I fear a little out of fashion these days, more's the pity. But in a woman of her age it's astonishing. . . .'

"For some time he went on with his description, becoming more and more enthusiastic, and as I listened, not without embarrassment, I could not help remembering young Mrs. Bartram's remarks about Mrs. Kynaston's childless state, when she had implied that the doctor 'was not capable'; as I watched his face I could well believe that his interest in life was bounded by the science of his profession, and I could understand that perhaps anyone married to him might have cause for bitterness. He did in the end seem to remember to whom he was speaking, because for a moment there came onto his face a look of almost comical dismay.

" 'My dear vicar,' he said, 'I really must apologize. Sometimes I'm liable to be carried away by enthusiasm for my subject. For a moment I forgot I was not in the hospital. But I assure you——'

" 'Don't apologize,' I said. 'It's good to see somebody with such an interest in his chosen profession. I can quite see that you had no time to take an interest in any other aspect of Mrs. Robinson——'

"Dr. Kynaston laughed.

" 'You have a sense of humour, Vicar. But joking apart, there is obviously a perfectly simple explanation of Mrs. Robinson's unpopularity—jealousy. The others are jealous of a woman able to attract the other sex at her age. Why, if I weren't so hardened a case myself, I would be attracted. No doubt you yourself have felt the power of her—how shall I put it?—her animal magnetism, to use popular language. After all, you're a young and healthy man——'

"Whilst saying this, he had stood up, and as he accompanied me to the door, he added, looking at me hard:

"'Mind you don't let your natural instincts play too large a part in your concern for her welfare——'

"'I don't understand you, Doctor.'

"'This is a hint for your own good, for what it's worth, as you seem so inexperienced in the subtleties of feminine intrigue. Apparently it has already been hinted that you are not impervious to the physical charms of the lady we have just been discussing——'

"'That, Kynaston, surely, is an example of your wife's imaginaton running away with you?' I said sharply.

"'Not my wife's, Ash—Mrs. Carrington-Smith's and her cronies'——'

"'Allow me to assure you, Kynaston, that I have certain mental reserves that render me proof against promiscuous physical attraction——' I said stiffly, pausing on the threshold of the surgery.

"'Now don't be annoyed, Ash. I'm only telling you what others say.'

"With an effort I forced down my anger, an emotion I never like to feel, and made myself speak more lightly, as if taking the whole matter as a joke, which I was far from doing.

"'Well,' I said with a smile, 'then I shall have to take care not to find myself walking up the aisle, instead of standing at one end of it——'

"'Not a bad walk to take, either, one of these days,' he said quietly. 'Though I'm not suggesting you take it with Mrs. Robinson. The discrepancy in age would be a little too much. But I always prescribe marriage to men between twenty-five and forty-five, if they are in any way inclined that way——'

" 'Do you think I need such a prescription?' I asked as we walked along the passage to the door.

" 'It is one few men can do without.'

" 'I, Doctor, am one of those few. Any such relationship would be a distraction from my vocation.'

"The doctor stopped and stood staring at me for a moment, a look of unexpected seriousness in his eyes.

" 'Look here, Ash, I am a doctor,' he said. 'We all see life in the way we have trained ourselves to observe it. When you look at a person, you probably see their souls; when my wife looks at them, she sees their minds; when Mrs. Carrington-Smith looks at them, she probably tries to see their family trees; when I look at them I see their bodies. To me, actions are guided by glands, not souls. I may be wrong. But one thing I do know. There is one instinct in man which is more powerful than any other, and it has a physical cause. Now take the advice of one considerably older than yourself and who knows what he is talking about in this particular respect—look out for some suitable young woman who will provide the worldly wisdom you lack, and give you the emotional stability which before long you will need. Believe me, my friend, we are all at the mercy of our bodies, however strong our belief in God. You are in the world now, Vicar, not a monastery....'

"And without waiting for me to reply, he closed the door and left me standing in the street.

"Almost, I knocked at the door in order to confute the argument of this man of science with a single phrase. But I resisted the temptation. For one thing, I did not know what my single phrase would be. Slowly, I walked back to the vicarage, trying to collect my thoughts without passion. I suspected Mrs. Kynaston's hand in the surprising advice just given me, it was so obviously Freudian. At the same time I felt anger that the arguments of these people should be capable of rousing my anger. So I tried to look upon it all from a rational point of view, always my refuge when my emotions were disturbed. It was they, I told myself, with their obsession with worldly things, who were making the mistake; they were judging me by their own standards, leaving out of consideration my faith, which they did not understand. I remembered Mrs. Kynaston's over-emotional manner on the evening I had nearly quarrelled with her; it had been almost as if she were jealous of my interest in Mrs. Robinson. It might even be that I was myself an object of interest to her . . . . I remembered also Mrs. Robinson's manner to me on some occasions, and I felt oddly disturbed at the thought that possibly I was able to inspire in women an interest other than the spiritual, this being something I had never felt for them in return; this was something I had left out of consideration when I had made up my mind to enter the world. . . . But at the same time it was additional confirmation that these people, lacking faith, inevitably attached themselves hysterically to any object that took their fancy; perhaps these two women, emotionally unstable, found something attractive about my own emotional stability. Do not think that this was a conceited thought; I knew there was nothing personal in it, that it was only my faith in God, which, unknown to them, made me attractive to them.

"With these thoughts I managed to some degree to calm my roused emotions, though the idea that I might be capable of attracting women came as a profound shock to me. It made me realize how much more I would have to be on my guard in order to avoid becoming emotionally entangled with individuals, which I knew would have a disastrous effect on my impartial view of mankind. Almost fervently, on that walk back to the vicarage, I thanked God for the faith which prevented me from becoming thus emotionally entangled; always, I assured myself, I would be able to remain detached, my task being to console humanity in general rather than any individual in particular, and so Dr. Kynaston's worldly advice would never be needed.

"What I then left out of consideration is that the world is made up of individuals. . . ."

Mr. Ash stopped speaking and for a moment was silent.

"You know," he said, "I think that after all I could sleep. . . ."

"Then do so," she said softly. "But stay where you are. To go down would wake you. . . ."

And almost before she had stopped speaking, she felt his body relax beside her, and was aware of his steady breathing. She pulled his one blanket closer over him and wished she could pull her own from under her and put that over him too, but was afraid that this would waken him. So she lay as she was, listening for some time to his breathing. Then she too fell asleep.

She was awakened the next morning by his stealthy climbing down to the floor. Without speaking she watched him quietly open the panel which hid the wash-basin, take out his shaving materials, and start shaving.

"Did you sleep well?" she asked.

At the sound of her voice, his razor slipped, and for a moment she thought he had cut himself, and sat up in alarm. But he had not.

"You are awake?" he asked without looking round. "Yes, I slept well. Better than I have for weeks, strangely enough. And you?"

"Yes, I too slept well," she said.

Having finished shaving, he went into the corridor, saying he wanted to get his first glimpse of Italy. She washed and dressed and soon afterwards joined him there. After a few moments they went along to the dining-car and found that Italian staff had taken the place of the French, and that the food was different, with much fruit, stronger coffee, and pencil-thin rolls. They did not talk much but watched the scenery as the train drew out of Turin, staring at the villages so different from those of France. She sensed that a new stage in their relationship had been arrived at, and with a kind of inward glow was conscious of a deeper sense of companionship with him, one in which experience could be shared without the need for speech. She felt that only one more barrier need be surmounted before their relationship became complete, and was more hopeful than ever that before long this would be done.

When they returned to their sleeper they found that the beds had been folded out of sight and that it had been transformed into a small private railway carriage of their own. They continued to watch the scenery for some time, and then she became aware of a distraction in his eyes; he

ceased to look out of the window, but stared in front of him, his face
grave.

"Would you like to go on with your story?" she asked.

He gave her a quick look of gratitude, and leaning back, started once
more.

"On reaching the vicarage," he said, "after my talk with Dr.
Kynaston, it was with feelings of some relief that I found waiting
for me someone who temporarily distracted my thoughts from
the people of Carlton Court, in the person of Tom White,
sitting stiffly on a hard chair in my study, with Mrs. Taylor
hovering suspiciously near him. It was a strangely anxious, almost
agitated Tom who stood up to greet me and who waited impatiently for Mrs. Taylor to go, which, at a signal from me, she
at last did, sniffing disapprovingly.

" 'Well, Tom,' I said, perhaps a little coldly, because since the
evening of the fight, I had come to distrust him a little, 'what can
I do for you? Sit down, won't you?'

"But he continued to stand.

" 'She's gone, Mr. Ash,' he said.

" 'Who's gone, Tom?'

" 'Ruby. She's done a bunk. Left 'ome.'

" 'You mean run away?'

" 'That's it.'

" 'Are you quite certain? When did she go?'

" 'Yesterday. You know she 'ad 'er calling-up papers to go
into the A.T.S.?'

" 'Yes—Mildred told me.'

" 'Well, she was due to go to the depôt next week. I knew she
didn't want to go, cut up about it, she was. Matter of fact, I
thought it a lot of bunk, seein' as the war's as good as over, but
you know what the Brass 'ats is, they goes on calling people up
up to the last minute—must give themselves something to do.
Would you credit they think Rube can be more use to 'em than
me? I thought I'd cheered 'er up when I told 'er it wouldn't be for

E

long, that the war wouldn't last more'n a few weeks longer, and once it was over they wouldn't want no more women in the Services, but would let 'em all out quick so's they could go into the factories. I thought she'd go off quiet when it come to the point. But it seems she 'adn't no intention of goin', 'cos when I come 'ome yesterday afternoon, she was gone. First I thought she'd just gone off to the cinema with one of those Yanks 'oo've been 'angin' around, but when she didn't come 'ome at night I searched 'er room an' found all 'er best clothes gone. If Millie 'ad still been there, perhaps we'd 'ave known somethin' about it,' he added resentfully, 'but she was away workin' for Mrs. Robinson—'er first day, it was. Rube must 'ave planned it all without sayin' anything to me. I can't understand it—never kept nothin' from me before. Best of pals we've always been.'

"I was surprised by the emotion behind his manner; if nothing else about him were sincere, there was no doubt about his affection for his eldest daughter.

" 'Have you informed the police?' I asked.

" 'Police, Mr. Ash? Not me. No good don't ever come of getting mixed up with them. An' they'll be round soon enough when she don't turn up at the depôt.'

" 'What exactly do you want me to do, Tom?'

" 'Well, Mr. Ash, seein' as she's always been friendly with you, I thought p'raps she'd said something to you, dropped a hint like.'

" 'Don't be absurd, Tom. You know quite well I haven't seen her for some time. I haven't been round to your place since I called for Mildred to take her to Mrs. Robinson.'

" 'Then I don't know what to do, Mr. Ash,' he said helplessly.

" 'Look here, Tom,' I said sharply, 'there's only one thing to be done—get in touch with the police at once. She's probably with some friend or in some lodging-house near here, and the police will pick her up before she's due to report. They won't do anything to her.'

" 'No, Mr. Ash—she ain't in no lodging-'ouse nor with no friends near 'ere.'

" 'Then you have some idea where she is?'

"He hesitated.

" 'Look here, Tom—just what are you afraid of?'

" 'Well, Mr. Ash, it don't take much imagination to know the easiest way for a girl like Rube to make a livin'—the only way, I might say. 'Cos she ain't 'ad no trainin' for a job and she ain't got the temperament to go into a factory or domestic service or anything like that. You see, Mr. Ash, I ain't ever intended Rube to work—'er face is 'er fortune, as you might say, that's why I've always bought 'er good clothes, to make the most of 'erself.'

" 'Just what are you suggesting, Tom?'

" 'Only that I gave 'er every chance to make a good marriage, Mr. Ash, the right an' natural career for a girl. I've introduced 'er to a lot of decent men—young N.C.O.s I've brought round to the 'ouse, men with a future in the Army, an' that's why I ain't objected when she's gone out with these Yanks—there ain't many as ain't got money in the States.'

" 'You mean you think she's run away with an American?'

" 'Maybe, Mr. Ash—maybe not.'

" 'Come on, Tom—out with it. Just what do you mean?'

" 'Well, Mr. Ash, I think maybe Rube's got some silly ideas into 'er 'ead. She knows 'ow men run after 'er—an' she knows from a certain person 'ow that can be put to financial advantage as you might say. You've met that there Mrs. Cohen in my place?'

" 'Yes,' I said, 'several times.'

" 'Well, she's an ex-pro., she is.'

" 'Ex what, Tom?'

" 'Prostitute, Mr. Ash. Street-walker. Made a fortune at it, she 'as. Reformed, though, now, never talks about it, but Rube knows about 'er. She's seen 'ow Mrs. Cohen's sittin' pretty now, with a nice little packet in the Bank, an' no 'ard work done for it. At least, that's 'ow it might seem to Rube. I don't know as it ain't 'ard work. Sometimes, when she's 'ad a few, Molly tells us about it—'ardest work of any profession, she says it is. But that's neither 'ere nor there, Mr. Ash. I'm just tellin' you so's you'll know why I think Rube might be followin' in 'er foot-steps—or tryin' to.'

" 'I'm surprised, Tom, that you should mix with such people.'

" 'She ain't what you'd call a friend of mine, Mr. Ash,' he said, and there was a slightly cunning look in his eye. 'But you know 'ow it is—she's good company, and you know 'ow you pick up people when you've 'ad a few. An' she's a good-'earted woman 'oo ain't ever known no better. I didn't intend Rube to mix with 'er—but things get out, you know. Somehow or other Rube got to know that Molly keeps an 'ouse.'

" 'A house?'

" 'You know, Mr. Ash—you was on the Continent with us. An 'ouse where women take men.'

" 'You are not suggesting there are brothels in London, Tom?'

" 'Not exactly a brothel, Mr. Ash. Just an 'ouse—an 'ouse where rooms is let out to girls.'

" 'You mean Mrs. Cohen procures women?'

" 'No, no, Mr. Ash,' he said, and again there was the cunning look in his eyes. 'She just owns the 'ouse, an' lets the rooms. She just don't inquire too closely into the occupation of 'er tenants, that's all. It ain't a crime, Mr. Ash. All quite legal. There's lots of 'ouses like that in London—Soho mostly. Well, Rube, she's learnt all about this, and I think it may 'ave put ideas into 'er 'ead.'

" 'Then you think this Mrs. Cohen may have had something to do with her disappearance? If so, I shall inform the police at once.'

" 'No, no, Mr. Ash. Molly wouldn't do nothin' to a daughter of mine. It wouldn't do 'er no good—business associates, we are. Quite concerned about it, she is, knowin' the ropes, as you might say. She knows almost everyone in the business, all the 'ouses—not that she's mixed up in it personal now, as you might say, but she keeps in touch. She'd know at once if Rube was knockin' around the West End—no, she ain't nowhere around there, Mr. Ash. She ain't no fool, our Rube, She's gone up North some-where—Manchester, Birmingham, Liverpool, maybe Glasgow

—somewhere Molly won't be able to trace 'er. Maybe she's gone up there with some Yank—but not to marry 'im, Mr. Ash. Look 'ere, Mr. Ash——' he leaned forward over the chair in which I was sitting. 'I'm tellin' you all this 'cos I'm real worried about Rube. I know you won't let it go no further, Mr. Ash. I know I ain't all I should be—maybe I'm mixed up in one or two rackets with Molly Cohen an' Al Manteli an Les Jenkins, an' a few others —but that don't concern you. But I'd give it all up, Mr. Ash— go straight as a die, I would—if I could get Rube back before she comes to 'arm. It's for 'er I did it—so's I could get 'er good clothes to make 'er into the real smasher she is. So you see why it is I don't want to get mixed up with no police, Mr. Ash. I want to get my Rube back without the assistance of the law. . . .'

" 'I see, Tom,' I said quietly. 'You've certainly put your cards on the table. But if you think that because we shared certain experiences in the war, that I would close my eyes to any kind of criminal activity you may be engaged in, you are quite mistaken. I am concerned with the good of the whole community, and if you are opposed to that community, I would sacrifice you without thinking twice about it.'

" 'Yes, Mr. Ash, I know that, and quite right you are, too. An' if I get my Rube back, I'll go straight as a die—I promise that.'

" 'Why did you ever go crooked, Tom? I have evidence of the fact that you were a brave man in the Army—why are you a coward out of it?'

" 'That's just it, Mr. Ash. They done me a bad turn. They chucked me out on my neck—five years before my time, after I'd given 'em the best years of my life. Fit as a fiddle, I am—but they chucked me out to mess around with these old men playin' at soldiers. They ain't played fair with me, Mr. Ash—so I ain't got no cause to play fair with them.'

"For a moment we stared into each other's eyes, and it was Tom who lowered his first.

" 'That, Tom,' I said quietly, 'is a point of ethics we will discuss some other time—we have a lot to discuss at some other time,

Tom. Now we must get back to the subject of Ruby. Just in what way can I help?'

" 'You 'as influence with Millie, Mr. Ash. She ain't got no feelings for me—I can't make 'er do nothing nor say anythin' she don't want to. She's as 'ard as nails, that girl, an' no one don't ever know what she's thinkin'. But she 'as feelings for you, Mr. Ash. You've made a hit with 'er. Maybe you can get 'er to talk.'

" 'You think she knows something?'

" 'Yes, Mr. Ash, I think maybe she does. Rube's always been frightened of 'er—funny seein' as Rube's the eldest, but then Millie's got what you might call a strong character. She's always bullied Rube—jealous, maybe, of all the things I give 'er. I 'ave an idea she persuaded Rube to take this step—to get 'er own back on me, like.'

" 'What on earth makes you think this, Tom?'

" 'It's an idea I 'ave, Mr. Ash. Millie weren't surprised like the rest of us when she learnt Rube 'ad gone—when she come 'ome from Mrs. Robinson an' found 'er gone, she seemed almost as if she expected it. And she looked kind of pleased—kind of exultant, Mr. Ash. She looked at me out of those dark eyes of 'ers as if to say—"there—that's my revenge." And nothin' I could do, Mr. Ash, would make 'er talk.'

" 'You didn't lay hands on her, did you, Tom?' I asked quietly, the idea having come to me from something in his manner.

" 'What, me, Mr. Ash? Me lay 'ands on me own daughter? I ain't that sort of swine, Mr. Ash.'

"But from his tone of voice I was quite certain he had in fact laid hands on her. I stood up.

" 'All right, Tom,' I said sharply. 'I will question Mildred. I will go round to Mrs. Robinson's tomorrow. And if I find you have in fact laid hands on her, I will get in touch with the police at once. You'd better go now.'

"Again we stared into each other's eyes, and again it was his that were lowered first.

" 'Don't worry, Mr. Ash,' he said, with a strange softness in his voice, a note that was almost menacing. 'You won't find I've

done 'arm to Millie. You misunderstand me, Mr. Ash. You an'
I ain't ever what you might call got on together, 'ave we?' He
walked slowly to the door, but on the threshold turned round
again. 'I'm fond of my kids, Mr. Ash, even if I ain't brought 'em
up right. But I ain't 'ad much assistance—the missus bein' what
she is.'

"'All right, Tom. Don't try to blame other people. You
married her, you know.'

"'We all make mistakes, Mr. Ash. 'Specially when we're
young.'

"'All right, Tom,' I repeated. 'Will you please go now. I have
a lot of work to do.'

"But still he did not move.

"'What shall I do, Mr. Ash—come round 'ere tomorrow
night—if the police ain't come by then?' And it seemed to me as
if there was again the mocking look in his eyes which I had seen
on the night of the fight, and often when I had visited his Company in France—a look which seemed to despise me.

"'No,' I said. 'I'll come round to your place on my way back
from Mrs. Robinson—you'll be in at five, won't you?'

"'Yes, Mr. Ash.'

"And with a nod, he at last left the room.

"That evening I was late going to bed. I sat for a long time
in my chair, thinking. In a short space of time I had learnt much
about human nature that surprised me. These two talks, first with
Kynaston, then with Tom White, had left me, for the first time,
spiritually tired. But though feeling disillusioned, I was at that
time more than ever convinced of the rightness of my decision
to come out into the world. I was needed, and felt more than
ever determined that, somehow, I would be of use. But that
night I once more found difficulty in sleeping.

"I had not visited Mrs. Robinson since the day I had introduced Mildred to her, and as I rang her bell the next afternoon,
I was a little ill at ease without quite knowing why. And her
appearance, when she opened the door, did not make matters any
easier for me; for she was dressed in a brightly-coloured overall,

pulled tightly round her waist, which gaped alarmingly in front; her hair, usually so impeccably set, was tied in a head-scarf, her cheeks were unusually flushed, her face almost without make-up, she was breathing rather heavily and there was a sparkle in her blue eyes I had never seen before.

" 'Oh, Mr. Ash!' she said, making a half-hearted effort at pulling together the bodice of her overall, 'how pleased I am to see you. You've caught me in the act of giving a demonstration of floor-polishing to Mildred. But do come in, my dear, don't stand on the threshold looking so taken aback. I know I look an absolute fright but a woman must do her housework sometimes, you know.'

"Actually, I thought she looked considerably better than when in her full war-paint, but I did not say so. Putting out her hand as if to shake mine, she pulled me gently into the hall, relinquishing me only to take my hat and hang it on a peg, talking the whole time.

" 'You didn't know I was a house-proud woman, did you, Vicar? I suppose it never occurred to you that ninety per cent of the work in this flat is done with my own fair hands. That kind of thing never occurs to a man. Your Mrs. Taylor only comes to me once a fortnight for three hours and not much can be done in that time. . . .' At this point she started to lead the way towards the kitchen. 'Having only seen me dressed to kill,' she went on, 'you've probably never suspected that I spend at least half my waking hours in the kitchen, often on my hands and knees. And I positively enjoy it, my dear. And now I've got Mildred I find that I still do all the work, whilst she watches. Not that she's unwilling, but somehow I can't bring myself to let anyone else do the work. And of course I want her to learn properly. Secretly, I believe she thinks me quite mad. Don't you, dear child?' she said to Mildred, into whose presence we had now arrived.

"The girl was rather surprisingly sitting very upright on a kitchen chair placed so that it faced one side of the room, which, completely denuded of furniture, showed a clear stretch of linoleum, shining like glass. In fact she looked for all the world like a student of domestic science receiving private tuition. She made no reply to her mistress's somewhat rhetorical question, but stared at me out of her large eyes, quite expression-lessly.

"'Talkative child, isn't she, Vicar?' went on Mrs. Robinson. 'But she was quite chatty to me this morning, she actually said three consecutive sentences. Oh, we shall be getting on like a house on fire soon. Well, Vicar, you can see what I've been doing —all this polish is my own work. In fact to prove it I'll do just a little more, and then Mildred will get us some tea, which for the last three days I've been teaching her to do, for just such an occasion as this, only no one's dropped in. . . . They don't often, these days. . . .'

"And without further words she went down on her knees and started strenuously polishing, a position which caused her overall to gape even more shamelessly, involuntarily affording me a very good idea of what Dr. Kynaston had meant when he had described her 'magnificent' body to me. Quickly I averted my eyes, and instead of at Mrs. Robinson, I looked at Mildred. The girl, I thought, was a little pale, and though her face was as much without expression as ever, it seemed to me that there was about her a certain air of strain; she was watching Mrs. Robinson unblinkingly as she continued her polishing, and from her expression I could not tell what the real relationship of these two was.

"At last Mrs. Robinson finished, and stood up, assuming her feet with a lightness surprising in one of her age.

"'I really enjoy this sort of thing,' she said, breathing only slightly more heavily than usual. 'It's a good way of getting rid of energy, of which I have always had a superabundance. Now for tea. This will be Mildred's first chance of assuming the guise of parlour-maid. Come and rest yourself in the sitting-room, Vicar, whilst I go and tidy myself up.'

"But I excused myself on the plea of wanting to have a word with Mildred.

E*

" 'As you like, Vicar,' she said, giving me a rather curious glance, in which there might have been a touch of jealousy, as she left the room.

" 'Alone with Mildred, I found her most uncommunicative. She would hardly answer my questions, and seemed in fact to resent them. All the trust I thought I had succeeded in building up in her, seemed to have gone, and she spent most of the time with her back to me, busying herself at the cooker.

" 'I don't know, Mr. Ash,' was all she would say on the subject of Ruby, and it was only when I asked her if her father had questioned her about it that she showed any animation. She looked round at me then, and in her eyes there was a look of malicious satisfaction.

" ''E went near mad when 'e found she'd gone,' she said.

" 'What did he do to you, Mildred?' I asked, watching her face closely.

" 'Do to me, Mr. Ash?' she asked. 'Nothin' more than what 'e usually does.'

" 'And what is that?'

" 'Nothin' you need worry about, Mr. Ash,' she said.

"And when I pressed her on this subject, her only response was a shrug of the shoulders. I decided that to persist would be useless, and I must confess that I had my first feeling of despair as far as Mildred was concerned. For the first time I felt that I might not, after all, be able to do anything for her. I did not stay with her much longer, and after asking her a few questions about how she was getting on with Mrs. Robinson—to which her replies were as guarded as ever—I left her. I went into the drawing-room, where, distractedly examining a Renoir nude which seemed to have been transferred from the bedroom, I awaited Mrs. Robinson. She came into the room so quietly that my first indication of her presence was when I heard her say from within about a foot of my shoulder:

" 'Charming, isn't it?' Such a rhythm of curves, such a nice, plump body. I've always had a soft spot for Renoir, because I feel I would myself have been such an excellent model for him.

My first husband, who was rather artistic, used to tell me so. The flesh seems almost to live, doesn't it?'

" 'It does indeed,' I said, without turning round. 'Pleasing composition, but very sensual.'

" 'But isn't a large part of life sensual, Vicar? Come and sit down and discuss with me the sensuality of life.'

"Turning round, I found that she had transformed herself from the perspiring and domesticated housewife into a sleek and sophisticated woman of the world, by merely changing into a frock, applying a little make-up, and doing something to her hair. And though she was now beautiful, a work of art indeed, I preferred her as she had been a few minutes before. Slowly I crossed the room and sat down in an easy chair opposite her, not beside her as I suspected she wanted, wondering as I did so whether this woman was in fact overflowing with generous impulses as I wanted to believe her, or whether she was as hard and worldly as her detractors would have me think, and which her appearance seemed now to confirm. Yet a few minutes before she had seemed so simple and unaffected. Women are complicated creatures, I decided.

" 'I prefer the housewife in you to the sensualist,' I said, in reply to her question.

" 'But, Vicar, surely a woman should be all things to a man? Sometimes the domesticated housewife, at others the lover, at still others the sympathetic companion. To my husbands I was all these things.'

" 'But I am not your husband,' I said lightly.

" 'No, Vicar, indeed you are not. I wonder sometimes if you will ever be a husband to anyone. All your emotions, if you have any, always seem so neatly docketed and placed in compartments, to be taken out as circumstances require. How you must despise such poor mortals as myself, so much at the mercy of our emotions, whose lives are so confused. . . .'

" 'No, I don't despise you,' I replied. 'But I keep my emotions strictly under control in order to be of use to such people as you.'

" 'Then you do feel what we feel, only you can control

yourself. Sometimes, when you look at a woman, she seems to you beautiful and desirable? When you look at that Renoir over there, do you feel, as I do, that he has captured one of the beautiful things in life—the beauty of the body?'

"I felt ill at ease; there was in her manner something uncontrolled, and I felt as if she were letting me down, behaving exactly as Mrs. Carrington-Smith and her friends would expect her to behave. I was about to reply coolly, which I did not really want to do, when Mildred came in, rather precariously carrying a loaded tray. At once Mrs. Robinson became the motherly, generous-hearted woman I knew and liked, fussing round Mildred, helping her with the tray, showing her where to put things, treating her with a gentleness and consideration that quite charmed me, though I was not sure that this was the way Mildred should be treated; already I was beginning to change my ideas about Mildred. For the moment, Mrs. Robinson seemed to have completely forgotten her mood of a few minutes before. And when the girl had left the room the mood did not at once return; she was again cheerful, the bright hostess intent on entertaining a guest. For some time we chatted about everyday things, and I felt glad to be in her company, once more almost convinced that the stories I had heard about her were slander. But before I left her that afternoon she was to provide me with another shock.

"Suddenly, during a pause in the conversation, she said with an unnatural tenseness:

" 'My elder son is coming home in a week or so, with his fiancée. . . .'

" 'You have two sons?' I asked, surprised.

" 'Oh yes. Surely you knew that, Vicar?' she asked, her eyes wide with a surprise a little too complete to be genuine.

" 'No,' I replied. 'You have never mentioned him to me, and as far as I know I've never heard anyone else mention him.'

" 'He's no secret. I . . . just never had cause to mention him before, that's all. To be quite honest, we've been a little estranged, and I have hardly heard from him since the beginning of the war. I was married twice, you know. . . .' She was talking

PARIS   135

quickly, in short sentences, not looking me in the eyes. 'My first
husband's name was Schofield—I divorced him—and of course
that's Bill's name too. Bill is a hero, like you, Vicar. He volunteered for Special Service early in the war, and is now a Lieuten-
ant-Colonel—one of the youngest in the British Army, I believe.
He's been awarded the M.C. As a matter of fact, I hadn't seen
him for five years before the war—he was abroad, globe-trotting.
He left at the tender age of twenty—now he's thirty. He suddenly wrote out of the blue, saying he was posted to England,
and was returning with this fiancée—some girl he met in India,
where he's been lately. She's a nurse, I think. It will be an experience, seeing him again. . . .'

"As she spoke I watched her very closely, and I could see she
was oddly nervous; as she kept putting her cigarette to her lips,
I saw her hand was trembling. And the smile, with which she
looked through the tobacco smoke at me, was strained, though
she was obviously trying to make it seem natural. And somehow,
I did not want to make things easier for her.

" 'You have certainly been very secretive about him,' I said.
'When does he arrive?'

" 'Almost any day. He posted the letter just before he sailed,
and with the war-time postal delays, he may arrive within a few
days of it. It was several weeks old. . . .'

"She looked at me almost piteously, and I just could not understand why she should be in such an emotional state about the
arrival of this son. It occurred to me that she might be nervous
about meeting him after so long, and this made me feel that
perhaps my manner was a little unsympathetic. So I tried to
make amends.

" 'I must say,' I said, 'that I would never have thought you
could have a son of thirty. . . .'

"She seemed to seize this as a chance to change the subject.

" 'It's sweet of you to say that, Vicar,' she said. 'And I honestly
believe you mean it. Most men when they make that sort of
remark are only being self-consciously gallant. But I honestly
believe you've never thought me more than, say . . . forty-five?'

" 'It would have surprised me to learn you were more than forty when you first walked into my study at the vicarage,' I said, and this was perfectly true.

"At once her whole expression softened.

" 'Of course,' she said, 'I was extremely young when I married the first time—cradle-snatching it was really, which was one reason why it broke down. Perhaps I'm not very much over forty. . . .'

" 'I'm sure you're not.'

" 'You're sweet, Vicar. Come and sit beside me on this sofa. I hate talking to people across a room.'

" 'There's nothing I would enjoy more,' I said, standing up, 'than to go on with this conversation. But I just have to go. I have an appointment at five—it's now ten to.'

" 'Oh well,' she said, and it seemed to me there was a look of disappointment in her eyes, 'perhaps some other time.' She stood up and came to within a foot or two of me. '*You* don't disapprove of me, Vicar, do you?' she asked suddenly.

" 'What reason would I have to disapprove of you?' I asked, more stiffly than I wanted to.

" 'Oh, things are said about me. I'm not thought quite nice. But I can't help it if men . . . are attracted to me, can I? Women like Mrs. Carrington-Smith can be as friendly as they like to men, and no one says a word. But as soon as I am even ordinarily polite, things are said about me. I'll give you an example. At a canteen dance a year or so ago I was normally polite, acting more or less in the capacity of hostess, to Mrs. Bartram's husband— a young puppy almost of an age to be my son. And immediately he asked me to dance—not once, but several times. What could I do—refuse? Well—I didn't. I danced—as often as he asked me. And for months afterwards there was a whispering campaign against me—it was said I flirted madly with him, that I made myself quite ridiculous. As a matter of fact I didn't enjoy dancing with him particularly—he was as clumsy as an ox. In fact he said his wife wouldn't dance with him because of his clumsiness. So there you are—a perfectly innocent piece of common politeness, and I'm a husband-stealer.'

"She was looking hard into my eyes now, with a kind of desperation; hardly knowing what I was doing, I put out my hand and patted her comfortingly on the shoulder. Immediately she burst into tears, and before I knew what was happening she was weeping on my shoulder, almost with her arms round me. Instinctively I drew away from her, and she seemed to pull herself together, smiling up at me apologetically through her tears, dabbing at her eyes with a handkerchief. And at that moment it seemed to me that I caught, in the depths of her eyes, for a fraction of a second, a look of annoyance.

" 'I do apologize for this foolish outburst,' she said, 'but to be quite honest I'm a little overwrought—what with Bill coming home, the end of the war at last upon us, and this . . . this changed atmosphere of everyone towards me. I thought for a moment, Vicar, you spoke so coldly, that you too were beginning to disapprove of me. And I had been so . . . flattered . . . when you chose me for Mildred's employer . . . I was afraid for a moment you'd come to take her away from me. . . .'

" 'Take her away from you?' I asked. 'My dear Mrs. Robinson, why should I do that?'

" 'Well—perhaps my outlook's becoming just a little distorted. Perhaps I'm developing a persecution complex. You must come and give me some serious advice one evening, Vicar—you have such a sane outlook that I'm sure you'll be able to make me see things in a better light. But I mustn't keep you any longer. . . .

"And, almost her old self again, she accompanied me to the door. Just as I was taking leave of her, however, she said something which made me wonder whether the whole business of her telling me about the imminent arrival of her elder son had not been from ulterior motives. For she said:

" 'If by chance anyone—Mrs. Carrington-Smith for instance— mentions to you anything about Bill's coming, you will tell them you know all about it, won't you—that I haven't kept it a secret from you?'

"I was about to show my irritation, but the expression in her eyes stopped me. For suddenly I felt compassion for her.

" 'Of course I will, Mrs. Robinson,' I said, and we parted.

"As I went along the corridor I knew there was some justification for the rumours about her—that she had some secret to
hide; though what it was I had no idea. As I went down in the
lift—thinking of Mrs. Carrington-Smith and her friends as well
as their victim—the words of Christ on the Cross occurred to
me again. . . . 'Forgive them, for they know not what they
do. . . .' For some reason, I felt more moved to pity than
ever before since coming out into the world."

"I went quickly to Tom White's flat to keep my appointment,
and found him alone in the kitchen, sitting at the table. He did
not stand up when I entered and looked at me with a morose
expression. I told him at once, rather brusquely, that I had found
out nothing about Ruby from Mildred.

" 'If you take my advice,' I added, 'you'll go straight to the
police. There's nothing else to be done. . . .'

" 'I ain't worried,' he said.

" 'What do you mean?'

" 'Ain't you 'eard the news, padré? The war's over.'

" 'What?' I asked.

" 'They've took Hamburg. Couple of days more an' it'll be
all over. An' no one won't care where Ruby is. Reckon she
done right to disappear like she did for a few days. If they'd once
got 'er maybe they'd 'ave put 'er in the Army of Occupation or
something. Ruby in the Army of Occupation! She'd 'ave the
Russians an' Yanks fightin' over 'er in no time an' start another
war.'

" 'Where did you hear this news, Tom?'

" 'On the one o'clock news. Surrendered 'amburg to the
Seventh Armoured. Trust the bloody armour to get there first
these days. They get all the bookays after the P.B.I. done all the
work. It ain't an Army now, Mr. Ash—just a question of droppin'
bombs and takin' pot-shots at each other from behind six inches
of armour-platin'. The side what's got the biggest guns and the

biggest tanks is the side what wins. No more Infantry, Mr. Ash, like you an' me was in. Good job they kicked me out on me neck, like they did, five years before me time.'

"The idea that the war was really over caused me a sudden happiness; I had never really contemplated the possibility before, though I had known for some time that the end was in sight. I felt a sudden comradeship for Tom—a strange, warm feeling. I leant over the table towards him, meaning to shake hands with him, and as I did so I caught a whiff of beer on his breath.

" 'You've been celebrating already haven't you, Tom?' I asked.

" 'Celebratin'?' he said. 'I ain't got nothin' to celebrate. When it's all over I won't even 'ave the poor old —— to look after— out on my neck, it'll be, drawin' a few bob pension. I ain't 'ad no trainin' for a civvy-street job. What do they expect me to do? Stand outside a cinema with one of them uniforms on, showin' off a row of medals? At least mine'd be real which most of those boys' ain't.'

"And as he sat glowering in front of him I could see that he was hardly aware of my presence. He was drunker than I had thought, in fact I realized he was probably hardly able to stand. I felt both anger and pity for him. But before I could say anything he continued his monologue.

" 'Since a boy I've bin in the army, Mr. Ash, an' me father before me. Born in married quarters, I was. My father ended up R.S.M., an' I would 'ave done too—but they chucked me out on me neck, five years before me time. And I don't play fair with those what don't play fair with me. They chucked me out five years before my time so's they wouldn't 'ave to pay me full pension. . . . An' they expect me to go straight! I've told you a few 'ome-truths about meself, Mr. Ash, 'ome-truths what won't go no further, will they, eh? You an' me was out there together, in the thick of it. Wounded together, we was. You seen a bit of action, Mr. Ash, you ain't a bad sort of padré, as far as padrés go. Not that any of 'em's any good—use up valuable vehicles, they do, and they give 'em batmen! Able-bodied men what could be in the front line instead of runnin' around polishin' boots. But I ain't got no grudge against you personal, Mr. Ash. You saved me life. Maybe you thought you was doin' me a good turn, eh, Mr. Ash?'

" 'I thought nothing of the kind, Tom. I saved your life because it was my duty to do so.'

"For a moment he looked at me hard as if making an effort to understand this; but the effort seemed too much for him, for he looked down again, and went on talking.

" 'It didn't do me no good, Mr. Ash, savin' me life. Nor givin' me that medal, neither. They give me that medal so's I could stick it on me chest an' stand outside a cinema for a lot of little kids to come along pointin' their fingers an' sayin': "Where d'you get them medals, grandpa? At Waterloo?" An' they'd run away laughin' their 'eads off thinkin' I'd bought 'em in one of those second-'and shops round the Angel. An' I might as well 'ave, for all the good they'll do me, Mr. Ash—just bits of coloured ribbon to most people, they are. An' what good d'you think you done savin' me life, eh? Me life ain't no good to me, Mr. Ash, nor to no one else, now that I ain't got no soldiering to do. That's my job, Mr. Ash. Been in the Army since I was a kid. Out East ten years—that's where I met the missus. Real beauty, she was. The Queen of Hong Kong, they called 'er. I married 'er, Mr. Ash, an' brought 'er back 'ere. And that's when me troubles started. She ain't no good as a wife—she don't know the first thing about makin' an 'ome. All she done is give me these four kids of which none ain't no good 'cept Rube. A real beauty, she is—do anythin' I say. Millie, she's a real 'ard little bitch. She 'ates the sight of me, she does. She 'ates 'er ma too, an' Rube—she ain't got no 'eart in 'er, that girl. Like 'er ma, she is—you can look into those great eyes of 'ers, an' you don't see nothin'— all the bints out East is like that, Mr. Ash—they ain't got no souls. An' then there's Jill. Real fast bit of stuff, she is—only fourteen an' already she's chasin' the troops. There ain't no 'ope for that girl. An' then there's that boy. Least, the missus calls 'im a boy. 'E ain't no boy, Mr. Ash—skin an' bone, that's all 'e is.

All 'e does is snivel round 'is ma. Imagine that kid in the British Army, eh? To think that's the only son I've got! I was in the Army as a kid, Mr. Ash, an' me father before me. An' I goes an' gets a kid like that to carry on the family tradition. . . .'

"He looked up at me, his little blood-shot eyes vindictive.

" 'I knows 'ow to get me own back, Mr. Ash,' he said. 'I don't play fair with those what don't play fair with me. Threw me out five years before me time, that's what they done, Mr. Ash. I won't do no standin' outside cinemas showin' off rows of medals. . . .'

"He leaned forward over the table and looked at me with extreme cunning.

" 'You know all them fine clothes Rube 'as?' he asked almost in a whisper. 'Where d'you think they comes from, eh? Out of me pension, out of the miserable few bob they gives me? Not on your life!'

" 'Well, Tom,' I asked quietly, as he paused, 'Where did they come from?'

"But he looked at me with sudden suspicion, and I saw distrust in his eyes.

" 'You wouldn't 'alf like to know, wouldn't you?' he asked. 'You 'oo comes creepin' round other people's 'ouses askin' questions. You an' the police, there ain't nothin' to choose between you. In league, you are. You can't fool me, Mr. Ash. I told you a few 'ome-truths about meself the other night, an' you think you can come creepin' round an' get some more, eh? You think that becos' I've 'ad a few I don't know what I'm sayin'. Well, you're wrong, see. I ain't told you nothin' you can take action on, Mr. Ash. It's only been between you an' me—no witnesses—and in law you must 'ave witnesses. . . .'

"I suppose there must have been something in my eyes that caused Tom to stop speaking suddenly; I must have looked at him more in sorrow than in anger, for though I knew he was not really responsible for what he was saying, I could not help resenting his insinuations. I intended to stand up and take my leave and return on some day when he was not drunk, because there was much I wanted to say to him when he was capable of understanding. But something about his manner, when he stopped speaking so suddenly made me pause. I hoped his better nature had been roused. But I was wrong.

" 'Maybe I didn't oughter 'ave said that, Mr. Ash,' he said. 'But sometimes I feels that angry about everything I can't 'old me tongue. And Mr. Ash——' here he again leaned forward towards me across the table and spoke almost in a whisper, 'I've said one or two things about meself in the last few days, I've dropped a few 'ints about not goin' straight, 'aven't I? Well, Mr. Ash, don't you believe 'em. It ain't true, Mr. Ash. I ain't done nothin' what puts me on the wrong side of the law, honest I ain't. You believe me, don't you, Mr. Ash? I wouldn't tell no lies to the man what saved me life, cross me 'eart I wouldn't. You won't go tellin' no stories to the police, will you, now? I know you're pally with that there George Baker, the copper 'oo does this beat. Don't you listen to nothin' 'e says, Mr. Ash. 'E don't like us—jealous, 'e is, 'cos 'e ain't done much in this war— just sat on 'is backside at the Station runnin' in little kids for stealin' lead off of the roofs, an' thinks 'e's a blinkin' 'ero. Don't you pay no attention to nothin' 'e says, Mr. Ash——'

"At last I stood up and took my leave. I could bear no longer the sight of a man I knew to be so brave so debasing himself. I left him sitting there staring after me with a slightly puzzled but still crafty expression on his face. I would return in a week or so, and try by reasoning to rouse in him a little of the self-respect of which he had had so much in the Army."

"Well," said Mr. Ash as if suddenly returning to reality, "I would say that at this point I've reached the end of the first part of my narrative. Because from here onwards the whole complexion of things changed. . . ."

"Why?" she asked.

"Because an evening or so later you appeared on the scene. . . ."

"You're not telling me that I at once made such a difference?" she asked, a slightly mischievous look in her eyes.

"*I do indeed,*" *he said, and for the first time in their relationship it seemed to her that he reacted to her mood and that there was a look almost of flirtatiousness in his eyes.*

"*I don't believe you,*" *she said.*

"*It was so,*" *he said, his manner becoming serious again.* "*Of course it was a long time before I admitted it to myself. In fact——*"

"*In fact what?*" *she prompted, as he paused.*

"*In fact I realize I have only really begun to admit it since embarking on this extraordinary orgy of talk which you have borne so patiently——*"

"*Then it is doing you some good, this orgy of talk?*" *she asked softly.*

He looked at her quickly and for a moment she thought he was about to say something which would have made unnecessary the rest of his narrative. But as his eyes met hers, he seemed to lose his courage, or his self-confidence, or whatever it was he still lacked in relation to her. He looked away again, out of the window.

"*We must be nearing Florence,*" *he said.* "*These look like the hills surrounding the city——*"

"*Yes,*" *she said, succeeding with an effort in keeping a note of disappointment from her voice. She looked at her watch.* "*We are due to arrive in less than an hour.*"

"*Then I will spare you any further—how shall I describe it?—any further efforts at self-orientation until we are settled in our hotel.*"

And at once he reverted to the manner he had almost lost since the beginning of this train journey, that mixture of formal politeness and over-anxiety to please, as he pointed out the landmarks he remembered from his previous visit. "*It is landmarks only that I remember from that visit,*" *he said a little ruefully.*

And patiently she fell in with his mood in order not to make matters more difficult for him.

Part Two

FLORENCE

Florence

THEY reached Florence's startlingly modern station—a relic of Mussolini's effort to make his country forget a glorious past in an awareness of an inglorious present—at one o'clock in the afternoon, too early to have lunch on the train and too late to have it in their hotel. So after rather hurriedly depositing their luggage at the hotel, they went out into the streets searching for a restaurant still serving lunches, too hungry even to linger over the beauties of the ancient city.

Eventually they found one, and had their first taste of spaghetti served in the Italian style which took them a long time to eat, for neither was experienced with this food which required, as well as the necessary appetite, a certain amount of manual dexterity to eat. They accomplished it eventually and were then able to sit back and become aware of their surroundings. They were in a little restaurant beside the Arno, from where they could look up the river towards the Ponte Vecchio, the only bridge still remaining after the attentions of war. And as she relaxed, her head slightly befuddled from the effects of a half-bottle of the stronger, cruder, Italian wine, the charm of Italy began to steal over her. They sat there for some time, hardly speaking, watching the people outside, the flow of the clay-coloured river, and the ancient roofs and towers on the other side.

At last they left the restaurant and spent what was left of the afternoon wandering through the narrow, kerbless streets of the old town, through which the noisy progress of many tiny motor-cycles and small cars seemed a somewhat dangerous impertinence.

For some days he seemed so charmed by his surroundings that he was lulled into temporary forgetfulness of his obsession with his immediate past, and it was not until an evening three days later, in the quiet of their bedroom, that he resumed his narrative.

"I did not like Bill Schofield from the moment I met him," he began at once. "It was soon after that talk with Tom White

that we met for the first time. I had received a 'phone call from
Mrs. Robinson in the course of the afternoon, in which, with
excitement in her voice, she had asked me over to meet Bill. It
was not altogether convenient, but having a great curiosity to
meet this young man, I was able to arrange it.

"I arrived at about six and found the flat already crowded.
Mildred opened the door and gave me the impression of being
just a little flustered, this being her first experience of one of
Mrs. Robinson's parties—as you well know, there were to be
many others—and she gave me the impression of not quite
knowing what she should be doing. However, she looked at me
as inscrutably as ever as she took my hat, and after hanging it
up left me to find my own way to the sitting-room from where
all the noise was coming.

"I entered to find there almost everyone I knew in Carlton
Court, as well as several people I had not met. The entire W.V.S.
Committee was present, including Miss Cooter, and both the
Kynastons. I was somewhat taken aback because I had thought
I was being invited to meet Bill on my own, flattering myself
that Mrs. Robinson had taken me into her special confidence
on the occasion of her revealing his existence to me. But it
seemed she had taken everyone else of her acquaintance equally
into her confidence: this was the first of several little shocks I was
to receive with regard to her character before I finally came to
know her.

" I could not see my hostess nor anyone who could conceivably
be Bill Schofield, but after a moment I saw, to my surprise,
Peter, presiding over a kind of improvised bar in a corner. At
first I did not recognize him, he was so changed. I had not seen
him since I had so unexpectedly persuaded him to accept his
scholarship instead of going into the Army, and he had spent the
intervening six months up at Cambridge. Had I met him then
for the first time, I would have taken him for a very sophisticated
twenty-six or twenty-seven, instead of the mere twenty which
was his real age. With his slim figure, his small, neat features so
different from his mother's, his black hair smoothed back over

his skull with rather too much hair-oil, and his over-immaculate
clothes—he is a very clothes-conscious young man—together
with his air of self-confidence, and the almost wicked look in his
intelligent eyes, he looked anything but a boy just out of his
'teens. . . ."

*"I know," interrupted Katharine, "I had exactly that impression of
him. I disliked him from the moment I met him, just as you seem to have
disliked poor Bill. . . .'*

"But the strange thing is, I have never been able to dislike
Peter," replied Mr. Ash. "I have always sensed in him a courage
which I admire. And I always admire courage—of the moral
rather than the physical kind. Also, he had a kind of fundamental modesty which is the very antithesis to Bill's attitude to
life. I still feel that in the end Peter will make something of his
life, and that when you know him better, you'll tolerate him
more. An example of that modesty of his which amounts almost
to self-immolation occurred on that very evening—but of that,
in due course.

" Before I could make myself known to Peter, Mrs. Robinson
came into the room—apparently she had just been called to the
telephone. She had the air of someone who had been in a considerably agitated state, but who had just heard something to
relieve her mind.

" 'That was he,' she said to the room in general, 'he's met
her and they're on their way here now. I don't expect they'll be
more than fifteen minutes or so. I'm so terribly sorry for this
delay and am so terribly grateful to you all for waiting so
patiently. . . .'

"The appropriate murmurs of 'not at all' were silenced by
Mrs. Carrington-Smith's clear voice from where she was seated
in the best arm-chair, looking very much like the most important
guest:

" 'My dear Marjorie, we would wait all night to meet this mysterious and heroic son of yours, whose existence you have so modestly kept a secret. . . .', and she smiled sweetly across at the other woman as if she had never in her life spread an unpleasant rumour about her.

"I sensed at once a feeling in the room of Mrs. Robinson being on one side and everyone else on the other, and at that moment I wanted very much to like my hostess, because I pitied her. But strangely, on that evening I found it particularly difficult to do so, because from the moment she came across to me, there was something about her that embarrassed me. She took hold of my hand with such an exaggerated air of warmth, as if it were I and not her son who had returned after ten years' absence, and I sensed from her almost convulsive handshake that her nerves were very much on edge, as if she felt that these people who had come as her guests were in fact enemies come to spy, and that I was her only true friend. For some reason I found myself wondering whether this had been her manner to every guest in the room. . . .

" 'Vicar,' she said, 'I'm so glad you've managed to come. There's been a most unfortunate hitch—Bill received a telegram an hour ago announcing that his fiancée was arriving at Victoria at seven-thirty, and he had no alternative but to go straight over to meet her. Most thoughtless of her, I think, at such a time. But he's just 'phoned, and they're both on their way here now. My dear, what a shock! We didn't expect her to reach England for another three weeks—she's been a V.A.D. nurse in India, you know. . . .'

"And she led me across the room in no particular direction in an odd kind of panic, as if she had only the vaguest idea of what she was doing. This was my second little shock concerning her, for though I had received a hint as to the hysterical undercurrents in her character in the evening she had confided in me, I had no reason to expect the almost complete demoralization I now observed. Even her appearance had deteriorated; her lipstick was clumsily applied; her clothes, for the first time since I had

known her, were somehow wrong, perhaps because she had so
obviously made a special effort to look smart and young; but
somewhere—I am not enough of an expert to say where—she
had made an error of judgement, and looked like a woman in
clothes ten years too young for her. Or possibly the clothes were
the same, but she herself looked ten years older, for her face was
drawn and anxious and her eyes looked sleepless. . . . And suddenly, in the middle of telling me something, she abandoned me
—she made a kind of panic-stricken rush from the room on
hearing the door-bell, though it was obvious that Schofield
could not have arrived so soon—and I found myself in a group
in front of the bar, being looked at by Peter with a smile that was
partly ironical, but which I felt, somehow, was not entirely unfriendly.

" 'Well, Vicar,' he said, 'once more I meet the man responsible
for preserving me from the hazards of war. What will you have
—there is sherry, of a kind, gin in various disguises, beer, and a
cocktail of my own invention which I certainly do not recom-
mend. . . .'

" 'But, Peter,' interrupted young Mrs. Bartram, who was in
the group I had joined, in the affected, specially refined accent
she had been acquiring in recent months, 'but, Peter, you malign
yourself. It's a most wonderful mixture, the best war-time cocktail I've tasted. The boy has genius. Do have one, Vicar—they
are really original. . . .'

"Peter then did something which I am sure was for my particular benefit, intended to shock me, and which, for that very
reason, completely failed in its object—Peter never was able to
grasp the fact that I always saw through these little attempts of
his. He put his arm round Mrs. Bartram's waist and hugged her
to him, saying:

" 'Take no notice of Norma, Mr. Ash—she's the most in-
sincere little bitch who's ever fallen in love with me. Aren't you,
sweetheart?' he asked, pinching her cheek, and though Mrs.
Bartram pretended to be indignant, she obviously enjoyed this
treatment, and made no very violent attempt to remove herself

from his arm. They stood there, looking at me, both with eye-brows raised, as if awaiting some kind of shocked reaction. But I was probably the least embarrassed person present for the others in the group laughed uneasily and looked at me out of the corners of their eyes as if not knowing what to do.

"So I ignored this little bit of flirtation put on for my benefit, and asked for a cocktail, which Peter sprang to get for me, abandoning Mrs. Bartram without any visible sign of regret. And as he handed it to me I saw again the slightly baffled look in his eyes, as if he did not understand me.

" 'Well, Vicar,' he said, 'you are about to meet my heroic brother. I'm glad to say you'll find him a healthy contrast to myself. He has all the manly virtues—he spent the war being dropped behind enemy lines, armed only with a dagger which he used to great effect, pouncing on guards armed to the teeth whose only weakness was that usually they had their backs to him. He's an expert in all forms of silent killing, from the swift knife-thrust between the second and third ribs, to the sudden blow on the back of the neck. You'll learn all about it after five minutes' conversation with him. He is a man completely lacking that defect of the imagination known as fear—unlike his brother who, as you well know, kept as far away from all shooting as he possibly could. Oh, you will have much in common with him, Vicar—for you are one of our heroes, too, aren't you?'

"And as he looked at me with his mocking smile, I suddenly remembered him standing at the window of that same room, looking calmly out at one of London's heaviest air-raids, whilst I lay under the table holding my breath. I knew that in thus mis-representing himself he was indulging in a form of self-immola-tion which gave him a perverted pleasure, and I felt pity for him in much the way I had felt pity a few moments earlier for his mother, and which I was to feel, months later, for his brother. I was trying to think rapidly of a way to at least give him credit for his courage to the group surrounding us, who, with the possible exception of Mrs. Bartram, took him at his own valuation; but at that moment the door opened and there appeared a large young man ushering before him . . . well, you know who. . . ."

"And from that moment," murmured Katharine, "you were aware of no one else in the room?"

"On the contrary, I hardly saw you. I concentrated my attention on Schofield about whom I had heard so much. . . ."

"If you have a fault, it is over-honesty. Surely you noticed me just a little?"

Mr. Ash allowed his lips, as if unwillingly, to relax into a smile.

"Well—I did afterwards remember your face as I saw it in that first moment."

"Tell me—what did it seem like?"

For some seconds he was silent, as if struggling with his memory; then, with the utmost seriousness, this time not sensing the mischievousness in her manner, he said:

"I had the impression of a broad brow, light gold hair which I was convinced was artificial, and violet eyes whose main expression was one of extreme ill-temper. . . ."

"And with this repulsive vision you at once fell in love?"

"On the contrary—for the first half of the evening I was convinced you were a hard, brassy young woman intent on ruining Schofield's life. . . ."

For some moments they went on talking like this, she trying to make him respond to her mood, he ill at ease though making a great effort not to show it. She sensed he was a little put out about her having interrupted his narrative, and determined not to do so again.

But the next day, which they had decided to spend walking to Fiesole, she found him trying to draw her into his story, as if he were aware of having almost snubbed her on the previous evening, and wanted to make amends. So, as they walked through the old city, out through the modern, characterless suburbs, he started talking in a way that was

*half-narrative, half-conversation. As they climbed the hill leading to
the beautiful little town that could claim an even greater antiquity than
Florence itself, and the famous view, perhaps the finest in Europe,
began to unfold itself, they paused sometimes and looked back at
Florence, and for a while would stop speaking. But soon they would
resume their way, and he would continue to talk, and continue to draw
her into his talk, in a way that puzzled her a little. After a while she
began to realize something she hardly dared believe, for it began to
seem to her almost as if he were jealous of her previous relationship with
Bill; for he seemed to labour too much the point of his dislike of the
other's character. He had struck this note immediately on resuming his
narrative.*

"I at once knew," he said, "when Schofield came into the room,
that he was aware of being the centre of the stage, and liked it. It was
not until later in the evening that I realized it was the same awareness
in yourself that was the cause of your look of ill-temper . . . that
you disliked being the centre of attention as much as he gloried in
it. . . ."

"It was that," she said, "and my fatigue. I had only just come off
the boat-train—and you know what war-time boat-trains were—and
he insisted in my going straight into that drawing-room without even
powdering my nose. . . ."

"Yes, that was thoughtless even for Schofield. But I suppose he
wanted to display you, to show us all what a beautiful fiancée he had,
in the same way he would have displayed an expensive new motor-car,
or any other possession that did him credit. . . .'

"I hardly like that simile!"

"But it shows his exact state of mind—he had not the smallest
consideration for your comfort—only his own vanity. Another thing
I could not like about him was the way he seemed to display that uniform with all the modifications which I suppose his branch of the Special
Service was allowed to carry out. . . ."

"Don't be too hard on him for that—he always had an adolescent
mind in some ways. He always loved dressing up in uniforms."

"A dangerous mentality—which a certain other nation was rather
too fond of. . . ."

Soon after this they reached a small café on the outskirts of Fiesole,
and it was here that he resumed his narrative proper for a while.

"The strange thing is," he said, "all these things about Schofield that prejudiced me against him, prejudiced me against you,
too. I thought that the fiancée of such a man must be objectionable. So I hardly looked at you, beyond taking in the fact that
you were undeniably beautiful, but, I thought, artificially so.
I only realized gadually that all your features existed in their own
right, that the kinds of effect other women had to call upon the
paint-box for, were yours by natural right. Do you know, for the
first half-hour you were in the room, I thought your finger-nails
were scarlet! It was only when you almost forced me to get you
a glass of that terrible sherry, and you took it from me—and
actually thanked me for bringing you the stuff—that I realized
they were a natural colour. I then looked at you, I suppose, for
the first time. I remember we then started to talk, and I could not
think why you singled me out in this way. Perhaps you thought
that, being a vicar, I would perhaps not try to flirt with you, as I
had noticed nearly every other man in the room had tried to do.
Anyhow, as we talked, I became aware of your tiredness, and it
occurred to me that perhaps you had had nothing to eat, because
the two glasses of sherry seemed slightly to have gone to your
head, for you sat staring into your glass, sometimes closing your
eyes, and talking, giving me a detailed account of your life from
the moment you stepped onto that troopship for the East. And
then, when you came to your meeting with Schofield, you had
no more to say, and even in that early stage, it occurred to
me that all was not right between you. . . . For it seemed to me
that a look of sadness crossed your face, and for some reason
I realized that throughout your narrative about your life in India,
you hadn't mentioned a single relative—nothing about letters
from home, or about looking forward to getting home. Then,
suddenly, I became interested in you, and in the same moment,
for reasons I still do not fully understand, from disliking

F

Schofield I began almost to hate him. For the first time in my life I felt I really disliked a man, and I did not enjoy the sensation. . . .

"It was then that I came to realize how long we had been talking; until that moment I had only had a vague impression of other people occasionally coming up and attempting to join in, but that we had ignored them. It was as if suddenly I came to my senses. I looked up and it seemed to me that we were being stared at, that everyone had noticed our tête-à-tête, that we were being watched covertly. As I looked round the room, heads seemed to turn away. I remember specially looking towards Schofield, and getting the impression that he seemed about the only person in the room unaware of our engrossment in each other—because he was talking so eloquently about himself. He was standing quite close to us, surrounded by about half a dozen people, and I remember hearing him say, in a sudden silence that fell on the room, '. . . he was a big fellow, bulging with muscle, but the knife slipped in as if he were made of butter. . . .' and I felt a sort of loathing for him. I felt appalled that such a man would one day be your husband—or the husband of any woman. I felt in that moment a desire to annihilate him, and was as horrified at myself as if I had committed blasphemy, as indeed I had. I made some involuntary movement and knocked a glass off the arm of the sofa, and this caused everyone to look at us, including Schofield.

"He stopped speaking and stared at me, and for the first time I saw come onto his face that special expression with which he always looked at me—the look in which there was a little amusement, a little mild scorn, and a great deal that was patronizing. He had been told by Mrs. Robinson when he was introduced to me about my little exploit at Dunkirk for which the War Office had misguidedly given me the same award that he had himself, and I always felt that secretly he looked upon it as something of a joke, as if he couldn't understand how a padré could get such an award; there was something in his attitude to me similar to Tom White's—the scorn of the fighting soldier for the padré.

"As I bent down to pick up the glass, you no doubt remember how, with one of those athletic, rapid movements he was so proud of, he forestalled me, and neatly took the glass almost from out of my fingers, and put it safely on the table beside us.

" 'Padré,' he said reprovingly, and no doubt jokingly, 'you're drunk.'

"This, though a rather stupid remark, was one anyone might have made without annoying me, but as he said it, it seemed to me that he exchanged with you a tolerant, faintly amused smile, and though I saw only *his* face, I imagined you returning his look—it did not occur to me that you might not have done so. This brought home to me the fact that it was you and he who were on terms of intimacy, not you and I. It was as if suddenly a spell were broken. You were again for me what I had first thought you—the rather brassy fiancée of an objectionable man. As he stood beside us, looking at you with a kind of smug, proprietary air, it seemed to me that you were both in league against me, showing amusement at a slightly squiffy parson. It seemed to me that the intimacy of my talk with you had been an illusion, that secretly you had been laughing at me. Indeed I did feel slightly the worse for drink, and wondered whether I had in fact been making a fool of myself. I could stand it no longer. With an effort I stood up, offered Schofield my seat beside you, made some excuse about an imaginary appointment, and left the flat. I had felt in the course of the previous hour or so two of the most violent of human emotions which I had always condemned in others—hatred and jealousy, and I began to wonder whether I understood myself. . . . Were you at all aware of what had been going on beneath the surface in that little scene?" Mr. Ash suddenly asked his wife.

"Not altogether," she replied. "I knew that something in Bill's manner had irritated you, but I did not know what. You see, I thought that in talking to me as you had, you'd merely been showing a professional interest in the state of my soul. I imagined you as a parson

skilled at getting people's life-stories out of them, and that I was just one of thousands. I thought that you'd been exercising a little charm on me. But you were the cause of my feeling my first real irritation with Bill. It was the way he was amused at you that irritated me—for I found nothing amusing about you, only something rather interesting. It made me aware for the first time of a certain insensitiveness in him. . . ."

For some time they talked desultorily, and then left the café, and went on into Fiesole. So enchanted were they by the little town that for the rest of the afternoon they ceased talking about themselves, and explored the area; they stayed there so long that they missed the last 'bus back and had to hire a taxi. They arrived in their hotel just in time for a late dinner, and after the meal, they went out again. They crossed the Ponte Vecchio, marvelled at the flood-lit Pitti Palace, re-crossed the river, and found themselves, without knowing where they were, in the Piazza della Repubblica; here they saw an aspect of Florence new to them, noisy and a little vulgar, with flashing neon lights, and gay, musical cafés. For a while they wandered round the square, enjoying the gaiety, but soon they tired of it, and instinctively made for the quietness of the Piazza della Signoria, where, seated in a café, they absorbed the atmosphere of serenity which this ancient place, once the scene of so much bloodshed, managed to convey. Here as the moon rose over the massive strength of the Pallazzo Vecchio and started to cast shadows over the paving, Mr. Ash went on with his story.

"That evening," he said, "I went back to the vicarage determined to do everything in my power to avoid meeting you again. And for some time I succeeded. I threw myself into the work of the parish. I visited the sick and the aged, redoubled my efforts to make myself felt in the slum area where I had had so little success, and to my astonishment found that I had almost ceased to care whether I succeeded or failed; and even more to my surprise I found that at once I began having more success, perhaps because of something new in my manner which these people understood.

For my manner no longer conveyed my pity for them because I no longer felt it. I now regarded my visits to them as work I had to force myself to do, and they liked this better. I feel now that it was only during those few weeks, and the even shorter time when you and I worked together in the parish, that I was really equal to the task I had taken on. . . . I explain my success during those first few weeks during which I avoided seeing you, to the fact that those people, who spent the major parts of their lives working in one way or other—even if in some cases it was avoiding work, which some did with great energy—sensed that in my new frame of mind I was merely doing a job of work, and not a particularly pleasant one, and this they sympathized with. They found me more businesslike, more abrupt in my manner; I no longer asked to go into their houses, but demanded entry as my right, and more often than not they let me in. And when in their houses I questioned them tersely about their lives, and did not hesitate to tell them off when I thought it necessary. And often when walking round the district in the evenings I passed pubs, with babies in prams outside, or with small children hanging about on the threshold—a common sight in any of the poorer parts of London. At such times a kind of cold rage would seize me and I would enter the public bar and demand who the parents were, and almost invariably they were pointed out to me; then I would go up to them and give them a lecture and often I was astonished by the bitterness of my own words. And it had a remarkable effect: a silence would fall on the bar, the parents would look ashamed; of course sometimes they would give me back as much as I gave, try to bluster it out, even swear at me, tell me to mind my own business; but almost always I found that most of the others in the room were on my side— always there was someone who would support me against their own kind. In this way I began to make a reputation for myself. Some hated me—especially the publicans—they thought I was taking people out of their bars. Whether or not I did, I never knew; I never even knew whether a single parent ever left a bar due to my influence and took their children home—I very much doubt it. But I probably left some argument in my wake—I made them think.

"The kind of success I had in those weeks is the sort of effect priests dream of having, but are never able to achieve in practice, and I have no doubt whatever that if I were to do the same thing again, in cold blood as it were, I would be a disastrous failure. It is a question of one's frame of mind, and perhaps the strangest, and most bitter thing about it all is, that I didn't care what effect I was having. I just took delight in venting this strange bitterness that was in me upon someone; sometimes I would pause and ask myself what manner of man I was; and then I would feel a little afraid, a little unsure, as if I were aware that there was within me an element I did not understand, something more powerful than myself. But these moods did not last long. On the whole I was rather pleased with myself, as if I were indulging a side to my nature which all my life had been starved.

"So for the next few weeks this was my mood. As you know, eight days after the evening on which I met you, Germany capitulated, and there started that series of parties held by Mrs. Robinson and Mrs. Carrington-Smith in which they vied to out-do each other in the lavishness of their entertaining, a rivalry which lasted until—well, you know when. The end of the war in Europe had comparatively little effect on me; I more than once remembered the flash of joy I had felt on that afternoon when Tom had told me of the fall of Hamburg, with a kind of astonishment—for now that it had actually happened I felt as if it were something that hardly concerned me. I had assumed a new personality, and I neither liked nor understood it, though it was bringing me more success with my work than I had ever had before. At that time I in no way connected my mood with you—I hardly ever thought of you. You know that I attended Mrs. Carrington-Smith's dinner-party which was, as it were, her opening salvo against Mrs. Robinson, and you know what happened across that dinner-table, an event which complicated rather than otherwise my mental confusion. But I will tell you about that in a moment, because before that evening something else had happened which drew tighter the skein which was finally unravelled at that remarkable party of Mrs. Robinson's on VJ night.

"For I had again visited the Whites. This had occurred on the evening preceding the dinner-party, two days after Germany's capitulation. It was about seven in the evening when I once more descended those stone steps and crossed the yard to the kitchen-door. As usual I opened the door without knocking, and found a party in progress—but this did not surprise me, for parties were going on everywhere that week. A fortnight previously I would probably have turned back, but in my new mood I welcomed the presence of so many people. I felt an odd kind of recklessness, and pleasure at inflicting what I had no doubt was my damping presence on them.

"Everyone who had been present on the evening of the fight was there; as well as Tom and Mrs. White, I saw the plump, rounded figure of the Jewess Molly Cohen, the tall, swarthy Al, and Les the little cockney. Mildred was as usual busy by the gas-stove, and there were about half a dozen others in the room, including a tall, smartly dressed blonde girl who seemed to be the centre of attention, but who had her back to me. I had not made much noise on entering and at first hardly anyone noticed me. But gradually people became aware of my presence, and as they did so they stopped speaking to stare at me, those who did not know me no doubt curious to see a member of the Church present, and those that did know me, feeling, I fear, even less friendly sentiments, as I had no illusions concerning Moll's and Al's feelings towards me. The Whites themselves were among the last to realize my presence; Mildred was too busy at the stove, whilst Tom was talking to the smartly-dressed blonde. Mrs. White was the first to see me. She was sitting, as usual, in the arm-chair, apparently oblivious to her surroundings, nursing the boy, gently rocking him to and fro on her lap. I saw her suddenly sit up and stare at me. I did not move, in an odd way enjoying the hostile stares that were being directed at me from all corners of the room. Suddenly Mrs. White leaned forward and plucked at her husband's arm—almost the only independent action I ever saw her take. By then silence in the room was complete, except for Mildred clattering crockery in the sink. Tom slowly looked round at his wife, and then in the direction in which she was staring, straight at me. Our eyes met. He stared at me blankly, as if completely taken aback by my presence, or by something new he saw in my manner, something more dangerous, perhaps, to himself. But before he could speak, the smartly-dressed girl, who had swung round to see what everyone was staring at, and to whom I had paid no particular attention, suddenly broke the silence.

" 'Well," she said, 'if it ain't the padré! Where you been, padré?'

"And looking at her, I recognized Ruby.

" 'So you've come back, Ruby?' I said quietly.

" 'Yes, padré, I've come back,' she said, walking slowly towards me in the silence that continued in the room. But before she reached me she suddenly swung round on the rest of the room, and said loudly, almost menacingly:

" 'Well—what's the matter with you all? Ain't you pleased to see the padré? Mr. Ash 'oo saved Dad's life? On this night when we're celebratin' the end of it all?'

"But they continued to stare at me with hostility. Even Mildred who had turned round from the sink, and was standing with her back to it, was looking at me in no very friendly fashion. Then, to my astonishment, Ruby flung her arms round me and kissed me on the lips. I had a powerful whiff of perfume and gin—she was half-tight. I tried to loosen her arms, but she held on.

" '*I* welcome you, padré,' she said. '*I* know an 'ero when I see one. You're the only 'ero 'ere, you are. What's the rest of them done in this war? They 'aven't even noticed there's a war on, 'cept to take their pick of the black market. . . .'

"She turned round to the others, still with one arm round my waist.

" 'Come on, you bastards!' she said. 'Give a welcome to the padré!'

"Again there was silence, and I knew my reception was in the balance; they seemed to be waiting for some lead as to how to receive me. I stood waiting with what I like to think was a mocking smile on my face. And at last that lead came—not from Tom, but from the person whom I had observed on a previous occasion to be the strongest personality among them. The Jewess Moll suddenly raised her glass in the air and said:

" 'Three cheers for Mr. Ash—but for 'oo one at least of us wouldn't be 'ere now!', and she looked round the room almost commandingly, and little Les, as if mesmerized, let out a loud 'Hip—hip—', and though there may have been something ironical in the cheer that followed, it was none the less vociferous, and immediately restored the convivial atmosphere of the room. Those who did not realize the tension between me and Tom, welcomed me wholeheartedly. A glass of beer was thrust into my hand, half a dozen people slapped me on the back, and some-one started singing 'For he's a jolly good fellow', and before I quite knew what was happening, I found myself in the midst of an uproarious party.

"I discovered that one or two present had heard of my ac-tivities in the slum area, and when they had heard the story of my saving Tom's life—told to all and sundry by Ruby, who seemed suddenly to be my champion and in some way hostile to her own family—I became a kind of hero in practice for the first time. I was in fact the only male present, besides Tom, who had seen active service, Les and Al both having some physical defect which had prevented their being called up—one of them had two fingers missing from his right hand—though I never discovered what was wrong with the other. All this amused me, especially when I noticed that Al was staring at me surlily and whispering to Molly Cohen, who appeared to be trying to calm him. I began to enjoy myself enormously, and the mood of recklessness that had been in control of me since I had entered the room increased. In fact, I was in great form; I felt as if I had discovered the secret of how to treat these people; at that other party I had let them dominate me; now I was under the

F*

impression that I was dominating them. I told myself that like all people ignorant of the Church, they were astonished to see a Minister behaving like a human being, drinking beer and cracking jokes with his arm round the prettiest woman in the room. I felt as if I were doing wonderful things to increase the prestige of the Church. They gathered round Ruby and me and roared with laughter at my jokes, though I wonder now how much was laughter at me and how much with me.

"In fact, I was not altogether keeping my head. For instance, I did not give due significance to looks I saw exchanged between Molly and Tom—the fact that I remember them now proves that I noticed them—which should have told me that my success was very much an affair organized by those two, and especially by Molly.

Meanwhile I had learnt from Ruby that she had, of all things, joined a music-hall company, and since her disappearance had been touring the country. Tom, who was standing near when she told me this, joined in our conversation; he was in the last stage but one of drunkenness, which with him invariably meant he was cheerful. He put his hand on my shoulder and said in slurred tones:

" 'Yes, padré, our Rube's an actress now. In the West End, she'll be, one day—up at the Windmill. Success of the family, that's Rube. You should see 'er Show, padré—it'll be up 'ere soon, won't it, Rube? "Legs and Laughter" it's called.'

"He leaned forward so that his mouth, from which there issued a mingled smell of gin and beer, was only an inch from my ear.

" 'If you go, padré, you'll see more of 'er than you've ever seen before—stark, she is!' He winked at me. 'That'll suit you, eh, padré? You like to see a bit of leg, whatever you say. I've seen you lookin' at Rube in 'er bathin' suit! . . . . She's only in the chorus so far—you know, standin' at the back of the stage in arty poses. But she'll be the lead one day—she's learnin' to dance, aren't you, Rube?' And he gave her a nudge, which she did not receive in a very friendly fashion.

"I looked at Ruby with greater interest. She was certainly

changed. There was already a theatrical air about her—or so it seemed to me who knew nothing of the theatre. She was as heavily made-up as ever, but without the old crudeness—there was more art in it now; she had learnt how to accentuate her good points and tone down her bad ones. And she looked more affluent —her clothes were expensive and her hair was obviously receiving professional attention. She no longer tried to hide her Eastern blood—she accentuated her slanting eyes, her dusky skin, which provided an extraordinarily effective, if bizarre, contrast to her blonded hair; her always impressive figure was now helped by carefully designed clothes, and was positively obtrusive. She looked a completely artificial production, but was most striking. And she looked happier, more self-confident, as if sensing her own success. And strangely enough she seemed spiritually more wholesome, as if her naturally generous instincts were now receiving greater satisfaction. She reminded me strangely of Mrs. Robinson—she had the same animal magnetism.

"When Tom had left us, Ruby said to me with a quaint air of self-defence:

" 'This ain't really a bad show I'm in, padré. It's sexy, of course, but that's what draws the boys. It's just a start, see, whilst I learn the ropes. A bloke's teachin' me to dance—says I got talent. Don't ask what I pay 'im with. But 'e says with my looks I'll go a long way. . . . I can sing too, a little—you know, croon. . . .'

" 'I hope you will go a long way, Ruby,' I said sincerely, for it occurred to me that this was a far better path for her to tread than the one I had feared she was heading for. I felt rather naïvely that if she took up the theatre, even that sort of theatre, at least she would have some kind of professional code—for all professions have their codes which gives to all who take part in them a certain pride in themselves.

"One other odd little incident occurred that evening before I left, and which almost caused Molly Cohen's carefully engineered plan of lulling my suspicions to fail. There came a sudden rap at the door, and when it was opened, a small man in a cloth cap, carrying a large suitcase, entered, and becoming aware of the crowd, stopped dead and glanced round suspiciously, almost like a rat caught in a room when the light is suddenly put on; he seemed about to back out again, when Tom strode across the room, seized him by the arm, and almost dragged him into another room, shutting the door behind him. This little incident caused a sudden silence, and I noticed Molly Cohen and Al exchange glances, Al's eyes showing a fury that was quite startling. But once more it was Moll who was mistress of the situation.

"She looked round the room with a smile, and winked.

" ''E's the boy we like to see,' she said, nodding towards the closed bedroom door. ''E's in the liquor racket—an' we ain't the ones to inquire into 'is source of supply. No 'arm in it now the war's over, eh, Vicar?'

"This seemed to satisfy everyone present, including myself, to whom it seemed a very probable, if not very admirable, explanation. Someone shouted through the closed door 'bring it out 'ere, Tom—don't drink it all yourself!' and one or two of the guests made as if to enter the room; but Al was leaning, as if casually, against the door, lighting a cigarette, and I noticed him glance at the two men coming towards him in a way which made them veer off in another direction. The two men grumbled, though quite good-naturedly, as if sympathizing with the Whites' desire to keep their liquor to themselves. And so the incident passed off smoothly enough and I would probably not have given it another thought had not Moll rather overdone things by deciding it was necessary to give me a fuller explanation. She came up to me, the first and only time she ever directly approached me.

" 'Don't think we're in the 'abit of doin' this, padré,' she said ingratiatingly. 'Durin' the war we wouldn't touch the black market—not us. Ain't fair to the boys up at the front. But now it's all over—just the once—to 'elp celebrate—there ain't no 'arm in it, is there?'

"I thought this rather odd—it was so uncharacteristic of Molly Cohen to approach me at all, and people never behave uncharacteristically without some very strong reason. However, even this did not really rouse my suspicions, so obsessed was I with my own success that night. I do not remember quite how I reacted to her explanation, but I do know we ended by toasting the 'boys still fighting in Burma' together, and that gravely she clinked her glass with mine.

"I did not stay much longer after this; I tried to get a few words with Mildred, but when I approached her she looked at me with such hostility that I soon left her alone. I wondered whether she had observed my friendly relations with Ruby and was jealous, so inflated was my ego. So I went straight back to the vicarage and to bed, where I fell asleep before my conscience was really able to begin functioning.

"And then, on the next night, there was that dinner-party of Mrs. Carrington-Smith's. But I shall have to leave the telling of that until tomorrow. They seem to be closing the restaurant. . . ."

They spent the next morning in the Uffizi Gallery, and in the afternoon took a bus to San Miniato, where, after exploring the Church, they sat down outside, entranced by this other view of Florence, almost as fine as the one from Fiesole. In fact she preferred it because from here she could see more clearly the ancient heart of the city, whilst from Fiesole she had been able to recognize only the Cathedral and the Campanile of the Vecchio Palace, and of course Giotto's Tower. But he preferred the Fiesole view, and about this they argued a little. From Fiesole, he contended, one was more aware of the unique setting of the City, in its hollow among the hills, as if God with one hand had scooped out a depression, and there set down the city; to which she replied with a twinkle in her eye that she had to confess sometimes to a greater interest in the works of man than in those of God, upon which he asked gravely:

"What is the difference?"

To which she replied that in the way she looked at it, God created the hills round Florence, but man the buildings that made up the city.

"But," he protested, "God made man."

"Then," she replied, "I prefer the works of God once removed. . . .",
and she looked into his eyes, on the verge of laughter.

For a moment he hesitated, and she held her breath, wondering
whether he would take her seriously or fall in with her mood; and for
some reason she did not fully understand it seemed to her that upon his
reaction depended whether their relationship was making progress or
otherwise. But after his momentary hesitation his face broke into a
smile and he laughed aloud at her reply, and upon this their argument
ceased to be even superficially serious, and even verged at one period on
the flirtatious. But at once, as if sensing this and afraid of himself, he
became serious again, and it was here, seated in the warm afternoon
sun, that he went on with his story.

"I had accepted Mrs. Carrington-Smith's invitation," he
began, "almost against my own inclination. But it had occurred
to me suddenly that in normal circumstances I would not have
hesitated to accept it, and this caused me to wonder what I
meant by 'normal circumstances'; I then realized, suddenly, that
by 'normal circumstances' I meant the time before you had
appeared in our community. This in a sense startled me, because
it forced me to admit to myself that somewhere, at the back of
my mind, you were playing an important part. This my intellect
refused to believe, and so, to prove it to myself, I accepted
this invitation to a party at which I knew you were to be
present.

"The invitation had come over the telephone by Mrs. Carrington-Smith herself; she told me she was having a few people
to dinner to celebrate the end of the war in Europe.

" 'Just a very small affair,' she said, 'but, I think you will find,
very pleasant.'

"And she went on to say—in the intimate manner which only
she knows on occasion how to assume, as if the person she is
talking to and herself have some special understanding denied
everyone else, which is the first line of attack of the born gossip

—that for some time she had been wanting to show 'these people' the kind of dinner-party she had been in the habit of holding before the war.

" 'You know the sort of thing,' she said, 'no vulgarity, no pretentiousness, but everything in the very best of taste.'

"I did not realize then that this was a remark aimed at Mrs. Robinson, though it was not long before I grasped the significance of this and many another remark of hers in the same vein. I was about to refuse the invitation rather coldly, because at that time Mrs. Carrington-Smith's snobbishness was beginning to be too much for me, when she casually mentioned some of the others who were coming, and among these was you.

" 'Young Colonel Schofield,' she said, 'and his charming fiancée. . . . To be quite honest, Vicar,' she went on, 'one of my objects in holding this little party is to show that child that some of us here know how to entertain. . . .' And she went on to hint mysteriously that she had reasons for suspecting you were accustomed to a way of life far superior to that of the family you were about to marry into. She had, she whispered into the telephone, 'come across' your parents before the war, and at the same time she gave me the impression that for some reason known only to herself she considered you especially deserving of sympathy . . . . And whilst she talked on the thoughts concerning you, which I have just mentioned, occurred to me . . . so it was that without further hesitation I accepted her invitation. In fact she spoke to me quite seriously and sincerely, as she usually did when we had no audience.

"So much for my feelings before the party; the party itself you experienced as well as I, and I daresay I have given you some idea of the unusual mental state I was in when, a little late, I entered the room. . . . What kind of an impression I gave to the assembled company is another matter. . . ."

And Mr. Ash paused, looking at his wife, as if inviting her to comment.

"I shall never forget," she said, "the impression you made on me...."

"Tell me about it," he said.

She paused, her eyes closed, as if re-creating the scene.

"I am not so good at describing things as you," she said at last.

"That doesn't matter, do your best. Take up the narrative for a while. It will help me to see things through your eyes."

"Well," she said, "I remember you were the very last to arrive. We were all sitting round that over-refined drawing-room in which nothing was in either good or bad taste. I had been sitting there for fifteen minutes, looking round, and wishing there was in the room—if not a spark of originality, at least some effort at it—even something in appallingly bad taste would have been a relief. But there was nothing—everywhere the same dull, middle-class monotony. I found myself longing for the vulgarity of Mrs. Robinson's flat—at least her place had life and energy, an honesty that reflected a personality. And then there were my fellow-guests—but I have no need to enlarge upon them—you too experienced them. They suited the environment. They were so afraid of committing some offence against etiquette that their conversation was almost meaningless. Unfortunately Bill and I had arrived early, and as each new guest arrived, we had to endure the same inane pattern of conversation; first the weather, then the usual thanksgiving that the war was at last over, and finally the inevitable paying of court to Bill. This last I found the most difficult of all to bear; because to everyone who came in Mrs. Carrington-Smith made sure of showing that she had as her guest one of the war heroes.

"'And this,' she would say, smiling as if she were herself responsible for Bill's existence, 'is Colonel Schofield, M.C., one of the heroes who made victory possible....'

"And of course Bill basked in it.... Each time there came onto his face the same look of modesty, there was the same shrugging of his shoulders as if he were trying to dissociate himself from the universal flattery, though each time he responded

eagerly enough—though pretending to give no value to them—
when asked to relate his experiences. Slowly, as people came in,
a crowd began to surround him, and there he stood on the hearth-
rug in that rather slovenly stance which at the same time manages
to suggest so well his athletic build, his blond hair slightly ruffled,
his boyish face flushed, the scar which made his features so
interesting showing in a white gash across the width of one cheek,
his blue eyes looking frankly, eagerly, into the eyes of his
questioners . . . yes, there he stood, the whole magnificent,
detestable six-feet-two of him. . . ."

"*Detestable—at that stage?*"

"Yes—at that stage. Though I didn't know then that already
I was detesting him, I was in fact already doing so. You see, I
had had it ever since arriving in England. I must have been
present during fifty introductions—and each time he had reacted
in the same way, each time there was the same modest smile, the
same shrug of the shoulders, and the same eager response to that
first question—invariably about the scar on his cheek. And always, afterwards, when we were alone together, the same apologetic grin, the same boyish laugh as he confided in me that he was
fed up with all this hero business. Oh! that boyishness! But of
course I hadn't yet reached the stage of admitting all this to
myself. You see, always there was the undeniable fact that he
had been a hero, that he *was* one of the men who had made
victory possible, that he had deserved every mention in dis-
patches he had had, and more than the M.C. which they eventually gave him. Physically, he was a very brave man. But you
see at that time I hadn't realized he had done all these things not
for his country but for the medals. . . . But on that particular
evening I had had enough. Which was why, when you entered
the room, I may have given the impression of at once starting a
flirtation with you . . . did I give you that impression?"

"You did, and because I thought it evidence of your true character—that of a flighty, shameless hussy—I responded. I told myself, with what I thought was relief, that in this way I would get you out of my system. For as I came into the room I saw at once that little tableau you have just described—Schofield surrounded by admirers, Mrs. Carrington-Smith looking proudly at her satisfied guests, and you sitting in splendid isolation in the best arm-chair, with a sulky look in your eyes. That was the first time I had seen you in evening dress, of course. You looked magnificent, and to my eyes extremely bold. Incidentally, I haven't seen that dress since. . . ."

"You won't. I got rid of it soon afterwards. It was one Bill had sent over from America—he ordered it before leaving India. And he insisted on my wearing it—and on my hair-style, and that almost theatrical make-up. Oh, I realize I looked a tart. But it was all vanity on his part, and foolishness on mine—he wanted me to be seen to my best advantage, as he called it, no doubt so that everyone could see how successful he was in love as well as war. I hadn't realized then that, as far as I was concerned, he valued only my appearance. So for a while I fell in with his ideas. But that evening my eyes were opened. I became aware suddenly that that gown was too much. . . ."

"It was indeed. It made you more beautiful than any woman has a right to be. When physical beauty reaches that level it becomes a social menace. It becomes a challenge to men and incites them to thoughts they do not find easy to control anyhow. In this case it seemed to me to prove conclusively that you were the kind of woman I half-hoped, half-feared, you to be. I felt I no longer had serious cause to fear you—that your attractions were only those of the flesh, and I believed myself able to resist those. It was the appeal you had had to my emotions that I had most feared during the preceding days—that starved instinct within me of which I had been growing conscious during the last months. For I was beginning to suspect for the first time that unless this instinct was roused in me fully it would wither away altogether, and that without it I would lack some human quality

—would in some way be inhuman, like those cold, ambitious clerics one sometimes meets. And you had appealed to that instinct. But now I saw you as I had always imagined beautiful women to be—and still think most of them are—as a woman seduced by her own beauty, unable to resist exercising its power over men, and become devilish cunning in its use, of which your disturbing of my emotions on that evening had been an example. So, after I had been introduced to the company, and they, after paying the minimum amount of attention to me compatible with good manners, had turned back to Schofield, and I found you smiling at me, inviting me to cross the room to you, I accepted your invitation and in a spirit of bravado crossed over to you, feeling rather as if I represented the powers of good advancing to do battle with the powers of evil. . . ."

"It was then," she said, "that you made such an impression on me. I had noticed how the others had given you the minimum of attention, and then turned quickly back to Bill, and how you had reacted to this. A look of faint amusement had come into your face, and in that moment I saw reflected in your face Bill's true nature; you who had met him only once, already saw through him, and I too saw through him—for the moment. For the first time I saw him as the egoist he was. And as I looked at you I saw that faint smile on your face, not despising—but tolerant, and faintly amused. It seemed to me suddenly that here was a man of great understanding and wisdom, possessing every-thing that Bill lacked. Suddenly I wanted to gain your good opinion. And when you looked at me your expression had in it none of the obsequiousness which I was accustomed to see when men looked at me, their tribute to that beauty which you say exists, and which had in fact haunted my life, and to which I had myself been on the verge of giving in to. . . . You looked at me as if you saw not my body but my soul, and did not think much of it. At once I became aware of that gown I was wearing, of my shoulders, my hair, my make-up. In this man, I said to myself, is strength; he has control over his emotions. I wanted des-perately to make you realize that I was not what I appeared to be, and so I beckoned you over. . . . I assure you there was no coquetry in that invitation. . . ."

"To me it had every appearance of coquetry. As I sat down near you I almost pitied you; I pitied you and felt full of self-confidence. I was aware of you as exercising all the feminine arts and wiles to gain my interest, and that they were having absolutely no effect. But this impression did not last for long. For soon I found myself once again losing my awareness of the rest of the people in the room as we started talking. Once more your power over my emotions was taking effect. I do not know what we talked about—I know only that in me all the time there was a core of resistance—I kept telling myself that you were putting on an act, that you were determined to amuse yourself with me and were adopting tactics which you thought would suit this particular prey. . . . I was aware of fighting a battle which I was losing confidence in my ability to win, and all the time we talked—what did we talk about?"

"The first time we had talked about me—that time we talked about you. You told me your complete life-history, and then started describing the parish, and the way you did it enthralled me—you have an extraordinary gift for describing people, you know, which is why your sermons are so good. And I was more than ever aware of the contrast between you and Bill. Because, you see, on the rare occasions when Bill told me anything about his past life—I mean his early past life, not his war-time experiences—I knew always that so much was being kept back, that there was so much to *keep* back—with you it was obvious there was nothing you had the slightest need to keep back. Knowing what we now do about poor Bill, we realize there was a lot he could hardly help keeping to himself, at least from a stranger, though not from his fiancée. . . . I was flattered by the way in which you told me so much about yourself, and was beginning to think that my appearance could not be having quite such a bad effect on you as I had thought, when something happened to stop our conversation. I don't remember what it was. . . ."

"It was just one of those changes in the atmosphere of a room" he said, taking up the story again, "of which the subconscious mind is always aware, for I remember suddenly looking up and seeing that the group round Schofield had broken up, and that everyone seemed to be looking towards us. I realized that everyone was in fact politely waiting for us to finish our conversation so that we could all go in to dinner. I had to make some effort not to show embarrassment, but I was helped by the fact that, with my return to reality, there flowed back into me my conviction of what I thought to be your true character—that of a coquette trying to add another scalp to her collection. So I was able to say to Schofield, whom I saw looking at me with some curiosity, some trivial remark which passed off the situation. . . ."

"What you said may have been trivial, but it is a sentence I shall never forget because of the pain it caused me. It showed me that I had failed utterly to overcome the prejudice against me which my appearance had caused in you. First of all you apologized to Mrs. Carrington-Smith for keeping her waiting, and then, turning to Bill, you said with remarkable pomposity: 'Your fiancée is so skilled in the feminine art of dissembling, that for the last half-hour she has quite convinced me that her one interest in life is the trivial affairs of a parish priest. . . .' And you looked down at me with an ironical smile. . . ."

"Of course. . . . I remember now. I thought that in this way I would show you I wasn't quite the simple parson you thought me, and that you would not so easily add my scalp to your collection. . . . Well, as you know, we did not sit together at dinner, but opposite each other, so there was no chance of our carrying on our conversation. You were sitting next to Schofield, and for some reason, perhaps because he had noticed how wrapped up we had appeared to be in each other, he suddenly started to show you great attention, to make a display of his affection; and it seemed to me that you responded. . . . You whispered to each other, laughed at some private joke, and generally made a display of your intimacy. I noticed other guests exchanging looks with that absurd sentimental smile which people of a certain age—you will remember that they were all, with one exception, past middle age—put on when observing the antics of lovers, and I heard old Lady Moon, who was on my right, observe to Major Calthrop on her other side that you made 'a very handsome pair' . . . . Of course the old lady was right, you were indeed a handsome pair, and there was no reason why her remark should have angered me. But it did, and I felt that powerful and unpleasant emotion I had felt before—jealousy.

"I managed to suppress it, or at any rate to prevent it from being visible, and proceeded to play my part in the dinner-table conversation which then took place. Now that meal was to me a strange experience; for normally, however dull and stupid my companions may be, I am never irritated by them; always I am aware that they are a reflection of the divine spirit of God, and if sometimes this reflection is a little dull and tarnished, then I think of all the circumstances beyond their control which have made them as they are, and I feel pity for them, and try in my conversation—usually unsuccessfully—to bring out the best in them. But to me that evening everyone sitting round that table seemed worthy only of either derision or scorn—which is strange because each of them, with the possible exception of our hostess and her young satellite Mrs. Bartram, had more good than bad qualities. Take old Lady Moon for instance; a snob, admittedly, and no longer in full possession of all her faculties, but an old lady of great courage who had continued to live in her old decaying mansion throughout the blitz, refusing to take refuge with relatives in the country which she could easily have done, because she had been born and bred in that house in the days when it had been a fashionable district, and loved it; every Sunday she had regularly attended Church, gave generously to collections though she could ill afford it, and did a power of good in the parish . . . yet to me that evening it seemed that all her good qualities sprang from one despicable motive— pride. . . . And there was Major Calthrop on her other side; a product of Sandhurst of the old school, with all the merits and defects of his kind; I knew him as a man of unswerving

honour who would have kept his word if it meant dying for it;
I had seen him walking through showers of shrapnel in the blitz
without a tin-hat as if it were so much confetti, joking with
terrified mothers and weeping children, helping them into
shelters though he could himself hardly walk for gout. He was a
great nuisance to the air-raid wardens, but everyone respected
him . . . yet to me that evening he seemed a silly, pompous old
man who drank too much and who could talk of nothing but the
Indian Army. And so with them all. I had great difficulty in
preventing myself from making sarcastic remarks to everyone,
and to prevent myself from doing so I kept as silent as possible,
and listened.

"And this did nothing to soften my mood. Never, it seemed to
me, had I heard so many people try so hard to impress each other
with the eminence of their social positions; each was aware of
having been specially selected as representatives of the élite of the
district, and each tried to justify their presence. Only Lady Moon,
secure in the possession of her title, was exempt, and said little,
but what she did say put everyone else in their place; she had
reached the age when the manipulation of her knife and fork
required all her concentration, and also she was so deaf that she
could understand very little of what was being said around her;
she would, however, occasionally make a quite irrelevant pro-
nouncement, which usually began with the magic words 'when
I was presented . . .', which at once silenced the entire table. Major
Calthrop too was past the age when social position continued to
mean much to him, but he made his contribution to the snob-
bery of the evening by shouting across the table at Schofield,
asking him about various places in India which I am sure the poor
fellow had never heard of, whilst Mrs. Carrington-Smith kept
her end up by referring loudly every so often to her friend Lady
So-and-So, and when one of the more humble guests timidly
referred to some holiday she had had abroad before the war, as
if to go abroad were in itself a social distinction, our hostess was
quick to mention that she herself had regularly spent 'the season' in
Monte Carlo. . . . And I myself was being bombarded most of

the evening by a middle-aged woman with an aggressive manner, sitting on my left, with details of her adventures on the backs of various horses before the war each of which she seemed to remember by name. And so it went on; no subject was mentioned which did not have some bearing on social position, and I grew more and more morose. I was too far away to hear what you were talking about, but you seemed engrossed with your left-hand neighbour, now that Schofield was involved with Major Calthrop, and I was sure that you too were boasting about your pre-war social conquests. . . ."

"I fact I was being told exactly how to breed fox-terriers."

"Then you were comparatively lucky. At least you didn't have to endure this obsession with social position."

"Oh, but I did. All dog-breeders, I was informed, come from County families. . . ."

"Well, well. Anyhow, you no doubt remember that it was I who eventually introduced the one discordant note into the conversation, and caused everyone to feel uneasy. . . ."

"Do tell me how it started. I remember suddenly hearing you holding forth about the old people of the parish in your best pulpit manner, with everyone listening uncomfortably. . . ."

"Our hostess was the direct cause, but of course it was the cumulative effect of all the conversation going on round me that really started it. She had noticed I was not joining in the general conversation and wanted to put me at my ease. Around me at that moment people had begun discussing what they most looked forward to in the peace-time world, and my neighbour had just been holding forth on the pleasures of riding, and the 'nice' people who went in for it. Someone else had talked about French food, another about ski-ing in Switzerland, a third about shooting in Scotland, and a fourth about getting her car on the road again—'my dear, this public transport—I just can't put up with it any longer'; and our hostess had kept her end up by saying dreamily that she had made up her mind to indulge herself 'just once more' in a little *haute couture*—'just one little frock, nothing really extravagant, perhaps somewhere in the region of fifty guineas. . . .' And the other women had looked at her round-eyed. Oh, how those misguided women swallowed everything our hostess said. . . . It was after this silence that she asked me what *I* most looked forward to doing, and I found I could control myself no longer. The subject I then embarked upon was the last I would have mentioned on such an evening in normal circumstances—there is a time and place for everything, and a celebration dinner-party is not the time to appeal to people's consciences—but as I say, I had had too much. I said very gravely that the thing I most looked forward to was organizing a service to look after the aged of the parish, and at once I was aware of everyone who heard me looking down at their plates uneasily, and there formed round me a little area of silence, which I filled by holding forth in my—as you describe it—best pulpit manner. I described to them these old people, laying it on as thick as possible, giving details of their plight, the fact that they rarely had any relatives, lived alone, and were often found dead in their beds through being unable to attract attention when they fell ill. I believe your side of the table joined in the general silence about half-way through this part of my speech, and by the time I had finished, everyone was sitting staring in front of them as if they were in fact in Church. This lasted for some seconds until it was broken, as no doubt you remember, by young Mrs. Bartram saying in those bored tones of hers and that newly acquired accent:

" 'Surely the place for such people is in homes. . . .'

"This caused me to see red. From then on I spoke with complete sincerity. I forget what I said—one never does remember what one says at such times. . . ."

"You were really impressive," she interrupted. "I could see you had lost your temper, but I doubt whether anyone else realized it. Coldly and quietly you demolished Norma Bartram. You explained with great eloquence—no longer with a pulpit manner but like a normal man passionately moved by his subject —how it was that suggesting these people went to homes was equivalent to a sentence of death; for, you said, those who have the courage to go on living alone, without asking for help, are invariably those with more than average pride, for whom forcible removal to the 'workhouse'—for to these people, you said, any home was the workhouse—would mean an instant collapse of all their self-respect, without which life is insupportable. People who before had been listening to you uncomfortably, now listened with enthusiasm, and poor Norma began to grow pink in the face. And when you had finished she, being the cocky little monkey she was, and no doubt wanting to regain some of her lost face, tried to be so sophisticated by saying, still in those bored tones to show how unmoved she was, something about it being the kindest thing to put them out of their misery by letting them die if that was what they wanted; to which you merely said, very gently, 'But that is not what they want,' and everyone looked at the girl as if she were a rather nasty and stupid child, and I have never seen anyone look so very small . . . by that performance you made an enemy for life of Norma Bartram and . . . more than a friend of me. . . ."

For a moment they both were silent, and then he said:

"I remember it all ended on a note of bathos. I remember apologizing to Mrs. Carrington-Smith for introducing so gloomy a note, actually feeling very pleased with myself . . . but my ego was somewhat deflated when old Lady Moon, obviously not having heard a word I had said, greeted my apology with a loud 'hear, hear' . . . . But at least it neatly changed the subject, and I have no doubt she voiced, if unwittingly, the sentiments of the entire table. . . ."

"With one exception. . . ."

"An exception which I did not, on that evening, suspect. When you came up to me after the meal and so charmingly expressed an interest in the old people, and offered to do what you could to help in the work, I thought to myself, has this woman no shame . . . this, I said to myself, is surely taking hypocrisy to absurd lengths . . . . And I decided to call your bluff, so I told you about my visits after morning service on Sundays to certain of these old people, and, on your saying you would be interested in accompanying me, suggested that if you were to attend the service, we could go straight on together afterwards."

"And when I accepted, you looked at me so ironically, that I knew you didn't believe me. And then you gave me that advice about clothes . . . quite the rudest thing you ever said to me. . . ."

"Well, in the most unlikely event of your turning up, I did not want you to arrive looking like something out of Hollywood; the old people would have thought I had taken leave of my senses. You see, I was judging you by that evening gown. . . . Anyhow, I did not take you seriously. I was sure you would either forget all about it because of some more interesting prey turning up in the meantime, or else you would send round some apologetic note on scented notepaper about a headache. . . but at the back of my mind there was a faint feeling that you might come, that you might be so keen on getting my scalp—a clergyman was probably something you had yet to add to your collection—that you would even go to the lengths of attending morning service . . . hence my advice about the clothes, because I had, as well as the feelings of the old people, the dignity of the Church to consider. . . ."

He paused, looking at his watch.

"We had better descend the hill and find somewhere to satisfy our English craving for tea," he said. "If they have yet imported any into Italy for the benefit of English tourists. And for the rest of the day the subject of the parish will be forbidden. . . ."

The next day was wet, so they spent the afternoon bringing up to date their correspondence, and in the evening settled down in a quiet corner of the hotel lounge, where he resumed his narrative.

"The day after that party," he began, "I was a little easier in my mind. I was able to tell myself I was playing a game with you, that soon, by seeing you in an environment where I was sure you would not come off very well, I would once and for all be able to rid my mind of you. This, I told myself, is my final test, that after it I shall be able to attain complete tranquillity of mind.

"Meanwhile I was aware of having neglected some of my duties, and in this mood of optimism felt more able to resume them, and chief among the items that lay on my conscience was Mildred. I had been uneasily aware during the past few weeks that since her employment by Mrs. Robinson she had become if anything more surly and unapproachable. So I decided to visit her in Mrs. Robinson's flat, an environment preferable to her own home for this purpose. I rang Mrs. Robinson up, told her what I wanted to do, and she invited me to tea the next day.

"I arrived rather early—not long after three—and the door was opened to me by Mrs. Robinson herself, who escorted me into her sitting-room. And there, once more seated in that highly-coloured room, I had an odd sensation of returning after a long absence; it was as if suddenly I had been reminded of things which many months ago had been my chief interest and concern. In fact, it was less than three weeks since I had last sat in that chair.

"Mrs. Robinson at once began to question me about the party on the previous evening, to which she had not been invited. She was obviously very hurt at not having been asked, and I must say I had thought it odd that she was not there, in view of the fact that the principal guests had been her son and future daughter-in-law. But apparently Mrs. Carrington-Smith had been quite open with her about it, telling her that she was not being asked because she was sure that 'Bill and Katharine' would for once like to 'get away from the family', and that she was sure Mrs. Robinson would understand in view of the length of their friendship. I could just see Mrs. Carrington-Smith saying this, with her tongue in her cheek, and then immediately asking all her most superior friends whom she had never allowed Mrs. Robinson to meet. The closeness with which Mrs. Robinson questioned me as to who had been there, told me that she was well aware of these wheels within wheels. It was in that moment that I realized fully the bitterness of the rivalry of these two women. However the subject was at last changed, and she then said something which startled me.

"'How changed you seem, Vicar,' she murmured, looking into my eyes.

"'*I* changed?' I asked. 'In what way?'

"'Well—you look tired, and worried. I've always envied the peacefulness of your eyes. Now they are no longer peaceful.'

"'I assure you I am not aware of having changed,' I said.

"'You have,' she insisted. 'You're restless, unsure of yourself. Though of course you won't admit it—not to a middle-aged woman who's no longer any use in the world. . . .'

"At once I realized with some relief that she was probably not conscious of any change in me, but merely wanted to gain my sympathy.

"'You—middle-aged?' I asked automatically.

"'Yes,' she said almost harshly. 'Don't pretend you're not aware of that.'

"'In our last talk together,' I said as gently as I could, 'I gained the impression that you did not always like to hear the truth on that subject.'

"'The truth, Vicar?' she said, staring in front of her. 'No. The truth and I are not altogether friends. . . .'

"'Is that wise?' I asked.

"'There is much in my life that has not been wise, Vicar,' she said.

"'That applies to many lives,' I said quietly.

"'But to mine more than to most. . . . Vicar . . .' she said, leaning forward and staring into my eyes. 'Sometimes I read reports of murder trials in newspapers, and in those books that are published about them—you know, serious books giving a word-for-word report of the trial and then the opinions of experts of various aspects of the murderer's character. And often one of the characteristics those murderers are described as having is 'no moral sense'. When a murderer is described in this way I have great sympathy for him. Because I too have no moral sense. . . .'

"'Nonsense,' I said, trying to speak lightly but in fact rather ill at ease, so serious was her tone. 'I would say that if you have any fault at all, it is over-generosity. . . .'

" 'Yes, Vicar, I have that too, but combined with no moral sense, it adds up to something dangerous. . . .'

"She paused, but before I could speak, she went on again.

" 'Vicar,' she said, 'I want to tell you the story of my life. I need moral advice. I've never told my life-story to anyone—always I've kept it bottled up and now it's beginning to destroy me. You see, I can't even tell it to my children, it concerns them too much. Let me tell you something. . . . Once, when I was a girl just starting out on her career—yes, I'll call it a career—I had a friend, an Irish girl just over from Ireland. She was very beautiful—you know, black hair and blue eyes and a lovely soft brogue—and she was religious, went to Church several times every Sunday, a Roman Catholic. But during the rest of the week she led a life of shocking immorality. One day I asked her how she could lead such a double life; she looked at me and laughed softly, that lovely deep laugh of hers. . . . 'Why, my love,' she said, 'once a week I go to confession—and everything is made fine. . . .' I envied that girl, Vicar. She had a conscience, and was able to put it at rest so easily. Ever since, I've wanted to confess, too. Will you act as my confessor?'

" 'I will listen to anything you have to say to me, and give what advice lies within my power. But I will not be able to ease your conscience merely by prescribing some simple penance, which seems to have been good enough for your Irish friend. . . .'

" 'As long as you give me advice, that's all I want. You won't just condemn me, and have nothing more to do with me?'

" 'Don't you know, Mrs. Robinson,' I said, again trying to speak lightly, 'that I am here to lead erring sheep back to the fold?'

" 'But suppose I don't want to go—that I'm too weak to change my ways—will you tell everyone what I tell you so that they'll keep away from me and not be contaminated by me? Isn't that what the Church does? Wouldn't it be your duty to stand up in the pulpit and denounce me to the congregation?'

"I stared at her, amazed by the agitation in her voice. No longer could I continue to speak lightly.

"'Mrs. Robinson,' I said quietly, 'if what you told me convinced me that you are such a danger to the community that your continued presence in it was liable to corrupt others, I would do what I could to restrain you, and if the only way I could do this was by letting my parishioners know of your crimes, then as a last resort I might do so. But I would take this step only in the direst need, and I would have to have either proof or your permission, otherwise you could sue me for libel. Also, I would like to impress upon you the fact that the Church is far more broad-minded than you probably realize. Secondly, I would remind you that during the last eighteen months I have had continual evidence of the good you have done our community, by your courage, your cheerfulness, your generosity. Such qualities as these I would set against any crimes you might have to confess, and if I found they outweighed them, I would consider myself justified in leaving you at large. God, Mrs. Robinson, has infinite wisdom. He puts into the world all kinds of people. He creates, for instance, women of strong sensuality and light morals—or at least He allows circumstances to breed such women—and so long as such natures are not combined with vicious instincts, such women have a place in the community. On the balance, they may do more good than harm, and I would certainly not take it upon myself to remove such a woman from among my parishioners, even if I had the power. . . .'

"And I looked steadily into her eyes, into those eyes in which always I had seen the simplicity which had caused me to trust this woman; and I saw it still, and at that moment something else too—a look of relief.

"'Vicar,' she almost whispered, 'in spite of your innocence, I believe you understand me. . . .'

"'Perhaps I do, Mrs. Robinson,' I said. 'Do you still want to "confess" to me?'

"'Perhaps it's not necessary now.'

"'It is up to you.'

" 'I no longer feel such a need to confess, but I still want advice.'

" 'And to obtain that advice you have to tell me your life story?'

" 'Yes.'

" 'Then tell it me.'

" 'There is not time today, Vicar. Besides, you came to have a word with Mildred, not to listen to me. I'll go and fetch the girl.' And almost hurriedly, as if not wanting to be pressed to tell her life-story, she left the room.

"Mildred came in alone a few moments later, and I had my talk with her, but we made no progress. She was surly and unresponsive. She looked at me with those inscrutable Eastern eyes and said nothing. I wondered whether I had in fact ever made progress with her—whether I had wrongly interpreted those talks we had had in her home when I had seemed to be gaining her trust. Had my mind at that moment been as free as it should have been, I feel little doubt I would have been sufficiently responsive to her mood to grasp the truth then; as it was I had only an uncomfortable feeling that somewhere in the depths of those mysterious eyes there was an appeal for help. But I allowed this suspicion to die before it became a definite thought, for that evening my mind was not wholly at the disposal of duty—it was restless and preoccupied, not sufficiently under my control. An element of distraction was entering into my absolute awareness of my vocation. . . .

"So I did not pursue this faint suspicion aroused in me by something in the girl's manner, and so missed a chance of saving her from . . . well, you know what. . . ."

Abruptly Mr. Ash ceased speaking. Involuntarily his wife put out her hand and touched his, but withdrew it quickly when he seemed almost to wince when she touched him.

"You don't—in any way—blame me for that?" she asked.

A faint smile appeared on his face, which touched his lips only.

"My mind is not quite so illogical as that," he said, "In spite of your being the direct cause of my preoccupation, no blame whatever

attaches to you. This I understand with my intellect, but not entirely with my emotions. It was just one of those unfortunate combinations of time and circumstance. I was human and therefore fallible. Had my mind been as free as it was before I met you, I might not have failed with the girl, that's all. But let me get on with my narrative, and please do not interrupt again."

She sat back in her chair.

"Go on," she said gently.

"It was nearly six before I was able even to consider leaving Mrs. Robinson's flat," he went on, "and then, as I rose to go, she offered me a glass of sherry. At first I refused, wanting to get away, but then something in her eyes made me change my mind. For there was an appeal in her eyes, one too strong for me to ignore. So I sat down again and accepted her sherry. She seated herself beside me on the sofa.

" 'Vicar,' she said, 'could you spare me some time, now?'

" 'Yes, Mrs. Robinson,' I said. 'Do you after all want to confess to me?'

" 'Yes—I feel as if I am in the mood to do so, and it is a mood which might never come to me again.'

" 'Is it altogether wise?' I asked. 'Afterwards we often regret succumbing to moods.'

" 'I won't regret it,' she said. 'It'll give me great relief and enable me to get a full night's sleep for the first time in weeks. . . .'

" 'Then go ahead,' I said. 'I promise to do my best to give advice that will be of use to you.'

" 'Thank you, Vicar,' she said. For a length of time that became almost embarrassing she stared in front of her, saying nothing. Then she said suddenly:

" 'I was born, before the beginning of this century, in a house— or perhaps I should call it a hovel—which stood where this block of flats is now standing. . . .'

"And she looked at me as if expecting some kind of dramatic reaction.

G

" 'Go on, Mrs. Robinson,' I said.

" 'Mrs. Robinson!' she repeated. 'I've been called that so long now that I almost believe it myself. . . .' And unexpectedly, her eyes filled with tears which at once overflowed and ran down her cheeks, and she made no attempt to dry them; she just sat staring at me with an expression of grief that was suddenly pathetic. I felt that to show sympathy at that moment would have perhaps precipitated an attack of hysterics, so all I did was to repeat, almost severely:

" 'Go on, Mrs. Robinson.'

"She quietened a little, the tears stopped flowing, and she leaned forwards towards me, but before she could go on speaking, we both heard the sound of a key in the lock of the front door. The effect on her was startling; a look almost of terror came into her eyes.

" 'Oh God. . . ,' she said.

"She stood up with a look of panic on her face, and then went quickly over to a mirror on the wall and started to dab at her cheeks with a handkerchief to remove the traces of tears; I could see from her shoulders that she was taking the long deep breaths of someone trying to suppress sobs. I heard the door open and looked round to see standing there, his raincoat hanging open, Peter; at once I looked back at Mrs. Robinson expecting to see relief in her eyes that it was only her son. But when she turned and looked at Peter there was in her face no relief, no surprise, only a strange wariness. I sensed at once that she had known, when she heard the key in the lock, that it was he, and that it was of him that she was afraid.

"It was then that I had what I feel even now might have been a form of hallucination, for it seemed to me that as I looked again at the son, that this young man, after glancing at his mother, looked at the indentation made in the settee by her body where she had been sitting close to me, and that onto his lips there came the trace of a sardonic smile.

"There was a moment of silence during which he stood staring at his mother, mockingly.

"At last Mrs. Robinson said:

" 'Hello, Peter, you're early. . . . Mr. Ash and I were just discussing the party. . . .'

"Slowly Peter turned and looked at me, inspecting me almost impertinently.

" 'Indeed,' he said coolly, and looked back at his mother.

" 'What's happened now?' he asked. 'Have you taken on a religious phase?'

" 'Don't be rude, Peter,' she said. 'Mr. Ash dropped in for a word to Mildred and has very kindly agreed to help with the arrangements for the party. . . ,' and she looked hard at me, as if asking me to be a party to her lie.

" 'Oh,' said Peter, as if suddenly disinterested. 'What are you drinking?' he asked. 'Oh God, sherry. Still got some of that stuff left?'

" 'The last dozen bottles,' she said quietly. 'Don't you remember, when war was declared, we put all those bottles away, and said we'd open them the day peace was declared?'

" 'No, I can't say I remember that particular incident. But it was a good idea. What else is there?'

" 'Besides the sherry, half a dozen port, half a dozen gin, three bottles of liqueur, and some sauternes.'

" 'No whisky?'

" 'No, Peter,'

" 'Pity, I drink nothing else. There's a place in Cambridge where it can be got under the counter.'

" 'How very manly of you, Peter, to drink nothing but whisky,' said his mother, with a touch of irony.

"A look of slight annoyance crossed Peter's eyes, but he quickly controlled it. He was still standing with his raincoat on just inside the door, as if he intended going out again. There was a moment of silence which I began to find embarrassing, and suddenly I decided to go, feeling that it might be partly my presence that was causing this tension between mother and son. I stood up, whereupon Peter said:

" 'Going, Vicar? Please don't do so on my account—I'm going

round to the local to have some of that whisky I can't get here. Stay and continue your discussion about the party.'

"And he looked over to his mother, again with a glint of irony in his eyes.

" 'No,' I said. 'It is time I went.'

"" 'Then I'll come with you. Perhaps you'll drop in and have a drink with me.'

" 'No thank you,' I replied. 'I am not in the habit of "dropping in" to the Carlton Arms.'

" 'Really, Vicar? I had heard that lately you had been carrying the pulpit to the public bar, and thought you might like the opportunity of doing a little more evangelism. I would like to witness it.'

" 'On the rare occasions when I carry the pulpit to the public bar, as you call it,' I replied, 'I prefer not to have disciples with me.'

" 'Oh, Vicar,' he said, 'how witty you are. I like very much the picture that conjures up—myself as disciple. But if you will not come in, I hope you won't refuse to allow me to walk a little way with you.'

" 'Of course not,' I said, rather surprised at his insistence.

"Without further word to his mother, he went out into the hall. I turned to her, holding out my hand.

" 'Goodbye, Mrs. Robinson,' I said. 'Perhaps we shall resume our discussion at a later date.'

" 'Yes, Vicar,' she said, 'I'll give you a ring.'

"But her hand in mine was oddly limp, and her face, now that Peter was out of the room, had lost all effort at self-control. She looked middle-aged and tired.

"I followed Peter out, and we hardly spoke until we were in the street. Then he said:

" 'Well, Vicar, have you too fallen for those lovely blue eyes of dear mama?'

" 'What do you mean?' I asked sharply.

" 'Oh, I've heard quite a lot about you, Vicar.'

" 'From what source, might I ask?'

" 'Oh, I'm around here more often than you think. Most week-ends, in fact. Unbeknownst to Mother, of course. And more interest is taken in your career than you probably realize. Do you know, Vicar, that your every move is watched with the greatest interest?'

" 'By whom?'

" 'Oh—certain rather nosy ladies. Or so one of them tells me.'

" 'Which one?'

" 'Norma Bartram. A lady, I regret to say, who does not love you. A bit of a bitch, actually, but in some ways most amusing. After all, it's a very feminine characteristic to be a bit of a bitch, and I find it rather attractive. You should get to know her better, you know. In fact I should advise it—for your own benefit. She has a very large vocabulary which she uses to all and sundry against anyone she doesn't like. She is excellent at damaging reputations—and there is always a grain of truth behind her slanders. It is quite fascinating to see her at work. Of course she served her apprenticeship with Mrs. Carrington-Smith, an excellent teacher, but she has now surpassed her mistress. For instance, Vicar, it would never have occurred to me how susceptible you are, but for Norma. It was she who pointed out to me how all your special converts—or would-be converts—are of the female sex. Dear Mama, for instance. And the mysterious Mildred—a not unattractive young girl, if you go in for extreme youth. And last but not least, my most beautiful future sister-in-law. . . .'

" 'You are talking not only nonsense, but offensive nonsense,' I said, really sharply this time.

" 'Oh—so that last barb went home, did it?' he asked. 'At last I have succeeded in moving you to anger, Vicar. Always I have wanted to do so. Don't think I blame you for falling for Katharine. I don't think I have ever seen so beautiful a woman. Not my type—too angelic. But just the type for you, I should have thought. I would be quite proud to have her for a sister-in-law—if I ever do. . . .'

" 'What do you mean—*if* you ever do?' I asked.

" 'Oh, I don't expect that marriage to come off. I hope for her sake that she soon sees through Bill. And then, if she has enough strength of character, she'll drop him like some kind of particularly poisonous snake. My heroic brother is an absolute egoist, and egoists are useless to women. They make very bad husbands. In fact I'm surprised he's gone as far as getting engaged, and frankly, if she doesn't break it off, I've little doubt he will before it comes to the point. . . . You see, he has been mixed up with girls before—and always very beautiful girls. He likes the limelight he gets by taking such women about with him—but he likes even more his personal freedom. So always he breaks with them. But as I say, he's never gone so far before as actually getting engaged. . . . So perhaps this time it will come off. But here we are at the pub, Vicar. Are you sure I can't tempt you to come inside?'

"Suddenly I changed my mind—I would go in with him, and continue this conversation. When I told him so, a look of both surprise and slight vexation crossed his face; but quickly he controlled it, and held open the door for me.

"Once inside, I realized immediately that I had made a mistake; for it would be impossible here to carry on any sort of conversation. For though it was still early—not an hour after opening-time—the place was already crowded. Of course all public-houses were crowded to capacity during those early weeks after the end of the war in Europe. I had only been in the public bar on two or three previous occasions, and never had I seen it so crowded. I was almost stifled by the smell of beer, tobacco, and human bodies. Everyone seemed to be shouting at once to make themselves heard. As Peter pushed his way through the crowd to the bar, I stood inconspicuously near a wall, with my mackintosh turned up to hide my clerical collar, not particularly wanting to be recognized as a member of the clergy. I wished I had not come but at the same time felt the odd excitement which always comes to me on the rare occasions I enter one of these places. I have never been able to explain this feeling, but it has something to do with anger at the spectacle of sentient human beings deliberately dulling their intellects—the most precious gift of God—in order to escape reality—and stimulation at the sight of so much vitality.

"I watched the milling crowd, the gesticulating arms, the flushed faces; I watched the skilful movements of the three barmaids as they weaved their way through the tables, coldly sober among this crowd of half-drunk, artificially merry men; as one of them came near me, I saw the damp patches of sweat beneath her arms and the perspiration standing in beads on her face; I caught too the calculating look in her eyes as she avoided the limbs of customers some of which seemed to be deliberately put in her way; as she leaned over a table to gather mugs I saw her press her bosom—deliberately? I wondered—against an American soldier, and her grin as the man put his arm round her and whispered something to her; I saw her take the pound note he carelessly offered her and go off to get change, and wondered whether the change would ever reach him. I saw the unusual number of young girls present, many of whom I was sure were under age; how they were giggling and holding glasses of gin-and-orange and sitting on the arms of chairs, almost on the laps of some of the men in uniform. There were men in uniform everywhere, officers and other ranks in mixed groups, Americans and British, Free French and Poles, airmen and A.T.S., shouting, singing and holding hands.

"Peter, as he pushed his way back to me precariously holding two glasses of whisky, looked conspicuous in his immaculate grey civilian suit. His thin lips were twisted into a slightly contemptuous grin as he elbowed his way through, as if pretending to himself that he despised these soldiers with girls on their arms, but probably secretly envying them. He reached me with most of the whisky still in the glasses, and putting his lips close to my ear, said with a note of satisfaction as he handed me my glass:

" 'From under the counter. Pretty good, don't you think, with all these heroes about? Evidence of the goodwill I've built up with Meg. . . .' And he indicated the barmaid behind the counter.

"For some moments we were silent, partly because of the difficulty of talking in such a noise, partly because he was himself looking round the room still with the contemptuous grin on his face. After a few moments he seized my arm and nodded across the room towards the bar.

" 'Did you ever see such a beauty?' he asked.

"I looked without much interest in the direction indicated, and for a moment failed to recognize the big blonde girl in a tight black skirt with a slit in one side almost up to her thigh, in the centre of a group of American N.C.O.s. Suddenly however she happened to glance our way and I recognized Ruby; an expression of astonishment came onto her face as she too recognized me, and to my dismay she at once abandoned her American friends and started to make her way over to us. The expression of surprise on her face was nothing to the look on Peter's when he realized I knew the girl.

" 'You know her?' he asked.

"I had to admit that I did.

" 'Well, well,' he said, 'being an evangelist seems to have its compensations. Another of your special converts, eh?'

"As she approached I saw the men in her path stare at her and wink at each other. She was indeed an arresting sight with her mass of artificially blonded hair, her slanting Malay eyes, her figure which her clothes did everything to accentuate, and her air of almost queenly self-possession—gone completely was her teen-age self-consciousness which I had known, no doubt due to the confidence given her by her stage success. And I do not mind admitting as she approached me across that crowded barroom, her white teeth flashing in a smile, with almost the entire room watching and wondering who it was she was showing such an interest in, that I had never in my life felt a greater desire to take to my heels and flee, not even on that road in Belgium when I had realized that the troops approaching me were German. . . . But having virtually no alternative, and thinking with a kind of metaphorical shrug of the shoulders that I would now indeed provide the parish with something to gossip about, I steeled myself to receive her.

"And I think I would have succeeded in greeting her with no show of unusual emotion—if she had let me. But she did not. No doubt aware of being the centre of the stage, with her sense of theatre having been developed in the last few months, she was determined to make an impression.

" 'Why, padré,' she said, "ow nice to see you—so unexpected.' and she took me by the arm and planted a kiss on my right cheek. Some of the licentious soldiery whistled.

" 'Hello, Ruby,' I said, a little weakly, doing my best to ward her off.

" 'Not Ruby, Mr. Ash,' she said. 'That's not my name no more. Lola Labelle, that's 'oo I am, of Sid Cohen's Musical Rep.'

"And I saw her, out of the corner of her eye, taking a hard look at Peter.

" 'An impressive name,' I said, recovering myself a little. 'I'm very pleased to have met you, Ruby. But we can't stay, unfortunately—we were just about to go. . . .'

" 'Oh, Mr. Ash,' she said, 'what a disappointment. Aren't you even going to introduce me to your friend?'

"And she gave Peter a kind of sidelong glance and a half-smile. This was the last thing I wanted to do, but really I had no alternative. And so it was that I tied the final string which brought about those events at Mrs. Robinson's party. I did not actually introduce Peter—he did it himself, forestalling me. But it was my presence which caused the two to meet.

" 'Let me introduce myself,' he said, doing his best to bow in that congested space. 'Peter Robinson—not nearly such an impressive name as yours, I fear.'

"But Ruby was determined to be introduced properly.

" ' 'Introduce me, padré,' she commanded.

"I made some kind of an introduction, upon which Ruby formally held out her hand which Peter took with equal formality.

" 'Pleased I'm sure,' said Ruby.

" 'Delighted,' said Peter.

"There then took place an oddly formal, disconnected conversation with Ruby on her best behaviour and speaking in most ladylike tones, and with Peter playing up to her but beneath whose mocking manner—quite lost on her—I could sense an interest I far from liked. However I could do nothing about it and my part in the conversation grew gradually less until, despairing of persuading Peter to come away with me, I took my leave alone, a departure hardly noticed by the other two.

"I could tell by the way Peter had quickly put Ruby at her ease that he was by no means unaccustomed to girls of her kind, and she was no doubt impressed by his immaculate appearance, and easy, confident manner. So I left them, and at the door turned to look back at them, and I saw them standing close together, delighted with each other's company, obviously not aware that I had left them. . . ."

Mr. Ash stopped speaking, and looked at his watch.

"*It is late,*" *he said a little wearily.* "*I have been talking for two hours.*"

"*I have been quite enthralled,*" *she said.*

He looked at her quickly, and then away again.

"*From now until the end is the most difficult part for me to get through,*" *he said.* "*It is difficult to describe one's own mental deterioration. But at least it was quick. So please do not interrupt me at all, whatever I say. I should finish in the next two days, before we go on to Venice. . . .*"

"*I am sorry I interrupted you when I did,*" *she said.* "*It was quite involuntary.*"

Still not looking at her, he said:

"*I admire enormously your patience. I can think of no one else who would not have been annoyed by my impatience a moment ago.*"

"*I am learning to understand you,*" *she said.*

He looked at her, and for a moment, for the second time in their relationship, she thought the barrier between them was about to fall.

But once more it was as if he withdrew into himself. He stood up, saying politely:

"Then if you go up, I will smoke my final cigarette."

And alone in their bedroom, she prayed that the barrier would really fall the next time this moment of contact was created between them.

The mornings of the remaining two days of their stay in Florence were spent in the galleries, but neither of them was much aware of the glories around them; even in the presence of Michelangelo's David they were only distracted from themselves for a brief moment.

In the afternoons and evenings, he went on with his story.

"After that visit to the Carlton Arms," he began on the first afternoon, "there began those few days between my visit to Mrs. Robinson and your appearance in Church. I spent the time restless and dissatisfied, telling myself I was not in the least pre-occupied with wondering whether you would in fact appear among my congregation on the following Sunday, but in my heart knowing that I thought of little else. There is no doubt that Peter's hint about the possibility of the marriage not taking place, had a considerable effect on me. Although at that time I did not consciously think of marriage with you or anyone else—I still looked upon myself as a dedicated celibate—I would catch myself out (in the middle of something that did not require all my concentration) visualizing myself in the future in your company . . . and when I realized what I was doing, I would take myself severely to task, accuse myself of daydreams unworthy of my vocation, and vow to discipline myself more strictly in future. Or I would try reasoning with myself and argue that if I were even contemplating marriage, you among all women were the least suitable, that you were worldly, irreligious, scheming, inconstant, and many other things. I told myself that all women were at heart like you, that even their love was an act of possession, that they wanted to possess a man heart and soul until he had nothing of himself left; I tried to tell myself that my temptations as far as you were concerned were only those of the flesh, and that this I could easily overcome. . . . I tried to see myself as being faced with a final test, the passing of which would at last see me face to face with God. . . . And for a few hours I would in fact forget you completely, only to find myself staring sightlessly out of a window or into the darkness of my bedroom at night, imagining myself in your company. It was a grim battle, but throughout those few days I was still optimistic, though to remain so I had to a certain extent to cheat; you see I was so convinced that time would show you as a scheming promiscuous female interested merely in adding my scalp to your collection. I did not even consider what I would do if it turned out that you were what my instinct already knew you to be, and what I was to find you out to be on the following Sunday; for this my conscious mind did not even consider as a possibility. . . .

"On a practical level, I spent those few days filling my time as much as possible with parochial duties. I found out without understanding why that I had passed through my phase of violent evangelism—that reckless mood that had enabled me to rise above myself and take the poorer quarters by storm; no doubt the psychologists would have an explanation for this, but I feel it was something to do with the fact that in those days as far as you were concerned, I had no hope—so my actions had been the recklessness of despair, activities outside my normal mode of behaviour. Now I had hope though I did not realize it—for the first time I was faced with the possibility that your marriage would not come off, and so my despair was incomplete.

"So I found myself going round, not the poorer quarters, but the homes of people acquainted with you, almost as if hoping to hear something about you. I went to Mrs. Robinson on the excuse of finding out more about this party she had so suddenly sprung on me; I went to the Kynastons, to Mrs. Carrington-Smith, even to the Bartrams—to the latter in a fit of temper that ended up more tamely than I had expected. And in visiting these people I learnt more about the growing prejudice against Mrs. Robinson than about you. The hints about her were stronger than ever, and now having reason to believe that these rumours were not entirely without foundation, I found myself less able to combat them wholeheartedly, and more inclined to listen. Anything was welcome as a distraction from my obsession with you —I was having my first taste of how selfish an obsession can make one.

"On my visit to the Kynastons, Mrs. Kynaston had looked at me with those bright little eyes of hers and said mischievously:

" 'I hear your study of female psychology has been advancing by leaps and bounds.'

" 'What do you mean?' I asked.

" 'You must admit, Vicar, that your record in the last few weeks has been pretty good. You have become the champion of a middle-aged lady of dangerous reputation; you've taken under your protection an exotic young creature of the East; and now you're trying to steal the affections of the fiancée of our local hero. . . .'

" 'I see that you too,' I had replied, more in sorrow than in anger, 'are a friend of Mrs. Bartram. . . .'

" 'Not a friend. I fear I am the friend of no one. My tongue does not allow that. But she amuses me, as nearly everyone amuses me.'

" 'And you listen to her?'

" 'Of course. I listen to everyone.'

" 'Then listen to me,' I said. 'There seems to be a campaign of idle gossip against me in certain quarters, and I take this opportunity to refute it. I am not, and never have been, interested in any woman more than is justified by my parochial duties. I am not as far as I know particularly susceptible, and am firmly resolved to remain celibate because I am convinced that in this condition I am more able to follow my vocation. It is the one aspect of Roman Catholicism that I agree with. If I do appear to have paid more attention to some of the female members of my congregation it is because I feel your sex to be more in need of salvation. . . .'

" 'What a pity, Vicar,' she replied, 'that you said that last

sentence so seriously. Said in lighter vein, it would have been
almost witty. . . .'

"I left her with hardly another word, aware of once more
having allowed her to cause me to lose my temper. It is
strange how easily that woman could do this, but on looking
back I realize it was because she only from among them all
really understood me, or at any rate a part of me . . . better than
I understood myself. . . .

"Anyhow I left her flat with my temper once and for all lost,
my mood not having been improved by the fact that she had not
been in the least ruffled by my loss of self-control but instead
had looked at me with keen interest as if I were providing her
with more material for her study of psychology, and she showed
me to the door with a show of imperturbable good manners
which to me seemed mocking. . . . I went straight from her to the
Bartrams where I was received by the young couple with some
surprise and the offer of a glass of sherry. I had intended accusing
her at once of being the source of the malicious gossip about
myself, but at the last moment, no doubt fortunately, something
prevented me. Perhaps it was the sight of this young couple
together at last—he had just been demobilized—and the realization that such an accusation would almost certainly involve me
in mentioning my conversation with Peter, and I did not want
to do this. I felt she would not want her husband to know of her
friendship with that young man, and being a realist in such
matters, now that these two were together for perhaps the first
time since their marriage, I wanted their union to have as much
chance as possible. To have caused the young husband on his
return from war to be suddenly faced with the possibility of a
slander action against his wife would hardly have helped a
marriage which I felt had not a strong chance of success anyhow. . . .

"So I left them after drinking a glass of their not very good
sherry, having contrived to give the impression that I had called
for the purpose of making the acquaintance of the husband—
who seemed able to talk of nothing but tanks and rugby

football—and as their flat was next door to Mrs. Carrington-Smith's, I next dropped in on that lady. Having failed to achieve my object with her young satellite I was determined to have it out with someone.

"As usual when we were alone together, she talked sensibly, and it needed some effort for me to introduce a jarring note into the conversation, which I did by informing her rather coldly that I was finding myself the victim of malicious gossip and that I was determined to find out who was at the back of it. She had stopped speaking abruptly and a wary look had come into her rather prominent eyes.

" 'How very distressing, Vicar,' she said. 'What kind of gossip?'

"I told her, and the expression of sympathetic surprise she now assumed looked completely genuine.

" 'You have heard nothing of it?' I asked.

" 'I?' she asked. 'Not a thing. It comes as a complete surprise to me.'

" 'Really?' I asked drily. 'That is strange for I have reason to believe that the main culprit is your friend Mrs. Bartram.'

" 'Norma? Impossible. She's a sweet child. So naïve. Not accustomed to our world at all, you know, but she's learning rapidly. I'll make a little lady of her yet. And she's not in the least bit vindictive.'

" 'Vindictive?' I asked. 'Has she cause to be vindictive?'

"For a moment she seemed to hesitate, then said, as if thinking better of it:

" 'None at all, as far as I know. It was only a figure of speech I was using. How sharp you are tonight, Vicar.'

"Suddenly I realized the futility of my accusations and my indignation left me as quickly as it had come. I realized that women such as Mrs. Bartram, Mrs. Kynaston, and the one now in front of me were skilled in the art of spreading rumour and creating gossip and that in their hands I was as helpless as a babe. I realized too late that in mentioning the subject at all I had been playing into their hands; that now they would feel that the rumours of their own creating had some foundation in truth, and that as soon as I had left her no doubt Mrs. Carrington-Smith would be round in Mrs. Bartram's flat discussing me avidly. I began to feel new sympathy for Mrs. Robinson—I was beginning to suffer in their hands as she had been suffering for months.

" 'Oh well, Mrs. Carrington-Smith,' I said, controlling myself with an effort, 'I expect this talk is harmless enough. As far as I know I have not been accused of any very dreadful crime. . . .'

" 'Of course not, Vicar,' she said; and then, after a pause, as I was about to leave, she added, with a glint of undisguised curiosity in her eyes:

" 'I hear you are helping Marjorie with her party.'

" 'She has asked my opinion on one or two points,' I replied, feeling a little uncomfortable and wondering how the bush-telegraph had functioned rapidly enough to put her in possession of this information so soon—only to realize at once that no doubt it had come to her from Peter via Mrs. Bartram.

" 'Is it to be a large party?' she asked.

" I gave her a rough idea of the numbers expected.

" 'Oh dear,' she said. 'We are all very fond of dear Marjorie but she is so inclined to overdo things. I do hope you will be a restraining influence. Vicar. She thinks so much of you. . . .'

"And she went on to enlarge on the vulgarities of Mrs. Robinson and hinted at the respect that lady had for me, and though never saying so, suggested that she had more than respect for me, and from this she went on to mention certain indiscretions 'dear Marjorie' had been guilty of in the past, and left me in no doubt as to what exactly her innuendoes really meant; at the same time she said nothing sufficiently definite for me to take her up, and I began almost to feel admiration for the way in which she seemed able to make words mean the exact reverse of their true sense. I left as soon as I could, feeling oddly apprehensive, as if I were surrounded on all sides by malicious gossiping women. . . .

"This feeling persisted throughout the few days which intervened before the following Sunday, yet I continued to seek the company of these people as if they were exercising some kind of hypnotic effect on me.

"Well, that Sunday morning came, and as I prepared for Church I did my best to banish from my mind all thought extraneous to the Service ahead, and was pleased to find that as usual I had no difficulty in this, though on looking back I realize that the fact of it even having occurred to me that I might on this morning have exceptional difficulty proves that my mind was not entirely in the service of God.

"However by the time I came to walk up the aisle between the two blocs of the congregation—it was an unusually large one on that morning—I was as always conscious of nothing beyond the fact that I was in the house of God and the centre of a communal act of devotion. For every Service is a separate artistic entity designed to create in the congregation an awareness of a certain aspect of God, and if the priest in charge is not himself in a mood of absolute devotion, then the Service is a failure. Everything, from the first note of the organ, through the reading of the text, the chanting of the psalm, the delivery of the sermon—which is as it were the intellectual content of the Service—to the last note of the final hymn, should be a harmony of sound and thought tending to increase the absorption in God. And if the priest, the conductor of the Service, allows thoughts unconnected with it to enter his head, this is at once apparent to the congregation in the form of a relaxation of tension. It is the moment at which children begin to fidget and adults to cough.

"So always when possible I prepare myself mentally for an hour or so before each Service and enter the Church with my mind at one with God as much as it is possible for me to make it. And this occasion was no exception. As you know, as I walked up the aisle I passed within a foot of you, yet I did not see you. During those moments God had cast out from within me my great obsession. And I continued in this mood through-out the psalms and devotions, and the reading from the Bible, until I climbed the few steps to the pulpit before delivering my sermon. Now it is at this moment only that I am in the habit of allowing my eye to wander over those present, not in a spirit of idle curiosity as to who has turned up, but in an effort to draw more closely to myself the attention of the congregation.

"It was then that, my glance wandering over the ranks in front of me, seeing no individual but only a mass of upturned faces, I became aware of you. It was seconds before I realized your identity, in spite of having thought of little else but you in the past few days, but thought to myself merely how spiritual is that woman's expression, how wholly she is entering into the spirit of this Service; then suddenly a shattering awareness of who it was broke in upon me, and my immediate reaction was one of hatred for you. This woman, with her wiles and artifice, I said to myself, has succeeded even in breaking my contact with God—and it seemed to me that at once the grip in which I had until then held these people, suddenly relaxed, that they had become aware of something unconnected with the Service entering my mind. I had to take a strong hold on my senses to deliver my sermon at all, and had even to look at my notes which I take with me through habit rather than because of any need I ever have to consult them. . . .

"I managed somehow to get through the rest of the Service, trying to force my mind to resist all thought but my devotion to God, and only partially succeeding. I did not again look at you. So it was not until I made my way round to the front of the Church for a word or two with those members of the congregation who make it their habit to linger behind after Service to speak to me, that I gave you any direct thought. Then I wondered whether you would be among those waiting, but almost at once dismissed the thought, telling myself that no doubt your vanity had expected some special glance of recognition from me during the Service, and not having received it, that you would have gone off in a huff. So it was without really expecting to see you that I reached the front of the Church and saw the usual little group of people waiting for me, and even though I saw the solitary figure of a young woman standing some distance apart from them, I did not look directly at her, and so was not absolutely sure it was you.

"Instead, as I did every Sunday, I greeted those waiting for me, consisting without exception of dear old ladies who formed the nucleus of my knitting-group, of my Mothers' Union —though most of them had been mothers so long ago that they had almost forgotten the fact—and of my Sunday School teachers, and each of whom was inclined to regard me as her own particular property and none of whom I dared offend because I had no doubt that their tongues, though usually in the service of God, were capable of becoming as vitriolic as Mrs. Carrington-Smith's, if ever I gave cause for offence. Though I held all these ladies in great respect, they were inclined to waste my time in a way I found very trying, vying as they did with each other to capture my attention, seeming to regard it as an especial triumph to be the last to speak to me and so be the one who accompanied me down the path to the street. And this time they seemed especially inclined to linger, perhaps because they were as conscious as I of the young woman waiting patiently a few paces away. In fact finally I was forced in desperation to abandon the odd reticence which prevented me from looking at you; I looked straight at you as if suddenly aware of your presence and replied in kind to the faint smile you gave me, which caused the last two old ladies who had seemed determined to outstay each other and probably you too, to finally take leave of me—in each other's company, no doubt for the purpose of discussing you as the next best thing to meeting you. In fact, out of the corner of my eye, as I walked towards you, I saw them making slow progress to the gate, looking over their shoulders at you every few paces.

"So at last I was forced to approach you; exactly which of us was the first to speak when finally I came up to you, I do not remember. . . ."

"It was I who spoke," she murmured. "When you reached me you looked slightly angry, and I thought you didn't want to speak to me, that perhaps I had driven away some important parishioners with whom you had been discussing some serious business. In fact I had very nearly fled long before you finished with the old ladies. So there was an awkward silence during which you eventually held out your hand, which I took awkwardly, and we solemnly shook hands. I felt slightly scared, especially after having heard your sermon by which I had been greatly impressed. You seemed to me to be so many worlds above me, scarcely human, a being more than human. I remember a strange irrelevant thought came into my head: 'Here,' I said to myself, 'is a man of God who will one day be Archbishop of Canterbury.' And I looked at you in awe. But at last I mustered my courage and said, in a voice which I was sure was trembling with nervousness, 'Well, Mr. Ash, I have attended your Service as I promised. Did you expect me?'—or words to that effect. . . ."

"Yes, I remember now,' he said. "And it's true that in a sense I did not want to speak to you. I was far more afraid of you than you were of me. Your appearance was so different from what I had expected."

"How—different?"

"Well, I hadn't really given thought to how you would dress for Church, but I had expected some incongruity—some failure of taste, some vulgarity—which would provide me with a weapon with which to protect myself against you. Had you provided me with something of the kind I would not have fallen so easily under your spell again. But your appearance was so exactly in accordance with how I liked a young woman to dress for the purpose of entering the house of God, that the wind was taken out of my sails. The sober two-piece linen suit, the almost total lack of make-up, the discreet hat which entirely hid your hair, and your whole subdued, almost grave manner—was the exact antithesis of the sexually obtrusive young woman of Mrs. Carrington-Smith's dinner-party. I tried to whip up a feeling of antagonism towards you by telling myself that a woman so adept at playing many parts must be artful indeed. . . . But by then another feeling, until that moment suppressed, began to assert itself—the instinct that wanted to like you, that wanted to approve of and admire you . . . and under the influence of your presence it began quickly to take command. . . ."

"So that," she murmued, "was why your manner was so strange during those first moments. I sensed I had had some kind of effect on you, but was by no means sure it was one flattering to myself. You see, I did not think you capable of being affected deeply by a woman—I thought you way up in the clouds above such influences. And I thought always that you were judging me —calmly and sternly, that to your eyes my soul was exposed, naked and faulty. But at that moment I sensed an uncertainty in you, and I suppose it was then that I began to feel hope—hope that I could be of use to you. Until then I hadn't considered you as a man at all—only as a remarkable being far above me in whose work I might be able to assist in a very small way. I had come to your Service without the slightest idea of interesting you in me— I hadn't considered this even as a possibility. But suddenly, in those few moments after we shook hands, I realized you were approachable as a man. . . ."

"Yes," he said. "I suppose it was in those moments that my resistance to you was broken down. Of course I didn't admit this to myself then—that did not come until after we had visited old Kennedy—but from that moment onwards I was fighting a losing battle without being aware of it. Had I been capable of a sufficiently objective view of the situation I would have known then that the entire way of life I had planned for myself over the whole course of my adult life had been thrown overboard in a matter of minutes, because of a hint in a woman's manner that she was interested in me . . . a change in my life to which I have yet to reconcile myself. . . .

"But let me give you my version of the rest of that morning. Like the slow removing of a film from before my eyes, your true nature was revealed to me. The whole time I was on the watch for some insincerity in your manner, some artificiality which would allow me to wriggle out of the spell under which I was falling. But I could find no sign of it. There was no suggestion

of coquetry in your manner, no hint that you were aware of
me as a man, only a sober interest in my work. As I walked
with you through the streets to the vicarage—you remember I
had to collect some articles before we went on our round of
the old people—I was aware of a certain embarrassment at being
seen with so attractive a woman, a sensation I had never had on
doing the same round with other of my voluntary helpers—
generally ladies hardly younger than those we were visiting, or
so plain that there was no risk of their exciting rumour.

"I remember the stare of Mrs. Taylor when she opened the
door to us—I did not realize then that she was well up in the
rumours concerning me—and the way she fussed round you
almost as if you were already the vicar's wife. I remember feeling
illogically glad that she liked you; and the way you started
chatting to her with such ease surprised me—I had for some reason
expected you to be stiff and formal with someone in her station
of life. But when I came back into the study and found you in
possession of all Mrs. Taylor's worries, prejudices, and con-
victions—which it had taken me six months to elicit—it occurred
to me for the first time that there was a place for a wife in the
life of a vicarage. . . .

"And as we did the round of the old people I found the same
kind of thing happening; some of the old dears whom I had had
the greatest difficulty in handling, and with whom my female
helpers had had no more success, seemed, after the first few
moments of suspicion, to become almost tractable in your
hands; and the way in which, in one or two cases where it was
necessary, you set about tending to their physical ailments made
me ashamed of my own natural revulsion from such tasks.
Slowly, as we went from one house to another, up and down
those grimy stairs and through those dirty streets, you told me
something about your early training as a nurse and I realized
that with you nursing had not been merely a war-time expedient
but something of a vocation. And there was more to it than
efficient training; I began to sense in your handling of these
people a depth of sympathy superior to my own; mine was on an

intellectual plane—something theoretical—whilst yours was on a physical plane, practical, something that shared with them their age and their sufferings. This was an attitude I knew I could never achieve, and was the reason why I had never really succeeded with these people. I began to realize that a woman such as you could bring to my work as a parish priest something I lacked, and there were opened before me new vistas of meaning in the relationship of man to woman. It could mean more than a mere coming together of the sexes for the purpose of reproduction and then a more or less harmonious remaining together for the purpose of bringing up their issue. This was what I had always thought of marriage as—a kind of necessary evil tolerated rather than blessed by the Church, and from which I, as a member of the Church with higher aims in life, was mercifully exempted. Now I realized that marriage could be more of a fulfilment of two people in each other. . . . But still in my mind there was a sneaking doubt concerning you—a doubt which, when we parted later in the morning, became dominant—a doubt springing from fundamental distrust of women which was a part of my nature. You see, the uncle who had brought me up and for whom I had always had a respect amounting almost to reverence, had been a woman-hater; a man—though I did not realize it then—unnaturally sexed, who would never have a woman near his house, even in the capacity of a servant. Not that I believe he ever gave in to his instincts—he was too good a Christian for that. But it warped his nature—this I have never told anyone else. So I still thought that possibly you were merely a very good actress intent on amusing yourself with me. And that was the main reason why I took you to see old Kennedy.

"I looked upon it as a kind of test for you. I thought that if you were able to enter his room and approach his bed and even to touch him, without giving some hasty excuse for leaving, that you could not be putting on an act. So it was that, rather unfairly, I gave you no hint of what to expect beyond suggesting he was one of my most difficult cases. When I opened the door and the usual overpowering stench greeted me, and I saw across

the room his great head lying on his pillow, I watched your
face closely, expecting you to turn pale or at least to look dis-
gusted; but I saw on your face only the pain caused by compassion; and as you walked slowly across the room towards the bed,
I looked at his face—or rather at the eyes, which, because of the
grime and beard which covered his face, was his only feature
capable of expression. I knew those fierce blue eyes so well—
eyes which on all the occasions on which I had taken one of my
voluntary helpers to see him, had blazed with anger. For always
from their manner he had sensed their revulsion. But this time
I saw no anger and for a moment wondered whether he was at
last so far gone that he had failed to realize there was a stranger
present. For it had never even occurred to me that you might
have an effect on him—I thought only that he would have an
effect on you. But his eyes were as bright and as intelligent as ever
and had in them a look more of wonder than of any other expression as he watched you approach—I have thought since that
he had just awoken from a pleasant dream to find you approaching, which accounted partly for the way we achieved our success with him that morning. Your face as you crossed the room
I could not see because your back was to me. I felt excitement as
if knowing something exceptional was about to happen, and
quickly crossed the room so that I could see both your faces.
You stopped close to the bed, and said quietly;   ,

" 'Hello, Mr. Kennedy. How do you feel today?'

"He said nothing, continuing to stare at you warily. Then
you leant over the bed and touched his hand—that hand that had
not been in water for months. I saw then a transformation in his
face—the wary, wondering look changed to one almost of
reverence.

" 'You have come from Him?' he asked, in the fine, deep voice
and cultured accents which had so startled me when I first heard
them.

"I knew what he meant and prayed that you too would grasp
something of his meaning, and it was in this moment that I
wished I had told you something about him, for I knew that if

you now showed indecision, or even surprise, that those blue eyes would at once flash with anger.

"But all you said was 'yes', continuing to look into his eyes with your hand on his.

" 'You know who I am?' he asked.

" 'Yes,' you replied without a hint of doubt in your voice.

" 'You are the Archangel Gabriel?' he asked then, and I saw a look of cunning in his eyes, and thought with despair that now you would fall into whatever trap he had laid for you. But you said calmly:

" 'No—I am mortal. I merely received the call to visit you.'

"At once a look of gratification came into his eyes.

" 'If you'd said you were Gabriel,' he said, 'I'd have known you were lying, because Gabriel was male, and you are female.'

"He continued for some moments to stare at you silently, and now there was a look of trust in his eyes.

" 'I knew Gabriel,' he went on suddenly. "In the days before I was cast down from the heavens with Beelzebub and the rest. He was a fine fellow, a great friend of mine.'

" 'You must have ranked high in the conclave of angels,' you said.

" 'I did indeed. Only He and Beelzebub were higher. But I fell out with Him, and then, after crossing the Stygian waters, I fell out with Beelzebub. So I was sent here to Earth as a place not so bad as Hell, where Beelzebub was sent, and not as good as Paradise, where He remained. And here ever since I have been expiating my great sin. On Earth only *he* knows this,' he said, suddenly pointing at me, 'but he can tell me nothing. He is very low ranking in the Servants of Him. He can tell me nothing of what they now think of me up there; perhaps . . . '—and here that look almost of fear came into his eyes—'perhaps you have a message for me?'

" 'Yes,' you said.

" 'What message?'

" 'I have come,' you said steadily, 'to warn you to prepare yourself.'

" 'To prepare myself for a return to Paradise?'

" 'Yes,' you replied.

" 'When will the call come?'

" 'I do not know,' you replied. 'It may be in a few weeks, or a few months, or even a few years.'

" 'Let it be soon.'

"It was then, you will remember, that I joined in the conversation.

" 'But not too soon,' I said.

"He turned his fierce blue eyes on me, and now there was no trust in them, only suspicion.

" 'How dare you break in upon the conversation of immortals?' he asked. 'What do you know about it?'

"You will no doubt remember how I spoke to him as if I were dealing with a man of exceptional intelligence, trying to give you a lead as to how to treat him.

" 'My contact with the Almighty may be slight,' I said, 'but I have been trusted sufficiently to have been allowed a consultation with my companion before coming to you. You will remember that it was I who brought her.'

"Slowly he turned his eyes back to you, interrogatively, and it was only when you nodded that he looked back at me.

" 'Then proceed,' he said with dignity. 'You may say what you have to say.'

" 'My companion has been instructed,' I said, 'to tell you to cease forthwith your expiations. You are now to rise from your bed and cleanse yourself in preparation for your entry into Paradise, so that for you it will be no longer Paradise Lost, but Paradise Regained.'

"I added this last in order to make quite sure that you realized from which book he drew his particular fantasy, and I prayed that you too had read Milton.

"Once more he looked at you.

" 'Is this true?' he asked.

"Again you nodded.

"The look of cunning came back onto his face, to me a well-known warning.

" 'But I do not take my mortal body with me to Paradise,' he said. 'So why then should I cleanse myself?'

" 'Because——' I began, but peremptorily he cut me off.

" 'No,' he said, 'I will hear it from the emissary of the Almighty herself. Why should you speak for her? You—a mere mortal!'

" 'I too am mortal,' you said quietly.

" 'I am not so sure,' he said. 'There is a kind of beauty that shines from you that is not mortal. I who have mixed with the greatest know more about these things than you. I think that possibly you are not mortal at all, but have not been allowed to realize the fact. However, proceed. Tell me why I am to cleanse myself.'

" 'You must cleanse yourself,' you said clearly and firmly, 'so as to put in order your affairs on Earth. Since you began to make reparation for your fall from Paradise, you have been a sore burden to us mortals. Now you have sufficiently mortified your flesh, and during the short time that remains to you here on Earth, you must make yourself less of a burden to your hosts. It is also a test to see whether your pride has yet been humbled.'

"This last point seemed to go home, for he looked at you with respect in his eyes.

" 'These,' he said after a moment, 'are hard terms. But He is a hard man, and it does not surprise me. It was such arrogance as this which caused us to leave Paradise. I am not sure that I shall accept them. I have disobeyed Him once and can do so again.'

" 'Then your return to Paradise will be indefinitely delayed.'

" 'I have been here on Earth for close on two thousand years and can remain a few centuries longer.'

" 'You may have to remain for ever.'

" 'For ever?'

"He looked at us uneasily, and seemed to consider, his great head sunk onto his chest. For some moments he was silent; then slowly he raised his head again.

" 'I will consider the terms,' he said. 'Go—and return after two nights and one day. Then I will have ready my reply.'

"And with that grand gesture of dismissal, a relic of the days when he was a Shakespearean actor, he waved us away.

"In the street, I noticed for the first time that you were looking a little pale.

" 'Are you all right?' I asked.

" 'Yes,' you replied. 'But it was a bit of a strain. I was trying so hard to remember my *Paradise Lost*. And that atmosphere—I could hardly breathe. Is a window ever opened— is his room ever cleaned?'

"I then told you what I knew about him—how I had only rumours and his delirious mutterings to go on, how I had built up from this what little I knew about him, how sometimes he seemed to wander in his mind, as on this morning, and how at other times he was practically sane; how it was from his delirious moments I had formed the opinion that he had at one time been a Shakespearean actor with what had seemed to be a real love, almost an obsession, with great literature, especially Milton; how some said it had been the raids that had finally sent him off his head, which seemed to be likely enough, for it had only been during the last two months, since the flying-bomb raids, that he had succumbed so completely to this Miltonic fantasy, believing he had to expiate his act of rebellion which had caused him to be ejected from Paradise with Beelzebub and the rest, an expiation which took the form of keeping to his bed and eating only what was brought to him; and he told me once that the flying-bombs were sent by the Almighty specially to punish him, but that so far he had dodged them. Before this stage he had occasionally gone out, and come back with money, obtained, I have been told, by declaiming Shakespeare to theatre queues. I believe he still has hidden in his mattress quite a quantity of silver and copper. I found him on the verge of starvation, because none of his neighbours had raised a finger for him. I believe I told you how, strive though I did, I could not get him to touch soap or water. He would however accept food from me, only bread and milk, believing that I was some very low-grade messenger from the Almighty, sent to show that there was still hope that he might one day be re-admitted to Paradise. It was the remarkable way in which you grasped the situation and inspired trust in him, that gave me the idea of a way to get him to wash himself, for uncleanliness was beginning to endanger his health. At the back of my mind I had intended leading up to suggesting, even in that interview, that he should allow himself to be removed to some home where he would receive medical attention. But our peremptory dismissal made this impossible. . . .

"So it was," concluded Mr. Ash on that afternoon, "that old Kennedy made it necessary for us to meet almost every day during the coming week to work out some means of saving his life, his grasp upon which I knew was weakening. . . ."

During the evening, a few hours later, Mr. Ash went on with his story.

"I need not go into details concerning that week," he said, "possibly it is clearer to you than to me, for I can remember little about it beyond atmosphere; I recall that you came each afternoon to the vicarage where in the study over a cup of coffee served by a delighted Mrs. Taylor, we discussed our approach to old Kennedy, according to how the previous day's visit had gone; I remember how we gradually gained his confidence until on the Thursday he agreed to start the cleansing process, and how, on our taking up to him a bowl of warm water, soap, and towel, he once more peremptorily dismissed us, insisting on looking after himself unassisted, to at any rate my great relief. . . . Then, an hour or so later, after we had parted, I went back alone in spite of his strict instructions not to return until the next day. I found him sleeping, and satisfied that no ill had befallen him I left him, removing the bowl of water and towel, which I saw had been used, though I had been able to detect no lessening of the grime on his face.

"Then there came the Friday—the day before Mrs. Robinson's party—when as usual we met in the vicarage and I told you how I had returned to the old man and found him sleeping peacefully . . . how then, more optimistically than ever, we once more climbed those stairs to his room intending if possible to broach the subject of getting him into a home . . . little did I think that this was the last time we were to do this together and the last time but one that I would see you for many months to come. . . .

"At first when we entered his room I did not see him and was merely rather surprised at finding him no longer in bed; it was only when I felt the grasp of your hand on my arm—the first time you ever touched me—that I saw him there on the floor, as I followed the direction of your eyes. Even then it was you who acted first, going down on your knees beside him, unbuttoning that shirt grey with dirt, and with a nurse's efficiency feeling for the beating of his heart. Then you looked up at me and shook your head.

" 'He is dead,' you said.

"We stayed there long enough only to lift the body onto the bed—you remember how light he was though he had always seemed such a large man?—cover it with a sheet, and open the window. We then locked the door in silence and went down to the street.

" 'So we failed,' I said, to which you did not reply, only nodding.

" 'Perhaps we shouldn't have allowed him to get out of bed,' I said after a moment.

" 'It may have accelerated the end,' you replied, 'but the heart must have been weak. . . .'

"And as far as I remember we said hardly anything else until just before we parted. Then it was you who said:

" 'I suppose I shall see you at Mrs. Robinson's tomorrow. I more or less have to go.'

"I could see you did not want to go, and certainly I didn't. But I said:

" 'I shall probably look in. I promised to. . . .'

"And on that we parted, I to inform the proper quarters of old Kennedy's death, an office of a kind I had had to fulfil more than once among the old people of the parish during my eighteen months there.

"I have no doubt that but for your remark on parting, I would not have gone to that party; and had I not done so, I wonder what difference it would have made to our lives?

"Early in the evening of the day Mrs. Robinson rang me up in a state of considerable agitation and asked me to go round as soon as I could. Apparently Peter who was to be in charge of the bar had not been in since the day before and as far as I could gather she wanted some male presence to give her moral support. And if I required any further evidence as to the deterioration in the poor woman's nerves, here it was; this was a very different Mrs. Robinson from the calm self-possessed woman of the war years who had been able to quietly put Mrs. Carrington-Smith in her place by offhandedly correcting her about some Paris fashion-house or hairdresser in the South of France. Now she seemed frightened of the other woman, and on the few occasions I had seen them together in the last few weeks she had been cowed, almost as if the other had some hold on her. Previously she would have laughed at the idea of wanting Peter to help her run a party; now she seemed almost to regret having taken it on.

"So it was that I went round to her half an hour before the party was due to begin. Mildred opened the door to me and showed me into the drawing-room where her mistress was. As soon as the girl had gone Mrs. Robinson turned to me with a look almost of fear in her eyes.

" 'That girl. . . ,' she said. 'She terrifies me.'

" 'Why?' I asked.

" 'She stares at me in such a peculiar way. And there is no heart in her—whatever I do I can't get a word of gratitude out of her or a sparkle into those expressionless eyes. . . .'

" 'She hasn't been brought up to respond to affection,' I said.

" 'Even so, she should show some human feeling. . . ,' she replied, and gave a slight shudder, and quickly changed the subject, at once talking about Peter's absence. As she did so I looked at her curiously, amazed at the change in her. She was dressed ready for the party wearing the gown she had had made specially for the occasion. No doubt your memory of that creation is more exact than mine, and I would certainly not be able to describe it now if I were asked; I remember only that it was mauve in colour——"

"Lilac," interrupted Katharine.

"Lilac then. And for some reason it looked terrible on her. This I could not understand because on examining it in detail I remember I found nothing very different from the usual kind of things she wore. The reason for this is now obvious to me— simply that the personality that normally made it possible for her to carry off clothes even outrageous in their vulgarity had now deserted her, and she looked merely a worried woman past middle age trying to look twenty years younger than she was. Even her make-up was more crudely applied; she had too a florid look about her which I had never noticed before and which caused me suddenly to wonder whether she suffered from heart trouble. But her eyes—those mirrors of the soul—were what I noticed most; they were the eyes of an elderly woman who could no longer sleep and from which all humour had fled—that sense of humour which had always been one of her most attractive features had completely gone, and I realized she was on the brink of a nervous breakdown. Her looks filled me with dismay and caused me to have almost clairvoyant powers, because at once I was able to visualize the torment she was about to undergo in the hands of Mrs. Carrington-Smith and her cronies, all of whom, rather quixotically, she had invited to the party. I could almost see in advance the scrutiny she was to be subjected to, the whispered comments behind her back, the criticism of her looks, the loudness of her furnishings, even the hospitality that had been accepted and which was being enjoyed.

"So when she confided in me her fears about Peter, I was sympathetically disposed to listen, and fears which on any other occasion I would have dismissed impatiently, I saw through her eyes. I sensed that the absense of Peter was a far more serious matter than the inconvenience of not having a barman, being in some way connected with the whole business of the persecution she was being subjected to, as if the attitude of her sons to her was one of the weapons her enemies were wielding against her. I remembered at once various hints made by women of the district about the attitude of both her sons to her, and in particular the quarrel which was supposed for years to have estranged her from Bill—it never occurred to anyone that the fault might have been on Bill's side, because he was the hero of the moment— and what I had myself observed between Peter and her. I felt suddenly a violently protective instinct towards her and so when she asked me to do what I could to find Peter I determined to fulfil this impossible task to the best of my ability. But even so it was more in order to ease her nerves by giving the impression of doing something that I set out from her flat to look for the boy, and it was an absolute shot in the dark that caused me to go straight to the Carlton Arms, which, because of the familiarity he had shown with some of the barmaids there on the night he had met Ruby—or Lola Labelle as I suppose I had better call her from now on—was the one place I knew he frequented in the district.

"When I entered, the public bar was quiet, it being only just past opening-time, and I thought at first it was empty. Then from an alcove near the bar I heard voices, one of which I thought was Peter's, the other I knew to be Lola's. I walked quietly up to the bar from where I could see them sitting with their backs to me, very close together. There was no one behind the bar at that moment, and I don't hesitate to tell you that I made no effort to make myself heard. I just stood there listening. There are certain moments in life when to spy on others is permissible. I heard Lola say:

" 'And what experience of women 'ave you 'ad, may I ask?'

" 'You'd be surprised,' replied Peter and there was unusual feeling behind his voice, normally so ironical.

" 'I would too . . .,' she replied sarcastically.

H

" 'What do you mean?' he asked in a low voice.

" 'Come off it, boy. You ain't 'ardly grown up. . . .' And she added something I was unable to hear. I saw Peter's thin, muscular hand grasp the fleshy part of her leg above the knee.

" 'Do you really believe that?' he asked.

" 'Well. . . ,' she said, her face very close to his. 'Maybe I don't . . . maybe I do . . . it all depends. . . .'

" 'On what?'

" 'Well—you know what they say—those as talks big often don't act according to their words. . . .'

"He leaned closer to her and whispered something.

" 'Well!' she said. 'Ambitious, aren't you?'

"At this point my attention was distracted by a barman who asked me for my order. As I gave it I was aware of a silence behind me and had no doubt my presence had been realized; having paid for my drink I turned round again and saw they were not sitting so close together.

" 'Good evening,' I said. 'May I join you?'

"Neither looked round at me. But Peter said to Lola:

" 'May the gentleman join us?'

"Lola shrugged her shoulders.

" 'It's all the same to me,' she said, not very graciously. At this Peter looked over his shoulder at me and said:

" 'My lady friend says she would be delighted by your company, sir.'

" 'An invitation so charmingly made cannot be resisted,' I replied, and sat down at their table, facing them. I looked from one to the other, smiling. Peter stared back at me insolently, whilst Lola looked down at the table in a manner I can only describe as sulky.

" 'Well, Vicar,' said Peter after a moment, 'to what do we owe the pleasure of your company? Are you here on one of your pulpit-to-the-public-bar visits, or were you by chance sent by dear Mama?'

" 'Your ma?' asked Lola, looking up suddenly. 'Does 'e know your ma?'

" 'Of course he does, Lola. They are friends of old standing. At least eighteen months' standing. Quite intimate friends. Eh, Vicar?'

" 'Yes, indeed,' I said mildly. 'I've known Mrs. Robinson longer than I've known you, Lola. As a matter of fact,' I said, turning to Peter, 'I have just come from her, and she did ask me, if I happened to meet you, to remind you of your promise to perform certain duties at her party tonight.'

" 'I thought as much,' said Peter. 'She's got you very well trained, hasn't she, Vicar? Extraordinary how she still has the power to make some men run round her in little circles. They have to be rather innocent men though, these days.'

" 'I wasn't aware of running round your mother in little circles,' I replied, still mildly. 'I've known her as you say for eighteen months now and I've had experience of her behaviour during some of the worst blitzes on London, and developed a considerable admiration for her. Her calm and humorous acceptance of certain situations prevented many a panic in an air-raid shelter.'

" 'Oh, she has guts all right,' said Peter, and I could see a certain unwilling admiration in his eyes. 'A quality inherited by my heroic brother, and which I sadly lack.'

" 'I remember a certain air-raid in which you can hardly be said to have panicked,' I said quietly.

" 'Oh that,' said Peter. 'I was only trying to show off in front of our allies, the Poles. In fact, I was scared stiff.'

" 'Without fear there can be no courage,' I said.

" 'Stop moralizing, Vicar. I know it's your trade, but for heaven's sake spare us in a public bar. Have another drink?' he asked, standing up. I realized suddenly that already he was half-tight, though where he had got the drink from at such an hour I could not imagine.

" 'No thanks,' I said. 'I'm going in a moment.'

" 'Same again, Lola?' he asked.

" 'Don't mind if I do,'' said Lola, giving him her glass.

"Whilst Peter was at the bar, she said to me:

" 'What's 'is ma like?'

" 'You should ask Mildred that,' I said.

" 'Millie? Why?'

" 'Don't you know she's employed by Mrs. Robinson?'

" 'By 'is ma?'

" 'Yes, Lola.'

" 'Blimey.'

" 'Did you really not know that?'

" 'No. Why should I? I ain't 'ardly ever at 'ome now. I live in digs. I knew Millie was workin'—but not 'oo for. And she never told me.'

" 'I don't suppose she has the slightest idea you know Peter.'

" 'No—I s'pose not. She never tells anyone anything, any'ow.'

"At this moment Peter rejoined us.

" 'Lola has just made the discovery,' I said, 'that her sister works for your mother.'

" 'Her sister?' asked Peter.

" 'Mildred is Lola's sister.'

"For a moment he stared at me.

" 'Good God,' he said.

"He looked slowly round at Lola, and I could see him scanning her face.

" 'So that's where you get those remarkable eyes from,' he said quietly. 'I suppose your mother's coloured?'

" 'What of it?' asked Lola truculently.

" 'Nothing,' said Peter lightly. 'If anything it adds to the interest you have for me. I should of course have realized it before. But in you the two races have combined remarkably well—unlike in little Mildred where they are uneasy partners. . . well, well. . . .' He put his head back and tossed off his drink— a double whisky—in one gulp. 'This calls for another drink. I've never met a Creole before.'

" 'A what?' asked Lola.

" 'A word used to describe a person of mixed race.'

"Lola looked quickly from one to the other of us.

" 'It ain't a crime to 'ave a coloured mother,' she said.

" 'A crime? Good heavens, no.' said Peter. 'It is only our un-
enlightened society that discriminates in such matters. And with
the skill you have employed in disguising the fact—at any rate
as far as the hair is concerned—you would succeed in passing the
portals of even our best hotels. They'd see through you in two
seconds in South Africa though—there you'd have to travel in a
different part of the 'bus. And in the States you'd be excluded
from the best society. . . . In England you are fairly well off—
some people would even make a point of being specially kind to
you, in a condescending way, out of pity. But they'd think twice
before letting their sons marry you. I believe in France there's a
more genuinely enlightened attitude to the colour-bar, whilst in
the West Indies they tell me everyone mixes together with great
enthusiasm with creoles often belonging to the oldest and most
respected families. But even there the texture of hair plays an
important part in social life. Your hair, dear Lola, in spite of your
skillful bleaching—' he leant forward and gently touched her
ash-blonde hair, 'would give you away in no time. And your
eyes—those lovely dark slanting eyes——' he leaned closer to
her, almost as if he had forgotten my presence, and there was an
odd mixture of tenderness and cruelty in his manner, as if he
both enjoyed and pitied the look of bewilderment tinged with
fear in Lola's eyes as she looked back at him. 'No, Lola,' he went
on, 'it's no crime to have a coloured mother . . . but it sets you
apart . . . it makes you just that amount more pregnable . . . you
have been born with skin that is not pure white and therefore
your more fortunate sisters will try to pretend you are their
social inferior because everyone likes to feel himself superior to
someone. . . . And you, dear Lola, will come to believe them, as
we believe anything if it's told us often enough, as the Germans
believed Hitler was an inspired leader—you believe them already
in your heart, and so there is born within you an inferiority
complex which eventually will *make* you inferior . . . and so
there will exist on this earth yet another half-caste at whom
people will be able to point their fingers and say "it is always
so". . . .'

"I watched Lola as she stared at Peter, God knows how much of what he said was comprehensible to her, but I believe she understood the cruelty in his eyes, and was fascinated by it. His flow of words seemed to have a mesmeric effect on her, and I have no doubt she was by no means impervious to the boy's good looks—because with his neat, small-boned features, his smooth black hair, pale eyes, and immaculate appearance, he was a striking-looking young man. They stared into each other's eyes for some moments as if I were not there, and I felt quite uneasy. Then suddenly the girl stood up, clumsily put her glass on the table, made across the room and disappeared through the door marked 'Ladies'; Peter looked at me.

" 'Well, well, Vicar,' he said. 'Do you think she's gone to have a good cry? Surely not the worldly Lola. But tell me about her, Vicar. What do you know about her?'

"I told him roughly what I knew about the family, and when I had finished he stared for some moments into his glass.

" 'I see,' he said at last. 'So you have some hopes of reclaiming Mildred, but Lola you think is a hopeless case?'

" 'I don't quite know what you mean by hopeless,' I said.

" 'Well—beyond the reach of your moralizing influence.'

" 'I think,' I replied quietly, 'that she is a girl of violent animal instincts which would control her destiny whatever outside influence were brought to bear . . . but I think also that she has the virtues which usually go with such a physical make-up, in full measure—that she is generous in much the way your mother is generous.'

"He looked up sharply and was about to say something when we were rejoined by Lola who sat down in her chair looking much more herself. But Peter strangely took no notice of her, continuing to stare at me.

" 'That is a very acute comparison, Vicar,' he said. 'There is a great resemblance, closer than you realize . . . dear Mama . . . in fact, a most exasperating mama. . . .'

"He stared into his empty glass, and as if suddenly realizing its emptiness, signalled to a barmaid—there were several about now as the room was filling up—and when she came over, handed her his and Lola's glasses.

" 'She has great hopes of me,' he went on. 'She tells everyone I'm going into the Diplomatic Corps. Diplomatic Corps! What hopes!' For some moments he seemed to be lost in thoughts not too pleasant. Then he laughed, ironically. 'I'm afraid I'm destined for a very different career—something less exacting, something calling for not quite such high moral character. . . .'

"And again he paused, this time to take his refilled glass from the barmaid, and putting it straight to his lips, he drank more than a half at a gulp.

" 'You see,' he continued, 'I've never in my life wanted to do anything that doesn't give me, personally, pleasure. I just don't understand the impulses that make people do selfless actions . . . they seem mad to me . . . up at Cambridge I'm told that if everyone behaved as I do, civilization would crumble. What the hell do I care? It wouldn't crumble in my lifetime— and if it did I'd have had my whack of enjoyment. And anyhow, everyone *doesn't* behave as I do, and presumably there will always be enough people around to counteract my particular hedonism . . . education will see to that. . . .'

"He put his head back and drank off the remainder of his whisky, and again beckoned to the barmaid.

" 'Same again, Daisy my sweet,' he said, when she came up. 'And another gin-and-orange for the lady. What about you, Vicar? Have a whisky? Have something to fortify you for the party. . . .'

" 'No thanks,' I said. 'I rarely drink spirits. . . .'

" 'Oh God. What do you drink?'

" 'Anything that comes from the grape—and in moderation. I respect my liver.'

" 'Oh God. He respects his liver. Hear that, Daisy?'

"He giggled and aimed a smack at Daisy's buttocks, which she skilfully avoided.

" 'Bring the Vicar something from the grape, Daisy—

anything, port, sherry, brandy—something to make him merry. But in moderation.'

" 'A sherry, please,' I said, more to keep Peter quiet than because I wanted it.

" 'Nice thighs that girl's got,' said Peter, as Daisy walked away, and winked at Lola, who looked the other way, an expression of pique on her face. 'The grape, eh?' went on Peter after a moment. 'You've got something there, Vicar. "O for a draught of vintage, that hath been cooled a long age in the deep delved earth. . . ." Keats, in case you don't know. But I get a bit bored with vintages. It's a cult—before you know where you are someone says "Enough—you'll spoil your palate—your sensibilities will be numbed. . . ." To me that's the only object in drinking—to numb the sensibilities, so that I am less vividly aware of this world in which we live. That's the reason why everyone drinks. Eh, Lola?' He turned suddenly to her, really looking at her for the first time since she had rejoined us. 'Eh, my beautiful, black-eyed Creole? That's the only reason to drink, isn't it? So's to forget wars and the colour of our skins and the natures of our mothers. . . . That's the reason, isn't it, sweetheart? You've got a black mother, I've got a—well, perhaps I'd better not tell you what I've got. . . .'

"And he put out his hand and touched the girl's hair. This time she sat impassive, her eyes inscrutable and Eastern, reminding me suddenly of Mildred, the first time Lola had ever reminded me of her sister. I knew she had been drinking glass for glass with him, and seemed of the two to have weathered the storm the better. I felt that now of the two of them she had the upper hand. I tried from her expression to read her thoughts, but was baffled, as I had so often been by Mildred, and I wondered suddenly which of these two was in the greater danger from the other. . . . And as I looked from one to the other I felt both pity and disgust; pity for these two children sailing rudderless in the sea of crude emotions into which they had been cast too young, and disgust at the emotions to which they were subject.

"I drank my sherry and stood up.

" 'Peter,' I said gently, hoping to break the spell under which they both were. 'Shall I tell your mother you'll be round soon?'

"He looked up vaguely, as if not recognizing me.

" 'Vicar,' he said, 'you can tell mother just exactly what you like,' and he turned back to Lola who continued to stare back at him without expression. For a moment I hesitated, wondering whether I could do any good by appealing to her; but something told me that her inscrutability was a mask hiding an obsession with him as great as his with her. . . . So abruptly I left them."

It was on the next afternoon, the day before they went on to Venice and the final part of their honeymoon, that Mr. Ash continued his story.

"As I made my way back to Mrs. Robinson's," he went on, "I felt a sudden wave of depression; I had been able to see no way in which to influence those two young people. I was leaving them to continue on the path to perdition, which was how I saw it. However I remembered then that in a few moments I would probably be seeing you again, and at once my depression lifted.

"When I reached the flat I found that about half the expected guests had already arrived. Mrs. Carrington-Smith was installed in the best arm-chair surrounded by a little group of her friends to whom she was talking in a low voice. Dr. Kynaston had taken over the bar from where he seemed to be dispensing neat spirits as if he were in his surgery, not even attempting to mix cocktails, the mysteries of which were a closed book to him. People were standing about in groups, whispering together, looking ominously like rival factions at a political meeting; I satisfied myself that you and Schofield had not yet arrived, and scarcely had I done this when Mrs. Robinson herself came up and drew me to one side. I saw at once that she was in a most distressed state, her face flushed, her eyes oddly feverish, and I felt she was near to tears.

" 'Did you find him?' she asked.

"I hesitated, not knowing whether to lie or to tell her I had indeed found him, drunk and in the company of a chorus-girl. I decided on the former course, feeling as if I were by now so contaminated by the world that I could lie glibly when the occasion demanded it.

" 'No, I did not find him,' I replied.

"Again a look almost of tragedy came into her eyes, indicating emotion far stronger than would appear to be demanded by his mere absence from her party. However she made a grave effort at pulling herself together, and said next in a voice she tried to make gay:

" 'Please help me to get these people acquainted. Not even Bill has come yet so I'm quite without a man, though the Doctor's doing his best. Everyone's standing about in groups whispering together as if they were surrounded by enemies, and every time I approach a group silence seems to fall on it—and when I try to break them up, they give me dirty looks . . . almost as if I were an unwelcome guest in my own house. . . .'

"At this moment the door-bell rang and without another word she hurried off to answer it leaving me to fulfil her instructions as best I could. I decided that the group surrounding Mrs. Carrington-Smith was the most dangerous, and moved over to join it, hoping that at least my presence would divert conversation from the poisonous gossip I was sure was going on. But as I reached them all conversation ceased as everyone looked towards the door to see who the new arrivals were; these turned out to be the Bartrams.

"Norma Bartram came into the room as if she were making an entrance on the stage. On her rather deceitful but pretty face there was a sweet smile and she was holding her husband's hand as if to accentuate her delight at being reunited with him; and as she gushed over Mrs. Robinson in the doorway—to all the world as if her hostess were her best friend—she studiously avoided looking at the rest of the room, like a poor actress trying to ignore the audience. For some reason she was in full evening-dress, a flame-coloured backless gown which was obviously, even

to my inexperienced eyes, expensive—but no doubt you remember it better than I do. She then proceeded to lead her unwilling husband—the only man in the room in a dinner-jacket,
and looking very conscious of it—round the room, introducing
him to everyone because not many had met him since his return.

"It was then that Mrs. Carrington-Smith started talking again
and at once I realized that she and her group had been discussing
everyone as they entered the room; I was astonished by what she
now said, because I was unaware of any break between her and
her principal satellite.

" 'Silly, conceited little fool, that girl,' she said. 'She knows
perfectly well one does not dress for a cocktail party, but of
course she wants to show off her new dress . . . that gown cost
forty guineas if it cost a penny . . . she can't forget that for the
first time in her life she's got money to play with—she must be
spending her husband's gratuity like water . . . it's the old, old
story, you know, marrying the boss's son . . . her father-in-law
is some kind of city merchant where she was a typist, though she
calls it private secretary—and there she met the son on leave—a
susceptible young fool interested in nothing but rugby football
and the insides of tanks . . . she can't forget the fact that he went
to a public school, though he's probably the first member of his
family to do so . . . and of course she lost no time in getting her
talons into him. Now he's back she no longer works but stays
at home all day polishing her nails and going round the shops
with her new cheque-book, or visiting beauty-salons—do you
see that new hair-do? She's too selfish to start a family, though
they could well afford it . . . in fact she's nothing but a common
little gold-digger with a bewitching smile . . . try though I have
during the last few months I've been unable to make a lady of
her . . . oh, there's going to be trouble there when she grows
used to her new situation and gets bored—already I've caught
her flirting with young Peter Robinson . . . she used to let him
spend hours in her flat, but now ignores him . . . she's now got a
husband to take her out . . . oh, good evening, my dear. . . .'

"Suddenly her voice had changed as the Bartrams reached our

group and she greeted the subject of her commentary in honeyed tones, and for a moment there was a scene of almost touching sentimentality between them as they kissed and made much of each other. Young Bartram was then introduced to those who did not know him and Norma gracefully accepted a chair offered her next to Mrs. Carrington-Smith, and the two of them proceeded to chat together as if they were still the best of friends, and I realized that there had in fact been no break between them, but that Mrs. Carrington-Smith had merely been expressing her friendship in her own way. Young Bartram stood behind his wife's chair looking round him morosely, speaking to no one.

"Realizing my presence would have no effect on whatever gossip was going on, I left the group, and was making my way across the room to have a word with Kynaston about old Kennedy—whom he had once attended—when I was intercepted by Mrs. Kynaston, who was standing alone by a window, smoking, and watching with a smile the behaviour of the rest of the guests.

" 'Good evening, Vicar,' she said. 'It's an age since we met. Do you still believe yourself to be among the best of possible people in the best of possible worlds?'

" 'I never have,' I said.

" 'I'm sorry we seem to have quarrelled, Vicar, you and I,' she went on. 'I always enjoyed your visits, and crossing swords with you. Shall we kiss and make up?'

" 'By all means,' I said gallantly. 'Though perhaps we had better leave the kissing until we are alone together. It might cause a little gossip in this crowded room. But I trust you will not persist in instructing me in the facts of life as if I were a two-year-old.'

" 'But you still are a two-year-old in some ways, Vicar. And surely all I said has turned out to be true?'

" 'In what way?'

" 'Why, the disillusion you have experienced. I see already a certain desperation in your previously innocent blue eyes. I'm sure you're beginning to realize that the teachings of Christ cut distressingly little ice these days. And then don't forget I predicted

that before you knew where you were you'd be succumbing to
the charms of some seductive young woman. . . .'

" 'Well?' I asked. 'And have I?'

" 'But of course . . . how about the lovely Katharine Pemberton who has just entered the room?'

" 'Has she?' I asked involuntarily, and looked quickly round.
But at once I looked back again at Mrs. Kynaston, aware that
I had to a certain extent given myself away. I found myself
looking straight into her intelligent, slightly ironical, but by no
means unkind eyes, and as she looked away past me I sensed she
was watching you and I longed to follow the direction of her
glance.

" 'Come, come, Vicar,' she said. 'Shall we be honest for once?
I'm not your enemy, you know—I like you. Although not quite
old enough to be your mother I feel almost maternally disposed
towards you. You are so innocent. And I sympathize with your
passion for Miss Pemberton. She is quite the most beautiful girl
I have ever seen, and completely wasted on that local hero of
ours who so loves himself and so delights in sticking knives in
people; I quite agree with sticking knives into Germans and
especially Japs but one should not *like* doing it. You know what
he is, don't you? This is where a study of psychology could help
you. He is a sadist—possibly a sexual sadist who would delight in
horrible perversions like flagellation; he's a classic case, they're in
all the psychological case-books, and they always do well in
war. Look at him now, preening himself in the public adulation.
And why is he still in uniform, with all those medals up? And
look at *her*, Vicar—go on, turn round, don't be afraid. You
needn't worry, she's not dressed in that vulgar dress she wore at
Mrs. Carrington-Smith's party—oh, I heard about it though I
wasn't among the honoured guests. Probably *he* made her wear
it. Well, Vicar, if you haven't the courage to look at your be-
loved, I'll tell you what she's wearing. She has on a neat little
green cocktail dress, in the most excellent taste, modest but at the
same time doing justice to her figure. And she's looking at you,
Vicar . . . .'

"Suddenly she stopped speaking, and was staring across the room, an odd look on her face.

" 'What's the matter?' I asked, still forcing myself not to look round.

" 'Vicar,' she said, almost beneath her breath, putting her hand on my arm. 'That girl's in love with you. . . .'

" 'Don't talk nonsense,' I said.

" 'Vicar, I'm a student of human nature. There is only one interpretation to put on the way she looked anxiously round the room, how her anxiety suddenly left her when she caught sight of you . . . it was the same look that was in your eyes when you came in, only your anxiety didn't fade because she wasn't here. . . . Oh! how foolish of her not to disguise her feelings! . . . she's putting herself into the hands of that Carrington-Smith bitch . . . it shows how innocent she is, as innocent as you, Vicar . . . odd, in a woman who has been in the Services . . . but I've always thought from her eyes that she has a sort of spiritual innocence, which is why she has not seen through Schofield sooner . . . look at the Carrington-Smith now, her head down, staring gloatingly at the poor innocent . . . yes, and turning her head this way, looking at you . . . for God's sake go over to her, before she starts expounding to that gang of hers, before the whole room is told you're having an affair with Miss Pemberton . . . quick. . . .'

"And she almost pushed me over towards Mrs. Carrington-Smith. I went, hardly knowing what I was doing, and as I joined the fringes of the group I paused before they realized my presence. I was in time to hear Mrs. Carrington-Smith say, as she watched your progress round the room:

" '. . . she has a really remarkable resemblance to her mother, and I only hope she doesn't take after her in character. . . .'

"I remembered the hint she had given me over the 'phone when inviting me to her dinner-party, about knowing something concerning you. I listened with all my concentration.

" 'You knew her mother?' asked Mrs. Bartram.

" 'Why, my dear, of course—who didn't? Or rather who hadn't heard of her? Every errand-boy who reads the Sunday

papers had heard of her at one time. I did actually meet her once
—at a party at one of the Embassies—I forget which. At the
Swedish probably, because she was half Swedish. But the whole
country had *heard* of her. Surely you remember the divorce of
Lydia Pemberton? It was about fifteen years ago—the biggest
society scandal of the decade. She was of good family, you know.
A title somewhere. She was the most beautiful débutante of her
year—she won that unofficial poll held each year by some evening paper. She was presented a few years after myself. She married a Guards officer—he was a colonel at the time of the divorce.
My dears, the things that came out in Court! Sodom and Gomor-
rah wasn't in it! Women, as well as men, she was mixed up with;
she was a—what are they called?—a heterosexual. Of course we
didn't hear the half of it, though I, who was in that particular set
at that time, heard more than most. She was known to be one
of the most—' here she whispered something to the women
nearest to her which I was unable to catch, '—and with that
angelic face, too. . . . And that poor child had to give evidence—
she must have been about fourteen then . . . and the evidence
she gave, apparently quite unwittingly, ruined whatever case
her mother had. An experience like that *must* have left *some*
traces . . . and she's exactly like her mother—perhaps a slightly
stronger mouth which makes her a little less beautiful, but the
same eyes, the same hair, the same broad brow. . . . I'm sure I
can't be mistaken . . . . And already I've noticed, that whilst
engaged to one man, she is already casting eyes at another . . .
that too is evidence. . . .'

" 'Evidence of exactly what?' I asked.

"I should of course have interrupted much sooner, but had
been unable to speak, almost mesmerized by what the woman
was saying.

" At the sound of my voice, silence descended on the group,
and Mrs. Carrington-Smith looked towards me, for a moment
slightly put out. But only for a moment.

" 'Why, Vicar,' she said, with a special, almost menacing
gentleness, 'doesn't it strike you as odd that she is still unmarried?

Girls as marriageable as she, in her walk of life, are usually married before they are twenty. Such marriages are arranged—mine was. But here she is, engaged to a young man who, though one of our national heroes and a perfectly charming young man, comes of the most obscure parentage. I don't know who his father was, this Schofield—no one does. Personally I'm very sorry for the poor girl—' here she gave a deep sigh, '—but if I were a man I would certainly think twice before marrying her . . . as apparently have all the really eligible young men . . . .'

"And she smiled sadly at me, but deep in her eyes I detected a look which mocked me. In that moment I knew that not only she, but the whole group, knew already of my interest in you. And at that moment you joined us.

"You came up smiling and it seemed to me that your whole manner would confirm to these people our relationship. And I swear to you that the coldness of my manner to you then was due to this feeling rather than to the fact that Mrs. Carrington-Smith's poison was beginning to work in my mind; for it had not, at that time, begun to work. So that was why I, in your own words, almost snubbed you; and whilst doing so I prayed you would understand, whilst at the same time another part of me, a self-immolating part, hoped you would not, that this action of mine would end this complication that had come into our lives. Because at that time I did not know you had already ceased caring for Schofield.

"So I said to you as little as possible compatible with good manners and saw come onto your face a puzzled look, which made me turn away for fear you would give away more, and started to talk almost wildly with whoever was standing next to me—young Bartram, I believe. Yes, it was young Bartram, for I remember he looked rather startled at being suddenly talked to about tanks on the Normandy beaches, the first thing that came into my mind. And when I next saw you, you were with Schofield at the bar, which he had taken over. I watched you, and it seemed to me you were entirely devoted to him. You were standing beside him, laughing up into his eyes, and it was then

that Mrs. Carrington-Smith's poison began to work in my mind.
You see, I was aware of my own inexperience with women, my
inability to judge them. What, I asked myself, if all that Mrs.
Carrington-Smith had said were true? What if there were some
truth in heredity? Would it not explain the way in which you
were carrying on with two men at once? What sort of a woman
were you, I asked myself? Had you indeed merely set out to
captivate me, and becoming convinced this evening of your
success, had returned to Schofield? And were now flaunting
your relationship with him before my eyes? As I watched you,
I became almost convinced of this, and to make matters worse,
Mrs. Carrington-Smith, beside me, began to continue her
commentary about you; I do not know to this day whether she
had grasped my state of mind, but what she then said had the
effect of increasing my distrust of you. She kept drawing the
attention of her listeners to the way in which you resembled your
notorious mother; the way you looked into Schofield's face was
'the exact replica' of how your mother had looked into the faces
of her suitors when she was a débutante; and the way you 'had a
smile' for 'any man who talked to you' was a characteristic she
remembered vividly in your mother. Some of the other women
too began pulling you to pieces; Norma Bartram just couldn't
see the beauty everyone raved about; you might, she said, have
been quite attractive 'six or seven years ago', but that now you
already had the 'frustrated' look of a spinster of thirty. Another
woman thought you had a sly look, and a third murmured that a
woman who had been abroad in the Services could surely not be
as virginal as you looked; this raised a titter. A fourth criticized
your dress—'such an undistinguished frock—almost dowdy.'

"I hated these women for their poisonous tongues, but at the
same time what they said gave me a perverted pleasure. Slowly
I was working my way into a frame of mind in which I felt
justified in despising you. The women then went on to praise
Schofield, to say how lucky you were to have 'got' him, a view
fully concurred in by Mrs. Carrington-Smith in spite of her
previous comments about his 'obscure' origin. The fulsome praise

which they then began to heap on Schofield's head was too much for me, and I moved away; for whilst I could get perverted pleasure out of hearing you insulted, I could not bear hearing Schofield praised.

"Meanwhile Schofield had succeeded in getting the party going with a swing. He had established himself behind the bar where he was busy pouring out drinks, talking ceaselessly the whole time, and, in a way which I half-admired, was acting the clown in a wholly effective manner. Soon after I began watching him, he indulged in a piece of clowning typical of his whole behaviour. Having gathered a crowd round the bar, he suddenly made a melodramatic gesture, entreated his audience to wait, and left the room; almost at once he reappeared, jauntily carrying an officer's hold-all. This he placed on the bar in front of him and opened, and then began to take from it one by one a dozen bottles, giving a running commentary on each, explaining how he had acquired each bottle—all, of course, during his expeditions behind the enemy lines; a bottle of mavrodaphne he had acquired in Greece, some Yugoslav hock had been presented to him by 'poor old Mihailovitch himself'; a bottle of vintage champagne he had raided from a German H.Q. in North Africa, some Chianti had come from Italy, and two bottles of claret he had taken from the cellars of a French collaborator whom he had 'unfortunately to liquidate'; all of which adventures he made light of, pretending it was the bottles, not his own exploits, that he valued. Having dealt with the last bottle, he invited his audience to sample the contents; and as people queued up he continued his commentary, making such remarks as 'it is one of my invariable maxims to always hold a bottle by the neck and a woman by the waist, never the other way round,' a remark greeted with a roar of laughter. By now he had reached the state of the professional humorist who has only to wink an eye to be greeted with a roar of laughter, and soon, aided by the alcohol he was so liberally dispensing, his corner of the room contained most of the guests who were positively jostling to get near him, and from which, every minute or so, there came a burst of laughter. So lost was I in the torture of watching this man's exhibitionism, that I did not know you had left that part of the room, and when suddenly I heard your voice beside me, I was startled. I think your exact words, referring to Schofield, were:

" 'In good form tonight, isn't he?'

" 'You sound almost ironical,' I said, I suppose stiffly.

" 'I am,' you replied.

" 'Why?' I asked.

" 'I think I hate him,' you said, beneath your breath, in a whisper I could scarcely hear. I felt suddenly great hope leap within me; but at the same time I did not allow myself to believe in the sincerity I knew was in your voice.

" 'You sounded almost as if you meant that,' I said.

" 'I did. Do you think I lie?' you replied.

"I looked into your eyes and saw pain there; suddenly I wanted to hurt you more.

" 'Yes,' I said harshly. 'I find that members of your sex usually say what they think their audience wants to hear in preference to the truth.'

"Had I hit you, you could not have drawn back more sharply, and what your reaction would have been after your moment of astonishment, I do not know; probably you would just have turned on your heel and left me, perhaps left the party. But whatever you were going to do, you were prevented by Schofield. Suddenly he shouted across the room at me. What he said then, was, I know now, due to the poor man's fury of jealousy, for as you have since told me, he already knew he had lost you to me, and, half-drunk as he was, he chose this moment to have some sort of revenge.

" 'Hey, you two over there,' he shouted, causing everyone to look at us, 'break it up, won't you? This isn't the first time I've caught you making love to my fiancée, Mr. Ash!'

"His voice was facetious with a touch of drunken hysteria in it, an odd combination which caused the crowd to realize that this was more than one of his jokes, and though one or two isolated laughs greeted his words, there was on the whole a sudden quiet in the room. For a moment he and I stared at each other and I felt my anger mounting. And in that silence the door opened and there appeared through it, staggering a little uncertainly, almost as if pushed from behind, Lola, and behind her, clutching the doorpost, Peter.

"Lola stopped just inside the door, her hand on her hip, looking at us almost belligerently, her ash-blonde hair ruffled, her make-up smeared, the two top buttons of her blouse undone, looking indeed as if she were following the profession her father once confided in me he feared was her destiny. The stupefied silence which this apparition caused was then broken by Peter.

" 'Go on in, Lola my sweet,' he said in slurred accents, 'Don't be afraid, everyone's waiting to welcome you . . . they've never seen anything like you before . . . have you, eh? Ladies and gentleman, let me introduce you to Lola Labelle, the most beautiful girl in London at the present time—though that's not her real name according to Parson Ash who knows more about her than I do. She's a member of the oldest profession of all, and my dearest friend. Mother, where are you? I brought her specially to meet you—I thought you'd have much in common. . . .'

"He stopped, swaying slightly in the doorway, staring round the room, as if looking for his mother and suddenly afraid she was not there. His glance travelled slowly round, and then seemed to focus on someone, and a look of unholy pleasure came onto his face. Everyone followed the direction in which he was staring, and there we saw Mrs. Robinson, standing very still, her face white, looking at her son. She closed her eyes for a moment, then drew a deep breath, as if pulling herself together.

" 'Bill,' she said, and her voice was quite calm, 'will you please see to Peter—I think he is unwell. . . .' Again there was a pause as Bill hurried across the room and hustled Peter out; then Mrs. Robinson walked quietly over to Lola, and in that moment I felt admiration for her.

" 'Miss Labelle,' she said, 'please don't go.' She put her hand on her arm. 'My son says he thinks we might have something in common. Does that mean you were on the stage?'

" 'That's right,' said Lola, looking at her warily.

" 'You are an actress?'

" 'Call it that if you like. I'm a strip, mostly.'

" 'Well—I was myself a chorus-girl, only in my day we were not allowed to take off so much. But times change. Do, my dear, go over to the bar, someone will get you a drink. . . .'

"Suddenly Mrs. Robinson swayed slightly and put her hand up to her head.

" 'I feel a little unwell,' she said. 'Perhaps someone . . . Katharine . . .', and it was then that you and Kynaston rushed to her side, and each with a hand under an elbow, escorted her from the room. Once the door closed behind you, a buzz of conversation arose, and Lola stood where Mrs. Robinson had left her, in a space in the middle of the room, looking round with hostility, being stared at by everyone.

"Keyed up though my emotions were, I found myself feeling pity for her. I was aware of the rest of the people coagulating into little groups, whispering excitedly together, with many sidelong glances at Lola. No one had the initiative to get up and leave, which would have been the right thing to do under the circumstances. I sensed the speculation going on as to the real cause of this scene; for I had no doubt that everyone was aware of something far more disturbing in the relationship of Mrs. Robinson and her sons than appeared on the surface, and that the real significance of Peter's little scene rested in his reference to Lola as belonging to the 'oldest and noblest profession of all' and that in doing so he had not been referring to the stage; and I had no doubt that I too was being included in the speculation for I was conscious of being looked at by more than one person. I felt hatred for everyone in the room except Lola, an emotion which in my vocation I should never have felt. . . . But I was aware almost of an atmosphere of delight around me, delight at this tremendous scandal in which everyone could share. These people, scenting that at last the façade of respectability that Mrs.

Robinson had built up was crumbling; these supposed friends, who had come to her party and partaken of her hospitality, felt a ripple of excitement in their humdrum lives which stripped off the veneer of their good manners. . . . I, who had always despised so-called County society and its snobbishness, felt suddenly that these middle-class people were no better; here they were, it seemed to me, secure in their own hypocritical goodness, despising someone who dared to be different, regardless of that person's virtues—her courage, her generosity, her natural goodness. I felt myself in the presence not of individuals, but of a mob, a cruel mob which in the past would have lynched someone, but which now was intent on social ostracization. In the bitter mood I was in I felt violent loyalty to Mrs. Robinson and for this girl who stood in the middle of the room and who somehow seemed to represent the older woman; as Lola stood there in her pathetic clothes, the gaudy blouse open at the neck, the tight skirt with its slit up one side showing a lace-edged petticoat, clothes which showed off too well her fine, strong body, and with her head thrown back and an expression on her face difficult to define—a mixture of fear, pride, and wariness—as she stood there, I felt for her a kind of protective affection.

"Quietly I crossed over to her, and said to her gently:

" 'Hello, Lola. So you decided to come after all?'

"She looked at me almost as if she didn't recognize me.

" 'Let's go over to the bar and have a drink, shall we?' I suggested soothingly, and holding her by the elbow I guided her through the crowd still surrounding the bar, aware of being stared at by everyone in the room. At the bar, she seemed to regain her confidence.

" 'Pink gin, please,' she said almost haughtily to the young man who had taken Schofield's place, and who proceeded to serve her with exaggerated politeness. Glass in hand, she stood surveying the company. Suddenly she nudged me.

" 'I know 'im,' she said, indicating a very respectable, middle-aged citizen.

" 'Really?' I asked.

" ''E's one of the regulars—front row every Monday, first 'ouse. Bet 'is old woman don't know.'

" 'You mean he regularly visits your show?' I asked.

" 'Sure. Mostly middle-aged men, our audience. Laps it up, they do. 'E won't reckernize me though—don't you worry. 'E ain't ever looked at my face. . . .'

"The buzz of conversation which had almost ceased when I had gone up to Lola, now started again, and I was aware of comments being made by several of the women, in particular Mrs. Carrington-Smith's group which had now moved over to the bar. Norma Bartram in particular was loud in her indignation; I heard her say, in a voice obviously intended for Lola's ears, that it was disgraceful they should be expected to meet people like this Miss Labelle or whatever she called herself. I saw Lola beside me take notice. She turned round and slowly looked Mrs. Bartram up and down.

" 'I 'eard you,' she said.

" 'Indeed?' asked Mrs. Bartram.

" 'What, might I ask, 'ave you against me?'

" 'Nothing in particular.'

" 'But a lot in general, huh? Well, I 'ave a lot against you too, I might tell you, in general and in particular. You an' your kind what ain't done a day's work in your lives, lookin' down your noses at honest workin' folk. 'Ow would you like to stand for hours on a stage in an artistic pose—never movin' as much as a finger, mind you, winter and summer, freezing sometimes? Not that anyone'd want to look at you—too skinny. Let me tell you somethin'—we're all workin'-class now, see? Only some don't work.'

"And she looked round triumphantly, as if expecting applause. But everyone was hostile, some grinning openly. Mrs. Bartram exchanged amused smiles with some of her cronies.

" 'I advise you to control yourself, Miss Labelle,' she said. 'You're not in a pub now, you know. Violence may be effective where you come from, but it does not amuse us here.'

"I saw Lola's right arm stiffen, and I have no doubt she would have thrown the remainder of her drink into the other woman's face, had I not stepped between them.

" 'Please remember, Mrs. Bartram,' I said, 'that before God we are all equal. And what is perhaps more to the point, Miss Labelle is as much a guest here as you. . . .'

"At this moment the door opened, and Dr. Kynaston hurried over to where we were standing.

" 'Mrs. Robinson has had a heart attack,' he said. 'She thinks she's going to die though that is very unlikely. But for some reason she wants to see you, Vicar.'

" 'Strangely enough, Doctor,' I said, 'some people when they believe they are going to die, still turn to the Church.'

"I thought quickly, looking round the room, wanting a friend in whose hands I could leave Lola, before she started pulling Mrs. Bartram's earrings out. My eyes encountered Mrs. Kynaston's, where she was standing, still near the window, watching everything that went on; she seemed to read my thoughts, for she came over and took Lola's arm.

" 'Come over here, my dear,' she said, 'and let me talk to you.'

"As I crossed the room with Kynaston, I saw Lola being led unwillingly across the room by Mrs. Kynaston, and there seemed to be a general movement among the guests to take their leave. Some of the more decent people had in fact already left, and the last thing I heard as I left the room was Mrs. Carrington-Smith's drawling voice say that 'it seemed to be about time for a general exodus'.

"Kynaston showed me into Mrs. Robinson's bedroom where she was lying on her back looking rather blue in the face, but not so ill as I had expected; you were standing beside the bed watching her, and did not look at me as I entered. Mrs. Robinson said, in a voice with almost a note of melodrama in it:

" 'I would like to be alone with the vicar.'

"Kynaston held her pulse, and after a moment nodded to you, and you both left.

" 'Vicar,' said Mrs. Robinson, 'will you take my confession?'

" 'But you are not a Roman Catholic, Mrs. Robinson,' I said. 'I do not take confession in the sense I think you mean.'

" 'That doesn't prevent you from hearing something I have to confess, does it?'

" 'Of course not,' I said.

" 'Then sit down in the chair beside the bed and listen to me carefully. I may not have many hours to live.'

" 'My dear Mrs. Robinson, it's not as bad as that. The doctor is quite optimistic about your health.'

"It seemed to me that a look of slight disappointment came onto her face, but I may have imagined this.

" 'But I still think I had better confess, Vicar,' she said. 'You never know, with heart trouble.'

" 'Very well, Mrs. Robinson,' I said, not altogether liking the idea; but I seated myself and gave her my whole attention.

"She leaned across the bed towards me and said in what was almost a whisper:

" 'I have led an immoral life.'

" 'Indeed?' I replied. 'So have many people who have later become worthy citizens. It is what we are now, and intend to be in the future, that matters.'

" 'Is that really so, Vicar? Can one really live down one's past?'

" 'If one genuinely repents, most certainly.'

" 'But one cannot live down its effects, Vicar. During the war, I thought I had succeeded—at last; what I thought to be decent people seemed willing to know me. But now it's over, I know it isn't so. In a few hours now, the whole truth about me will be out. The Carrington-Smith woman will ferret it all out, now she has something to go on. She's been trying long enough. But fortunately I shall probably be dead then.'

"And she looked at me mournfully.

" 'Nonsense,' I said. 'You'll be on your feet in two days. Now tell me all about it.   What is so terrible about your past?'

"Again she leaned over to me.

" 'I have never been married, Vicar. I was the kept mistress of two men. And before that I was little better than a prostitute.

Both my sons are illegitimate. I . . . went with several men . . .
for money. . . .'

"I admit I was a little taken aback; but I believe I succeeded
in not looking too surprised.

" 'Tell me the whole story, won't you?' I suggested gently.

" 'I was born,' she started, almost eagerly, as if she had many
times rehearsed her story in her mind, 'in a house—or a slum—
that stood on the very site of this block of flats. And I swore to
myself that if ever I made good, I'd build a mansion where the
old house stood. Tenement block, it was. My parents were
paupers—father kept a barrow in the market and was a drunkard.
My mother too drank gin. They had seven children of which
I was the youngest. Father was in and out of prison, and when I
was fourteen, he died there. Soon afterwards, Mother became
mentally deranged—started breaking the house up and screaming
in the street. She would go out shopping quite normally and then
suddenly start this screaming, startling people out of their wits.
So she was taken away to an institution. We children went to
work, those of us who weren't already working. I had a job
in a tailor's, sewing on buttons. But that didn't last long, Vicar.
There was a young Jew there, son of the tailor himself. About
sixteen he was at the time. He told me how beautiful I was—the
first ever to do so. He said he knew someone in the theatrical
world who would give me a job in the chorus—that I'd make
two pounds a week instead of eight shillings—two pounds was
good money then. He said he'd introduce me but first had to
make sure I had the right figure. Accustomed as I was to un-
dressing in front of my brothers at home, this meant nothing to
me. So one night at the back of the shop after the others had
gone, I undressed in front of him—took off everything. He then
said that to get this job I might have to be 'kind' to the proprietor, and that it would be a good idea if I had some experience
first. Now I'm not saying that what was done then, Vicar, was
done without my connivance—I knew what I was about all
right. In fact I knew in theory far more than my Jew boy. But he
offered me money and—the temptation was too great. Well,

afterwards, that boy kept his word. He was a good boy. He introduced me to the manager of a music-hall. The manager was some kind of cousin of his—you know what Jews are, all sticking together. I was fifteen then, and was at once accepted. But only on condition that I did for the manager what I had done for my Jewish friend. I did so—but didn't have to often. You see, there were fifteen chorus-girls, and he had the same arrangement with each. So my turn didn't come round often. It was there I met this Irish girl—the beauty I told you about. She was already on the way up by then and no longer had to give her favours to the manager. She was understudying the lead. And she had contacts with influential people. She was a career girl with her head screwed on. She didn't give her favours for nothing—first she got something useful from each man she gave herself to; and afterwards she would go to confession, as I told you, and everything would be all right. I envied her that, as I envied everything about her. She was nice to me, and I admired her greatly. Soon she got her real chance, for the lead fell ill. My friend was so good that when the lead recovered she was dismissed and the part given permanently to my friend. But she didn't keep it long —she had other ideas. Three weeks later, she was engaged in the West End. And within a year she was married . . . well, I won't tell you who to, it wouldn't be fair. Anyhow, she's now mistress of one of the largest estates in the Home Counties, and head of a family that is a household name. And she still keeps in touch with me, bless her. Well, before she left that music-hall she'd taught me all she knew—and that was plenty. She taught me to use my power over the male sex as other people use their capital. Our beauty, she said, is our only capital, and used properly could go a long way. But I wasn't so lucky as she. For one thing, I wasn't so beautiful—she was the most beautiful thing you ever saw; and for another, I was always a little heavy on my feet. So no West End for me. But the men liked me—though I wasn't able to get into such exalted company as my friend. But I had plenty of followers, among rich tradesmen. Unfortunately for me, Vicar, I had one fault—which I still have: I've too soft a heart. Always

I seemed to choose middle-aged men whose wives misunderstood them. I was so sorry for them. So, unlike my friend, I was never able to marry. And after three or four such men, I met Hector Schofield. . . .'

" 'Hector Schofield—the politician?' I asked involuntarily.

" 'None other, the old dear—he's seventy now and as fit as a fiddle. He still gives me an allowance. But in those days he was still married to his first wife—she was a chronic invalid, you know, bedridden. And Hector was—well, warm-blooded. He was almost middle-aged then, and I—seventeen. Sweet seventeen. He set me up in a flat in Bayswater. I adored him. I stayed with him for seven years. Then he was in the running for Prime Minister, and it became advisable for him to marry again—his wife had died in the meantime—and this second marriage was to be a political one. He swore he'd still be faithful to me. But the unexpected happened—he fell in love with his wife. He told her all about me—and she didn't cut up too nasty about it. Not a bad woman, but a bit horsey. She agreed to him giving me an allowance—you see, in the last year he was with me—1914— Bill was born. So I got out of that quite well. Not only the allowance, but he educated me—taught me to speak the King's English. From being a little guttersnipe I could now pass myself off as a lady—or almost. For a few years I had no one in particular. I led a quiet life, bringing up Bill. By that time I was twenty-six. Then, in 1917, I met Robinson. He was a business man, and rather badly shellshocked. He was just my age and I fell in love with him at once—a kind of maternal love, for he needed looking after. He also had a bitch of a wife, who wouldn't divorce him. So once more, no wedding-bells, and I became his unofficial 'wife'. And he did very well for himself—with a little assistance from me. He worked like a slave, and built up a little string of grocery shops. We were wealthy, though not as wealthy as we should have been, because he had to give his wife an allowance. He worked so hard that he literally worked himself to death; two years after the birth of Peter—who was born when I was thirty-five—though I looked little more than twenty-five,

though I say it myself—he died. That was in 1927. After that,
Vicar, I turned over a new leaf. I'd been left half Robinson's
estate, consisting of the shops. I set about managing these, and
made a go of it. They are still a flourishing concern. You've
heard of Robinson's Stores?'

" 'Of course,' I said.

" 'They're mine—every one of them. And together with
Schofield's allowance—which he still insists on giving me—they
make me a wealthy woman. I needn't live here—I could live in
Park Lane. But as I told you earlier, I once swore that if ever I
made good I'd build a mansion where the house I was born in
stood. But unfortunately these flats had been erected—so the
next best thing was to live in one of them. So here I am, Vicar—
trying to be respectable.'

" 'And your sons?' I asked. 'Do they know about your past?'

" 'Bill does—I could hardly keep it from him, especially as
his father recognizes him. He's eleven years older than Peter,
you know. The knowledge seemed to have a queer effect on
Bill, which frightened me. He's always been very unstable; kind
enough to me when he remembers my existence, but often going
away for long periods—years at a time, and never communicating
with me. I've never had a letter from him—only an occasional
card. He's been a rolling stone, depending on his father's allowance, never done a day's work in his life, and quite irresponsible.
Always I've wondered how much of this is due to his knowing
he's illegitimate. Robinson was sure it had a lot to do with it,
which was why we made up our minds we'd keep the truth from
any child we might have. In fact we had no child until 1925,
when Peter was born; it was Robinson's fault we didn't have any
earlier—he suffered from a nervous complaint. Often I think
Peter's inherited this, in a different form. He's very like his
father in many ways, only without his gentleness; Peter is cruel.
So I never told him the truth, and until recently he's behaved as
if he didn't know it; but lately he's been very curious—sarcastic and bitter to me. At one time he had ambitions to go into
the Diplomatic Corps; but for the last year he's laughed at the

idea, in a strange sort of way. And I've suspected him of living an immoral life during the last few months. . . I believe he's often in London without my knowing . . . of course, it's obvious he's found out the truth, or some distorted form of it . . . and tonight . . . he's had his revenge on me. . . .'

"There were tears in her eyes now as she looked at me.

" 'He was very drunk,' I said. 'I've no doubt when you've had an explanation with him he will be very different.'

"But she seemed not to hear me, and was staring in front of her sadly.

" 'You haven't heard the worst yet,' she said.

" 'Then tell me,' I said very quietly.

" 'I'm not cured. I still get ridiculous passions for men. At my age! Perhaps you've noticed it yourself, Vicar. I . . . have more than once found myself flirting with you. Only you very properly ignored me. All my life I've looked forward to the time when I would get peace. But it seems I never will. It's the wages of sin, I suppose. I thought . . . everyone told me . . . that when I'd passed a certain age, I would find peace . . . but I haven't . . . in a way it's worse than ever . . . as a young woman I could have an affair, and get it over quickly, forget it for a while . . . now, there is no satisfaction . . . always searching, trying to look younger than I am. . . .' She was openly weeping now. 'I just can't hide it. That's why these women hate me so . . . they look upon me as unnatural . . . and I am, Vicar . . . in me certain instincts are extended beyond their natural span, . . . and I am an unnatural mother . . . look at the effect I've had on my children . . . what can I do?'

"This was an appeal to me, the most sincere and tragic that had been made since I had taken Orders, and I felt a great compassion for her. And I wanted passionately not to let her down. I could see how she hated herself for the instincts that had made her what she was—the instincts which sprang from her greatest virtue, her generosity. I saw suddenly the falseness of the premises on which all my life I had been brought up—to believe the virtuous wholly good, and the immoral wholly bad. For in my heart I knew this woman to be not so bad as the other whose poisonous tongue had made so many people unhappy, and who was so virtuous; this one had given much pleasure and happiness in her life. I realized how shallow was my understanding of human nature, how slight my experience of life. All my principles seemed suddenly to be worthless. I knew not what to do. I took her hand to give her comfort of some kind, and have no idea what I would have said—that I would have been any use to her I very much doubt.

"But I was interrupted by the opening of the bedroom door and the entry of Kynaston. Seeing his patient weeping he quickly crossed the room uninvited and took her pulse. I felt anger and knew that my proper course was to order this man of science out of the room whilst I tended to her soul which in that moment was more necessary than his futile ministrations to her body. For this woman's body had always been healthy, and her soul sick. But being uncertain of myself I took the weaker course, and allowed him to remain. I stood aside, saying nothing. And when, after satisfying himself that there was no immediate physical danger, Kynaston said I was wanted outside on rather urgent business, all I did was to look rather hesitantly at Mrs. Robinson, and when she nodded, as it were giving me permission to go, I went. I felt in that moment as if my soul was as sick as hers. As I crossed the room I heard Kynaston ask me to send you to him, and meeting you in the hall, I gave you this message, not looking at you, and without a word you went into the bedroom.

"I tried then to pull myself together, wondering dully what this 'urgent business' was, and thinking that probably it was non-existent, a ruse to get the useless man of God out of the room. But then I became aware that there seemed still to be a number of people in the flat, that excited voices were coming from the sitting-room where the party had been held. I went into that room and found there a number of women, among whom was Mrs. Carrington-Smith. In fact all the tenants of Carlton Court who had been to the party seemed to be there still, as if not having had the decency to go. But I realized suddenly that they had already gone, but had come back again. And then I saw coming towards me across the room the figure of George Baker, the constable, whom I had not noticed seated at a table in a corner. My first thought then was that there had been an accident—that perhaps Bill had been exercising his love of violence on Peter.

" 'What's happened, constable?' I asked rather wearily.

" 'Don't you know, Mr. Ash?' he asked, surprised. 'There's been robberies.'

" 'Robberies?' I asked. 'Is that all?'

"I nearly laughed; this was an anticlimax. I had expected something so much worse, and could not see for the moment how robberies could involve me.

"But almost at once we found ourselves surrounded by the women.

" 'We've been robbed,' said Mrs. Carrington-Smith. 'Every one of us who lives in these flats and who came to the party, has been robbed.'

"And then all the women started to talk at once, like a chorus of cockatoos.

" 'Now then, ladies,' said George Baker. 'Talking won't do no good. Be quiet now whilst I have a word with the Vicar.'

"Having achieved a certain degree of silence, he took me to one side.

" 'The Inspector's in the room next door,' he said. 'He would like a few words with you. This is a big thing, this robbery, and not the first, not by a long chalk. There's been a whole series of them in the last few months, and we 'as our suspicions. This time we think we 'as a real clue, and the Inspector thinks you might be able to help us. Would you care to step in and 'ave a word with 'im, sir?'

" 'Of course,' I replied.

"And as I stepped into the hall, I saw the whole thing, I saw just how I was involved in these robberies. I had before my eyes a kind of vision of Mildred—Mildred and Tom White and Les and Al and last but not least Molly Cohen. Facts seemed suddenly to fall into place. Mildred's surly unapproachable manner since she had taken service with Mrs. Robinson; Tom's eagerness for her to go into that employment; the way in which Al, the big Italian, had looked on me with suspicion, almost fear; I remembered the evening of the party at Tom's when the little man had suddenly arrived furtively with the big suitcase; of course it had not contained black-market gin, but the proceeds of their latest robbery, stolen goods of which Tom was the receiver. He was the fence for the whole gang. All this passed through my mind in the moment it took me to cross the hall, and as I entered the spare room where the Inspector had established himself, looking somewhat incongruous seated beneath a Renoir nude, I tried to dismiss it all as hallucination. But it remained with me as I entered the room and faced the Inspector, beside whom there was a plain-clothes constable taking notes. I do not remember what the Inspector's preliminary words were, I was almost too tired to hear. But almost at once he asked the question I was expecting.

" 'There's a girl employed here, Mr. Ash,' he said. 'No one here seems to know who she is. If possible we don't want to disturb Mrs. Robinson with this fresh trouble, and thought perhaps you could help us. One of the tenants, Mrs. Carrington-Smith, believes you had something to do with introducing the girl to Mrs. Robinson.'

" 'Her name is Mildred White,' I said. 'She lives at 27, Carlton Terrace, where her father, Tom White, is small-arms instructor to the local Home Guard. I know Tom White as a brave and gallant soldier, we served together in the same Battalion at Dunkirk.'

"As I had expected, my words had an immediate effect on the Inspector; in fact I doubt whether he heard my last sentence.

" 'Well, well,' he said, 'how very short-sighted of them to plant one of the family. But it's not Tom White we hope to get, Mr. Ash—we could have picked him up any time in the last three or four months. He's been very clumsy. It's the rest of the gang we're after, especially a certain Molly Cohen, a very slippery customer. We shall be lucky if they haven't got away by

I

this time. So we shall have to leave you rather abruptly.' He stood up. 'Thank you, Vicar, for your information. We must now go into action quickly.'

"Suddenly his manner changed.

" 'Get down to the car,' he said to the plain-clothes man. 'I'll follow with Baker.'

"And they were out of the room before I could say another word. For a moment I sat still in my chair, feeling utterly weary. This news had come as a kind of final blow. It seemed to me as I sat there that I had failed from every angle; my whole theory of human nature had proved false; I had been disloyal to one of my firmest principles by falling in love, had not even had the strength of mind to pursue that love, and had lost it; I had had no effect on the parish in the eighteen months I had been there, and this very evening had failed to answer the first real call for help I had had; and now I had been the cause of giving away Tom White and Mildred, two people who in my heart I had been convinced possessed more good than bad qualities. And worst of all I was aware of a weakness in myself which made it impossible for me to rise above these disasters and conquer them. . . .

"Almost I felt as if I did not believe in God Himself, the final blasphemy.

"I stood up and went into the hall, and as I moved I felt strange pains in my knees of which I took no notice. As I went towards the front door Kynaston came out of the bedroom.

" 'How is she?' I asked automatically.

" 'It's an extraordinary thing, but she's perfectly fit,' he said. 'Her heart now seems quite normal. Yet less than an hour ago she had all the symptoms of heart-failure.'

" 'Science does not know everything,' I said.

"But Kynaston did not reply and was staring at me with some intensity.

" 'Are you all right, Vicar?' he asked. 'Here—let me feel your pulse.'

" 'Oh go away,' I said. 'You have a one-track mind.'

"But he put his hand on my forehead.

" 'You're feverish,' he said.

" 'Nonsense,' I replied.

" 'Give me your wrist.'

"But almost roughly I pushed him away.

" 'When I need a doctor,' I said, 'I'll send for you.'

"And I walked out of the flat.

"I have no memory of walking back to the vicarage, but I must have done so. I do remember Mrs. Taylor's look of horror when she opened the door to me. I believe I laughed at her. Anyhow I refused her assistance and got myself to bed. I remember nothing else until Kynaston visited me the next morning, sent for by Mrs. Taylor, and of the next four days I have only the most confused memory. It was only an attack of violent influenza, but at one time complications threatened, and I was in bed for ten days. . . ."

Mr. Ash closed his eyes, his face pale.

"Tomorrow," he said, "we go on to Venice. I will tell you the rest in the train."

They boarded the train shortly after breakfast the next morning, and almost at once, he leaned back in his seat and started talking, quietly.

"When finally I left the vicarage again," he said, "a fortnight after Mrs. Robinson's party, I found that indeed a transformation had taken place in Carlton Court society. Mrs. Robinson had gone, and with her both Peter and Schofield, and worst of all, you. At once I came to the conclusion that you had married him, and that I would never hear from you again. I tried to tell myself that this was a relief. Tom White had been arrested, and Mildred was already on her way to Borstal. Of Lola I could find no trace. The police had failed to arrest the remainder of the gang—when they arrived at Tom's house only he and Mildred were there.

with some of the loot. Poor Tom—he was a soldier, not a criminal. I questioned a few people discreetly, including Mrs. Carrington-Smith, but they knew nothing, or would tell me nothing. Mrs. Robinson, they said, had gone on a holiday, and it was Mrs. Carrington-Smith's view that she would never come back to Carlton Court.

" 'She wouldn't dare show her face again,' she said. Then her voice dropped to a whisper. 'Do you know, Vicar,' she said, 'that in her youth she was little better than a prostitute. I've found out everything about her. She was never married. . . .'

"But rudely I left her, and in so doing offended her for life. Finally, it was from Mrs. Kynaston that I found out something of the truth. This little woman, this cynical observer of human follies, who had a heart but who disliked admitting its existence, and whom for so long I thought I disliked, did in fact in the end salvage for me the wreck of my life.

"But before I had that first talk with Mrs. Kynaston, I had a letter from Mrs. Robinson. It was from an address on the south coast where she was recuperating, and in it she said she was much happier since she had told me everything; it was just like a confession, she said, and she understood now how her Irish friend must have felt. She referred only vaguely to her sons, as if not particularly interested in them. Peter, she said, was back at Cambridge—just that bald statement. Concerning Schofield, she merely said she had not heard from him at all. She then made a statement which I was to read and re-read during the months that followed. She had not heard, she said, that the marriage had come off, but with Bill 'you never knew'. He might quite well, one day, have casually stepped into a Registry Office, and got married. And then, giving no reason, she said she hoped it had blown over. She ended her letter by saying that as soon as the powers permitted, she would go abroad; she would probably settle, she said, in the South of France, or Venice. And that was all. Up to now I have not heard from her again.

"But to return to Mrs. Kynaston. One afternoon, three days after my recovery, I visited her. After inquiring after my health,

she at once set about relating to me what she knew of the rest of
that evening, and of the days during which I had been ill. She
told me how, soon after I had gone in to Mrs. Robinson, Schofield had returned, and found herself and Lola the only people
left in the drawing-room; how he had insisted on escorting
Lola home. He was, she said, rather drunk, and in a strange, reckless mood. Lola seemed quite willing to go with him. She had
herself left soon afterwards, before the excitement over the
robberies, about which she heard nothing until her husband
returned in the small hours. She then related in detail what I
already knew in essence—the arrest of Tom White and Mildred,
and their subsequent fate. She then looked at me strangely, and
said:

" 'No doubt you would like to hear about Miss Pemberton?'

" 'Oh yes,' I said, trying to appear only mildly interested.
'What has happened to her?'

"She smiled at me, her faint ironical smile.

" 'Why not be honest with yourself, Vicar?' she asked. 'You
know it's the one subject you're interested in, the only reason
why you came to see me.'

" 'On the contrary,' I replied stiffly, 'I have put her out of my
mind. I admit I was—how shall I put it?—temporarily enamoured
of her. But it is a crisis I've managed to get over. I am now more
determined than ever to devote myself to the Church and a life
of celibacy.'

"She then looked me straight in the eyes for some seconds,
and I did not flinch.

" 'You disappoint me, Vicar,' she said. 'I had thought you
were human.'

" 'I sincerely hope I am,' I said.

" 'No, Vicar—only half-human.'

"And she looked almost as if she despised me.

"Even then, in that first talk with her, I had an odd idea that she
knew more about you than she chose to admit, and I could not
bring myself to ask her. But this was only a passing idea, and
a few moments later, when I took my leave, it had vanished

altogether, and I left her still without any trust having been established between us.

"But I could not help remembering how, on my having answered her about you as I did, how suddenly she had become cold towards me—as if she had subjected me to some kind of test in which I failed. And in the weeks that followed, this impression kept returning, in such a way that I found myself going back to her again and again, ostensibly for an informal chat, but in my heart wanting to assure myself that my impression of her knowing more about you than she had admitted, was false. We would talk about nothing in particular and there would be sudden silences during which she would look at me with her ironical little smile, as if daring me to refer directly to you. But I never dared do so, so you were never mentioned between us.

"This went on for months, as I battled to regain my mental equanimity; but though my body completely recovered its health, my soul remained sick. I tried hard to interest myself in the parish, but could not. I slept badly and was always tired, and my sermons began to lose their power of holding the congregation. My Church began to be empty; I could sense discontent in the Parochial Church Council. And I became morbid. I visited Tom White in prison regularly, and did what I could for his wife. But she had degenerated from bad to worse. A month or so after Tom went to prison, the boy—the only creature in whom Mrs. White seemed to show any interest—died. He had always been weakly. Three days after this, Mrs. White was found dead with her head in the gas-oven. It was Jill, the youngest daughter, the only member of the family now at large, who made the discovery. She was just fifteen. She too then vanished from the district and was found a few weeks later consorting with lorry-drivers on the Great North Road; she was discovered to be with child and followed Mildred to Borstal. All this news I had to convey to Tom and Mildred and it did nothing to improve my own mental health. I visited Mildred quite often, and to do so had to travel fifty miles out of London. I was the only person who did visit her, and though I seemed to make little progress with her, she did, latterly, seem quite glad to see me. This gave me my only hope in a very gloomy period.

"There then began the final stage which brought about my downfall. The Bishop asked me to a special interview, and one afternoon, over a cup of tea, very charmingly, he told me there had been complaints about me; he hinted too that he had received anonymous letters accusing me of all sorts of iniquities, including—here he laughed uncomfortably—consorting with prostitutes! I remembered Mrs. Robinson's party and the way in which I had been stared at when I had gone up to Lola. I remembered how more recently I had offended Mrs. Carrington-Smith by not listening to her gossip. And I put two and two together. And I laughed.

"The Bishop looked at me more closely.

" 'This is not a laughing matter, Vicar. And you don't look well. Are you sure a London parish suits you?'

"Of course I knew what was expected of me, and I decided then and there to resign the living. I made up my mind to return to the life I had led before the war, cut off from the world. For in the world I was a stranger, and they took me not in. I told the Bishop of my decision. He tried to look concerned, but I could see he was relieved.

"After that, matters moved quickly. I formally resigned the living, and the time came for me to take leave of the few friends I had left in the parish. A week before my final Sunday—when I was to preach my farewell sermon and introduce my successor —I called again on Mrs. Kynaston.

"This time she looked rather grave as she led me into her sitting-room.

" 'So you are turning your back on the world again, Vicar?' she said.

"I achieved some kind of smile.

" 'I fear I am not suited to parish life,' I said. 'The Bishop told me so, and was much relieved when I resigned the living.'

" 'The Bishop is wrong,' she said. 'He can't see further than his big nose.'

" 'He has a rather small nose,' I said.

" 'Don't try to be funny, Vicar; it doesn't suit you. Would you like to meet Katharine Pemberton again?'

"For a moment I could say nothing, and was aware of her looking at me keenly. I made one last effort at appearing undisturbed.

" 'It would be pleasant,' I said politely. 'Do you happen to know where she is?'

" 'I've been in touch with her ever since she left the district.'

" 'Indeed?' I said. 'And is she now a happy wife?'

" 'Don't be absurd, Vicar. You don't think she'd marry that savage, do you? The last heard of him was that he'd gone off with that Lola girl of yours, God help her. No—Katharine is a nurse at Guy's. And she's been writing to me regularly, and we've met more than once. She's been quite eager to keep up the acquaintance; not, I suspect, because of the pleasure of my conversation, but because I am her only contact with you. It is almost pathetic the way she questions me. But of course I've always been able to tell her how completely you've put her out of your mind.'

"I believe I made no reply, but just stared ahead of me.

" 'It's true, isn't it?' she insisted.

"Again I did not reply.

"She looked at me silently for some moments.

" 'No, Vicar,' she said at last, 'it is not true. But you did for a while fool me into thinking you would in the end succeed in forgetting her. But when you kept coming back here to talk about nothing in particular, with those long silences, as if you were waiting for me to say something, I began to think differently. But I wanted to test you thoroughly. You see, I am very fond of Katharine. In the last few months I've grown to realize she's one in a thousand. And I don't often like people. I did not want her to throw herself away on someone who loves a mythical God more than he would love her. So I've been watching you. And if you had succeeded in making a go of the parish without her—I would have washed my hands of you. I would have

known then that you were a man who really did not need a
woman, as you have always believed yourself—in fact one who
loved his vocation more than life itself. Very fine, perhaps, for
the vocation, but not for the woman he would live with. It
would be a case of God help her. But seeing how you have
gone to pieces in the last few months, I've realized you are the
kind of man who must have a woman behind him, and a strong
woman. Katharine is just such a woman. So I'm giving you the
chance to meet her again.'

" 'Aren't you too late?' I asked.

" 'What do you mean?'

" 'Surely it's hardly the moment for a man to embark on
courtship at the very moment his career has come crashing about
his ears?'

" 'The very moment, when the woman is one like Katharine.'

" 'It is a risk I prefer not to subject her to,' I said. 'No, Mrs.
Kynaston. I am grateful to you for your concern for my future.
But I prefer not to meet Miss Pemberton again.'

"And without another word, I left her house.

"I did not hear from her again that week, which seemed to
drag more slowly than any week of my life. I wanted now only
to get away from the world and back to my life of seclusion.
At last that final Sunday came. I preached my last sermon and
introduced the new incumbent to a relieved parish. And then,
taking one last look round the congregation—bigger than it had
been for months—my eyes met yours. You were standing beside
Mrs. Kynaston about half-way up the nave, looking at me sadly.
As soon as you realized I had seen you, you looked down,
embarrassed.

"As I prepared to leave the Church I hardly knew what I was
doing. On this occasion it took me some time to get away because
I had to take leave of the verger—who had remained a good
friend of mine—and one or two others. Finally, I stepped out of
the Church. There were none of the usual old dears waiting for
me—they had been among the first to desert me. But standing
just outside the churchyard were you and Mrs. Kynaston.

"As I came up to you, Mrs. Kynaston said in matter-of-fact tones:

" 'Oh, by the way, Vicar, Miss Pemberton is staying with me for a few days, and I thought that as an old friend, you might like to meet her again. At the same time you can also do me a service by escorting her home, as I'm late already for a meeting of the Red Cross.'

"And before I could reply, she had left us. The rest, I need not tell you. You know it. . . ."

"*I know only,*" *said Katharine,* "*that we walked the streets for an hour, talking about nothing in particular. That we met several times in the next few days and still talked about nothing in particular, and that on the fourth day you asked me to marry you. . . . I know nothing about the state of your mind during that period. . . .*"

He looked at her quickly, and was about to say something, when the train started to slow down, and they saw that it was rolling over the bridge leading into Venice station.

Without a word he stood up, and started to get their luggage down. Soon they found themselves on the quay, looking out over the Grand Canal. It was just after dark, and as he stood there on the quayside beside her, experiencing the sudden transformation from the rolling train to the rippling waterside, and looked across the Grand Canal and saw the shifting lights and the strange silhouettes of the palaces across the water, he felt suddenly his heart leap with hope within him. It was as if, with the end of his story, a burden had been lifted from his heart. He looked quickly at her; she was standing motionless beside him, her head tilted slightly upwards; a shaft of light was falling on her face, catching the golden sheen of her hair and illuminating her features, her broad brow, her gentle mouth, her white, finely-modelled throat; and he felt an excitement new to him. And as she looked round at him she seemed to sense this new feeling in him, and put out her hand and touched his, and as he looked into her eyes he saw there a love such as he had thought could only be given to God, and he felt sudden revulsion.

He looked quickly away from her, signalling to a gondolier, and

*brushing aside the importunings of a motor-boat owner. Gently he
helped her into the deep cushions of the beautiful, slender craft, and let
himself down beside her, and as they glided away from the quay, he did
not touch her, but leant this way and that, conscientiously pointing out
the more famous palaces on their route; but in spite of the interest each
tried to show in them, they might as well have been passing through the
suburbs of London.*

*And so slowly life dropped back into the slower, sadder tempo which
had become normal to them, and which she was prepared to face in order
to continue living with him, for she realized the futility of being jealous
of God.*

*But in the evening they went out into the magic of Venice after dark,
and they leant over the parapet facing the lagoon in front of the Ducal
Palace, looking in the direction of the Lido. Suddenly he put his hand
on hers and squeezed it so hard that she had to control herself not to cry
out.*

*"I am sorry," he said, "for my performance as a bridegroom. But it
takes a man some time to be reconciled to the fact that he is not as strong
as he thought himself. That he needs a woman to make himself a
man. . . ."*

She remained still beside him, hardly breathing.

*"You see," he went on, "my whole sense of values has been turned
upside down. In the past ten days, in telling you everything, I have been
trying to get onto an even keel again. . . ."*

"And have you?" she murmured.

*"I feel much nearer to mental health, without which I would not
allow myself to love you. I thought that I could not spare from the love
I feel for God, any for you. But . . . now I see that in loving you I will
not cease to love God. I will love Him in you. . . ."*

*Now his arm was round her waist. It was then that they heard foot-
steps behind them, and he felt sudden annoyance that there should be
anyone else in Venice. And when whoever it was approached nearer and
seemed to be peering at them, his indignation rose. He turned his head
to see who it was.*

*"It is! It's the vicar himself! How are you, Vicar?" said a woman's
voice well known to him but which he could not for the moment place.*

*Peering through the darkness he saw a large majestic woman looking
rather like a musical-comedy version of a countess.*

"Have you left the Church, Vicar?" *continued this figure, and now he
recognized Mrs. Robinson; he tried to say something but she would not
let him.*

"But let me introduce you to my husband," *she said and indicated a
shadowy figure standing some yards away.*

"Jan!" *she said commandingly.* "Come here! This," *she said, introducing a bowing, gray-haired figure,* "is my husband Count Miszinski.
He belongs to one of the oldest families in Europe and is quite penniless.
He also speaks not a word of English. But he is a dear and I was so sorry
for him. He was struggling to make a living in Monte Carlo with a
tourist agency. We met in the Casino and he was most sympathetic
when I lost ten thousand francs in one throw. And the next day he asked
me to marry him. . . . But, Vicar, who is this with you? Why—it's Miss
Pemberton! Oh! I'm so glad! You're married, of course? Oh, I can't
say how glad I am. . . . My dear——"* she kissed a stupefied Katharine
on both cheeks,* "I've had nightmares thinking you'd married Bill. Not
at all your type, my dear. A rolling stone. He'll never marry. He loves
only himself. But the Vicar, now, he's different. I've always said to myself that if ever he took an interest in a woman—I was never sure he
would, mind—that it would be for life. . . . And where are you dears
staying? But do let's go into the light where we can see each other. . . ."

*And talking incessantly, she led the three of them to a restaurant where
they sat down at a terrace table, and the Count beckoned a waiter, order-
ing four of the most expensive drinks on the wine list, in very bad Italian.*

"My dears," *said Countess Miszinski, leaning across the table,*
"he's so pleased with the little annuity I've settled on him—it's quite
re-established his self-respect. He's so extravagant—quite an aristo-
cratic disregard for the value of money. And he's teaching me French—
already we can exchange simple sentences. I refuse to let him learn
English. I have cut adrift completely from England. I'm going to
become a citizen of Monaco—I've already applied for naturalization.
The Count is already naturalized. But you, my dears. Are you on your
honeymoon? How sweet. And are you returning to the parish? What
are your plans?"

And at last she paused to let the others speak. Briefly, Mr. Ash confirmed that they were on their honeymoon, that he was not returning to the parish, and had not left the Church, whilst Katharine made conversation in French with the Count. And no sooner did Mr. Ash pause than the Countess showered him with questions about the parish, whether Mrs. Carrington-Smith was still there, what had happened to the Bartrams, and what had been the fate of "poor Mildred". She shook her head sadly when told of Mildred's situation.

"A difficult case," she said. "A girl I could never bring myself to trust. So secretive. But perhaps, Vicar, if you persevere, you will make something of her."

Asked discreetly about her sons, she confessed she had no idea where Bill was, and had heard no word from him. He'll turn up one day, she said, when he wants to borrow money. Peter was just about to leave Cambridge where he had taken a very satisfactory degree; no, he was not going into the Diplomatic Corps, he was to be a scientist. He was studying nuclear physics and was going into a laboratory where he was to help make atom-bombs for the purpose of blowing up humanity; he seemed quite amused at the idea. She thought this a very suitable occupation for him, she added with the only touch of irony Mr. Ash had ever heard in her voice.

"Look," she said, changing the subject to one nearer her heart, "look how Katharine is getting on with the Count. Real ladies' man, isn't he, Vicar? And so handsome. Don't you think he's handsome, Vicar? And passionate, my dear. . . . He has the real middle-European temperament. . . ."

And so they went on talking for an hour. When they parted, they all shook hands heartily, promising to meet next day.

Later that night John Ash whispered to his wife:

"Now I feel nearer than ever to God. For now I have used all the senses He saw fit to bestow on me. . . ."

And in the darkness there came into her eyes tears of relief.